CW01457731

Makepeace

Taking Shield 03

ANNA BUTLER

**GLASS HAT
PRESS**

Copyright © 2016 Anna Butler

All rights reserved.

ISBN-13: 978-1542991834
ISBN-10: 1542991838

DEDICATION

For Dad
28 June 1931 – 12 May 2009

CONTENTS

PRAISE FOR MAKEPEACE

The world building is phenomenal…with a wide sweeping story and the book is heavy in detail. I highly recommend the entire series if you are a Sci-Fi/Spec Fic reader.

Love Bytes Reviews

Stunning battles scenes, harrowing confrontations and a well-balanced array of other things in the mix. This book will have you on the edge of your seat, holding your breath. It captures you from the start and does not let go until the end.

MM Good Book Reviews

This story was so powerful. It brings all of the wonderful space opera elements that I love about this series and the science fiction that is so astounding that you can't help but marvel at the world Ms. Butler created… I couldn't put the book down.

Molly Lolly Reviews

I adore space operas. I really and truly do. This one was perfect in all of its glory. The imagery was fantastic. The character development is wonderful.

Thorn and Ink Reviews

Just like the first two books, this was a very well written, epic sci fi drama, with plenty of intrigue, political games, tension between the crew and corruption.

Diverse Reader Reviews

I love this series. I not only have read the ebooks, but I own the paperbacks as well, and proudly display them on my very limited and very tight shelf space because I love it so much... Aside from the fantastic science fiction, Butler knows how to write characters well. In fact, it's hard to even call them characters. They feel so much like real people.... If you are a fan of hard scifi, this is the series for you... It rivals all of the "mainstream" science fiction I've read; in fact, I think it's better because it doesn't shy away from human sexuality of all kinds.

The Novel Approach Reviews

MAKEPEACE

PROLOGUE
Septimus 6217

Something small scuttled across the open space between the dark bulk of the buildings, pausing to settle onto long back legs with heavy, muscular thighs. Perfect legs for jumping. The front legs had well-articulated paws to lift seeds to its mouth and hold them. The gods only knew what the middle legs did.

Motion sensors triggered, the security camera tracked the animal. Not a real rat—this planet's equivalent—but a rat's long nose and big incisors, and a rat's dexterity with its front feet. It ate with dainty speed, nibbling at a seed and turning it in its paws. Whiskers bristled on the scaly face as the creature tilted its head this way and that, tasting the air. A big head for the size of the body, with large eyes set on the side of its head, like a bird's, and ears like radar dishes in constant, nervous movement.

Prey, not predator.

The big ears swivelled towards something to its left. Lightning fast, it pushed against the ground, leapt up and bounced into the shadows in a single jump. Safe.

The Maess drone came from behind the building to the left.

1

Not fully humanoid, but vaguely man shaped—head set direct onto the torso, short legs, low centre of gravity. No arms. Instead, each shoulder joint sprouted five tentacles of varying length. The longest was stiff, unmoving. The remaining tentacles on each side writhed with all the sinuous grace of a nest of snakes woken by bright sunshine.

For all its short legs it moved fast, cutting diagonally across the space to the right, towards the power generation plant. A corner of the building housing the plant, shadowy and windowless, loomed large in the camera field. The drone vanished around the corner and it, too, was gone. An instant later, the security vid feed stopped in a flash of yellow-edged white.

Twenty minutes later, the human colony on Makepeace was gone.

SECTION ONE:
PROJECT INITIATION

38 Quintus 7489 – 08 Tertius 7490

CHAPTER ONE

38 Quintus 7489: Military HQ, Sais City

"You're kidding." Captain Felix took the datapad Shield Captain Bennet offered him. Contemporaries when they were students at the Strategic Studies Institute, they had been working partners in the Military Strategy Unit for the last seven years. "Tell me you're kidding."

"Wish I was." Bennet picked up a duplicate pad and switched it on.

Felix peered at the screen. After a couple of seconds, he swore and flung open his desk drawer, rooting about in it for a connection lead. He keyed the datapad into the larger desk monitor, increased the magnification and stared again. "How did you come up with this?"

"I got a ship to go in and take a look at Makepeace."

"Shield, of course."

"Is there any other kind?"

Felix glanced at him and grinned. "*Hyperion*?"

"No. The *Dhow* went. General Martens told me I had to get over my mistrust of any ship that wasn't my own, and she couldn't spare the *Hype* anyway." Bennet caught Felix's sardonic gaze, and they both laughed. Bennet sobered first. "Still, the *Dhow* came back with the goods. I'm not complaining."

Still grinning, Felix went back to staring at the scan results, and for a few more minutes he bent his head over the accumulated evidence Bennet had been working on for weeks now. The grin faded as he went over it again, and then again. "I don't want to believe this."

Bennet didn't want to, himself. "I don't think we can avoid it."

"For fuck's sake, Bennet! Live human prisoners are unusual enough, but this many of them? It's unprecedented."

"Yes." Bennet put a hand on the pile of datapads. "Makepeace was a Nicaean colony, you know."

"I didn't know until I read this. I've never heard of it."

"An Albion-class planet with a good climate. Perfect for agriculture. From the maps, the colonists converted an area of about fifteen miles square into farms and gardens." Bennet picked up the relevant datapad, the one holding the history of a short-lived colony long since lost and abandoned to the Maess. "It wasn't a big place. They barely got it started."

"A rural idyll, I'm sure. If you like that sort of thing." Felix increased the magnification on the screen to peer at the advertising vid Bennet had found in the colonial archives. The land-girl waving cheerily at the camera, caught on film for eternity, would be a great-grandmother by now. Or dead.

"It only lasted a couple of years."

Felix grunted and turned back to reading the data. Bennet left him to it and idled away the time staring out of the window. While Albion's Military HQ was an undistinguished example of brutalist architecture, it was one of the tallest buildings in Sais. The views from Felix's office were superb, the vast city spreading out to the horizon. Three miles away, the sun struck the dome of the Thebaid Institute with a familiar flash of gold.

For a third of his life, the dome had been the first thing Bennet saw every morning from the window of the bedroom he'd shared with Joss. He'd always risen first, to be the one to throw back the curtains and take in the view; the park, lush and green, with the Thebaid's ornate, columned bulk on the other side of it. The Thebaid had always been a huge part of his life, more so after he'd met Joss there and fallen for him. He'd never tired of seeing it each morning. After the mission to T18, not to mention Fleet Lieutenant Flynn, had led to the cracks in his relationship with Joss blowing wide open, he'd missed the ritual even more than he missed Joss. His current flat, the one he shared with Rosie, who had once been his Lieutenant in Shield, was on the wrong side of the park to see the dome.

"Well." Felix cut off Bennet's unprofitable thoughts. "I think you're right. It's a Maess base and they definitely have a lot of live human prisoners."

"Yes." Bennet poked at the datapad as if he could wipe it clean of all the uncomfortable data. Scowled.

"How in Hades did you get on to this?"

"Felix, I've been on sick leave for over a year. I keep going between working here and teaching at the Academy, but I am desperate for something interesting to do until I go back to my proper job—"

"Any day now, for sure. But your emotional torment aside, how did you find this?" Felix was a bastard, sometimes. He had about as much sympathy as a block of granite.

"I was at a loose end after the Borealis project finished, so I started on the more obscure stuff in the T18 data. A lot of it's too technical for me—that's more your line. I started digging into the softer data. What there is of it, anyway. I didn't find a lot of what you could call social information, but I've been going over what there is. I'm not even close to convinced the translations of the Maess machine codes are accurate, not when it comes to this stuff where there are so many unknowns in the language, but it was enough to interest me in this place."

Felix nodded. "Well, you got the T18 stuff for us. I don't see why you shouldn't get some enjoyment out of it."

"Enjoyment?" Bennet shrugged. Felix always did have an odd

sense of humour.

"And what does our nominal overlord have to say?"

Bennet snorted. Colonel Jorgensen liked to think he was in charge of the Strategy Unit. Most of the Unit allowed him the illusion. "Jorgensen's focused on the technical data. He told me he wasn't that interested but to let him know if I found anything. I'll have to tell him. Eventually. He'll find out anyway if we push for project resources."

"Jorgensen's blinkered." Felix had as little time for the Colonel as Bennet did. "We know bugger-all about the Maess. We need more on the soft information. Much more."

"I can't get a handle on what their society is like. Well, nothing other than them being extreme xenophobes—closed off, think they're superior to everything else, with all that nonsense culturally encoded. Etcetera. Etcetera."

Felix gestured at his monitor screen, frozen on a still from the bitty, grainy security feed of the Maess invasion of Makepeace. "And yet they copied us, made their drones more humanoid. An interesting step for a race that thinks it's our superior. And they continue to develop them, which is even more interesting. The Makepeace drones still had tentacles, for the gods' sake, more like the first ones we ever encountered. These days the Maess make them look more like us."

"They don't really look human."

"No. But they're looking more human all the time. Have you noticed the reports show we've been seeing an awful lot of EDA drones recently? They're definitely another step up the evolutionary ladder—better articulated limbs, a larger neural node, smarter. The Maess evolve their drones to better match their enemies. Intriguing."

Bennet swallowed, still, after all this time, fighting a surge of revulsion as the memory surfaced. The thing he'd seen three years ago on T18 had been man-high. No fixed shape, no head or limbs, skin an oily iridescence overlying a pallid, greyish bulk that shifted and changed and grew his own face to scream at him. Not a drone, but a real live Maess. "At least we have something to go on now when it comes to what they look like and why they use drones. If the Maess don't have a shape of their own, it stands to reason they borrow shapes from others to make their drones. Like parasites. Chameleons."

"Good analogy."

"It hated me," Bennet said. "That thing I saw on T18. It screamed at me. It wanted me dead. Ever since the war started, they've operated one principle—all humans should be dead. Having live humans on Makepeace… you'd think it'd be enough to get even Jorgensen wondering."

"I can't imagine why they've kept them alive."

Nor could Bennet. "Well, we're paid to find out. I've booked some research time for a detailed analysis of the archives, to see if that can clue us in to why the Maess established a base on Makepeace. If I've missed the reason in the T18 data, it's because it's well hidden or I don't have enough understanding to get the references to it. A deep analysis may give us a handle on why they have live humans there."

"What a fucking mess." Felix spoke without heat, his tone weary. "How long is it since the Maess overran this place, did you say?"

"I didn't. It was quite early in the war; just over a century ago. There was a battle over the colony. Well, more of a skirmish."

"We lost, I take it."

"Don't we always?"

Felix chuffed out a laugh. "Not always. But often."

"And usually the big ones. Well, we lost Makepeace and the whole of the quadrant went shortly after. The colonists were evacuated just in time, though I'll bet we didn't get everyone. We never do."

As Bennet's experience on Telnos the previous year had proved. He'd been one of those left behind.

Felix frowned and gestured to the screen, frozen on the welcoming smile from the promotional land worker. "Do you suppose they're the descendants of original colonists who didn't make the rescue ships?"

"How the hell should I know?"

"You're the analyst."

"I don't think so. If—and it's a big if—I've translated accurately the little bit of the T18 data I've been able to decode, the Maess established the base relatively recently; within the last thirty years or so. I suspect that's when they started shipping in the prisoners."

Felix pushed the printouts, maps and datapads over to one side of his desk and planted his elbows in the space. "Solactinium extraction? They usually keep humans alive where they can't automate the mines. If the seam's too narrow, I mean. The ore's as useful to them as it is to us, especially weapons-grade."

"There's nothing to suggest it from the first scan I did of the data files. I don't know. We'll have to see if a deeper trawl of the archives comes up with something. The question is, what do we do about this now?"

Felix shrugged. "Nothing that will win us praise and a pay rise. Our beloved government never knows what to do with any prisoners we manage to retrieve. They won't make this a priority."

"I can't see the Ennead would want it known they've left a couple of hundred humans in Maess hands."

"Probably not, when they always have an eye to the next election. Mind you, Rets aren't a big vote winner." Felix caught Bennet's gaze and rolled his eyes. "Oh, all right. Returned prisoners. Must you always be so damned mealy mouthed? Anyhow, most people are ambivalent about them, at best. Of course they don't want humans left in enemy hands. But they don't want a Ret living next door, either. Just in case they come back indoctrinated, or something, and kill the neighbours while they sleep."

"Returned prisoners," Bennet said, ramming the point home,

"are still human and now we know they're there, we have to do something about them."

"The Management won't thank you for it. I'm not sure the Rets will either. They aren't exactly welcomed home with flowers and fatted calves, are they? Most are disowned by their families and, hell, it must be a shitty life."

"The thought crossed my mind a few times, stranded on Telnos last year." Bennet raised his hand, smoothing a fingertip over the Shield badge pinned on his uniform. "No one in Shield has ever been taken prisoner, and I wasn't going to be the first. Nor anybody on my watch"

"I don't know how the hell you managed to keep those farmers out of Maess hands," Felix said. "But don't let it colour your judgement now. Don't jump straight to getting those people out of Makepeace until we know what's going on."

"I've no intention of it. I'm a helluva long way from submitting any sort of recommendation. I want to be certain about the archive stuff, come up with some theory about why the Maess have taken humans there, and gauge the military significance for both them and us. I'd like your opinion on what I've got so far and your help with the rest."

"I'll do what I can." Felix swivelled his chair around and pointed to the star map pinned on his wall. "It's a long way from our space. It'll be one hell of a job getting enough ships in to rescue those people, if we decide it's feasible. Can Shield do it?"

"Too many of them. Our ships aren't big enough."

"So, you'd be talking about a full scale invasion."

"It will take a fair sized force." Bennet met Felix's arched eyebrow with a grin and a shrug.

"How do you want to play it?"

"Help me put the project initiation document together and put it to the Intelligence Committee for clearance to continue working on it."

"Couple of pages." Felix waved a dismissive hand. "All

IntCom can read before their brains get tired."

"You do recall my father is a member?" At a second dismissive gesture, Bennet let it go. His father certainly didn't need him to ride to the rescue. "I know IntCom won't like it, but we'll have logged the presence of the human prisoners and I can secure some of your time to work on it."

"You've got it."

Bennet didn't have time to respond. A messenger knocked at the door and stuck his head into the office. "There you are, Shield Captain. The Supreme Commander wants you."

"Now?"

The messenger smirked. "No, sir. About ten minutes ago."

"Hung and drawn by now and quartered when you get there," Felix said, as Bennet jumped up and pulled his uniform jacket straight. "It could be good news though."

"The only good news would be they're throwing me out of here and letting me go back to Shield." Bennet nodded to the messenger to lead on. "And he's not likely to yank me up there to tell me. That's Personnel's job."

"I dunno. You said your medical board last week went well."

Bennet spread out both hands in a 'whaddaya know?' sort of gesture and left to find out what The Management wanted.

The lift decanted him onto the top floor of the building, straight into the Supreme Commander's outer office, a huge space filled with desks big enough to use as shuttle landing pads. The chief office boy at the moment was a Fleet colonel: small, dark and intense, with a tic in one cheek. Bennet reckoned it came from working in close proximity to The Management. It would give anyone a few tics and twitches.

Bennet rated a swift glance from her papers and datapads. She acknowledged his salute with a nod. "Go straight in, Shield

Captain. He's been waiting for you."

It was good of her to deliver the warning. Supreme Commanders didn't expect to be kept waiting by mere captains, even the sons of old friends. Jak had commanded Bennet's father, Caeden, when Caeden had been fresh out of the Academy and they'd been close friends ever since. So close, Jak was Bennet's godfather. Bennet counted it as a mixed blessing. He was fond of his godfather and had no doubt it was mutual. But bad enough he had a father who was Commander of Fleet's First Flotilla. Adding the Supreme Commander to the mix made it more difficult for him to avoid the suspicion of nepotism. Both Jak and Caeden cast long shadows.

Jak was alone in an office so large the outer one inhabited by the Colonel seemed cramped. Bennet could have landed a dreadnought on the desk. The Supreme Commander sat with his back to the wide windows and their breath-taking view and returned Bennet's careful, by-the-book salute with a brief nod. "Where the hell have you been? Do you think I have nothing better to do than chase all over the building looking for malingering wastrels?"

"Of course not, sir."

"Why weren't you in your office?"

Bennet said, blandly, "I don't have an office, sir. I have a cubby-hole."

The gleam in Jak's hazel eyes was, Bennet hoped, amusement rather than venom. "So small the Animal Welfare people wouldn't let me keep a cat in it?"

"Yes, sir."

"Good," Jak said. "That's all a part-timer rates. And more than you deserve."

Another *Yes, sir* was probably safe. Bennet offered one.

Jak extracted himself and his gold braid out from behind the desk and onto one of the more comfortable chairs set around a low coffee table. He motioned to Bennet to join him, waving him into a seat. "Where were you?"

"With Captain Felix, sir, talking about a possible project."

It was enough to divert Jak. "What project?"

"I'm just getting started on it," Bennet said, cautious about saying too much. "It's some data I picked up on T18, to do with an old Nicaean colony the Maess overran a century ago. Place called Makepeace."

"Never heard of it. Interesting?"

"Yes, sir. I think the Maess are holding human prisoners there. We're putting together a preliminary report to ask for permission to raise it to project status."

"Prisoners?" Jak stiffened, his expression souring. "Oh joy. Do you have any idea what problems the thought of humans in enemy hands causes the politicians? And by extension, me? It's only marginally better than the problem of bringing the prisoners home. What the hell are the Maess doing with them?"

"I don't know, sir. The T18 stuff on this is obscure, to say the least. I'll need project resources for the analysis."

Jak snorted. "What you mean is you're so damned cautious, you won't commit yourself. You should have been an accountant. You have no sense of adventure."

"I can't add up, sir," Bennet said, meekly as he knew how.

Jak stared, fierce eyes unreadable. It could go either way, Bennet thought.

Then the Supreme Commander snorted again, but with laughter this time, choosing to be amused. "I want the project initiation document on my desk tomorrow, with an indication of when I can have the full analysis. To go no further than me, not even to Colonel Jorgensen, until I tell you differently. What's your gut feeling on this one, Captain?"

"I don't like it, sir. I can't see any reason for them being there."

"How many?"

"Difficult to tell. The preliminary scans I had Shield do indicate well over a hundred; nearer two. I think they've been on Makepeace about thirty years. The Maess' time measurements are different to ours, of course, but that's my best guess."

"And when will I get the full analysis?"

"Could be months, sir."

"Eats at you, does it? Well, if they've been there thirty years, a few more months won't make much difference one way or the other. And until there's a decision about what to do with them, you know the rules about any project involving potential returned prisoners. Highest level security." Jak indicated the coffee machine to Bennet's right. "Get me one of those and I'll tell you why I wanted to see you. Have one yourself."

"Thank you, sir but I'm fine."

"I forgot you prefer maundering your insides with tea. Effete nonsense only fit for old women."

Bennet thought about saying it came from not having a father figure in his life, but reflected it was unfair on Caeden who wasn't there to defend himself. So he contented himself by merely saying *Yes sir* again, and poured the coffee. His right hand barely trembled. He flexed his fingers once he'd set down the cup.

It was said around the place that the Supreme Commander never missed anything. He gave a laconic demonstration of omniscience. "The medical reports say that's as much dexterity as you'll get."

"It's pretty good, sir."

"If it's the whole price you pay for almost dying on Telnos last year, it's reasonable."

"I think so, too."

"I suppose you're wondering why you're here?"

Bennet smiled, keeping it deferential and polite.

"Your medical board came through. Full mobility on the leg and the hand's classed as a mild disability. Given you're left-handed anyway, you have no more excuses. Time to boot you back into a proper job instead of wasting your time and mine here." Jak smiled, the wolf's smile that had the spot between Bennet's shoulder blades itching with apprehension. "And it's my pleasure to do the booting."

CHAPTER TWO

Maybe Felix hadn't been facetious when he'd said the Supreme Commander would be handling Bennet's next posting. The old man, though, appeared to be enjoying it far too much.

"I suppose," Jak said, "you weren't expecting me to be the one to be giving you your marching orders?"

"No, sir, although I appreciate it." Bennet tried to force warmth into his voice. Jak's motives probably had more to do with a favour to Caeden.

Please the gods it wasn't a posting to the *Gyrfalcon*.

"And now you're wondering if I'm taking a personal interest in this because your father asked me to."

Bennet couldn't see a way out without downright lying and the old man would see through him in an instant. "The thought had crossed my mind, sir."

"It may come as a surprise to you, but I don't run the military to please your father." Jak grinned. "It may come as a surprise to him too, come to think of it. Nor do I run it to annoy you, tempting though it is. The only reason for putting up with all this bloody braid is so I can run it to please myself. You're my godson, Bennet, and I've always taken that seriously. If I left this to Personnel, they'd post you anywhere there was a space and you'd have no say at all in where you end up. I'm prepared to bend the rules and give you a choice. You've done pretty well with yourself so far, son. I want to make sure you still have the right chances in the future."

Bennet didn't know what to say for a moment, before settling on the simplest response. "Thank you, sir."

A part of him wanted to squirm with embarrassment and mutter something brash and cynical about the old man coming over all unnecessary. The other part, possibly the better half of him, had to clear its throat and felt a slight difficulty in speaking. He was fond of his godfather, knowing him better than many of his blood relatives and liking him better than most. If anyone had ever asked him and he was feeling more than usually truthful, Bennet would have said he was very fond of his godfather, but the underlying affection had always been that—extremely underlying. It was unusual for the old man to be so overt. Bennet hadn't expected it.

It appeared Jak hadn't expected it either. He crusted over and became rather gruff. "So what's it to be? Fleet or Infantry?"

"I'd like to go back to Shield, sir. It's home."

Jak regarded him over the coffee cup for a long and silent minute. "I expect you would. But I'm not bending the rules that far, even for you. We rotate you people out of Shield for very good reasons."

"I've had over a year of non-combat duty, sir, while my leg healed. Couldn't it count as extra?"

"No. Well, I might knock half a year off for good behaviour, but don't count on it. It all depends what holes I have to fill."

"Yes, sir." Bennet had only ever known Shield. Serving anywhere else was unimaginable.

"I can't hang about all day waiting for you to make a decision, son."

"I'd rather regain my flying privileges as soon as I can, sir, as long as—"

"As long as it's not your father's ship? I don't run things to please you, either, Captain. You don't get that much choice. Fleet or Infantry?"

"Fleet, then, sir." Bennet resigned himself to the inevitable. *Oh gods. Not the Gyrfalcon...*

Jak nodded. If the smirk was anything to go by, he was pleased. "I expected it would be. I have a year's posting in mind for you, then we'll see what comes up. Second Flotilla with the Dreadnought *Corvus*. What do you know about Commander Dalton?"

Jak liked nothing better than to wrong-foot someone. The smirk widened into a wide, open grin and Bennet acknowledged the little victory with a nod. "Mostly by repute, sir. My father knows her, of course, but I don't think I've met her more than once or twice. She took command of the *Corvus* about five years ago, didn't she? I remember some talk about the *Corvus* being in a mess and Dad taking temporary command to sort it out."

"I thought about it, but I'd have had to dynamite him out of the *Gyrfalcon*. I could hear the howls of pain from here." Jak smiled his evil-dictatorial-bastard smile. Bennet was willing to bet the old man practised it every day in his shaving mirror. "I didn't let him off the hook altogether though. He mentored Dalton over the first year while she pulled *Corvus* around. It was good for his soul."

They shared a grin, Bennet enjoying Jak's snide and wholly un-commanderly take on motivating his subordinates. As long, of course, as it wasn't him in the firing line.

"Because I'm in a good mood I'll allow you some multiple choice after all. Either you can take temporary command of the *Yaris* destroyer while her permanent captain is away on maternity leave, or I let *Corvus*'s flight captain have the *Yaris* and you take over the squadrons."

Bennet thought about it for a minute. "Running the *Yaris* will be like the *Hype*, the command I had in Shield. I know it's bigger and more challenging but not that different. Running the *Corvus*'s squadrons will be something new and it would give me some command experience on a dreadnought's Bridge and in running the flotilla's Flag Office. I'd like that, sir, if it won't put the current squadron leader's nose out of joint."

"Not him. He's gagging for his own command. He'll jump at the chance to prove himself, and Dalton will be pleased to keep him within her flotilla while he does it. You take the squadrons then." Jak took a datapad from his pocket and handed it over. "I thought you might take that. Here are your orders. You leave for retraining at Demeter flight school next month, on the eighth. That leaves you enough time to get your Academy classes through this year's exams."

"Yes sir." A week! Only a week. At least Bennet could attend Natalia's graduation from the Military Academy before being shipped out, but hell. Only a week. He'd have to get word to Rosie, fast.

Rosie. This would finish him and Rosie.

"My office has told the Academy you won't be back for next term and I've had to outshout the Strategy Unit about letting you out to play again. The usual arrangement applies. You'll continue working on the long-term projects in your own time. Things like this new problem. All right?"

"Yes sir. I enjoy doing them."

"Just not full time, eh?"

"No. Not really. I'm a warrior, and I want to get back to what I do best."

"I wish I was still out there, sometimes. And one other thing— I know how fond you Shields are of being all mysterious in black, but as long as you're in Fleet you'll conform and wear Fleet uniform. Pick up a kit at Quartermaster's on Demeter." Jak grinned, presumably at Bennet's expression. "All right. Back to work. You've slacked long enough for one day."

"Yes, sir." Bennet stopped at the door and decided to risk a little familiarity. "Uncle Jak?"

He didn't get his head bitten off.

"Yes?"

"Did you have the orders for the *Yaris* in your other pocket?"

"Of course," the Supreme Commander said. "And an infantry posting hidden away there, too. The reputation for infallibility is based on sound planning."

Bennet smiled. "Thank you, Uncle Jak. I appreciate it."

"Don't mention it." Jak re-established himself behind the massive desk. "Keep in touch. And Bennet?"

"Yes sir?"

"Try not to get left behind anywhere this time. I'm getting too old to stay up late for Midnight Watches. Besides, I can't always find excuses to send in ships to rescue you, you know. The Finance Committee asks such damn awkward questions."

"Fleet." Bennet dropped back into his seat in Felix's office.

"I'll bet you'll look lovely in grey." Felix smoothed both hands down the jacket of his own navy command uniform and gave Bennet a smug grin. "Which ship, I wonder?"

"Not *Gyrfalcon*, and that's all I care about. The *Corvus*. I'm out of here next week."

"I'd have thought the old man was so sick of you hanging around, he'd have had you out of here tomorrow."

"I have classes at the Academy, remember, and this year's tests are just starting. He didn't want to disrupt their education." Bennet grinned at Felix's expression, and gathered his datapads and maps together. "I'll be taking this with me. Will you take a look at the draft report?"

"I started already. I'll check the grammar and punctuation as I go. You overuse colons."

"I mentioned it to the old man. He says it's to go to him only. Not even Jorgensen, until he says so."

"Really? Well. That's different." Felix raised a quizzical eyebrow. "I'll start drafting the project initiation document and I'll run the archive searches. They'll take weeks and you won't be able to access it from Fleet."

"Thanks."

"Rosie's away, isn't she?"

Bennet stared at the maps and put them into a nice neat pile, each lined up down the left hand margin. It took a moment to get them just so. What a fucking mess. He'd been unfair to Rosie. And selfish. "Yes. We always knew this could happen. She should be back any day. I'll send a message to her, but I think she's on her way home. She should be back before I go. I'd better call my mother and tell her, too. I doubt I'll have to tell Dad. I'll bet the old man already sent him word."

"Such influence and connections! You'll have time to have dinner with Charis and me before you go? Rosie too, if she's back in time."

"I'd love it." Bennet had been what Felix described as 'unflatteringly astonished' when Felix's on-off-on again relationship with a civilian analyst had resolved itself into a formal engagement. "She's too good for you, though."

"So you keep saying. Have fun tonight with your family crying all over you."

"Not tonight." Bennet had yet one more ordeal to get through. "Tonight I'm having dinner with Joss."

"Joss? You two split up over a year ago. Why in hell are you having dinner with Joss?"

Bennet grimaced. "He was part of my life for nine years. You don't just cut that out and forget it. I've had dinner with him a few times."

"Oh boy. Mixed signals there, I suspect. I'm astonished Rosie hasn't brained you for it."

"She doesn't mind. It's only dinner."

"With an old flame." Felix gave him a long, steady look. "I can't work out if you're soft headed or soft hearted. Don't get burnt."

"Don't worry. I'm fireproof." Bennet laughed; partly at Felix's expression, but mostly at himself. "Believe me. I got burnt. It's all ash."

"Uh-huh."

Bennet looked down at the datapads and maps in his hands and banished Fleet Lieutenant Flynn from his memory. It wasn't Joss who could burn him. Not now. "Uh-huh. The fire's out."

Bennet met Joss in a fashionable restaurant in the heart of the old city, one they'd patronised often when they were together. As always, the meal was superb.

Joss's reaction to Bennet's news was less so. "Does this mean you won't be home at all?"

"Not for months. Probably not until they let me out of Fleet."

Joss pushed away his glass. Wine slopped over the rim, staining the tablecloth red. "So what's this? A valedictory meal, wrapping up all your inconvenient loose ends before you go?"

Bennet blew out a silent breath. "I thought you'd want to know, that's all. And I like having dinner with you."

This was an expensive restaurant, with hedonistic, luxurious décor. The tablecloth was thick white silk damask. Joss used the glass to grind the wine into it, heedless of the damage. Bennet kept his gaze on the thin, elegant fingers. When he'd been eighteen, and for years after, Joss's voice and mouth and those beautiful hands had reduced his bones to water. He'd tossed everything away to be with Joss, taking an enormous leap into a future that hadn't quite turned out the way he'd imagined. Not forever and ever, after all. He still loved Joss, and wanted him to be happy, but there was no going back.

"I don't get it," Joss said. "I don't get why you still call me up and suggest we meet for dinner. I assume when Rosie's away and you need company, you wheel me out as a sort of substitute? I don't understand what you think you want here."

Bennet picked up his own wine and sipped at it. It was better than throwing it, and hell, was he tempted for a moment. Joss just would not let things go, always picking at things to see how they came around to be about him. "I'm very fond of you, Joss. We were together a long time. That's incredibly important to me. I don't want to lose it."

"Fond!" Joss gave the glass another angry push, slopping out more wine to deepen the stain.

"Yes. Very."

"Thank you. That makes it all worthwhile." Joss released his death grip on the glass stem and stared at Bennet.

The light in the restaurant was kind to him, softening the signs of ageing he wasn't able to hide: the loosening of skin at the eyelids and the corner of the mouth that once Bennet had lived to kiss. The silvering hair, though, had been subtly dealt with.

"You know," Joss said, "I spoiled you."

"Spoiled me?"

"I gave you too much of a good thing. Too much, too easy. Too much… oh, everything. I think it went to your head."

What in hell was he talking about? It always had to be Bennet's fault, didn't it? Whatever went wrong it was never down to Joss. Oh no. Bennet bit back the impulse to snap back and kept it calm. "I don't know what you mean."

"Once you said to me, when we were talking about Shield— all right, when we were arguing about it—you said being in Shield meant you had it all: being the toy soldier, doing the strategy thing, being with me."

Bennet took another mouthful of wine. Gods, where was Joss going with this? "I don't remember, but yes. Being in Shield allowed me to be home with you. It was worth it. It made it work for us."

"For you." Joss threw himself back in his seat, frowning. "It made it work for you. That's what it's always been about, hasn't it? You getting it all. The job you wanted, me when you loved me. Oh, but I got that wrong, didn't I? You're fond of me."

Who had he learned it from, that having it all was a very good thing? The master of having it all was sitting right in front of him—or had Joss forgotten how many times Bennet had looked the other way while Joss took a trot around the block with one of his many playmates? Bennet pressed his lips together hard against the words that would tumble out if he let them. It was a moment before he was capable of a calm "Yes." He held out a hand. "I do love you, you know, Joss. I always did."

Joss hunched up one shoulder, ignored the outstretched hand. "Did you? Once? The way you loved him? The way you love Rosie?" And then, very abrupt, "Are you going to marry her?"

"What?" Bennet drew back his hand.

"It would please your father."

"I rarely do anything that pleases my father."

"And it would please her."

Bennet took his fork and started on the dessert he'd abandoned when he'd told Joss the day's news. It was good. His favourite.

Joss's tone was soft, malicious. "Ah. So she doesn't get you either."

"Don't be spiteful."

"Why not?" Joss drank off his wine and poured more, emptying the bottle into his glass. "I don't think we'll meet often from now on, will we?"

"Not for a while. I'll write, and I'm not disappearing forever, you know."

"You already have!" Joss's hands shook as he slammed down the empty bottle. Bennet put out his own hand, automatically, to steady the wobbling bottle. He ignored the scowl Joss shot at him. Joss gulped at the wine, staring at Bennet over the rim of the glass.

"Do you still have it?"

Bennet blinked. "Have what?"

"The heart scarab."

The heart scarab he'd given Bennet when they'd split up? Why in *hell* was he bringing that up? "Yes. Of course. I have it safe. I always loved it."

"You know what it means."

I have come in order that I may be thy protection. I gather together for thee thy bones, I draw together for thee thy members, I have brought for thee thy heart.

Regret flamed for everything they'd had. Bennet had loved Joss once, so much. And now... well, however fond he was of Joss, he had finally outgrown him. Joss could be right about him not having it all forever. No one could.

Or should.

It wasn't good for them. It hadn't been good for him, and he'd hurt Joss as a result.

"You were reminding me of what it was all about," he said. He felt dull, heavy. He should try harder not to hurt Joss. "Reminding me of what we had."

"And setting you free, to choose. You chose him. Flynn."

"Yes. I'm sorry." He was, too. He had never wanted to hurt Joss. But regret had to be ignored and stamped down and strangled unborn.

"Are you? Well, there it is. Done with. You know, you can't play with being free, Bennet. You have to make a real choice and stick with it. And I guess I'm not the choice you'll stick with. So take the scarab with you and keep it safe until you give it to someone else. Are you happy with Rosie?"

"Yes. Of course I am!"

"Really. Without him?"

Joss knew him too well. Bennet grimaced, but said nothing.

"No." Joss's smile was a thin, wintry thing. "I don't believe you. You aren't, really. Nobody's happy. Not me, not you, not Rosie, and not him." Joss didn't appear to expect Bennet to reply. "That's all right then. I couldn't bear it if I was on my own in everything. It looks like nobody gets what they want. Nobody gets it all. You know, I can live with that."

Bennet stared. A cord was being cut, and it hurt more than he could ever have anticipated.

Joss raised his glass in a toast. Whether to Bennet or to himself, Bennet wasn't sure. "Because I have to live with it, Bennet. We both have to."

CHAPTER THREE

01 Sextus 7489: Military Academy, Sais City

"Do you think it will rain?" Natalia sounded fretful. As usual.

Bennet glanced at the window. "No. The sky's clear."

His mother said something he couldn't quite catch, drowned out by the usual litany of nerves they got out of his sister. Bennet stared out of the window, letting both Natalia's complaints about the fit of her jacket and his mother's soothing murmur wash over him.

It had been a cool spring, and summer wasn't shaping up to be any better. In the unseasonable Sextus weather, the Military Academy compound was a pitiless grey. Only the slender metal flagpoles foresting one end of the parade ground, and the fresh wind that had each silk rectangle snapping and straining against its halyard, lent colour and movement to the overall dreariness.

If he pressed up against the window and craned his head to the left, Bennet could just see the familiar roof-line of the Strategic Studies Institute where it sat in a far corner of the Academy's extensive compound. Symbolic, somehow, the way SSI turned an elegant back on the more plebeian neighbour in whose grounds it was housed. Bennet had felt at home and at peace there, on the single teaching day he had at SSI each week. He didn't belong in the Academy. He'd turned his back on it a lifetime ago. He'd turned his back on a lot of things.

He focused on his own regimental flag, the sombre black and silver twisting against the halyard. Movement caught his gaze. Across at the far end of the parade ground, a dark mass resolved itself into a group of figures. Top Brass, given the amount of gold and silver braid bedecking them. One figure detached itself and walked towards Natalia's dorm building, threading a path through the growing crowds collecting nearer the buildings.

Caeden.

Bennet drew back from the window, turning to face his mother and sister. Natalia pulled at the collar of her dress jacket, out of cadet blue for the first time and in the brand spanking new Fleet grey, slashed across with the dark green sash representing her Engineering discipline. She had been assigned to their father's dreadnought. It astonished him she wanted that.

"Why didn't you choose combat duty?" he asked. "You're a fair pilot."

"I didn't want it. I'm an engineer."

"You're as good as Sioned is. She chose combat last year, didn't she?"

"I'm not Sioned." Natalia's dismissive tone indicated she had no wish to emulate the daughter of their father's oldest friend, Fleet Commander Warwick. She pointed to the ceremonial sword in his hands. "Are you going to give me that?"

She raised her arms to let him buckle on the sword belt. The sword was the family heirloom their father, and the gods only knew how many generations before him, had carried on graduation. Bennet hadn't worn it. He hadn't expected to. He hadn't asked. By the time it was offered to him, he already had the new and gloriously decorative sword Joss had had made for him, a sword untainted by family tradition. It hung on his belt now, its silver handle inlaid with onyx: black and silver, to match his uniform. He was making his own tradition, he'd said when he refused the old, useless weapon he'd never believed his father would let him touch.

He risked a kiss to her cheek when he'd fastened the belt around her slim waist. To his surprise, she didn't protest or wriggle. Natalia wasn't normally given to encouraging or offering stray embraces, but she hugged him back before shifting her belt to get the sword into place.

"You look lovely." His mother, Meriel, raised a ridiculous scrap of laced-edged linen to dab at one immaculately made-up eyelid. Bennet couldn't see any tears. She met his gaze without flinching, and he smiled. His mother was a genius at effective gestures. She smiled back, unblushing.

"Do you think Dad'll be here on time?" Natalia asked, once she had the sword settled to her exacting standards.

"Your father hasn't been late for a Passing-out Parade for over thirty years." The instant Natalia let go of the sword, their mother tutted and shook her head. Her small, beautiful hands twitched the sword a fraction of an inch to the left. Natalia's chagrined expression was priceless and this time Bennet shared the conspiratorial smile with his little sister. "His Transport shuttle was due in two hours ago. He'll be here."

"I wanted to see him before we have to muster for the Parade."

"He's on his way. He arrived with Uncle Jak a few minutes ago. I just spotted him." Bennet gestured at the window and the parade ground beyond.

Meriel tweaked Natalia's uniform into place. "Good. Well, we're all set then. Your father's here, and Thea and Al are keeping us seats in the spectator stands."

Natalia gave her a sharp glance. "But where's Liam? I'll bet he's off canoodling with that blonde he's been seeing. If he's late, I'll never forgive him."

"Liam is precisely where we want him." Bennet was as familiar as his sister with their younger brother's irritating habits. "He's under lock and key."

Meriel's sharp eyes brightened with amusement. "The brig?"

"Well, no, although I thought about it." Bennet had given his last lecture two days earlier, but he still counted as Academy staff, with all the duties and rights and privileges that entailed. Including the right to order punishment duty for defaulting cadets. He hadn't gone quite that far, but Liam was safely penned up in the office Bennet had used during his year as Strategy Tutor.

"You'd better go and collect him, and find Thea."

"Yes, Mamma." Bennet looked his sister up and down. If they were handing out prizes for the smartest turned-out cadet that day, she'd win. He saluted her. "Ensign."

For once, he'd said something that pleased her, using her new rank for the first time. Blushing, Natalia snapped to attention and saluted back. "Sir!"

Bennet grinned, wishing they could connect like this more often. He kissed her cheek and left her to their mother. When he reached the landing, Caeden had arrived at the foot of the staircase to Natalia's room, smoothing his dress uniform to repair the ruffling the sharp wind had given the parade-ground perfection expected of dreadnought commanders. He carried off the ensemble well, despite the yards of gold braid. Bennet ran down the stairs to join him.

"Tallie was worried you'd be late." Bennet stopped on the last step. That nod of approval had to be for his fast progress down the stairs. On Caeden's last brief visit home, Bennet had still occasionally used a cane.

"I'm never late." Caeden took a good long look at him and nodded. "You look better each time I see you."

Bennet grinned and took the last step down. "I couldn't look worse!"

"That's true. You looked terrible on the hospital ship." Tentative, as he always was when they were first reunited, Caeden raised his hands and rested them on Bennet's shoulders. "You look very well now, thank the gods. I'm delighted to hear you've accepted Fleet."

"I'm getting used to the idea, myself." Bennet made himself stand still, not flinch.

Caeden nodded, and for a second he pulled Bennet in close, his hand on the back of Bennet's head, smoothing his hair. Caeden had made two flying visits home since Telnos and Bennet had been touched by the length of time his father had tried to spend with him each time, and by the attempts at more overt affection. It was still awkward. Caeden had the air of a man trying to make up for lost time and not always knowing how to do it.

Caeden murmured something, his breath warm across Bennet's neck and ear. The muttering was Theban, but what the scholar in Bennet considered to be the bastardised version appropriated by the church, not the pure Theban he preferred. A blessing. Of course.

"And if you're both finished with this affecting reunion," Meriel said from the upper landing, "Natalia's waiting."

"Yes, dear." The Great Commander could be surprisingly meek. Caeden pulled back, straightening Bennet's jacket as he did so. "Just completing inspection."

Bennet grinned at his father, recognising maternal disapproval over their restraint. "She always cries when she first sees me after I've been away." It seemed only fair to let his father know the standards to be met.

"I can imagine."

"Daddy?" Natalia appeared at the head of the stairs, looking and sounding like the shy schoolgirl she'd been. She hadn't called their father by that childish diminutive for years, and Bennet raised an eyebrow in Caeden's direction.

Caeden smiled up at her. Meriel gave Bennet a pointed look suggesting his absence would be a very good thing indeed. She'd spoken to him about it earlier, and though he'd protested he wasn't in competition, he'd agreed to give Natalia a clear run.

He acknowledged the implied instruction. "I'll go and get Liam."

"We'll talk later." Caeden started up the stairs. He paused and turned. "Where is Liam?"

"He's locked up in my office."

Caeden paused, smiled. "Oh well done, Bennet. We should lock him up more often." He frowned. "Come to think on it, we should have done it sooner. From birth, perhaps. It would have saved me quite a lot of grief and grey hair."

Liam had whiled away his captivity rearranging Bennet's office furniture and drawing rude pictures on the white board. If he hoped for a reaction, he was doomed to failure.

"I don't think it's anatomically possible," was all Bennet said, herding Liam out the door and towards the parade ground. "Not even in my most limber days."

Liam was unrepentant. "You should exercise more. You didn't have to lock me in, you know. I do have some sense of family obligation. Much as I'd like to cut and run, I do know I can't do it. How's Tallie?"

"Nervous. You mustn't tease her."

Liam grinned. "It's irresistible. Only teasing Dad beats the thrill."

"Do you ever think about anything serious?"

Liam appeared to give this a micro-second's consideration. "Not if I can help it. I don't like thinking. I'm more of a feeler."

Bennet allowed him a half-smile for that one. "That explains some of your class ratings, then. You feel your way to a D grade."

"Your aversion to cutting me any slack in class took fair play and anti-nepotism to extremes, you know. I've done all right this year, haven't I?"

"Yes." Bennet dodged through the gathering crowds, scanning the spectator stands for Thea. Bless her, but she'd bagged the best seats in the house. Front row. Of course. "There's Thea. Come on."

It took a moment or two to greet Thea and her husband, Alain, and push Liam into the seat on Bennet's left. He left a seat clear between himself and Thea, for their mother when she arrived. Caeden, of course, would sit with the other commanderly demigods in the section reserved for the Supreme Commander and his acolytes.

"I did do okay, didn't I?" Liam asked, picking up where they'd left off and sounding subdued.

Well, that was out of character. The boy wasn't insecure about it, surely? Liam did more than okay. He was bright, probably the brightest one of them all, but a touch of Shield reticence would do him the world of good. Bennet nodded. "You did fine."

"Then be grateful I didn't blight your teaching career and don't make snarky comments when he gets here. Otherwise I'll be treated to another lecture about how hard I'll have to work to be posted to a dreadnought. Which, I might add, I'm not sure I want, anyway."

Bennet glanced sideways at him, but remained silent. On his right, Thea turned her head and raised an eyebrow. She'd heard, then. At his grimace she smiled and turned back to Alain, leaving Bennet to it. When it came to Liam, the entire family had a bad habit of leaving Bennet to it.

As Bennet expected, Liam was rather put out at the lack of fraternal interest. "What, no lecture on duty and honour and service?"

"It's your decision. You don't need me to tell you he'll be disappointed. He'll kick up a fuss if neither of us joins the family firm."

Liam ran a hand inside the tight collar of his dress blues. "Missing the entire point, big brother. Of course he'll fuss. That's what makes it fun. Mind you, I'm not so sure I want the same sort of fuss you got when you rebelled."

"I suspect you'd agonise over it less."

Liam snorted. "I'm cultivating the habit of sailing unscathed through life. It leaves more time for the important things. Anyhow, you escaped Fleet."

"Temporarily. I am going to the *Corvus* next week."

"At least it's not the *Gyrfalcon*. Just because you got away, don't think I'm going to be left behind to be your sacrificial lamb on the family altar. If I do decide I don't want it, then he'll have to make do with Tallie. That'll be nice for him, if she stays as snippy as she was at breakfast."

"It's a big day for her and she's stressed. You do know about the effects of stress? You have done human biology, haven't you?"

Liam smiled. "Oh yes. I'm making quite a personal study of it."

"Liam!" But Bennet couldn't hold back the laugh. "The blonde?"

"Leta. She's Galatian. They're all ice-blonde and statuesque." Liam raised his hands, cupping them around imaginary breasts. "Best developed mammary glands in my year."

Ah, that one. Bennet wasn't nearly as appreciative. "I'd wondered how the laws of physics have been bent to allow a body that slender to support a chest of that magnitude. I might have known you'd have been making a personal study of the phenomenon."

Liam laughed. "She has some impressive underpinnings. I hadn't realised you knew which one it was this week."

"I didn't. I'm not good enough at maths and the man hasn't lived who could devise a computerised tracking system with a sufficiently high data-handling capacity to keep up with your girlfriends. It makes me dizzy. Tallie mentioned her and then I worked it out."

"You're one to talk about dizzy," Liam jeered. "At least I know what I want! I don't bounce from Joss to Rosie."

"Oh, I know what I want." Getting it, was the problem. Bennet swallowed a sigh. Liam was far too sharp, and far too predatory, to be allowed into that secret. "You'd better not say anything in front of Dad about her, unless you want him in High Theban mode, lecturing to the spiritually fallen. He hasn't got over the last one yet."

"Which one was that? You're usually at least half a dozen girls behind me."

"If it comes to girls, I'm dozens behind you." Bennet laughed again.

"Yeah, but I bet you got a few lectures."

Bennet's smile didn't falter. "There's no lecture stern enough."

"I wish Dad came with a volume control some days."

Gods, didn't they all?

Bennet tried not to smile. Liam didn't need encouragement. "Keep quiet about your sins, then, and he may not find out."

"I don't want to keep quiet about Leta. I'm seeing her tonight."

"I doubt that. The old man won't let you off being family today, especially since it's his first day back. You know what he's like."

"Too true I do." Liam scowled. "Won't you help get me off?"

"No."

Liam sighed, accepting defeat gracefully. "I hate it when you come over all responsible and he comes over all paterfamilias."

"I'm not being responsible. I need an ally." Bennet gestured to the crowd. "Warwick's out there somewhere and you know what that means."

"Oh dee-light-ful!" This time Liam's scowl was a thing of magnificence. Impressive. "A family dinner with Warwick-the-Glorious. I can understand why people leave home."

"Warwick was little more than a contributory factor."

"Beautiful! Even I couldn't think of a better put down." Liam made another eloquent grimace and stared out over the gathering crowd of spectators all making their way to the stands. "Yeah. You were right. Warwick's with Dad and Mamma, heading this way. Aunt Beth's there, too."

"Is she?" Thea glanced up as she spoke, betraying she'd been listening in on the conversation. Bennet pointed out Warwick's wife, just then greeting his mother. "Move down a seat, you two, then. We'll have to make room for her."

Liam hmphed but did as he was told. Thea just laughed at his mocking, "What a lovely example of grace and etiquette you set us!" and turned back to give her attention to Alain. Liam returned to his original complaint. "Hell. Dinner with Warwick. We'll have to listen all night to him wittering on about how he won his bloody medals. You know, Dad thinks you influence me. Should I follow your example and get myself disowned?"

Over on the parade ground, Warwick was being his usual big, blustery self, slapping Caeden on the back and throwing back his head to laugh. Bonhomie personified. Bennet allowed his lip to curl in derision.

"You won't like it," he said. "I didn't."

CHAPTER FOUR

01 Sextus 7489: Military Academy, Sais City

As soon as Natalia, red-faced with excitement, had been sent off to the final year muster, Caeden had the chance to kiss his wife before taking her arm through his to escort her to the spectator stands. They moved through the crowds of parents and military top brass. Meriel nodded and smiled greetings, as usual managing to meet the social demands made on her with grace and charm. She was admirable, but Caeden suspected none of it impinged even slightly on what she was thinking.

"When Natalia was little and this excited, she'd be sick," she said. "I think she's grown out of it, but I'll be glad when the ceremony's over."

"It's the highlight of a cadet's career. She'll be fine." Caeden glanced over Meriel's head to watch his daughter join her classmates. "I'm delighted to see Bennet looking so well, Merry. When I think that when I saw him last he still used a walking cane, it seems a miracle."

"That was five months ago. He's pushed himself hard. Too hard, sometimes, I think, but his doctors managed to keep him under control. Tallie did well this year, don't you think? The commandant's been very complimentary about her."

"Yes. She did do well. It's just what I expected of her, but I'm pleased." Caeden frowned. "He doesn't look happy."

Meriel rolled her eyes at him. "Well, he wasn't happy with Joss, and he doesn't seem too happy without him. But I thought that was what you wanted, Bennet without Joss."

"Yes."

"Then you have to accept the consequences, which aren't all as beneficial as we'd like."

"I know you don't approve, but I wanted him to remember he had choices, and I wanted him away from that man."

"You never did forgive Joss, did you?"

"Did you?"

Meriel shrugged. "I'm better at compromise than you. You might want to think about whether you chose the best means to cut him loose. More people than Joss were involved, you know, and I dare say they aren't happy either."

"But he's cut Joss adrift. That's good."

"Bennet is the one doing the drifting, and in some odd directions."

"In some more acceptable directions." Caeden considered the outcome of his interference. He'd done well there, in the end. Bennet had turned in acceptable directions. "Rosie is a very nice girl."

He had to make an effort not to allow through a smile. If he were honest, he'd laugh at himself, that the thought of Bennet living with Shield Lieutenant Rosamund was a matter for congratulation. Most people wouldn't raise an eyebrow at it, of course but Caeden still had an old-fashioned reverence for the institution of marriage. Mind you, anything was better than Joss. As with everything else, sin was relative.

The sly look Meriel gave him, the slight smile, let him know she got the joke. Her hand tightened on his arm. "Oh, I don't deny that, although he's very close-mouthed about what's going on."

Caeden glanced at her. "He hasn't said anything to me, either.

I've not dared ask outright, because… well. I don't think I have the right."

"No. You don't." Meriel's tone softened the implied criticism, but still it stung.

"I thought since she's living at the apartment…" He allowed his voice to rise on a questioning note.

"I thought so too, but he doesn't say. Don't get your hopes up too high. She's spent all her leaves with him this year, but she hasn't been on Albion for weeks." Meriel paused, frowning. "I wonder how he likes being the one left behind while Rosie is away?"

"He left her the pendant in his will. That was significant."

"Yes, it was. All the same, I wouldn't expect a wedding announcement any time soon. I don't think it's Rosie, for him. I don't know what Rosie thinks, poor girl." Meriel tugged his arm and pointed. "There they are. Bless her, Thea got us the good seats. Bennet appears to have Liam corralled, which is no mean feat. I suppose you have to sit with the great and good, along with Jak?"

"Jak is the great and good." Caeden chuffed out a laugh. "He says it's the only compensation for the burden of overall command."

Meriel smiled, but her thoughts were evidently with their elder son rather than Caeden's boss. "I'm glad Bennet was home so long, though, and I'll miss him when he goes to Demeter next week. For one thing, Liam is so much easier to manage. He'll go out of his way to do anything Bennet asks him to."

Caeden snorted. That hit home and she had to know it. Liam went out of his way to do the opposite of anything Caeden wanted, or to do something he knew would send Caeden into a towering rage. Sometimes it infuriated him, seeing his elder son's influence over his youngest, as much as he gave thanks for the way it mitigated some of Liam's wilder flights.

Meriel softened the hit with another little squeeze of her hand on his arm. "Natalia's looking forward to joining you on the *Gyrfalcon*. It will be nice for you two to spend some time together."

"I won't be able to mother her, Meriel. Just because she's my daughter doesn't mean any special treatment—the opposite, in fact. I have to be fair. I can't be seen to give her more attention than any other engineering ensign."

Meriel's light tone was barbed. "Well, that'll be a great deal more than she's used to."

Caeden glanced sideways at her before being distracted. Up ahead was an unmistakable figure. His impatience smoothed out into pleasure. "There's Warwick and Bethany. We'd better join them."

"How delightful," Meriel said.

01 Sextus 7489: Mendes suburb, Sais City

Bennet had escaped his mother's drawing room and taken refuge on the terrace overlooking the sea. Caeden glanced at Warwick, who had Natalia in thrall. Bennet had the right idea. When had Warwick grown so pompous? Was it just as they'd got older? Who'd have thought the daring, devil-may-care cadet Caeden had befriended at the Academy would grow up to be such a... well, no need to sugar coat it. Warwick had turned into such a self-aggrandising windbag, boasting about past victories. Caeden had heard those stories a dozen times. No wonder Bennet always tagged *-the-Glorious* onto Warwick's name; a habit Liam had picked up, Caeden noticed. And getting back to Bennet, Caeden needed to spend time with his elder son. He grabbed a bottle and followed, leaving the rest of his family to Warwick's mercy.

"I appear to be in trouble with your mother." He took the chair beside Bennet at one of the small tables set to take advantage of the views of the bay. The evening was cooling as it inched towards sunset, the breeze coming in from the sea heavy with the taste of salt. He offered the liquor bottle. "Again."

Bennet shook his head at the offer and held up a glass still three-quarters full. "Fast work. You've only been home for about ten hours."

"Not quite my best, but close to the record."

Bennet laughed. "What have you done this time?"

"The usual."

Bennet stared out across the bay. "Ah. My fault then."

"Fault? Of course it's not your fault. But I have to admit the disagreements are usually about what your mother considers my interfering at times she deems I should stay right out of things." Caeden was quiet for a long minute or two, sipping on the liquor. "Are you angry about that?"

Bennet didn't answer straight away, apparently intent on the sunset.

Albion's sun was just dipping below the horizon. Caeden twisted in his chair to watch, waiting for the odd green flash, a green the colour of peridots, that slanted across the ocean the instant before the sun disappeared altogether and the bright Albion day melted into twilight. The killjoys who liked to explain everything would say it had to do with the way the light refracted on the horizon line or how the atmosphere scattered the sun's rays, or something. He'd rather focus on the satisfyingly beautiful instant when the green flash came. It didn't matter why it happened.

There it was. A flash of brilliance, swiftly over.

When it faded, Bennet said, tone thoughtful, "No. I'm not angry about it. I'd have left Joss eventually. We were heading for a crash. We wanted different things and I was tired of compromising. You added the catalyst to the mix, that's all. I'm not mad about it."

"But not happy either."

"I'm happier now than I was for the whole of the last year with Joss."

"I suppose that's some consolation." Caeden sat back. The last of the sun slid below the dark horizon line. Behind him Warwick's loud voice drifted out of an open window. He was talking about the Taxos battle. Not for the first time. "And the catalyst?"

He had never asked before. Whatever had gone on with Flynn—and he wasn't so naïve as to believe nothing had—so far he'd granted Bennet an adult's privacy about it. He'd never asked, never alluded to it, never hinted. Meriel's unusual sharpness had him wondering how affected Bennet had been by it, whether Joss had not been the only one to pay a price for Bennet's freedom.

Bennet reached for the bottle, using his right hand. It was a relief to see how easily his fingers grasped it as he poured himself a drink. He'd got back more dexterity than the medics had predicted, thank the gods.

"Catalysts come and catalysts go."

Another long uncomfortable silence. Well, that was significant. And a snub, if ever he heard on. Caeden sighed. "I'm sorry."

"I'm not."

"He's well. He's doing very well."

"Who is?" Bennet stared him right in the eye.

"Can I come and join the grown-ups?" Liam paused, his hand on the back of Bennet's chair, sharp blue eyes looking from one to the other. "Or am I interrupting something?"

Bennet caught at Liam's wrist. "No. Sit down."

The wink Liam sent Bennet's way was all too knowing and far too obvious. Was Caeden so impossible they had to ally themselves against him all the time?

"Good," Liam said. "Can I have some of that? You'll forgive me for saying this, Dad—"

"Possibly, but don't rely on it." Caeden's tone was sharper than he'd intended. "And water that down. You're too young to be drinking hard liquor."

Liam obeyed, adding soda to the small amount of liquor Bennet had handed him with no more comment than an exasperated roll of his eyes at his brother, who prudently took no notice of that or of Caeden's implied criticism of him for indulging Liam with spirituous alcohol. "All right, but you can't stop me from telling you Uncle Warwick is better than a sedative. He's telling the baby bedtime stories in there and it's putting me to sleep."

Bennet cocked an eyebrow. "Baby?"

"He's managed to reduce Tallie to a mental age of about twelve. She seems to think it her duty to fill in for Sioned and she's hanging on his every word. She hasn't the sense to run away. Mamma and Aunt Bethany have, though. They've gone off to talk about whatever it is women their age talk about."

"Lovers and new clothes." Bennet grinned at Caeden. "You do know my surgeon would have laid heart and scalpel at Mamma's feet if she'd given him a micro-gram of encouragement?"

Caeden smiled. "She told me all about it. I am, however, a devoted and careful husband."

"That was horrifying to see. Scarred me for life. I should be seeking financial compensation from somebody." Liam sipped at his drink. "Dad, is something wrong with Aunt Bethany? She doesn't look well."

Caeden shook his head. Warwick hadn't said anything, but he'd been shocked when he'd seen Bethany. She'd lost a lot of weight and she was greyed over, diminished. Meriel hadn't been as shocked, but she did look sad. "I don't know. I agree, though. She looks ill."

"Oh." Liam frowned. "I don't think Uncle Warwick's noticed."

Caeden stiffened at this infelicitous observation.

Bennet said, quiet and quelling, "Liam."

"Sorry. Sorry. So, what are the grown-ups talking about?"

"I was about to ask your brother how he is, not having had the chance all day," Caeden said, glad to change the subject.

Liam had always fought against any tendency to try and

reduce Bennet to invalid status. "He's fine, and not allowed any more sympathy for at least the next five years. He's had his quota. Sorry, Dad. You missed your opportunity to feel sorry for him."

That stabbed. Hard. "I usually do miss things."

Bennet spoke quickly, to fill up a space that might become maudlin and uncomfortable. "You wouldn't have wanted to be here when I was throwing up all the time."

Liam sniggered. "Gods, no! I've never seen you display so much creativity in anything before. And so sweet tempered!"

"But I'm fine now." Bennet rolled smoothly on over Liam's tactless interruption with no more than a flick of a fingernail at Liam's ear lobe. "They wouldn't let me back if I wasn't."

"I know. But all the same…" Caeden wasn't allowed to finish, any more than Liam had been.

"I've taken up Tierce again. That's partly why I went for the *Corvus*, rather than a destroyer—the attraction of a full-sized Tierce court. I'm enjoying playing again and I don't want to give it up."

"You used to be pretty good at that, once upon a time."

"When I was Liam's age. Do you remember coming to sports day in my last year at school?"

Caeden nodded. He smiled. "I remember wondering where my mild-mannered son had gone. You played like you were waging all-out war."

"I won, though."

"You did indeed. I was very proud of you." He rode out the look Bennet gave him, holding his son's gaze until Bennet's mouth gave the tiniest twitch in acknowledgement.

"Why'd you give it up?" Liam asked, rubbing at the afflicted ear. "You were good at it. I know you played right through the Thebaid and SSI but I can't remember you playing after you graduated."

"Shield ships aren't big enough to have a Tierce court."

"Well, okay. But you were home often enough to play in minor league, surely?"

Bennet paused, and shrugged. "Shield life meant I couldn't commit to any sort of programme of matches. Besides, I didn't have time when I was home."

"I'd forgotten Joss doesn't like Tierce," Liam said with his usual sweet malice. Caeden took a hasty mouthful of liquor to hide the grin.

"No." Bennet's serenity, Caeden suspected, was hard won. Impressive, though.

"Are you never tempted to brain the impertinent little beggar?" Caeden asked. He and Bennet exchanged grins. "You're out of order, Liam."

He was wasting his time there. Liam was immune to chastisement. Frankly, nothing short of a fusion bomb was likely to have much impact. Liam grinned to display how untouched he was by the rebuke and finished off his drink with a flourish.

"And don't even think about asking for more," Caeden warned.

That must have stung. Liam frowned. "I'm nineteen, not nine, you know. Nearly twenty."

"Not mentally." Caeden turned his attention back onto his elder son, who at least didn't show Liam's talent for stinging like a particularly irritating wasp. "Are your knee and hand really up to Tierce?"

"They are. I'm still pretty damn good at it. Of course, I haven't played competitive Tierce for coming up to seven years and you won't believe how slow I am these days. They paired me off with the beginners to start with."

"Shameful." Liam wrinkled his nose and grimaced

"Oh, I don't know." Bennet grinned at his brother. "What's really shameful is I'm still one helluva lot better at it than you are."

"Hey!"

"Less interest in Galatian ladies' underpinnings and you'd be a great deal healthier."

Caeden gave his youngest son a pained look. "Who is it this time?"

Bennet raised both hands to chest level, cupping them, and smiled when Liam glared at him. Caeden laughed, and replenished all their glasses. Even Liam's. All things considered, all the messy all-too-human relationships included, it was good to be home.

CHAPTER FIVE

01 Sextus 7489: Sais City

All right, perhaps it was unreasonable for Shield Lieutenant Rosamund to be disappointed that when she flung open the apartment door with a cheery "I'm back!", she found the place dark, empty and conspicuously lacking in Bennet. But then, reason could be over-rated.

She huffed to herself, carried her kit bag into the bedroom and tossed it into a corner. Neat freak Bennet would shove it out of sight when he came in, but it could stay there until she could be bothered to unpack it. She stared out of the window, across a park just darkening into dusk.

Where was he at this time of night? Working? She wouldn't put it past him if some problem at the Strategy Unit had caught his interest. At least he wasn't out with Joss. The planned dinner Bennet had oh-so-carefully told her about had been two or three days earlier. She should work on him to cut the ties there. He'd outgrown Joss. He said so himself, and it wasn't healthy to cling on like that.

Of course. Graduation Day at the Academy and Natalia's last day. He'd have been at the Academy for the ceremony and now the family were celebrating somewhere. It was bad timing. That was all. But she hated coming back to an empty flat. It wasn't a big apartment, the one she shared with Bennet when she was home, but felt cavernous when she was in it alone. She rattled around the rooms like a small ball bouncing in a big space. How did Bennet feel about it when she was away on jobs in the *Hype* and he was forced to live here alone? Did he rattle around too?

She couldn't settle to anything. Not a scrappy supper, not the vid, not a book. She dismissed the idea of an early evening run in the park. She turned on all the lights instead. Things were never so lonely when you weren't sitting in the dark.

She poked through the freezer to find something edible. He was out somewhere grand with fine wines and glorious food and here she was, facing a warmed-up frozen dinner, kicking her heels and waiting for him to come home.

How very little-woman of her.

She caught herself up, fast. It wasn't his fault. It wasn't as if he could have been sure she'd be back today. He couldn't have known the *Hype* would make it back to the Demeter transfer station a day early and free her up for a shuttle home. And of course he couldn't miss Natalia's passing-out parade. But still…

The food tasted like cardboard in a gravy whose only merit was being wet enough to wash the cardboard down. It turned to mush in the mouth. It tasted worse than being out on a job longer than expected and having to break out the emergency rations to tide them over. She'd have preferred emergency rations. Dehydrated meat dinners could give this crap a parsec's head start and still win the race. She dropped the half-eaten meal into the trashcan, fished a bottle of beer out of the fridge and retired to the living room sofa to wait for Bennet's return.

A very Bennet-ian sort of room this. A scholar's room. She was slowly having some influence, though. The two bold pieces of modernist painting that lent patches of bright colour to the plain walls, for instance. Her Yuletide present to Bennet. He'd put them up on the walls himself. That meant something, that he'd hung them and not once complained they didn't match his old bits of antiques or his old life. It meant something.

The one on the right was crooked. That probably meant something too.

She smoothed away the condensation on the side of the bottle with a fingertip. Better not go there. It didn't mean anything. Just stick with the notion that Bennet was no handyman. Couldn't put a picture hook in straight.

Apart from her paintings, most of the décor was ancient: framed papyri on the wall above Bennet's desk and ancient artefacts scattered on every horizontal surface, with a museum case of the finest ones over by the windows overlooking the park. And books. Real ones.

She jumped up, went to the bookcase. Shelves and shelves of books, books, datapads and more books; neatly lined up, brigaded by subject and then alphabetically. How many hours had she spent getting those books aligned to Bennet's satisfaction when he'd first moved in? She ran her finger along a shelf of them, following the topography of hill-valley-hill-valley of the book spines. She hadn't minded helping him unpack and sort them out. It stopped him from overdoing when he was still so very unwell after Telnos (and what a cock-up that had been, with Bennet getting himself left behind and then so badly injured protecting those religious nuts who masqueraded as farmers) and everything that brought in its wake in the way of him leaving Joss (about time, and Joss was ten kinds of idiot) and his time with Flynn (the ultra, ultra cock-up).

Her hand closed over one of the books, pulled it free of its row. A history, of course. *Colonisation in the Second Age*. She'd bet Bennet was word perfect in it. Rosie preferred something with more in the way of a plot. She shoved the book back into place on the shelf with a hard little push.

It had been worth it, helping him sort out the flat. They'd come closer together quicker than she could ever have anticipated. It brought opportunities. After all, if you've spent all day cataloguing a man's books, it would be downright churlish of him to cast you out into the night when you'd crashed, exhausted, on his bed.

Bennet was a lot of things. Principled, for instance; he'd not made a move on her when she'd still been his Lieutenant, for whatever noble reason he told himself was right and proper. At the same time, he could be as self-absorbed as any man, short tempered if people couldn't keep up with him, too proud to ask for help when he needed it. But he was never churlish with her.

Rosie went back to the sofa, took a swig of lovely, icy cold beer. It washed away the taste of the cardboard.

Nothing happened those first weeks when she'd sort of muscled her way into his life. She'd had a three week break with him before going back to the *Hype* for another job, and they'd been so platonic they could have been poster children for Good Book study classes. He'd still been in mourning for losing Flynn again, and she'd been too scared to push too hard, too soon. But when she got back again, four weeks later… well, he'd been more open then. More receptive.

Lonelier, and readier to grasp at something to dull it down.

She fingered the diamond and sapphire pendant at her throat, the one she'd been left in his will. He wouldn't take it back when he was resurrected. He'd closed her fingers around it and told her it was hers. Forever. No matter what. She wore it always, under her uniform. The little slip of paper it had come with never left her either.

For the only girl who could have straightened me out

She'd been there when he was ready to turn to her. Shoulder to cry on, hand to hold, arms to lie within, ears to listen, lips to soothe. The only girl who could ever straighten him out, he said, and she'd done it. But then she was Shield, and Shield never gave up, never gave in. Bennet should have known that. She grinned, toasting the room with her beer bottle. He really should have known.

By the time Bennet arrived back at the apartment, just before midnight, Rosie had exhausted all her strategies for killing time.

She'd had a reluctant run around the park perimeter (twice), followed by the luxury of a hot shower with real water, and had paged through most of the vid channels. Honest, there was so much crap on the vid it made her want to be back out on the line, deep in Maess space doing something mildly destructive involving enemy bases and a lot of explosive.

When the outer door opened, she was half-asleep on the big sofa, an inane space opera playing out on the big flat screen above the fireplace, the sound muted. When Rosie struggled upright, disorientated, the heroine was trapped in a burning space ship (type unspecified) under attack by the Fiesl, or whatever stupid name the writers had come up with that week, and was apparently accustomed to flying her space ship while dressed in nothing more than a bikini. Which was stupid. Especially where she was keeping her laser—the chafing would not fun. At all.

"Rosie?"

Bennet grinned down at her, his eyes crinkling in just the right way to show his delight at seeing her. His hands gripped her biceps, hauled her up to her feet, before he let go and planted them on her shoulders, warm and heavy. She raised her arms, reached up to curve them around his neck and clasp her hands together. He was in dress uniform, and hell, but he looked good. The gladness washed over her, made her giddy.

"Rosie." A tone of quiet satisfaction now, and his smile gentled into the contented look she saw so rarely. "Rosie."

He ducked his head and kissed her.

And whoa, but she'd missed that. It was several enthusiastic minutes later before she could pull back to smile at him. That was the sort of welcome a girl could come to appreciate. "Heavens, have you missed me or something?"

"A bit." Bennet grinned, and wrenched at his dress jacket collar. "Help me out of this, will you? And then I can see about a proper welcome home."

"Where's the fun in that?" Rosie wondered, starting on the silver buttons down the jacket front, easing them from their frogged fastenings. "I'm holding out for something improper. Scandalous, even." She tugged at a recalcitrant button. "I'd forgotten how sweet you look in dress uniform. And I'd forgotten it was Graduation Day today. Have you been with the family?"

"All day, gods help me. Then back to the parents' house for dinner. I wish you'd been there. As usual, Warwick came back with us, since he and Dad go back to a time before Earth went dark and Dad is appallingly loyal to his old friends. Even when they're windbags and braggarts. Believe me, an evening spent in Commander Warwick's bracing company tends to stretch itself out into a week or six. I could have done with the distraction."

"It's not like you to need protection." Rosie pushed the jacket back off his shoulders and dropped it over the sofa arm. He pulled her back in close, his hands smoothing down her sides to cup her bottom and she pushed back into them, grinning. She wore only a thin tee and sleep shorts. His hands were warm and she fitted into them perfectly.

"Oh, I managed to keep out of Warwick's way, mostly, but I wish you'd been home earlier and could have come."

"Well, it was really a family thing, wasn't it? I don't think Natalia would have been pleased if I muscled in on her big day. She doesn't like to share." She grinned up at him, and added before he could do more than open his mouth to protest, "I'm not family, Bennet."

"I'd rather have you there than most of them."

"Mmmn. So Warwick may have been wearing but your dad was more so. How was it?"

Bennet grimaced, but a grin lurked under it. "Spiky."

"You or him?"

"Me, I think. It was all right, really. Not too bad, I mean, but he did want to talk to me."

"Significantly, you mean."

"Very. I had to hide behind Liam a lot."

Rosie laughed. "You're more inarticulate than most men, and that's saying something."

"That's why I wanted you. Liam's inadequate as protection. I keep mentioning his philandering as a diversion, but I think Dad's beginning to see through that one. I'm not used to having him there to talk to. I'm not comfortable with it."

"Is he?"

"No. No, I don't think so." Bennet laughed. It sounded rueful. "He thinks it's his duty, though."

"Whether you want it or not? Ingrate. I like your father, you know. He doesn't strike me as the sort of man who gives up easily."

"Not likely. You don't get to be a dreadnought commander and not be a dozen shades of stubborn. I got the raised eyebrow and the imperious command to lunch tomorrow. Alone, he said. I don't think I can wriggle out of it."

"You and your father are very alike." And before he had time to be insulted, Rosie wriggled to remind him it was time for her improper welcome home. "Mind you, it's really odd talking about your dad while I'm trying to seduce you. Kinky."

He laughed. "All right. We have more important things to talk about anyway. At least… you did get my message, didn't you?"

"What message?"

He froze. Grimaced, and this time no humour lurked beneath it. His hands tightened on her a trifle. "Damn. I thought you would have got it. I sent it a couple of days ago."

"I've been in transit for the last two days, Bennet. I had the chance of an early Transport shuttle and I grabbed it with both hands. I had to run for it. I didn't have time to look at messages." And hadn't thought to since, while she'd been waiting for him to come home. What had she missed?

All he said was, "Oh."

Oh. It echoed in her head. He wouldn't send her any old

message. This was important. Serious. He drew his mouth into a line, and his brow furrowed. *Uh-huh.* That was the face he wore when he was looking for the right words.

It wasn't them. If he'd changed his mind about them being together, he wouldn't have kissed her like that when he came in. He wouldn't have kissed her at all. That wasn't his style. Self-absorbed sometimes, yes. But not consciously selfish. It had to be someth—

Her mouth was dry. She had to work her tongue for a moment to get the saliva flowing before she could moisten her lips. "Your medical board."

He nodded. "I was cleared for combat duty. They told me a couple of days ago."

Rosie pulled away, sat down plump on the sofa. She shivered. It was cold in the room. A draught? Bennet probably left a door open somewhere. Something fluttered in her stomach. Not something light and ethereal but something wearing hobnailed combat boots and dancing the tarantella. The sensation kicked up against her ribs. She pulled in a deep breath against the constrictions of throat and chest.

His medical board.

Damn.

The sofa cushions dipped under his weight as he sat beside her. He slid an arm around her shoulders.

She pushed the air back out, found enough of a voice to speak. "I suppose we should have expected it."

They'd only had half a year. Shit. Only half a year.

"Yeah." Bennet huffed out the word, as if the same hands constricting her had him in a choke-hold too. "I took a Fleet posting. The *Corvus*. Second Flotilla."

Well, it wouldn't be Shield and the *Hype*. It would have to be his rotation out.

Rosie's hands twisted over themselves. This was the end for

them. Bennet wouldn't consider not returning to duty, not even to preserve what they had. He wouldn't do it, and she wouldn't ask it of him. She'd be struck down first.

She could ask one thing. "When?"

"Next week."

She closed her eyes, pressing the lids down hard. She'd hoped... gods, it was stupid really. She hadn't hoped so much as been determined not to think about it. She'd be taking her own rotation out the following Septimus. If only he'd been home until then. They'd have had another year. But now... with him in Fleet and her going to Infantry the following year, they wouldn't have the chance to meet for years.

Ever.

"I'm sorry, Rosie."

She was too. She was very sorry. She should have known what she was getting into. She had known. And yet still she'd jumped in with both feet—fools rush in, they say. Well, lovers are all kinds of fool. Star-crossed lovers are the worst kind of fool of all.

Her throat was so tight nothing could get past it. Shield warriors didn't sob. She choked it back past a lump in her throat the size of the *Hype*. Her eyes burned, blurred.

"I'm so sorry. It wasn't fair on you. We always knew this could happen, and I shouldn't have taken advantage—"

"It's been worth it," she said, fierce and hot, slapping a hand over his mouth to shut up the futile regrets. Stupid, futile regrets. Stupid. "Worth it. What time we have... worth it. Every damn minute."

She looked at him. He was beautiful and he'd been hers. For a little while. Not long enough. She had to drag her gaze away before she cried, looking around at the room she was only starting to help shape, the one that would be taken from her now. She'd felt like she rattled around in here when Bennet wasn't there...

That was it. That explained them.

They both rattled around: sometimes separately, sometimes together. But the baseline, the ground state, was that they inhabited separate spaces that only came together every few weeks when she got home for a scant couple of weeks between jobs. The coming together was very enjoyable, no doubt about that. Exciting, like atoms pumped up with energy. But it wasn't steady state, it wasn't baseline.

Baseline was being apart.

She turned to him. His eyes were over-bright. Her own eyes burned, and she had to blink to keep back the tears. When he opened his arms, she went straight in, clinging, pressing herself in, moulding herself against him to get as much of him as possible for as long as she could hold on. Not that it would be long. She worked one hand in between them and let her fingers curve around her pendant.

Everything fell back to baseline, in the end.

CHAPTER SIX

02 Sextus 7489: Dreadnought *Gyrfalcon*

"I think he's been at the booze already," Flynn said, barely a whisper. "He must have it for breakfast."

Cruz kept her attention on their Captain as Simonitz finished the daily morning briefing, but Flynn read the minute changes in posture, the merest hunch of the shoulder nearest him. Cruz hadn't missed it either. Simonitz wasn't red-faced as if he were running a fever, his voice was normal and unthickened. But it was there all the same in the almost imperceptible pause between words betraying the care Simonitz took, in the slightest fumbling with the datapad in front of him as he read the daily orders.

A few months. No more than a year. That's all it would take and The Management wouldn't be able to pretend any longer it wasn't happening. One day they'd wake up and Sim would be gone and they'd have some smart-arse, shiny new captain to get used to, and another old-timer would have 'retired'. Well, a better fate than Simonitz going out into a skirmish so wasted on liquor that not even *Gyrfalcon*'s pilots could keep the Maess off him.

Someone coughed, and Flynn glanced across the table, distracted. The beta squadron leader, Kyle, covered his mouth with one hand. Kyle caught the glance and his eyes narrowed, rolling slightly in Simonitz's direction.

Flynn turned his attention back to Simonitz and reconsidered. No. Retirement might not be the best option. The instantaneous heat and flash of white, blood-tinged light and the long silence were better than a soused old age looking for long-past glories in the bottom of a liquor glass.

"And finally," Simonitz said, "You know it was Graduation Day at the Academy yesterday. We're getting six out of this new batch, to fill some of the holes."

Flynn's glance strayed to where Nairn used to sit, before he'd broken down. Nairn had seen three out of his squad blasted to blood and bone and atoms. The kid had lost it. His responsibility, his guilt. When he'd recovered, he'd been granted the downgrading he'd begged for. Flynn was grateful the Commander had understood that to send Nairn away somewhere his friends couldn't care for him was a far worse option than keeping him. Nairn flew as Cruz's wingman now, quiet and content to have the thinking done for him, no responsibilities. Flynn thought about taking half a dozen new kids, as bright and as enthusiastic and as naïve as Nairn had once been, and trying to make sure they survived their probationary year in one piece. He hoped they wouldn't fail these new kids the way they'd failed Nairn.

Simonitz voice cut into Flynn's thoughts, brought his attention back. "They're not all pilots. We get four; one goes to Isometrics and one to Engineering. The engineer is the Commander's daughter, by the way. Natasha or something. He seems to like fancy names for his kids."

Flynn mouthed the correct name. Natalia. But he didn't say anything aloud, too canny for that. Beside him, Cruz stirred and turned her head to look at him, but Flynn kept his eyes straight ahead, staring past Simonitz. If he stared long enough, it would all fade away again.

The one good thing about getting through another day was that the past was one day further behind.

"Is she anything like Bennet?" Cruz asked.

It had been easy enough to avoid Cruz when they were out on patrol—being several thousand miles apart and with a Comms officer who'd roast your nuts on a griddle for daring to misuse her precious airwaves for social chit-chat, gave plenty of opportunity for Flynn to hide away in the procedures and protocols that made up the military day. But they'd come off duty an hour ago, and any change in his routine of meet-Cruz-and-socialise and his friend would be after him like a Maess drone after a systems upgrade. He'd had to meet Cruz, play a practice Tierce game with her, walk and talk and act exactly as if there wasn't a thing in the Captain's morning briefing to bother him.

And, of course, there wasn't. Nothing at all.

He'd known that at some point in the evening, the topic would come up. It was inevitable, because the memory of the three weeks when they'd been commandeered by the Shield Regiment wasn't just his memory. He had his own unique memories, true, but some were shared. Someone was certain to hark back to it, prompted by hearing the Commander's daughter was on her way. "Remember when we went into T18 with the Commander's son? Three, four years ago? That was some mission."

He would meet any recollection, any talk of past glorious deeds, any enquiry from Cruz with his usual insouciant wit. He'd practiced it.

Bloody annoying that it crumbled at Cruz's first sally.

"Did you meet her on Albion last year?"

"I saw her. And the youngest one. Liam. At least, I think it was them. It was at the hospital and I was sneaking into an elevator on my way to see Bennet while hiding behind a bunch of flowers. I'm not sure if it was them, mind. We never met."

"Flowers? You?" Cruz blinked. "Surreal."

"You said it." Flynn wondered why the insouciant wit had gone into hiding. So much for practising his defences, here.

They turned into the OC. Cruz moved fast, backing Flynn into a corner table and trapping him behind it. "I've been very patient. Apart from you telling me you'd seen Bennet, you haven't said anything about what happened last year. It's not that I want to be personal—"

"But you're going to be, right?"

"Right. You've not been your old self all day. No, dammit, Flynn. You haven't been your old self for a year. You can't deny you had room for improvement, of course, so I'm not complaining about all of it. But I'm tired of being the strong, silent support and not know what the hell I'm being supportive about."

"Hey, even I'm entitled to some privacy!"

"Debatable. You've had a year's worth, anyway. I think that's more than enough for you. I've been good about not nagging you, but I've had it." Cruz's dark eyes were watchful. "You know, I swore I wouldn't do this. I swore I'd leave it, and let you get over it. I saw how you were the night of the Midnight Watch when we thought Bennet was dead, and I thought it was none of my business as long as you could cope."

"Thanks."

"Don't mention it. Because I'm changing tack. You're not coping. I've watched you, Flynn. You try hard, and I know you've been seeing one of the med-techs, and you still love taking our last credit at cards, but you're not actually enjoying any of it, are you?"

"I always enjoy taking your last credit, Cruz. The lost look on your face when I jingle the coins in my pocket is enough to keep me warm and cosy for days."

Pointless trying to divert the woman. She was on a mission, and rolled over all opposition. She gave him a kind smile. "Balls. You've been hiding ever since you came back."

"I don't know what you mean."

"Really? Well, let's see what we do know. One, you fell for him and fell hard. First time ever, wasn't it?"

"And last." Flynn kept it down to a mutter.

But Cruz heard him, and nodded. "I know. First and last. Two, you spent most of your leave with him, despite him supposedly living with some older guy, his tutor or something. Three, you're not exactly the happiest little pilot on the *Gyrfalcon*."

"I'm doing okay!"

"Okay, but not great. All day today you've wandered around looking like someone gave you a metaphorical kick in the balls, ever since the Captain mentioned that Bennet's sister arrives next week. Until then, I thought I was imagining it, because you're good at hiding, but now I'm sure I'm not. I need to do something about it."

"I don't see what you can do." Flynn opted against offering a comment on Cruz's analysis. It was pretty close to accurate.

"Me neither, especially since I have insufficient data to work with, here. So shall we start with you giving me the whole story about what really happened on your leave? And not the story of nightclubs and gaming hells you spun for the OC when you got back, where his name didn't feature once. The truth, if you remember what that is."

"I told you. I saw Bennet."

"That's all you ever told me. It's not enough."

"You're wrong. It's everything." Flynn bowed his head.

Cruz drew back. After a minute, she said, quietly, "I'll get the drinks."

Flynn nodded and went back to brooding. He was only roused by Cruz setting a full bottle of liquor in front of him.

"I thought alcohol might loosen your tongue." She poured a generous couple of glassfuls, chinked her glass against Flynn's in an airy toast, and sat back. "I know you were with him, but how can I help if I don't know what happened?"

"Do I want help?"

"You need it."

Flynn looked at her for a minute, then smiled. It didn't feel like much of a smile from the inside and from the wry twist of Cruz's mouth, didn't look too good on the outside, either. "I guess. All right. It bothers me, Natalia coming here. I don't know why. I know her coming here is… well, it means something significant. I just don't know what. It's getting to me, making me antsy."

"Because she's a member of Bennet's family?"

"So is the Commander and I see him every week."

"True. And he did take you to Demeter."

"We've hardly been best buddies since, now have we? I've seen no more of him than any other officer on this ship and less than some."

Cruz refilled the glasses. "Still true. He's always been distant, though. D'you think Bennet gets treated like an officer or a son? They didn't seem that close when Bennet was here."

"Don't think it's like that. They show the outside world something different, I mean. The Commander wouldn't have trailed all the way to Demeter for the chance of seeing him for a few minutes unless it was more."

"That makes sense. How does Bennet get on with Natalia, do you know?"

"I don't understand families," Flynn said. Hell, it came out as a whine. Mortifying. "How do you expect me to understand families? I've never had one. I'd have thought having a brother and sisters would be great."

Cruz snorted. "Not always. Depends where you are. Fourth kid of six, me. That's neither one thing nor the other."

"Better than being none of none."

"Yeah, and I guess I wouldn't really be without mine. It's just… well, it's often about jockeying for position, for attention. Everything's relative. There's no one pattern. Being eldest can be good, or being youngest. Sometimes it's about gender. Sometimes about who you look like, dad or mum. It can be messy."

"Boy, does this take me back to Academy lectures on group

dynamics." Flynn shook his head.

"It should. The same principles apply. Families aren't always safe places, Flynn."

"I wouldn't know."

For the life of him, he couldn't work out what significance Natalia's arrival might have. But having another one of the Commander's family around, someone else he couldn't talk to about Bennet, made him want to talk to Cruz instead. Cruz had no familial axe to grind, no familial alliances and feuds to build and maintain, no action or inaction or emotion to measure against her own place in the family unit. Cruz was safe.

"Did I tell you he met me at the landing station?" Flynn asked, at last.

"No. I assumed you'd found his address, somehow. And?"

"And he left his partner, Joss, the same day."

Cruz stared at him over the rim of the glass. "That was fast work. Even for you."

"It had been coming for a long time. I sort of helped things along, maybe."

"Uh-huh," was all Cruz said to that. She listened in silence as Flynn recounted something of those glorious, but too-short weeks in the Grande Hotel in Sais City.

"I did meet his mother, but I didn't see the rest of his family," Flynn said, winding up the tale, "because—well, first of all, I don't think they knew about me, except for his mother, and Bennet said he didn't see they needed to. He said they'd give him a wide berth until the Joss thing had worked itself, and they did. Second, his elder sister was married and working as a surgeon and the two kids were in the Academy, not underfoot all the time." Flynn paused, then said with a slight grin, "And third and last and most important, I didn't give a damn if I never saw his family. We were way too busy to go visiting."

Cruz said, after a long silence, "What's his mother like?"

"Beautiful. I liked her. She was very kind to me, and she must have wished me to hell and back. She was as worried about him, because he'd been so ill and breaking up with Joss... it's stressful to try and rip out nine years of your life like that. It upset him."

"Seems to have upset the boyfriend, too." Cruz was dry as dust.

"Yes." Flynn sipped at his liquor. "I think she liked Joss, too, so she was sorry for him. But she was very nice to me, and she didn't have to be."

Cruz waited. "That's it?"

"Yes." Flynn had already said more than he wanted, but he needed Cruz on his side to help keep up the protective boundaries as the Caeden family increased its presence on the *Gyrfalcon*. He needed... something. He needed Bennet, and he wasn't going to get him, so Cruz as protection would have to do. "Except, you're right about falling hard. I got in over my head, Cruz. Some days are better than others, but I still feel like I'm drowning."

"And Bennet?"

Flynn hunched one shoulder. "Oh well. He's no better at swimming than I am."

Cruz grimaced and nodded, and was quiet for a minute or two, concentrating on her drink. Relieved, Flynn let himself relax. It hadn't been too bad telling Cruz about it. He'd been able to say Bennet's name more than once, without feeling like someone was tearing his heart out of his chest with blunt instruments. Not too bad at all. He was getting used to this. Immune.

Then Cruz tore it all apart on him. "Have you heard from him since you got back?"

His stomach heaved with the suddenness of it. He stared at her until she looked away.

"Sorry." She winced.

"No." Flynn's chest thumped. His hands were so clammy the glass slipped in them. He put it down and rubbed his hands against his uniform pants. Gods, sweaty hands were disgusting. "No. It can't go anywhere. Seeing him… seeing Bennet for those weeks… well, neither of us ever expected it. It was wonderful, but what could come out of it? I'm here and he's in Shield and what's the chance we'll ever meet again? We decided it was better to make it a clean break, better not to pretend."

"You mean Bennet decided. I don't think that's your kind of thinking. Your whole life is about pretending."

Flynn shrugged. Cruz, bless her, just touched his arm, very briefly, and he could relax again.

"One thing that I don't understand," Cruz said, after a long, comfortable silence broken only by the occasional melodious chime of glass against bottle, "and that's what you said about Bennet meeting you at the Sais landing field. Explain that to me and I promise I'll leave you alone. How did he know you were going on a home leave, much less when you were arriving?"

"The Commander told him, of course," Flynn said, and watched with a detached and kindly interest as Cruz sprayed half a mouthful of liquor across the table, and showed every sign of choking to death on the rest.

Septimus 7489: The Office's Club, Dreadnought *Gyrfalcon*

Flynn kept his distance to begin with, careful only to observe until he decided what his reaction to this turn of events should be. Often, in those first weeks, he'd sit in his quiet quarters, holding Bennet's shield in his hands like a talisman, clutching it so tight that when he released it, its hard edges had imprinted themselves into his skin. The slight pain couldn't distract him from trying to decide what he thought about having Bennet's sister always in front of him, reminding him of what was over and done.

One blessing was she and Bennet had only dark hair and pale skin in common, when it came to looks. The shapes of their faces were different. Natalia didn't have Bennet's cheekbones and the eyes above them were blue not Bennet's grey. From what little Flynn had seen of them, the expression in them was a touch anxious. She had a brittle smile, as if she were uneasy and conscious she tried too hard.

They were an odd mix of their parents. Bennet was as tall as Caeden, although not as bulky and solid-looking, but his looks came straight from his mother. He had the same prominent cheekbones and wide-spaced grey eyes that made Meriel such a beauty, even in middle-age. Natalia was the opposite mix. She had all of Meriel's rather petite slenderness, emphasised by the unflattering engineering uniform, but she was the softened, feminised version of Caeden: same shape face and nose and eyes, although in the case of the latter, Caeden's eyes had certainly never been seen to be anxious.

Now, in the Officers' Club, Flynn turned his attention from Ensign Natalia sitting at the other side of the room and concentrated on his cards. It was all very well reflecting on the turn of the genetic dice, but he was better off not reflecting at all. The past was a dangerous country to navigate and he'd lost the route map long ago.

That game won, he riffled the cards in his hands. "Right, ladies and gentlemen, I believe some of you may still be in possession of some of your pay. Time to rectify that sad state of affairs. My deal, I think."

"You've cleaned us out, Flynn," Cruz said. "I have nothing left to lose. I have so little of my pay left, I'll be selling myself behind the refuelling stores just to survive to the end of the month."

Flynn sighed, looking at others. Kyle raised an empty hand in surrender. Jillia pouted and shook her head. Cruz stared at him, eyes narrowed, gaze accusatory. She glanced from him to the bar and back again.

Flynn sighed again and gave it up. "My round then."

Natalia reached the bar at the same time he did. He wondered if she planned it, given her uncertain smile. The one he gave her in return was his most dazzling and charming. The one he kept up with constant practice.

"We've not met yet. I'm Flynn."

"I know." Natalia regarded him, grave and serious. "I've been told all about you."

"All?"

"The other girls in the barracks had a lot to say."

Flynn smiled, relieved that was all she meant and no one else had talked to her. But then, what he knew of the Commander made him trust the man not to betray a confidence, especially his elder son's. And Bennet certainly wouldn't say anything. "What you mean is, you were warned about me."

She nodded.

He looked down at her, searching for the resemblance and seeing nothing to wrench at him. Too little to raise Bennet's ghost, in any event. He'd been foolish, putting this off for so long.

"Well, although you can ascribe the calumny to their jealous natures, let me assure you it's all true." He increased the smile's wattage when she laughed. "I know this is late, but welcome to the *Gyrfalcon*, Ensign Natalia. Can I buy you a drink?"

CHAPTER SEVEN

14 Sextus 7489 – Decimus 7489

Bennet got to the Demeter transfer station on the standard Transport shuttle run, docking at Airlock 20. Fifteen docks from Shield territory.

He hesitated, standing for a few minutes on the walkway, looking up-station towards docks 1 through to 5, where Shield and home were. People stepped around him, one or two grumbling.

It was a long time before he turned away, heading down into the heart of the station. The crowds thickened as he reached the central core, and though they tried to give him a wide berth, he felt the pressure of curious glances. Shield was apart and singular. Even here on Demeter where more Shield troopers could be seen in one place than anywhere else in Albion's star systems, his all-black uniform singled him out for attention. Dammit. He hated being this conspicuous. It was a relief to reach sanctuary in the compartments on level three housing Quartermaster's department.

The Corporal who shepherded him into one of the cubicles lining the compartment wasn't even slightly fazed when Bennet asked for a complete Fleet outfitting. Dozens of Shield warriors taking their reluctant, complaining rotation out had probably passed through her hands.

Mirrors lined the wall of the small cubicle. Bennet stared at the unfamiliar reflection for a long time. He didn't think Felix was right. He didn't think he looked too great in grey. He did look washed out and colourless.

Behind him, the Corporal folded the black uniform and put it into Bennet's kit bag. "I'll find another bag for your new kit. You may need to find someone to help you carry both bags and your case there."

She nodded towards the sealed case that held the datapads with the encrypted T18 Makepeace data, and which hadn't been more than a foot away from Bennet at any time since Supreme Commander Jak hadn't so much given him permission to continue working on it throughout his *Corvus* posting, as ordered him to.

"You're letting me keep my Shield uniform?"

She didn't glance up from smoothing the black flight jacket into neat folds. "You lot usually want to keep it. For when you go back."

Bennet watched her for a minute, then grinned. "Yes. Thank you. You never know when it'll come in useful."

One advantage of the scholarly mind was the capacity for sometimes quite frightening focus. If Bennet had to go to a Fleet ship for a year, the sooner he plunged into it, the sooner it was over. No point in putting off the inevitable by hanging about a flight school getting re-certified for flying. Regaining his wings in the fastest time possible was a reasonable goal. Theory and simulators first, because he was used to flying Shield's Mosquito fighters—Mozzies were smaller and a tad faster than the Hornets Fleet used, although both fighters used similar control boards and systems. He had to assimilate those differences, let them sink under the skin until flying was muscle memory and instinct, leaving his brain free to assess the threats the instructors threw at him. Then, finally, he was let loose on the real thing, taking out a Hornet on patrols and exercises around the huge space station.

He focused on getting his flying privileges back. He didn't

socialise with the half-dozen other pilots who were, for various reasons, seeking recertification. When he wasn't working on the theoretical aspects of flying Hornets, or drawing up new simulations manoeuvres to thwart instructors who appeared to be devilishly talented at testing pilots to the limit, he wrote to Rosie. True, he didn't always send the emails that were, he realised, full of whining self-justification about how selfish he'd been with her and how sorry he was, but those telling her about his day's training and ending in love to her... those he sent.

It didn't take long for it all to come back, despite more than a year away from flying. Fifteen days after his arrival on Demeter, Bennet pocketed his recertification papers, shouldered his packs and walked up the ramp of the cutter the *Corvus* sent to collect him. When he walked off the ramp at the other side, Shield Captain Bennet was (temporarily, he hoped) no more.

Flight Captain Bennet took his place.

Whoever *he* was.

CHAPTER EIGHT

Early Nonus 7489: Dreadnought *Gyrfalcon*

It just wasn't possible to avoid Cruz. Unfortunately.

Or was it fortunate? Flynn wasn't, at that moment, prepared to say. It was true that Luck was the only lady with whom Flynn had any sort of permanent relationship, and although She smiled upon him, he hesitated to make a value judgement about the way She let the cards fall from Her hands.

Well, no matter whether it was fortunate or otherwise, Cruz knew him all too well. Cruz knew all his shifts and evasions, every plate and greave of the armour, all the hiding places and what put him in them. Sometimes, she knew what to do and say to bring him out again.

In fact, given how well Cruz knew him, it astonished him the woman ever played cards with him. All she ever did there was give her pay into his erratic custody. She was a lousy card player. Flynn could only assume that this one, profitable blind spot was Lady Luck's way of weighting the dice in his favour: unaccountable, but useful and a boon not to be questioned too closely.

Hiding from Cruz was a non-starter. Not profitable. What was the point of betting on certainties? And it was certain Cruz would find him. Even if she had to lie in wait and ambush him when he thought it was safe.

Like the ambush she had just sprung on him outside the Officers' Club. And she was not pleased with him, if the glower was anything to go by. Her tone was hard. Accusatory. "I can't work out what you think you're doing with that girl."

Huh. Not so much as a how-de-do before launching all missiles at him. Flynn spread his arms and put on his most innocent face.

It didn't work. It never worked on Cruz. She snorted, and encouraged him into the OC by pulling him around forty-five degrees and applying a sharply-prodding finger to a spot between his shoulder blades. She ignored his yelp. "And that isn't going to help at all. Every time you look innocent as a choirboy—"

Flynn snorted, but went obediently to their normal table, staying out of reach of that prodding finger. "You obviously haven't met many choirboys."

Cruz waited for him to finish, then went on as if he hadn't opened his mouth, "—I check my wallet for leaks. You are not to be trusted, Flynn. What in hell do you think you're doing with Natalia?"

Good lords, was that a bad stain on his flight jacket, or what? Flynn rubbed at it as he sat down, making tsking noises.

"Flynn," Cruz said, in a hard tone. She wasn't going to be diverted with stains. Not even if it got him on report for bringing the service into disrepute with a grubby uniform.

When he glanced at her, she was unsmiling and her mouth had tightened into the sort of line he imagined mothers had perfected for dealing with irresponsible children. Shit. He hated it when she was this mad. There was nothing for it. Flynn puffed out a quiet breath. "Nothing."

"Nothing! C'mon, you aren't being fair on her. She's not her brother."

"I can see that for myself, thanks."

"It's not nice, Flynn, to use her to make up for Bennet not being here. It's a shitty thing to do. You're usually better than this."

Ah, the more sorrow than anger ploy. It made the back of his neck burn. Flynn glanced over to where Natalia sat. She had oversight of the engineering desk that month, taking her turn on Bridge duty, and sat with several of the Bridge crew rather than her engineering pals. She glanced up and met his eyes for an instant before looking away quickly, her face pink. Her confusion wasn't exactly subtle.

Beside him, Cruz huffed with impatience. "See? You've got her in a tailspin, with no brakes. She's a kid, Flynn. She's not up to the kind of game you play. She takes things seriously, from what I've seen, and she'll be easy to hurt."

"Friends, that's all."

That was a very unladylike snort Cruz had going there. "You don't do friends!"

"That's hardly fair," Flynn said, hurt because it wasn't true. "I have you. I've never made a pass at you."

"No." Cruz looked at him steadily until he squirmed in his seat. "Please stop before you get into trouble. I can't see the Commander sitting back and letting you seduce his little girl. Not with your history in the family. Besides, do you really want her?"

"No," Flynn said, after a long and resentful silence. "It's just that she knows what Bennet's doing, and I keep hoping she'll mention him."

Gods, he was whining like a hormonal teenager. Luckily for him, Cruz was inclined to support and sympathise, not treat his yearnings with scorn. Although she did say, tone as stern as a schoolmistress, "You're using her. It's not fair and it's not honourable."

Flynn looked over towards Natalia again. She must have been watching him, waiting for him to go to her, because she smiled the moment he glanced at her and lowered her gaze, looking at him through her lashes. Could be she was trying for demure, but what she managed was complacent. He'd seen that expression on many another before her, the *I've-got-him!* expression. She thought she owned him. But Flynn didn't do ownership and he didn't like the expression on her any more than he'd liked it on anyone before her.

With one notable exception.

Besides, he'd been the recipient of one or two hard stares from the Commander recently, and common sense suggested a strategic withdrawal. He sighed. "Yes, you're right. I'll be good."

Cruz laughed at last, relaxing the stern lecturing stance. "From what I hear, you're always good. That's half your trouble." She signalled to one of the stewards, waving a hand between her and Flynn and holding up two fingers. Good. The least she could do was buy him a drink.

Flynn laughed too, and turned in his chair, away from Natalia. Out of the corner of his eye he saw the complacency on her face fade into disappointment. She lowered her head, shoulders drooping.

He wouldn't let himself feel guilty. She'd get over it. They always did.

"So," he said, "What do I do instead?"

Cruz sighed. She took a pack of cards from her pocket. Her tone was sad. "Do you think the gods will take notice of this heroic sacrifice? What you do instead, old son, is what you always do. You win." She called over a couple of other willing victims and let the games begin.

Flynn sat back in his chair, ignoring the sighing glances Natalia gave him, and thought of the only Lady to whom he was constant. He watched as She scattered the cards in his favour and, as he won yet again, wondered if the old adage was true.

He'd gladly lose every card game he ever played if She would let him be lucky in love.

Cruz didn't ask.

I'm being nice to her because I hope she'll mention Bennet,

Flynn had said, inviting (in truth, almost begging) enquiry, but Cruz didn't ask.

Has she mentioned him? Does she talk about him? Does she tell you what he's up to?

Flynn would have had to say that no, she doesn't talk about him very often. It could be a protective thing, a shield to keep her family private and away from prying eyes that weren't interested in her for herself but because of whose daughter she was. Flynn could understand that, but it wasn't the whole story. She was reticent because the distance Bennet hinted at was real. She mentioned her mother, Thea and Liam, but seldom talked about Bennet.

Once, early in their... how would he describe it? Friendship? Mild flirtation? Well, whatever it was, she had said, without knowing the weight of it for him, "My elder brother was here on the *Gyrfalcon* a few years ago. Were you here then?"

"Well, yes. Yes, I was," he'd said, tamping down the rush of memories of T18, of heat and danger and two bodies entwined in the darkness of Bennet's quarters, sweat-sheened skin sliding against skin. "It was an exciting time."

She said no more, either not interested in the details, or because she knew the Official Secrets Act had everyone's lips sealed tight.

And once she said, in passing, when the general talk in the OC was of the other dreadnoughts in the Fleet, "My elder brother's on the *Corvus*. He's their Flight Captain."

Now that was momentous news. It meant Bennet was well enough to be back on duty. Flynn could banish the memories of a Bennet worn down by pain and illness, and replace it with the memories of T18, where Bennet was fit and strong. Flynn knew Bennet would be disappointed not to be allowed back into Shield but delighted to be allowed to do something. He must have chafed at a year's inactivity, teaching at the Academy and SSI.

But Natalia didn't seem to know how Bennet was doing on the *Corvus*. "Oh, all right, I think," was all she said in answer to Flynn's careful, casual enquiry.

And once in a crowded bar on Demeter, with the entire ship in for some repairs to a hull breach and a few days unexpected R&R for the crew, she said, tone doubtful, making something in Flynn's chest hurt with a stab of real pain, "For a moment, I thought that was Bennet's girlfriend, Rosie. But I don't think it can be. She's not in Shield uniform."

Girlfriend?

Girlfriend?

Flynn remembered Bennet's Rosie, of course he did. The mass of red curls, the fierce blue eyes, the savage undertone with which she warned him not to hurt Bennet. Her interest had been blatant. She wanted Bennet for herself. She hadn't needed to say so. Flynn might have been dazed with love and dizzy with the effects of days of incredible sex, but he had enough emotional intelligence left to work that out for himself. Had Bennet turned to her after Flynn returned to the *Gyrfalcon?*

Flynn didn't quite know what he felt about that. So he had bought Natalia a drink, and thrown himself into celebrating the unexpected holiday. The life and soul of the party, as usual.

Bennet's girlfriend, Rosie.

Wise old Cruz. Sensible old Cruz. She knew better than to ask what Natalia had told Flynn about Bennet. She already knew Flynn had nothing to tell.

CHAPTER NINE

13 Decimus 7489: Dreadnought *Corvus*

"Fuck."

Bennet closed down the datapad. It took him a couple of tries to secure it, his hands clumsy. Nausea welled up, burning his throat. His stomach roiled, sweat breaking out on his hairline, along the length of his jaw and prickling at the corner of his eyes. He wiped at his mouth, his hands trembling so badly it was like he had palsy.

Fuck. He couldn't be right. He just... he just couldn't.

16 Decimus 7489: Dreadnought *Corvus*

Sometimes it was hard to know whether being Caeden's son was an advantage or otherwise, and if his instinctive avoidance of Fleet to get out from under the parental shadow had been worth the aggravation and angst that came with the resultant breach with his father.

Commander Dalton had welcomed Bennet to her ship, all those months ago, with a cordiality he suspected most young officers would have to earn the hard way. She'd been genial and friendly, shaking his hand after he'd offered a by-the-book salute and settling in with him for what she called her 'orientation' meeting in an affable, casual, we're-the-same-species-you-and-I way. Almost her first words had been to ask after his father.

It paved his way into Fleet. Every Fleet officer could recite the names of the nine commanders and list the ships in each Flotilla. To be the son of the commander of First had a cachet all of its own. He'd been welcomed by Dalton, welcomed by his juniors in the Officers' Club, and, once he proved he could fly as well as any of them, he'd settled into Fleet life with little difficulty. He shook up his three squadrons of pilots, assessing skills levels and training until they were performing to Shield levels of efficiency, got them through several minor fire fights and one pitched battle. Each day he took overall command of the *Corvus*'s Bridge and the Flag Office for the Second Flotilla for several hours, sitting in Dalton's command chair and learning to manage both the huge ship and the fleet of smaller ones following in her wake.

And each day, he tried to live with being known around the ship as Commander Caeden's son.

Bennet took to grinding his teeth in private and keeping a neutral expression primed for any public mention of his illustrious sire. He could admit he loved his father—at least, he could now Joss wasn't there to give him knowing looks and sneers, and if he wasn't expected to say it out loud—but it was galling to be considered as a sort of adjunct to his father, a sort of mini-Caeden.

Everything a man was, was defined by something outside of him. After all, he was a dozen Bennets at least, each one different depending on whose eyes were on him. Shield Captain Bennet, who walked into Maess bases any day of the week, and twice on Tenth-day for the gods. Strategy Unit Bennet, who was given some interesting problems to solve, to worry at, building the bigger picture to keep their people safe; the Bennet who was Felix's work partner. Here he was Flight Captain Bennet, training and protecting his pilots, seeing them through fire fights and skirmishes, and making damn sure no one alive was ever left behind. He was the Bennet who was Meriel and Caeden's son, the Bennet who was brother to Thea, Natalia and Liam, uncle to Sairy. And once he'd been Bennet the young lover, who threw away everything he'd known for the first eighteen years of his life, to be with Joss. And Bennet, Rosie's lover, finally able to act when she was no longer under his direct command and who mourned her now, because he couldn't see a future for them.

And once he had been Bennet, Flynn's lover…

That thought was cut off, fast. No way was he going there. Instead, he went back to teeth-grinding and counting the days until he could return to Shield where he belonged. Where getting the goods in an infiltration job mattered far more than whose chromosomes combined with whose. Where he wasn't in anyone's shadow but his own.

But being Caeden's son had some advantages. Not least, when he had to go and talk to his Commander about a desperate need to contact the Strategy Unit. Urgently. Expensively.

Dalton had waved him into a chair when he came in, in her usual welcoming way. But now she frowned, lips thinning. "I'm not certain I'm getting a fair share of your time here, Captain."

And that was unfair. Bennet was careful to keep his various jobs in air-tight compartments and he didn't allow the Strategy Unit work to bleed out into the day job. Feeling challenged by Commander Dalton for the first time since he'd arrived on the *Corvus*—he was doing well as her squadron commander, damn it—the fingers of his right hand twisted in the fabric of his uniform pants. He didn't need this on top of the report he had to get to Felix. Dalton watched him, eyes narrowed.

"You know what I do, Ma'am."

She nodded. "The Supreme Commander made that very clear when he assigned you here. I accepted it along with you. But I've always been at a loss to understand where you find the time."

"I only work on long-term projects. Nothing that's time critical." Bennet glanced at her. Was this real opposition or just her making ritualistic noises? "I can get through a lot in the odd hour between patrols."

"Or even during them," Dalton said, as if she could see the datapad he always carried in his pocket. "And now this long-term, non-time-critical project has reached the point where you need to call home?"

"Yes, Ma'am."

"Using the incredibly expensive, top-security rated Gold Channel to do it."

"I don't want a verbal link, Ma'am, but yes."

"The taxpayers will be grateful," she said. "I'm told even text links cost the equivalent of a year's salary. My salary."

He sighed and waited.

"You need extremely high security clearance to use it."

She was fishing. She had to know this. Along with making clear that Bennet's little side job of working with the Strategy Unit was important, Jak would have told her his security clearance was high. Higher than hers. Wounded pride was a bitch, sometimes.

"Griffin Beta Seven, Ma'am." With that clearance, he could call in the *Corvus*'s security officer and commandeer the entire ship, and they both knew it. He hoped she wouldn't push him that far. It would make the day job difficult.

Her mouth quirked into a brief smile. "I know. All right, Bennet. I thought you'd avail yourself of the privilege long before now, but I concede you've been admirably restrained. I'm curious to know what it's all about."

"You really don't want to know, Ma'am."

"Which, given you certainly won't tell me, is perhaps just as well. And given the body language, all too true."

Bennet flushed. He hadn't realised he was so obvious.

"Something's been bothering you for the last few days."

"I finished the analysis three days ago. I've been reviewing it since then."

"Because you're meticulous and anal about these things?"

"Because I was praying I was wrong."

Her eyebrow curved up. She watched him for a minute or two. He could sense her unease, because she had to be picking up on his own, but she nodded. Her tone became formal. "Then let the record show you invoked Griffin Beta Seven clearance and I have acknowledged its primacy over any other communications activity. When do you want to do it?"

Bennet pulled the datapad from his pocket. "As soon as I can, Ma'am. It may not be a one-time thing. I'll need to use it again, as soon as the Strategy Unit's had the time to assess the report and get back to me."

She stood up, bringing him to his feet automatically. "You can use this office. I'll tell the Comms desk to make the link for you." She waved away the salute he offered and paused in the doorway. "Bennet, should I be worried?"

Fuck, yes. Any sane person would be.

He chose his words with care. "It isn't imminent and it's not in this sector."

"That's not what I meant, and you know it."

"Yes, Ma'am, I know."

Her expression was unreadable. "I see. Then perhaps I'd rather not know."

He nodded. That was wise.

She grimaced and left him to it. As soon as the door closed, he fitted the datapad into the computer monitor on her desk, logging himself in past its layers of encrypted security while he waited for the link.

Anything she or anyone else need worry about? Yes, Ma'am, just a little worrying. Enough to make sure he had trouble sleeping at night.

The monitor blinked at him. {{Gold link established. Enter initiation and destination codes}}

Bennet sighed and leaned forward. Time to tell Felix the good news.

~~~~~

Date and Time: 16-10-7489
From: Bennet, Flight Captain, Corvus
To: Felix, Captain, Strategy Unit, HQ
Status: Eyes only. Encrypted.
Urgency: Immediate
Subject: Project Makepeace

Report attached. SC Jak ONLY. Encoded – private cypher, tenth modulation. Security code to access attachment follows in three separate transmissions.

~~~~~

Date and Time: 17-10-7489   00.56
From: Felix, Captain, Strategy Unit, HQ
To: Bennet, Flight Captain, Corvus
Status: Eyes only. Encrypted.
Urgency: Immediate
Subject: Project Makepeace

Fucking hell, Bennet.

~~~~~

Date and Time: 17-10-7489   20.22
From: Felix, Captain, Strategy Unit, HQ
To: Bennet, Flight Captain, Corvus
Status: Eyes only. Encrypted.
Urgency: Immediate
Subject: Project Makepeace

SC Jak acknowledges. Authorises you to continue

work to secure confirmation. Highest possible security. Am working on supporting material. Will forward soonest for comment.

One hell of a theory.

~~~~~

Date and Time: 18-10-7489 02.45
From: Bennet, Flight Captain, Corvus
To: Felix, Captain, Strategy Unit, HQ
Status: Eyes only. Encrypted.
Urgency: Immediate
Subject: Project Makepeace

Received. I think I'm right. The gods help us all.

~~~~~

08 Tertius 7490: Strategy Unit Laboratory, Military HQ, Sais City

"You're late."

"And it's nice to see you, too, after all this time." Bennet pulled a stool up to the bench.

Felix's hand rested on Bennet's shoulder for a minute. For him, that was an almost fulsome welcome, all the emotion he'd allow himself on seeing his friend back and in one piece. Best friend? Were they that? Bennet thought they might be.

"How have you been?" Felix asked.

"Fine. You?"

Felix nodded. "Very well, thanks. Charis has set the date, by the way. Next summer. Apparently planning a big wedding takes time."

"I'd elope." Not that he'd be given the chance. Bennet had called in at the flat, but Rosie wasn't there. She was still out on a job somewhere. And even if she hadn't been, a relationship that now depended on email exchanges didn't exactly have a glittering future.

"I'm tempted. How's Fleet turned out? As bad as you expected?"

"Different. Not as bad as I thought it would be. Exciting, sometimes." Bennet gestured to his pale grey uniform. "Still not Shield, but Dalton's a damn good commander to work with. She's sharp."

"At least she's let you out to play for a few days."

"She rolled her eyes when she heard I was summoned back to brief the Intelligence Committee, but she's been good about things. I think she only mentions me being a part-timer once or twice a day now."

Felix grinned. "Well, thanks to her generosity in lending me her Flight Captain, we have today to prepare and go over everything."

"I don't see why Jorgensen doesn't do it all. He hates having to take us along to briefings anyway. Thinks it undermines him or something."

A grimace. Felix wasn't any more respectful about Jorgensen than Bennet was. "I'm not sure he buys the whole thing, to start with. He thinks it's too speculative. I don't think he'd do the briefing justice at IntCom. Besides, the Supreme Commander wants you there, since it's your speculation. You know this better than anyone."

"Sadly."

Felix pushed aside the equipment he had been adjusting. They stared at each other for a minute. "I think that's enough displacement and delay. I know what you want to know."

"Do you?"

Felix looked at him steadily. "To know if it's true. The answer's 'yes'. We've successfully integrated the tissue. Only a couple of weeks ago, as it happens."

"Oh fuck," Bennet said.

"We had to be sure. Now we are sure."

"Viable?"

"No, we didn't get that far. It will be years before we could, if ever. But it is possible, yes. It's all possible. Everything you thought about is possible." After a very long silence, Felix reached for a datapad. "I couldn't put the detail even into encrypted messages. I'll take you through it all now."

Bennet took the datapad Felix offered. It was an ordinary datapad; hard edged and smooth. He had no real reason to think it felt slimy, soiled. Still, he had to rub his fingertips together to rid them of the dirt after he touched it. "I don't think I want to know."

"You and me both, but what choice do we have?" Felix tapped on his own datapad to activate it. "You didn't have plans for dinner tonight, did you?"

"I'd thought about calling Mamma and seeing if I could cadge a meal out her. But I guess I can see her after IntCom tomorrow, if you think I can't make it now."

"Oh, you might make it," Felix said. "But I can guarantee you won't want to eat dinner or be able to keep it down if you do."

SECTION TWO:

CALIBAN

08 Tertius - 37 Quartus 7490

CHAPTER TEN

08 Tertius 7490: Mendes Suburb, Sais City

Caeden hadn't been certain that Meriel would be home from Cicilia. She had spent the last few weeks in Albion's southernmost province to be with his old friend Warwick's wife, Bethany. Literally the last few weeks for their long friendship: Beth had died in mid-Secundus.

Even after all their years together, it was sheer pleasure to walk into the house and find Meriel at home. She was dozing on a chaise in the big sun room overlooking the ocean when he walked in on her, and for a moment she stared at him blankly before jumping up to greet him. She was flatteringly delighted to see him. She said so, often, in the first few minutes; eyes bright and smiling, her arms flung around his neck. He kissed her again before depositing her back onto her chaise with an admonishment to put him down and stop being melodramatic.

"You're a cold hearted creature!" She dashed at her eyes with a scrap of a handkerchief.

"I'm not the one crying crocodile tears." He pulled a chair up close, raised her hand to his lips and kissed it. She was the most beautiful woman he knew. Neither of their daughters, pretty as they were, could hold a candle to her.

"Tears of joy," Meriel protested. "Although I'll be damned if I know why you deserve them. Why didn't you tell me you were coming home?"

"I didn't have time. I was called back by the President's office for a crash meeting. Unexpected and very hush hush."

"Then I won't ask."

The gods bless her, she never did. After more than thirty-five years of marriage, she was the best of military wives. She understood when Caeden wasn't able to tell her about the job. He switched subjects. She was more tired and drawn than he liked.

"I hope you've had time to rest since Bethany… well, since you had to go to her."

For a moment, with her mouth dragged down and her eyes filling with tears, Meriel looked older. The grip of her hand in his tightened. "It wasn't a good death, Caeden."

"Are any of them?"

"Some are quieter and quicker than others. She was in a lot of pain and she took a long time to die. At least Warwick and Sioned took compassionate leave to be with her. Poor Sioned. She was closer to her mother than I realised, and Beth's death was hard on her."

Caeden was touched to see that this time the handkerchief dabbed at tears that couldn't be laughed at. "She'll be missed. I always liked Beth. I'm glad Warwick and Sioned were with her."

Meriel rubbed her eyes. "Sioned kept it all controlled until Beth had gone. She broke down then, poor child, and I think she was glad I was there. The gods know Warwick wasn't much use to her. To either of them."

Meriel had never liked Warwick. She wasn't particularly fond of Sioned, either, who was too much her father's daughter for Meriel's taste. But she would always be kind, for Beth's sake.

"I can't imagine him being good in that sort of crisis." Caeden would be the first to admit Warwick liked simple solutions. Give him something to shoot at and he'd have been fine, but Bethany's illness would have left him rootless and helpless with no clear target to aim at. "Not his forte."

Meriel shook her head. "You're right about how bad he was at dealing with a sickroom. He was home with Beth for her last three months, you know, and it was rather like having a gadfly take up residence. Ah well. It doesn't matter. They're both back on the *Caliban* now, and their lives go on. Poor Beth. I miss her. We were friends for so long." She dabbed at her eyes again. She patted his hand and sat straighter, making an obvious effort to be cheerful. "Did you get the message I sent you yesterday then, or did you miss it? Thea's news, I mean."

Caeden let his smile broaden. "I'm to be a grandfather again, I hear."

Her answering smile was radiant. Genuine. Not the thin, frail thing of a moment before. "Wonderful isn't it? A boy this time, Thea says. She waited until she was sure before she said anything, but she's very well and blooming…"

And she was off on family news. Caeden sat back in his chair and let her talk, taking in news of Thea and Liam, giving some in his turn about Natalia's first year—although saying nothing of some rather undesirable friendships he had been watching with concern. He passed on some of Dalton's comments on how well Bennet was doing, despite Meriel jeering at Fleet commanders who gossiped more than old women.

Anything to take his mind off the unexpected meeting President Maitland had called. He didn't like being dragged back for unscheduled Intelligence Committee meetings. They tended to mean trouble.

Bad trouble.

09 Tertius 7490, Intelligence Committee Meeting

IntCom was set for 10.00. Not in the usual conference room in the Praesidium building, but in President Maitland's own office on the top floor.

Another reason it didn't smell right.

Caeden's two military colleagues were already in the outer office when he arrived. He wasn't late, although he'd cut it fine. A group of protesters in the square outside the Praesidium had caused an unexpected delay. The Phoenix League, strong in the settlement planets and outer colonies light years removed from the central government in Albion, appeared to be gaining traction and popularity here at home if the numbers out waving placards and looking earnest were any indication.

Field Marshall Klára, who headed the Infantry, stood by the window overlooking the square, tapping her swagger stick against her leg; tall, pugnacious, damned good at her job. That swagger stick was completely archaic. Perhaps she just needed to keep her hands busy. She nodded a greeting at him and the stick tapped with a more urgent rhythm. She didn't appear to like this unscheduled meeting any more than he did.

By contrast, General Martens of the Shield Regiment was the calm, still centre of the room. Bennet had described her once to Caeden as the epitome of Shield: quiet, reticent and watchful. Remote. Bennet was a touch starry-eyed in his admiration for her, but… well, perhaps he had cause. Nothing much ever shook Martens out of her serenity. Even when she was angry, and Caeden had heard and seen her in what in others would be a towering rage, she had been focused and outwardly unruffled. Her mouth may have tightened down and the expression in her eyes grown cold, but that was about it. She gave Caeden a slight smile and returned to whatever internal meditation occupied her. If she, too, disliked the smell of this meeting, she didn't show it.

No sign of the politicians yet, unless they were already in with Maitland, but Etienne was there. And that was another reason for the itch between Caeden's shoulder blades. Etienne, the head of the Ennead Secretariat and an old friend of Caeden's, often attended IntCom meetings, it was true, but always with one of his clerks with him to do the actual work of scribing. But this time Etienne was alone. He gave Caeden a grave nod and that alone was worrying. The unsmiling expression the old man wore signalled that he didn't anticipate a pleasant meeting.

Caeden joined him, when beckoned. He took one of the thin white hands in his own. How old was Etienne now? Well past retirement age, surely, but still showing no signs of stepping down, despite age and an apparent frailty that had to be illusory; the old man's grip was strong and his eyes still clear, bright with intelligence.

"What, no acolyte today?"

Etienne's smile faded quickly. "No. The President was quite clear. He doesn't want any underlings, shall we say, at this meeting. Just me."

Caeden glanced sideways at the old man. "You know what this is about."

"Yes. Jak shared the initial paperwork with me at the same time he briefed the President. It makes for uncomfortable reading." Etienne returned the glance. "You don't know? Interesting."

"I have no idea. And that alone makes me nervous."

Another slight smile. "Well. A gold star for young Bennet, then, for the exercise of discretion. I am impressed."

Caeden stiffened. Bennet. Bennet was involved with this?

"We are to be briefed by the Strategy Unit," Etienne said. "Principally by Shield Captain Bennet."

Oh hell.

The spot between Caeden's shoulder blades itched harder. What had his son got into this time? It was unlikely Etienne would tell him, but they were called into the inner office before he could frame the question. At least he'd been warned before following Etienne into the committee room to join the rest of IntCom.

Not all the Intelligence Committee, mind. The two Ennead Councillors who sat on the Committee—Seigneur Jethric of Illuria and Madam Beatrice, the Achaean representative—were absent. Caeden didn't miss Jethric, frankly. The man was a sharp-tongued boor with an ambition so naked it ought to have been ashamed to be seen out in public. Beatrice, though cold and calculating, could be a useful ally. If it were worth her while.

Jak sat at Maitland's right hand, and Etienne took the chair to the President's left. Maitland was almost testy when sending the military representatives to sit down one side of the table, leaving the seats on the other side empty. Whatever this was about, Maitland was so rattled even his considerable political skills couldn't gloss over it.

Maitland had grown heavy during his time in office. Given his size, it seemed ironic to reflect that there wasn't much left of the man who'd once commanded the Eighth Flotilla's dreadnought, *Isis.* Not enough exercise, probably, and all too many presidential dinners. Normally he had the polished look Caeden associated with politicians, using his personality and the voice many an actor would envy, to persuade, influence and sway. Not today.

Today, he looked drawn and didn't waste time beating about bushes. "This is a special meeting of the Intelligence Committee— the non-political part of it at least. There will be a verbal presentation only, with no minutes taken, and no more than a note in Etienne's files of what we eventually decide today. And Etienne will bury that deep for as long as possible."

Caeden frowned. Beside him, Martens drew herself up a fraction. On the other side of Martens, Klára shifted position in her chair. It creaked. Every eye went to her and she grimaced.

"These proceedings are unusual," Maitland said, drawing their gazes back to him. "Legally, we are quorate, even without my esteemed Ennead colleagues." He paused. Hesitated. Dropped the stern tone for something more human. "Listen. Things are… delicate right now. That's the best way to describe it. Of course, the Ennead's infighting and provincial-biased posturing is rife but that's normal. Business as usual. But with many of our colonies seeking more autonomy, political pressures are growing daily. We're under scrutiny as never before, with some very canny operators watching our every move and making capital out of every misstep. The Ennead is increasingly cautious about provoking discontent or firing up public opinion. That makes the problem we are now to consider, that certain people have tipped into our laps more than delicate." He looked from Jak to Caeden, who thanks to Etienne could at least work out why he had been singled out. "It's potentially the most difficult issue this committee has had to face in over a century of war. You will speak of this to no one outside this small group. And frankly, I'd rather you didn't talk about it even to each other. Understood?"

The three of them were rather too few to be called a chorus, but they mumbled something to signify their understanding. Almost in unison.

"If you're wondering about the legitimacy of whatever decision we take today, then be assured I intend to exercise executive action." Maitland's smile was wry. "I've been elected President three times now. This is my last possible term of office. I don't have to worry about re-election and I will take the risk, ladies and gentlemen. Etienne will record it as a presidential executive order."

Well... Hell.

Caeden was not normally moved to profanity, but this did not bode well. That Maitland even acknowledged a risk of this political magnitude was a concern. And one shared by his colleagues, if he read them aright. Martens had grown more than ordinarily still—never a good sign—while Klára laid the swagger stick on the table and linked her hands together, resting them on the stick and scowling down at them.

Maitland nodded. "Right then. Let's begin. We'll be briefed by the Strategy Unit, I think, Jak?"

"Better first hand, I thought," was all Jak said.

"Let's get them in." Maitland copied Klára's gesture, clasping his hands on the polished wood of the table top and keeping his gaze on them.

Caeden turned as Bennet and his Strategy Unit partner, Felix, came into the room with Colonel Jorgensen, who ran the Unit day-to-day as Jak's executive officer there. Caeden frowned. Bennet was too thin; not as thin as when he'd been after the Telnos adventure, when several weeks of inadequate rations, injury and fever had reduced him to skin and bone. But too thin for all that. And he looked tired.

Bennet glanced at him. Not a smile, but a quirk of the lips in acknowledgement, a slight widening of the eyes. Caeden nodded back. The boy's discomfort was evident to anyone who knew him. Caeden ran a finger around his collar. The room was too warm and he reached for the water carafe in the centre of the table.

Jak nodded at Jorgensen. "I think we know everyone from previous briefings, Colonel. Off you go."

The Colonel settled into his chair, Felix and Bennet on either side of him. "Right. Forgive me for the history lesson, but it's important for the context. Four years ago, Shield infiltrated a Maess base, designated T18, to test a device we hoped would connect to the Maess computer systems and mine them for data. The device was developed by Captain Felix, and the infiltration mission planned and carried out by Shield Captain Bennet, both members of the Strategy Unit." Jorgensen waved a hand left and right as he spoke. "The data has proved invaluable, but as we anticipated, difficult to translate. The schematics for battleships, fighters and bases were the most easily accessible, and have certainly helped improve our success rate against the Maess."

"Not a lot on drone weaknesses," Klára said, whose people faced them most often. Many a Fleet pilot only saw a drone on the ground if he or she were taking it out in a strafing run. The Infantry encountered drones up close and far too personal.

"That's true. We have some better information on how they create drones, but what you say about analysing weaknesses there is a case in point. It illustrates our problem with the data—the linguists are still struggling with decoding it. The data on drone production gives us a tentative lexicon for the processes the Maess use to create drones. But we have not been able to decipher the Maess language with any degree of confidence in the accuracy of our translations or our understanding of the linguistic concepts behind it. We're not sure they have a language, as we understand it."

"They must have something," Klára said. "You gave us so much intel, Colonel, it has to be based on some sort of understanding of their communications and how they do it."

Bennet said, tone neutral, "As you know, ma'am, the one I glimpsed on T18 grew a face and a mouth and screamed at me. So we know they're capable of producing sound, but there's nothing to confirm they have a spoken language. The Maess itself was fluid, with no fixed shape. The language could be based on shape variations, on changes in pigmentation or skin texture, on pheromones or scents, or telepathy for all we know. What we see in Maess bases on their computers, what the Link brought back, is a kind of machine code. Deciphering that is hard when we don't have the lexicon and the concepts are totally alien."

Klára nodded and raised a hand in acceptance of the point. She gave Bennet a glance that might have been sympathetic; the look Caeden gave him certainly was. Everyone there knew Bennet had glimpsed an organic Maess on T19. In the aftermath, the committee's debrief had been rigorous. That was the word. Rigorous. They had turned Bennet inside out to extract every scrap of information out of his head. Caeden had always regretted his part in the interrogation. That Bennet didn't appear to blame him for it was little consolation.

"So, we're still working on decoding the T18 data for information about the Maess themselves. Anything that will give us an edge." Jorgensen inclined his head to Klára. "We've been looking hard at drone production precisely to try and find Infantry the same sort of advantages that Fleet gained from the ship schematics. The other area of interest is, what in our terms, we'd call social data. Now, what Captain Bennet brought back from T18 four years ago is rich in technological information and we're developing the lexicon for translating that. In retrospect, that was relatively easy. The softer stuff is more problematic and sparser." He nodded at Bennet.

Bennet closed his right hand into a fist, opened it up and stretched out his fingers. Over and over. His tone, though, remained unemotional. "If the Maess record the things that anyone looking at our computer systems would discover about human society, we haven't found it. I don't think they see themselves in the same terms. As I said, this is all about alien concepts with no cultural correlations to guide us. I was looking into the data to try and mine social information from it, when I kept finding references—at least at a superficial level—to a place I was able to identify as one our ex-colonies. A planet called Makepeace in the Firenze Quadrant."

Caeden gave it a second or two's thought. "I've never heard of it."

"Makepeace? The Strategy Unit had a Shield ship look at it, last year." Martens glanced at Jak. "I wondered about that."

"We lost the colony to the Maess a century ago. It's well inside their space now. Using a Shield ship to gather more data was our only option." Jak nodded at Bennet. "Continue."

"Sir." Bennet took up the narrative again. "The data wasn't what I expected. If we look at how all the T18 data is brigaded and categorised, it wasn't in the area that dealt with normal drone production. And it wasn't in the areas where we found the technical schematics. The data sets were separate. Kept to one side and isolated." He shrugged. "I was curious. I gave up on anything to do with Maess social data and started analysing the Makepeace information instead. It is fascinating stuff." A minuscule pause. "It indicates the Maess have live human prisoners on Makepeace, held there long-term inside the only base on the planet."

This time the pause was longer. Bennet waited on their reaction.

Martens frowned. Shrugged. "I remember the *Dhow*'s Captain reporting human captives. Regrettable, but we know they sometimes keep humans alive for a short period. If they need to use them to extract solactinium, for example, in places their drones don't operate."

"Yes, ma'am. I agree. That aspect isn't unusual, but human prisoners have a very short life expectancy unless we manage to rescue them. The Maess kill them as soon as possible. The data sets suggest these humans have been on Makepeace for at least thirty years and quite possibly longer."

That *was* unusual. But what was Bennet getting at?

Caeden raised an eyebrow. "Constantly replenishing their

workforce, you mean? That's not unusual, if their prisoners don't live long. They'd need to restock, as it were."

"I know, sir, but I don't think that's what's happening here. First, Makepeace has no viable mineral deposits that either we or the Maess are known to extract and use. The presence of prisoners there doesn't appear to be explainable in reference to any situation we've come across before." Bennet paused. "The data, though, indicates some of them have been on Makepeace all the time the base has been in operation. That they've been allowed to live for years."

"Hell," Klára said, so softly Caeden barely caught it.

"It suggests the prisoners are being held on Makepeace for a special purpose." Bennet paused again. It struck Caeden that it wasn't for emphasis or effect, but to find the right words. "No, they're not being held. They are being bred on Makepeace. Deliberately bred. And more than that. If our translations are accurate, and they've been checked and rechecked dozens of times, the data uses the same terminology in regard to the prisoners as it uses for the programme for creating drones."

CHAPTER ELEVEN

l09 Tertius 7490, Intelligence Committee Meeting

They met Bennet's announcement with a short, but profound, silence.

Klára broke it. "Sweet hells," she said. Her hands clenched on the swagger stick.

"You never said a truer thing." Martens stiffened, raising her head to scrutinise Bennet. Her expression was grim, eyes narrowed beneath an unaccustomed frown and her lips pressed together.

Klára threw up both hands. "You're implying… what the hell are you implying, Captain?"

"You have to understand, ma'am, that we don't know anything for certain," Bennet said. "That's our only certainty, actually, that nothing is certain."

Caeden swallowed back bile. He glanced at Jak. The Supreme Commander's mouth twitched, that was all. He'd known, of course. And he didn't like it any more than Bennet did. Caeden turned his attention back to Bennet. "Some sort of breeding programme or experimentation or what?"

"Or all three or none, sir. This is analysis and speculation based on what I've been able to decode."

"What *do* we know?"

Bennet held Caeden's gaze. "We can eliminate all the things we're sure Makepeace is not. It's not mining, though the Maess have been known to use human labour in unshielded mines that would otherwise incapacitate their drones. Makepeace has limited mineral resources and the Shield scouting run showed no sign of any kind of mining or other industrial activity. It was a rich agricultural colony but not now. Some small scale farming, enough to feed the human population. That's all. Maess drones don't need food anyway, but a power source to recharge. We don't know about the organic Maess and what their nutritional needs are, but unless Maess farming looks entirely different to ours, it's not food production. I can't find anything related to the planet itself to account for the human presence there."

"And then there's the commonality with the drone terminology." Jak sounded serene. But glancing at him again, Caeden saw the set of his jaw.

Jak's disquiet was shared. The President's grimace spoke volumes of distaste and Etienne's air of relative youth vanished, leaving an old man in its wake.

"Yes, sir," Bennet said. "Indicative, to say the least."

"What do you think, Captain?" Maitland spoke for the first time.

Bennet spoke slowly, choosing his words with evident care. "I think, sir, that the terminology is too much to ignore. They create drones by implanting a few neural cells into the mechanical bodies, enough cells to grow some sort of rudimentary brain, a neural node. We think it allows an organic Maess to control the drones somehow. The node gives a drone just enough life to do what a Maess tells it to do. Drones don't show initiative, self-awareness or individuality. They appear to be completely subservient to the organic Maess. We've assumed control is exercised through the node, which is made of Maess tissue—that theory has driven the geneticists' research for the last century."

Jak grunted. "Not that it's got much to show for itself."

"We have no firm evidence for what they're doing," Jorgensen said. "Strategy Unit's best guess is that this is an experimental installation where they're building a new kind of drone."

"Dear gods." Caeden wiped his mouth with the back of his hand, swallowing down the bile and saliva. "And the human prisoners are involved?"

Jak nodded. "Give us the bones of it, Captain Bennet. This is your analysis."

"Yes sir." Bennet sounded tired now, worn out. "I think we're looking at two possibilities, each with more than one variant. Our baseline is that they keep their drones in a state of constant evolution. We've seen a recent surge in Enhanced Dactyl-Articulated drone numbers, for instance. The Makepeace base functions to either implement another step in modifying their drones, or they're trying to modify the human prisoners."

Oh dear gods. Dear gods.

Caeden wished he hadn't had the glass of water earlier. He felt sick. After a second he shook his head, like a man trying to clear the last remnants of sleep from his brain. "Modifying humans? This is hard to accept, Captain."

"I know, sir." Bennet's expression of anguish, the grimace and the hard jaw, had Caeden fighting the impulse to reach out to him. But it was only for a moment. His son straightened his shoulders, looked them all in the eye. "Let's take the first possibility; that they're trying to introduce some changes into drone production. As I said, they create drones by implanting a node of live tissue, mostly neurones, into the metal/plasteen body. One possibility is that they're taking human brain tissue as a source for the node."

Martens grimaced. "Is that likely? If the theory is right, about the node being the control point, would it work with human brain tissue?"

"I'm reluctant to rule it out without more evidence, ma'am, but the short answer is we don't know." Bennet glanced at Caeden as if for support. "The second variant within this option, is that they're using hybridised Maess and human tissue."

"That can't be possible!" Klára half rose in protest, tone

strident.

Captain Felix cut in. "I'm afraid it is, ma'am. We've carried out some experiments ourselves, using nodes from downed drones and human tissue. It's entirely possible to hybridise the two."

Caeden pushed his chair away from the table, the movement so abrupt the legs squealed on the polished wood floor. He mumbled an apology and walked to the window to stare out at a city that had no idea, no damned idea *at all*, what monstrosities their enemy might be planning. Or, for that matter, what monstrosity the Strategy Unit might be planning. He wasn't concerned about the source of the Maess nodes Captain Felix had found to play with, but the source of the human tissue? He was very interested in that.

Behind him, Felix carried on. "We know the organic Maess don't look anything like us, if the glimpse Shield Captain Bennet got on T18 was a real one—and we have no reason to believe it wasn't—but there are some basic similarities. T18 was an Albion-class planet with an oxygen-rich atmosphere. The creature Captain Bennet saw was probably utilising some sort of oxygen metabolism, possibly was carbon based. We can only theorise, but it's a reasonable place to start. Similarly, we can expect some sort of internal structure corresponding to our brains, hearts, lungs, and digestive tracts. They have to breathe something, eat something, pump round something that we can loosely call blood. At the cellular level, we're going to see basic building blocks similar to ours: proteins, carbohydrates, lipids—"

"Maess DNA is different, surely." Martens sounded calm and composed. When Caeden turned to face them all and return to his seat, under control again, he could only envy her serenity. He slid back into his chair. Jak and Maitland both glanced at him, and Etienne gave him the thin smile again.

"Alternatives to carbon-based life and oxygen metabolism exist in nature, of course," Jorgensen said. "On planets with a different atmospheric base, for example. But the optimal characteristics in all the Albion-class planets we have ever encountered support the similarities Captain Felix has mentioned."

Felix nodded at Martens. "You make a good point, though, ma'am. Strictly speaking, the drone neural nodes suggest Maess don't have DNA, but something similar; a peptide-nucleic polymer that we can't reproduce in a laboratory yet. But it appears to act in a comparable way to DNA, carrying the codes for peptide and protein production. We have DNA in a double helix, they have stacked octagons of fifteen nucleotides instead of our four." Felix shook his head. "Fifteen! It's almost unimaginable. It gives the Maess an incredible plasticity of genome and endless possibilities for protein genesis and combination. It may account for the fluidity of shape. The thing on T18 morphed and changed, didn't have a fixed shape—we can see that in the photographs Shield Captain Bennet took. Study those and you can see how it changed shape from one shot to the next. I can only posit they need very complex biochemistry for that."

"Indeed," Etienne murmured, breaking his silence.

"We hybridised the tissue, yes. Making it work in any meaningful way… making it *live*, is an entirely different proposition. We couldn't do it." Felix leaned forward, eagerness in every line of him. "But the Maess have centuries, probably, of drone production behind them. They adapt the outward appearance of their drones over time. You'll recall the first drones we ran into weren't humanoid and it's possible they were made to mimic the last race the Maess went to war with. The drones are humanoid now. If they've been working on the whole—how shall I describe it? The spark of life inside the drones. If they've been working on improving that, then there's every possibility they could hybridise the tissue and make it function. They have a technology and experience we don't."

Caeden was running out of exclamations of surprise. Even calling on his gods was failing him. He would have liked to put his head in his hands.

"Explain what would they get from it," Klára said, still strident. "Where's the advantage in using human tissue in any form?"

Felix glanced at Bennet and sat back.

Bennet's hand was opening and closing again. "We've been at war for over a century, ma'am. They haven't been able to destroy us, despite their advantages in numbers and technology. Captain Felix noted they were slow to change their drones to match us, and that's true. It was years before their drones morphed into human shape, and they've evolved the EDA drones, the ones with workable hands and arms, only in the last four or five years. Perhaps they have failed to wipe us out because we respond to change much, much faster." Bennet reached for the water carafe and poured himself a glassful. "We're more prepared to take risks, willing to sacrifice ourselves for something bigger. They hide behind drones. We have more spirit, perhaps."

"Dear me," Jak said. "We are like our father."

Bennet twitched but he glanced at Caeden and managed a wry little smile. "I probably am, sir. But the point is they know they haven't been able to defeat us and that has got to offend their sense of order—"

"Humanity offends their sense of order." Martens was back to her calm stillness.

"Yes. But it doesn't mean they haven't decided to see what… what system enhancements human tissue might give their drones, imbue them with some of the things we have that they don't."

"It's a disgusting concept," Klára said.

"Yes. It is, ma'am." Bennet glanced at them all. "Should I continue?" At the various nods and grimaces, he went on, "So, that's the first option, with two variants—they're harvesting humans for neural tissue to make drone nodes or to contribute to them." He took a deep breath. "The second option is that they're p-putting Maess m-material into humans, t-trying to m-modify the human prisoners using a variation on the t-techniques that produce drones."

Caeden gave him a sharp look. That little speech hesitation always returned when Bennet was stressed. His son grimaced, and pressed his lips together.

"Oh gods." Klára shook her head and clasped her hands

together again. Presumably to stop them trembling.

Bennet spoke with care. He had the stammer controlled again. "If successful, it would allow them fine control over the human prisoners. And again, there are variables on how they might do that. A hardware solution, if you like, or a cellular change."

"I don't like," Klára snapped at him.

Caeden gave quick glance around to garner reactions. Martens was expressionless. Jak's gaze was on the distant skyline. Maitland had returned to staring at his hands. Etienne, though, was studying Bennet, his expression thoughtful.

"Nor I, ma'am." Bennet took a quick drink of his water. "Okay, the hardware solution first. We create a sort of cyborg ourselves, you know. We can't do what they do, putting an organic node into a metal body, but we can do it the other way around." Bennet's smile was thin and humourless. "I have an artificial knee joint myself. It's mainly titanium, grafted into what's left of my right leg. They could be trying something similar to my knee, grafting in some technological components into living humans to over-ride human reactions and thought processes. We couldn't do that, but the gods only know how many years they've been creating cyborgs and what that's given them in terms of micro-technological techniques."

"You're saying they might be able to do it." Klára sounded more aggressive than usual. Although it may have been fear.

Bennet met her glare square on, Caeden had to give him that much credit. "Nothing is certain, ma'am. They also have real expertise at the cellular level. After all, they make those few Maess cells in the drone node function in a way we can't begin to understand fully, much less emulate. The alternative to the hardware theory is they're implanting Maess cells or some hybrid of human-Maess stem cells into the prisoners. Either process, hardware or cellular modification, would have one clear goal—to develop a host of subservient cyborgs that are human in appearance. The end products would look human."

There would be no way to tell. No way to be sure who was

human and who wasn't.

Caeden's gut clenched and his hands curled into fists. It could be Klára or Martens or Jak or anyone. Even Bennet or Meriel... No! Not going there. This was beyond foul. No one would be able to tell from the outside. No one would trust anyone else. Ever.

"We couldn't tell." Martens frowned. On her, that had to be an expression of hysteria.

"No. It's a frightening prospect." Bennet caught and held Caeden's gaze.

No wonder the boy had lost weight and looked so damned tired. Caeden didn't think he'd be sleeping too well himself now, thinking about the potential consequences if ever there were outwardly human-looking Maess.

Klára's hands tightened so hard on each other, her fingers were white. "You don't say."

Bennet's mouth tightened at the tone. "While none of the possibilities is benign, this is the most dangerous outcome in terms of impact on us and on the course of the war. There are arguments against it, of course. A human is more than just how we look. It's how we think, how we behave, the way we react to others around us. The social conditioning, if you like. Altered humans who've never lived in a real human society won't have any of that, and they would stick out, be eccentric, abnormal. But if the Maess can overcome that problem, then controlled human cyborgs would give them an infiltration force to destroy us from within."

"They'd look like us," Klára said. "Your second option. They'd look like us."

Bennet nodded. "Ideally, they'd retain enough humanity to be able to blend in and act with reasonable normality."

"Ideally!"

"In the context of the theory, ma'am." Bennet sat back and looked at Jorgensen.

Who took over smoothly. "In sum, then, we're looking at five distinct possible combinations of human and Maess. A drone node composed of human neural cells, a drone node composed of hybridised Maess and human neurones, a hardware implant into the humans, a Maess cellular implant into the humans, or a hybridised Maess and human tissue implant into humans. It could be any one of these. Or all of them. Or something else entirely."

"Is it possible?" Caeden appealed to the Supreme Commander.

"Yes," Jak said. "It all is. Theoretically."

Caeden glanced at Bennet, but his son had turned his head to stare out across the cityscape to the distant tower housing the Military HQ. Closer to hand, loomed the minarets and towers of the Theban temple.

Caeden turned to look at Sais. It was a beautiful city; a very human place, teeming with people who for all their unfamiliarity had at least a lot in common with him. It had been safely human, once. Now he'd never be sure that, even here in the heart of Albion, anything was safe or ever would be again.

CHAPTER TWELVE

26 Quartus 7490: Military HQ, Sais City

Four other captains waited in the Supreme Commander's outer office under the jaundiced eye of the current office boy, still the Fleet Colonel with the nervous tic. They all looked up as Bennet and Felix came in, most of them betraying some apprehension about the impending close-up view of The Management. Bennet had a slight acquaintance with one of them: Van Trion, the Captain of the Shield ship *Dhow*. She'd done the initial scouting run of Makepeace, and in the last seven weeks, as he and Felix had planned and refined and planned again while they waited for the President's final decision about what they were to do about Makepeace, she'd done several more. She smiled at him as he came in, although her eyes widened with a faint surprise. She hadn't known she was doing the runs for him, of course. The other three—one Fleet and two from the Transport Directorate—were strangers. Bennet knew who they were, but they'd never met.

The Colonel glanced at him and Felix. "He said to send you straight in when you got here. Take them all in with you." She touched the com unit on her desk. "On their way, sir."

Bennet hadn't seen the Supreme Commander since completing his posting to the *Corvus* and arriving back on Albion two days earlier. He wasn't looking forward to the meeting. He let Felix be the kind shepherd shooing the other captains in ahead of them, while he trailed along in everyone's wake.

The Supreme Commander sat at the conference table, flanked by Shield General Martens on one side and Commander Warwick of the dreadnought *Caliban*, Third Flotilla, on the other. The glare he turned onto the gaggle of captains saluting him was inimical. That was the word. Inimical. Jak didn't like this particular job any more than Bennet did. Protocol demanded the Supreme Commander accept and return their salutes but his response was perfunctory. Instead, he waved everyone into seats at the table with scant regard for ceremony. Martens' faint smile signalled approval, Bennet hoped, but Warwick stared in recognition and with what appeared to be dislike, if the narrowed eyes and wrinkled nose were anything to go by.

Jak turned the fierce gaze onto Bennet. "Well, I hear you didn't crap it up too badly on the *Corvus*."

Bennet had a copy of the glowing report from Dalton in his kit bag. He said, in the mild tone he often adopted with his godfather, "I didn't want to disappoint you, sir."

Jak snorted, eyes gleaming with sudden amusement. "Very laudable. Well, get to your seats. We've waited around long enough for you prima donnas to join us without you holding us up any longer."

That was rich, considering they'd all been held up for an hour because Warwick and the Fleet Captain had been late, and then another ten minutes while Warwick was given a fast, personal briefing by the Supreme Commander and General Martens. Bennet took the seat at the conference table beside the presentation system, putting the data crystal he and Felix had prepared into the slot, ready. Felix, eyes rolling, sat opposite him.

"Everyone knows the General and the Commander," Jak said, with a casual wave of the hand. "These two are Captains Bennet and Felix, from the Strategy Unit. This is Shield Captain Van Trion, from the *Dhow*; Captain Illych from the Third Flotilla's destroyer, the *Hertford*; and Captain Willem of the *Bryson* and Captain Mione of the *Smithfield*, both with the Transport Directorate." The Supreme Commander paused to allow the nods of greeting. "Right, Captain Bennet, this is all down to you. Get started."

"Sir." Bennet tripped the switch of the computer set into the table top, projecting a star map onto the screen at the end of the table. "This is the target—the Makepeace system in the Firenze quadrant, about six days' hyperspace journey into Maess territory. Epsis-Acteon is the nearest frontier system, within, as you see, the Third Flotilla's demesne." Bennet glanced at Warwick and Illych. "Which is why you're here of course, Commander. Third will be critical to this particular job."

He ignored Warwick's smirking nod, and returned his attention to the screen. He would only give them the bare outline of the Makepeace problem. They needed enough information to understand what this was about, but not the detail that could compromise security.

"Makepeace wasn't always in Maess territory. A century ago, it was in ours. It was a Nicaean agricultural colony, but it was never an important one. So far as Captain Felix and I can work out from the records, Makepeace doesn't have extensive deposits of useful minerals—although there is evidence of some solactinium and selenium, it's not in commercially viable quantities and is locked in the polar icecaps—and it didn't sit on any of the major trade routes of the time. It was a bit of a backwater. When the Maess overran it, we didn't put up much resistance. Some light skirmishes, mainly diversionary, to allow us to evacuate survivors from the colony and fall back to more defensive lines. We gave Makepeace up."

"Without a fight?" Warwick's tone proclaimed he would, as ever, have stood alone against the forces of the night and that every other member of the human race was a lily-livered coward.

Bennet liked his Fleet commanders to be predictable. Warwick showed a typical lack of finesse about it. Thinking about this job gave Bennet nightmares, depressing spirits that weren't, in any event, naturally high. Warwick's reaction cheered him up at once, although after one joyous second where he met Felix's delighted gaze, he hoped he hid it well.

"As I said, sir, light skirmishing," he said. "It was the *Caliban*'s territory, but although some of Third were involved, I couldn't find any record of *Caliban* herself being there. The Nicaean member of the Ennead made a ritual protest about giving up the colony, but the Ennead's view was there wasn't anything there worth fighting for."

"But they were wrong?" Mione guessed.

"The situation's changed. Four years ago we got hold of a significant amount of intelligence on the Maess, everything from weapons systems to battleship schematics—"

Illych cut across him. "We've noticed! Our kill rate went up by fifteen percent and is still improving. How did we get it?"

"That's not relevant to—"

"A Shield operation." Warwick nodded towards Martens.

"Of course!" Illych turned to Van Trion. "Yours?"

"Shield Captain Bennet's," General Martens said. "And, as he said, apart from giving us the initial data, it's not relevant to today's briefing and is still covered by security restrictions so secret that only four people at this table are cleared for them. Please continue, Captain."

Warwick scowled. He wasn't one of the four. Felix, who was, smiled across the table at Bennet.

"I'm on my rotation out." Bennet had caught Illych's glancing frown at his Fleet battledress. He'd decided that to wear his Shield uniform would be to tempt Fate, in the irascible form of the Supreme Commander, one time too many. And before Jak could remind him that no one was interested in his bloody life history or his fashion choices and to just get on with it, he went on, "Most of the information we got from the intelligence is hard. Weaponry, technological systems, ship schematics. We found very little soft data and it's taken a lot more translation and analysis than the tech stuff. About a year ago, I went over some of the data again, working with Captain Felix. I was interested in the indications that organic life-forms are being utilised on Makepeace."

"Prisoners?" Illych was quick on the uptake.

Bennet nodded and flicked onto the next scan image, the base itself.

A wide flat-bottomed river valley cut through a treeless plain, the river running west to east. In the middle of the valley floor it took a sudden bend, running south for about half a mile before turning sharply east again. The base sat in the first bend as if in the crook of a riparian knee, water on its northern and eastern borders. Two caged runs for the human population were set near the perimeter of the base, running down its western border and along the south. Three small buildings right in the crook of knee appeared to be re-charging stations for the drones.

And slap bang in the centre sat the low building where *something* was going on: single storey, a couple of hundred yards square. Scans showed the building itself and its rocky foundations were blooming with power signatures. Whatever it was, whatever the Maess were doing, whatever they were manufacturing in there, pulled a lot of energy.

Bennet could have drawn scale plans of the base in his sleep. He used a laser pointer to name off the various buildings, skating over the one that really interested him. "These scans were taken by scouts from the *Dhow*. The only ground facility is here in this river valley, and a substantial number of prisoners is being held there. It has standard ground defences—laser cannon here, here and here—and you can see on this scan, the power conduits for the defence grid radiate out from the base centre to the gun placements around the perimeter. Fighter defence squadrons are based on a platform in geo-stationary orbit above the base. Captain Van Trion estimated sixty fighters."

"Yes." Van Trion gave Bennet a tight smile. "It was an interesting challenge, getting scouting runs in and out unnoticed."

"That's a good number." Warwick nodded, his smile pleased and anticipatory. Already planning his assault tactics, probably.

"There are no ground-based fighters. The platform will have to be destroyed, of course. These two pens within the base perimeter—here—house the humans. We estimate numbers at two hundred. Give or take a few. We can't be absolutely certain whether they're the descendants of the original colonists who were left behind or if they've been recently shipped in, or a mix of the two. It looked to me from the T18 intelligence that some of them, at least, had been moved there over a period spanning the last thirty or so years."

Willem said, speaking for the first time, "With Mione and me here, I guess that points to a rescue operation."

Bennet nodded. "Yes. Yes, it does."

"Why us?" Mione sat back, folding her arms over her chest. "Why involve Transport? Why not load them all onto the *Caliban*? There's enough room, surely."

"We don't allow returned prisoners anywhere near our warships," Felix said. "Not until they've been debriefed and cleared."

Warwick snorted. "Damn right."

"Of course." Mione reddened, two angry spots of colour spreading over her cheekbones. "It doesn't matter if they've been turned, and they sabotage a mere Transport Fleet ship."

"We hope they won't do that, of course." The quirk of Felix's eyebrows was for Bennet alone.

When Jak spoke, his tone had all the weight of authority, drawing all eyes to him. He shed the irascible old warrior pose. He was cold. Threatening. "You are all co-opted onto this mission. It is not voluntary. It is covered in its entirety by the Official Secrets Act. The job is not to be discussed in detail with anyone, even your seconds, who may be told only enough to enable them to carry out their duties efficiently and that this is a prisoner rescue. For the entire duration of the mission, your ships will be on communications silence except for military channels and your crews will not be allowed emails home or contact of any sort. It is at that level of secrecy and that level of importance. It has the personal approval of the President. Am I understood?"

The red spots on Mione's cheeks deepened. She gave Jak a

jerky nod, and Bennet had to give her points for not cutting and running, because he sure as hell wouldn't like a slap down like that.

"Good. The only discussion I expect now is on the detail of the infiltration plan. Captains Bennet and Felix have been working on it for the last few months. They'll take us through it now, and then throw it open for debate. It is not set in concrete, and you are all experts and warriors so your views will be welcomed. Captain Felix, I believe you're explaining this part."

"Sir." Felix reached across and took the laser pointer from Bennet's slackened grip.

Bennet turned his head away as Felix started on explaining the mission plan proper, only glancing at the familiar maps and diagrams. He turned his attention to the audience, watching them as they were taken through the infiltration plan. He didn't feel guilty about not telling them everything. But as he watched their reactions, he wondered what they would say if they knew the truth about the horror that was Makepeace.

The Supreme Commander called a short halt after a couple of hours. Bennet and Felix had gone over the infiltration plan twice and the discussions had felt endless. Warwick's increasing displeasure at the roles assigned to *Caliban* and the *Hertford* had been amusing, if not unexpected. Warwick-the-Glorious was not at his best supporting a ground operation while he, in his own words, "tootled about in close orbit minding the shop."

Jak's ability to handle him was impressive. The Supreme Commander listened to him with every appearance of complaisance but whenever Jak summed up the discussion so far, somehow Warwick's suggestions for putting the *Caliban* at the forefront of all the action slid away and they got back to the existing plan that was mainly Felix's: a sneaking run in from Epsis-Acteon with *Caliban* and *Hertford* escorting the two slower Transport ships, the *Dhow* doing what Shield did best and ranging ahead to scout their way. It would be the *Dhow*'s warriors on the ground too, either to destroy the base or to shepherd the prisoners onto cutters up to the Transport ships and then destroy the base, while *Caliban* took care of the orbital platform and its fighters. And then a fast run back to Albion space, this time with Third Flotilla's Hornets surrounding *Bryson* and *Smithfield* like wasps around a honey pot, sneaking secrecy put aside in the race for home.

Just like T18, but with prisoners and Warwick instead of his father and… and other people. Bennet glanced down to hide his face and grimaced at the polished table top. Not so much like T18, after all.

Jak's office staff brought lunch in to them. The Supreme Commander tucked in with gusto, talking to Martens and Warwick in a corner of the room.

Bennet picked at the plate the orderly pushed into his hands, his appetite gone. He wasn't convinced about having to use Third for this. Warwick was… well what? Wrong for this sort of job? Too bullish to sneak? Too independent to follow a plan other people—and those other people a pair of mere captains—had devised? And was it worth Bennet's career to say so? The *Gyrfalcon* would be better, despite the disadvantages. Caeden had a more realistic political grasp than Warwick and no desire for personal glory. He wouldn't be looking at every plan put to him for signs he was being cheated of greatness or for opportunities to enhance his heroic reputation. Caeden knew what was at stake, too, and was as horrified as Bennet about it.

The little group of senior officers drifted apart, and he found himself near Warwick. The Commander nodded at him, looking less antagonistic. "Your father never told me you did this sort of thing. I knew you went to SSI, of course, but I hadn't realised you were involved in the Strategy Unit."

"I'm not allowed to talk about it, sir."

"No. No, I suppose not." But Warwick's expression showed his resentment at being left out of the loop. He put his plate onto the table and stood stiffly, his mouth pinched-looking and thin. "I haven't seen you since last year's Graduation Day. You're on the *Corvus*, aren't you?"

"I was, sir. I'm waiting for another posting right now."

"Dalton's a good commander."

"Yes, sir. She is."

"Liam's turn this year, is it? He'll be going to the *Gyrfalcon*, like Natalia."

"Next summer, sir. He's finishing his third year." And if they were now discussing family, Bennet hadn't seen Warwick's boisterous daughter for several years; he ought to show willing and ask after her. "How's Sioned, Commander? She's been with you for a couple of years now, I guess. Didn't she graduate the year before Natalia?"

"Class of 'eighty-eight. She's fine, just fine. She's a damn good Hornet pilot, one of the best I've got." Warwick coughed and added, his voice thickened, "She had a difficult time over her mother."

Damn. Bennet never knew what to say when faced with stuff like this. His face grew hot. "I was sorry to hear about Aunt Bethany. I'll miss her."

Which was true. He'd liked Bethany, and if nothing else, he'd miss her restraining influence. She'd at least kept Warwick halfway tamed.

Warwick nodded and put on what Bennet, unkindly, thought of as a 'troubled but dealing with it in a manly fashion' face. "Yes, you wrote to me, didn't you?" Warwick faltered just long enough for Bennet to register it as at least as accomplished as anything his mother could have done in similar circumstances. "I'm sorry not to have replied. Things were difficult."

"Of course. I wasn't expecting a reply." Which was true enough. Bennet wasn't in the market for opening up a correspondence with Warwick and only the manners instilled into him by his mother had had him writing a short condolence note in the first place. He wasn't in the market for continuing this strained conversation, either, and he was delighted when Illych joined them. He smiled at the *Hertford*'s Captain with excessive wattage, if Illych's surprised blink was anything to go by.

"You know," Illych said, "I'm looking forward to this. We spend too much time falling back and being defensive. It'll be wonderful to take the fight to the enemy for once."

"I know what you mean." It was inconceivable that anyone could look forward to Makepeace but Bennet could be open-minded with someone who'd rescued him from a tête-a-tête with Warwick.

"You Shield lot do it all the time." Warwick was abrupt and gruff again. "I remember when you graduated from SSI and took Shield. Your father's face was a picture."

Illych raised an enquiring eyebrow.

"Commander Caeden is my father," Bennet said, cornered.

"The *Gyrfalcon*." Illych nodded. "Of course. A damn good ship."

And just what was Bennet expected to say in response to that? He fought his baser nature into silence and said nothing at all.

"He'll be pleased you're in Fleet now," Warwick said.

Bennet shrugged, irritated, trying not to show it. "Only until this time next year, sir, when my rotation's finished. Then I go home. To Shield."

"I always envied the Shield Regiment." Illych put some effort into being conciliatory. With Warwick for a commander, he probably got a lot of practice. "You get all the excitement."

Excitement? Bennet shrugged. "We mostly get the crap."

That set Warwick alight. "No. Illych's right. We spend all our time on the defensive, falling back, giving up system after system without a real fight. You people are out there all the time, taking the fight to where it matters, kicking the Maess right in the balls."

Bennet hadn't ever noticed that Maess drones had balls. The organic Maess hadn't carried their metallic imitation of humanity to such a level of verisimilitude. The Maess themselves, the real ones like the one he'd seen on T18... he closed that thought off, sharp, and murmured something bland and conciliatory, aware that Warwick would roll straight over him anyway.

Warwick did, his voice low and intense. "We're pushed and trammelled by those god-damned politicians, more every day. Jak does what he can, but at the end of it we're hamstrung by the timeserving weasels. They never let us do what we need to do—go out there and attack until we grind those bastards into the dirt. They're too worried about casualty figures, finance, taxes, their PR, their public, getting elected, staying elected, getting a foot higher on the Ennead, those Peace fools out there in the square. They're going to get us all killed. They're—" He stopped short, pressing his lips together. He gave Bennet a hard look and stalked away to rejoin Jak and Martens.

Bennet blew out a soft, relieved breath. "Strewth."

Illych's expression, the brief grimace, betrayed his discomfort. "Sorry. He has some strong views, you know, on the conduct of the war."

"You don't say."

"He's not been himself since his wife died."

Bennet turned his head. Warwick stood beside Martens, stiff and frowning "I dunno. I think it's the opposite. I think he's more himself now than he ever was."

CHAPTER THIRTEEN

26 Quartus 7490: Military HQ, Sais City

When the Supreme Commander dismissed the junior officers at the end of the meeting, he held Bennet back. Felix played sheepdog again, ushering out the other captains ahead of him. He winked, leaving Bennet to it. Smug bastard. Bennet wasn't sure how Felix had managed to weasel his way out of this bit.

"Time for a more detailed briefing." Jak turned to Warwick. "I'm sorry we didn't have time to do this before the main meeting."

Warwick waved a lordly hand. "Propulsion problem with my cutter. I didn't intend to be late."

"You need to know what's really going on, more than the little I was able to tell you before we began. Besides, it's all this one's fault and he knows it better than anyone." Jak grinned at Bennet, fierce and unamused. "You can tell him the lot, Captain. I've given him the statutory warning about secrecy."

Warwick merely smirked. The warning must have been applied with a fair amount of ego stroking.

"Everything we just told you, Commander, was accurate." Bennet paused. "So far as it went."

"It didn't go all the way, I take it?"

Not even close. And it wasn't amusing any longer, baiting

Warwick-the-Glorious. Not when the colour drained from his face and his breathing sharpened as Bennet recited, yet again, his account of what he thought the Maess were doing on Makepeace. And just as IntCom had, two months before, Warwick exclaimed and protested, baulked, jibbed and resisted. And, in the end, had to face up to Bennet's analysis.

At the end of it, Warwick turned to Jak. "And we're going in to retrieve those things? Seriously? The risks—"

"You're going in to take a look. Captain Bennet offered IntCom two courses of action. Option one is to treat it as a normal rescue operation. That is, get out as many as possible and hope to the gods that the Captain has an overactive imagination, and there's some less terrible explanation. Option two was to destroy the installation and everything we find in it. Everything."

After a pause, Warwick said, "That's why you need the *Caliban*."

Bennet stirred. "Not for blowing up bases, sir. Shield does that every day of the week. But for firepower to protect a ground operation of this magnitude... yes, most certainly."

"Given you're sending the Transport Fleet ships along, do I guess which option we're going for?"

"IntCom didn't decide one way or the other," Jak said. "Or rather, the President didn't. This whole operation is mandated by his personal executive orders."

Bennet looked away again to hide his irritation. He'd been pulled back from the *Corvus* for three days for the meeting, and a frustrating experience it had been. The only compensation had been the opportunity for a quiet word with his father afterwards, and the unexpected comfort of Caeden's hand on his shoulder while they commiserated with each other over being caught up in something so monstrous.

"The President came to the conclusion there wasn't enough evidence to make a decision from this distance." Martens' smile was thin. "You're tasked with going in and making the decision on the ground, when you're sure about what's is really going on."

"The provincial government elections at the end of the year is on their minds, I suppose? Politicians!" The contempt in Warwick's tone would have stung even a political hide.

The Supreme Commander was smooth. "President Maitland is in an impossible position, of course."

Bennet said, keeping his voice quiet, tone serious, "Whatever happens, sir, we're destroying that installation. What we find will govern whether we bring back any or all of the prisoners."

Warwick's eyes were cold, calculating. "Worse than Rets usually are. Quite a hornet's nest you've stirred up, Captain. Even if you're wrong, we could never take the risk of letting those people live amongst us. We could never let them out of a high security compound."

He was right. None of the Makepeace prisoners could be reintegrated into Albion society. They could never be trusted.

"We aren't bringing them back here," Jak said. "Or anywhere near Albion. The transporters will take them to a former penal colony in the Boeotian sector. It hasn't been used for years and it's well away from most of our colonies and settlement planets. It's being converted into a special holding facility to receive them. Highest possible security."

"Even that's risky." Warwick scowled at Bennet. "What if your theories are right? Any of your theories. Can we bring any of them back, then?"

"Some of them have to be brought back." This issue concerned Bennet. A lot. "For investigation."

Warwick blinked. "Hell's teeth!"

Bennet avoided Jak's fierce gaze. "And as many Maess nodes as the ground team can carry."

"For investigation," Warwick said, toneless and flat.

"Yes, sir."

"I don't give a bent credit for the Maess nodes, but the rest—" He snorted. "That's unbelievable!"

"Immoral," Bennet murmured.

It didn't draw a reprimand his way, although Jak gave him a sharp look. "It has to be done, Captain."

When Bennet looked up, he saw the rough sympathy beneath the fierceness. He nodded.

Warwick huffed to himself, disgruntled, staring at Bennet as if it were all his fault. Well, in a sense it was. "One helluva hornet's nest! But President Maitland has left the outcome up to us, yes?"

Jak nodded. "Yes."

"But what was your recommendation, Captain? What did you advise IntCom and the President to do?"

Bennet moistened his lips again, the arguments he'd employed running through his head, flickering and fast. His stomach twisted into a knot. If the long-ago destruction of Earth had taught humanity anything, it was that life was precious and fragile. How long was it since humans had warred between themselves? Millennia? It went against everything humans were, everything they were taught.

What Makepeace meant, everything it could represent, everything it threatened…. He wasn't a religious man. The church's reaction to his relationship with Joss had seen to that. He went to Chapel now and then, for Midnight Watches for a fallen comrade, and that was about all. But he had never forgotten his upbringing in the Theban faith and, as well as he could, he lived by what he thought was the best of it. He didn't think he was an evil man, a bad one, or a cruel and pitiless one, but Makepeace had made him wonder. The immorality of every choice hit him in the face every way he turned.

The President hadn't taken his advice. He hadn't listened, in the end.

"Captain," Jak said, quietly.

Bennet couldn't delay any longer. "The thought of what may be happening there scares me silly, sir. The Supreme Commander will tell you I have no sense of adventure, and my recommendation reflected that. The President took another view. I can see that he and IntCom were caught—we're caught—on the horns of a painful dilemma. Elections are always chancy, and the Phoenix movement on Thorn is spreading, gaining influence with more planets and colonies seeking more autonomy. Even without that, either choice carries huge political risk, could cost votes and political influence in the provincial senates here on Albion and the colonial and settlement planet government. Even within the Ennead itself. Leaving people at the mercy of the Maess on the one hand, against the risk these people mightn't be human now on the other, that they might be the Maess' most terrible weapon and we must destroy them… a nasty choice to make. In the end, the President concluded he didn't have enough information to make a decision, and risk doing what I suggested; because the political fallout from that might be even worse. Too many variables, too many unknowns."

Bennet turned to stare out to the city skyline. It was very beautiful, each tower and pinnacle the outward manifestation of everything he was fighting to preserve, everything he'd sworn to protect. The old words in the Book—*Stand therefore… taking the shield of faith, wherewith ye shall be able to quench all the fiery darts of the wicked*—given new purpose by the oath he'd taken on joining Shield, promising never to count the cost, never to falter, to be prepared for every sacrifice *that I may be a shield between Albion and her enemies…*

Warwick waited with unusual patience. He nodded when Bennet turned away from the city to which he could no longer guarantee protection, his expression encouraging. Bennet's mouth was dry. He'd give anything for some water. Jak gave him a fierce, get-on-with-it look. No more delay.

"I advised him to fry Makepeace, sir. From space."

Warwick spent several minutes staring out over Sais from the windows behind Jak's desk, his hands behind his back. His hands were clenched tight together, fingers intertwined and whitened. Jak and Martens gave him the time, talking between themselves in low voices. Bennet, left to his own devices, reviewed the datapads. Again.

Warwick showed little outward emotion when he returned to his seat. "Well. I see now why you want the *Caliban*, Jak. No ordinary Rets, these."

"No." Jak glanced at Bennet, and nodded. "The rest, Captain."

"Gods, there's more?" Warwick threw up his hands. "More?"

"A different issue, sir. The Maess themselves. For the whole of the course of this war, we've had no more than a glimpse of them." Bennet looked down to hide his grimace; the glimpse had been his, and it still came between him and his sleep some nights. "Images of them are inexact and unclear and we've never had a body to dissect and analyse. All of our interactions have been with drones. Either the Maess are xenophobic to the point they hide away from contact or they're few in number and precious. In either case, the drones are their protective layer, the barrier between them and the races they encounter. But drones have no initiative, and don't show reasoning ability. Whatever the node does to link them in to the real Maess... well, we don't understand it. But, I do think one of our inferences in all this is right: the drones aren't capable of running complex bases and installations. Not even the EDAs, which are definitely a step up on the older models, and which we have seen as the most 'senior' drone, if you like, on automated bases."

"You think a real one could be down there? On Makepeace?"

"It's only a possibility, sir. It's dangerous to extrapolate from human behaviour, but it would be a dumb move on our part to set up an installation like that and leave it to low-level drones to run." Bennet made a gesture to encompass the whole of the base on the image on screen. "The power signatures and usage fluctuations mapped by the *Dhow* suggest the three buildings here, outside the holding pens for the prisoners, are drone re-charging stations. But no apparent command centre. In fact, that's always hard to distinguish in any Maess base I've ever been in. We don't know how the Maess operate, or even if they think in the same way about managing something like that. Perhaps their hold over the drones means they don't need something we'd recognise as a command centre, and everything is more diffuse. I don't know. The real Maess, if there is one, may be on the orbiting platform, not on the ground. But with a base as complex as Makepeace, we'll be looking for a real organic Maess commander somewhere. It's too sophisticated an operation to leave to EDAs and ordinary soldier drones."

Martens broke in. "While we're mounting this mission to find out what the Maess have been doing to the human prisoners, the fact is that Shield will be on the ground for far longer than normal. We'll be holding the base for hours. That gives us opportunities we don't normally have for a lengthier exploration of the facility. If we can get hold of a real Maess… well, the benefits would be incalculable."

This time Warwick nodded his approval. "More to the point than a few Rets, anyway."

Since there wasn't anything to say to that, Bennet didn't bother saying it.

Jak blew out a soft breath. "All right. That's it." He glanced at Bennet. "I'm feeling quite well disposed towards you at this minute, Captain. I'm sending you along on this little job."

Whoa, wait! He couldn't mean… "You're letting me go back to Shield, sir?"

"I didn't say that. I said you're going on this job." Jak waited until Bennet had subsided again. "Your lot are always so bloody keen to get back, Martens. Do you bribe 'em or something?"

"Something." The General's thin smile warmed a fraction. "I'd rather like the Captain back, though. I have plans for him."

Jak nodded, not taking his fierce gaze off Bennet. "Another year, and you can have him." To Bennet, he said, "You've done well in Fleet, but Martens seems to think you're a natural Shield. You'll get back. But I warned you, son, I'm not breaking the Regs for you. Three years out."

"Yes sir." Bennet hid the sigh. So much for the vague promise that Jak might try to find some way to shorten his exile.

"I do have something in mind for you, when this is done," Jak said. "But I want you on this job."

Unsurprised, Bennet nodded. He'd expected he'd be required to see it through.

"Commander Warwick has overall command of the Makepeace mission, of course, but we've agreed you will be second in the chain of command and have command of the ground operation."

When? When did they agree? Bennet knew Jak well enough to know the Supreme Commander would have presented Warwick with the decision and expected him to make the best of it, but Warwick didn't look surprised. The social chit-chat over sandwiches at lunch must have included the heads up about Bennet's being in on this little job.

Jak went on, "I want you to make the decision on the ground, Captain."

"Oh. Yes, sir." Bennet was hit by all the moral ambiguity again, that had plagued him for the last few months.

"You know this material best, better than anybody. And it means I don't have to brief Captain Van Trion about what may be really happening on Makepeace." Martens' thin smile reappeared. "The fewer people who know, the less likely it is we have a security breach."

"She'll have to know when we hit dirt, Ma'am."

"She'll have to know some of it," Martens agreed. "As much as she needs to know to help you do the job. No more."

Jak gave him a long, considering look. "It won't be an easy decision, Captain, but I trust you to make it on the basis of the data you get on the ground. I think you've as good a grasp of the consequences as anyone."

"Yes, sir," Bennet said. "I think I have."

Jak's gaze sharpened. "And you can deal with it."

It wasn't a question. Bennet knew what was expected.

Whatever needed to be done, he'd do: it was his project, his theory, his mess to clean up. It was only fitting.

"Yes, sir." Bennet glanced at Martens. "Do I go out with Van Trion today, then, Ma'am? Captain Felix and I still have some details to iron out."

"No." Jak rolled his shoulders and relaxed into his chair. He rubbed at his temple, pushing back the thick grey hair. "We need to send the *Dhow* back to watch Makepeace for you until you get there. You'll be going out on the *Caliban*."

Bennet let his gaze slip sideways, trying to see Warwick's reaction.

The Commander nodded to him. "I'll be delighted to have you on board, Captain."

Be damned if he didn't sound as if he meant it.

Bennet nodded back. "Thank you, sir. The pleasure's mine."

CHAPTER FOURTEEN

26 Quartus 7490, evening

Aegypta was the first and oldest of the nine provinces on Albion, the site of the original landing from Earth. It took outrageous advantage of its seniority. The Aegyptans had long ago ensured all the main governmental institutions were established in Sais City, and in some cases, established centuries before the other provinces were founded.

An outsider could be forgiven for assuming the other provinces were colonies not of the Earth that was long gone, but of Aegypta. The Ennead made a token gesture of a meeting in each of the provincial capitals over a two-year cycle and a few government institutions had been established in each of the other provinces as a kind of sop to nationalistic fervour. But if he were an Illurian, say, Bennet would be hard put to it to be excited about getting the Food Standards Agency when everything important, from the Praesidium to Military Headquarters to the main financial centre, was in Sais.

The cab dropped Bennet at the front door of his favourite institution. He'd long ago decided the other provinces could take what they liked of government and military establishments as long as they left him this one. He loved the Thebaid Institute and Museum; loved every stone, from the dark storage basements through the tiers of columns touched pale reddish-gold by the setting sun, to the huge and lofty dome. Every time he saw it, something in his chest tightened. In some peaceful parallel universe, Professor Bennet was in this place, happily dissecting a mummy, untroubled by war, never being called upon to make any regrettable and regretful compromises, and going home each day to gold-brown hair, a gold-brown face with a glowing smile, intense green eyes and a mouth that melted a little bit of his soul with every kiss.

But in this universe, Shield Captain Bennet might think wistfully of that alternate professor, but was here to meet with the greatest compromise he'd ever made. No gold and green for this Bennet; only a life that felt as if it had been bisected by the knowledge of Makepeace, cut in half by it. The Thebaid belonged to the half when all Bennet's knowledge had been about innocent things like population drift and mummy rites and how to build a pyramid.

The Thebaid never changed. It looked and smelled the same as the day he'd been brought here as a schoolboy for a birthday treat, and plunged headlong into a lifelong fascination with humanity's past. Still the same huge marble atrium with the carved pillars holding up a roof three storeys above his head. Every landing of the staircase showcased the best of the Thebaid's collection of millennia-old statues, some little more than huge heads, many times life size: the Pharaohs who'd brought humanity here to Albion from the wreck of Earth. He knew each one, loved each one: Sneferu, Ramesses, Seti, Djoser. He touched each Pharaoh as he climbed the stairs to the top floor, their smooth granite faces cold under his fingers, carved eyes expressionless. Because of them, he'd defied his father and refused to go to the Military Academy when he was eighteen, taking up his scholarship here at the Thebaid instead. He'd been so certain then he could bend the universe to give him the life he wanted, that he could serve both the Thebaid and the military, have Joss, have it all. It wasn't the pharaohs' fault he'd failed.

He passed the library door with only a sideways flicker of his eyes to acknowledge it. That was where his compromise had been made under the wrathful, disbelieving eyes of his father, who'd caught Bennet and Joss together there years ago; the compromise he'd found, years later, to be untenable. He didn't regret all the years he'd had with Joss. He did regret how they had ended.

Joss gave him a cool welcome. He offered his cheek for Bennet's kiss, but his smile was faint.

"I can't stay long." Bennet smiled as he kissed him. "I'm off on a job in a day or two. I wanted to see how you were before I went."

"I don't have long. I'm meeting Andy in half an hour."

"Andy?" Bennet looked around the big laboratory. He remembered examining a mummy here with Joss, long ago, more than a decade ago, the feel of Joss's hands on his as the older man guided him in the search for the sacred amulets under the linen. A few days later and he'd fallen into Joss's bed and stayed there, metaphorically speaking, for nine years. He wondered if Joss remembered the mummy, and searched his memory for its name. He gave it up. Probably best not to remind Joss of the past.

"Andy... well, Andy moved in a few weeks ago." Joss examined a fingernail, not meeting Bennet's eyes. "He's rather nice."

Moved in? As in, moved into the apartment Bennet had shared with Joss for so long?

Oh.

Joss looked at him now, his smile widening. "He's adorable, actually. Very sweet."

Bennet swallowed. "I'm... I'm glad. I'm glad for you, Joss."

"He's just what I needed." Joss's sideways glance towards his desk clued Bennet in.

A framed photograph on a small easel stood on the left side of the desk. Bennet had to look twice. The first casual glance had him thinking Joss had resurrected a holopic of Bennet at twenty, the one of him leaning up against the Thebaid doors after his graduation ceremony—young, untried, undamaged. Hell, he'd been impossibly young and innocent back then. But it wasn't Bennet. The boy in the holopic looked quite like him, mind, with the same dark hair and shape of face, but had to be a good decade younger than he was. A boy about the age Bennet had been when he'd first gone to Joss.

And that was a punch to the gut.

Come to think on it, two years before when they'd broken up… the playmate Joss had brought home that day couldn't have been twenty.

Joss liked his boys young.

He'd thought he'd outgrown Joss, but he hadn't considered it was true in more ways than one. He had grown too old. It was likely he'd left Joss before Joss could leave him.

It was an effort to sound pleasant and disinterested. "Does he work here at the Thebaid? A student?"

Joss shook his head. "I met him on the last cruise I took on the *Star Wanderer* liner. He was a steward. He's not really doing anything at the moment."

Except be spoiled and decorative and concentrate all his attention on Joss. Joss had always wanted that; Bennet had always failed to deliver. Like the Thebaid and the cold granite eyes Bennet had passed on the staircase, Joss hadn't changed.

If Makepeace had bisected his life, then all of them—Joss, Thebaid, mummies, statues—were in the cleaner half. A place where he, with his new knowledge, didn't belong any more. Bennet himself had changed too much, grown up too far, outgrown what had been important in the past. This was like the mummy he and Joss had examined together once: a dried out husk.

Time to close the door on it and go. And never come back, no matter what he found at Makepeace. This part was finished.

Bennet kissed the unresponsive cheek again. "I'm happy for you, Joss. I won't hang around then, if you're getting ready to meet him. I'll catch up with you sometime."

"Yes, do." Joss was polite and indifferent, returning the kiss as passionlessly as Bennet had kissed him. "Goodbye, Bennet."

Bennet glanced back when he reached the door. Joss had already turned away, head bent over an amulet, elegant hands turning it over as he examined it.

Definitely time to go.

The door closed with a hard, cold snick of the lock.

Bennet wasn't surprised when Jak called him to his office at a time when most sensible people would have gone home for the night. Apart from the fact Jak knew him well enough to know he'd rather work late than lie in bed in a fruitless attempt to sleep, Felix had already warned him Jak was on the prowl.

The Supreme Commander, Felix said, had suddenly loomed into his office ("I choked on the half-dry sandwich doing duty as lunch—a very late lunch, as I tried to point out to him when he yelled at me for eating at my desk. What sort of emotional crisis has the old man wandering the corridors like that, do you think?") and had made snide comments when he'd found Bennet absent, visiting old lovers at the Thebaid.

"I didn't tell him that, of course," Felix assured him.

Bennet shrugged, told Jak's outer office where he was and awaited the inevitable summons with no more than his usual nervousness around his godfather. He pushed all thoughts of Joss away with all his other regrets and failures, stole the other half of Felix's sandwich and they got back to work, going over the evidence and the plan, trying to iron out the last-minute changes and spot the potential for mistakes and crises. Hours and hours of it. They had dinner at their desks, delivered by a messenger.

The work took his mind off Joss and the past. By the time the Supreme Commander called him a little before midnight, he was as near equanimity as he ever was.

Whatever crisis had sent Jak looking for him earlier in the evening had passed. The old man gave him a mellow welcome and didn't mention Bennet's earlier absence. He had shrugged out of his uniform jacket and sat, not at his desk, but on one of the group of comfortable chairs set before the big windows. He glanced around from staring out at Sais and gave Bennet a twitch of the lips that approximated a smile. "Well, today went just about as expected."

He waved Bennet into a chair opposite and offered him a glass of liquor.

"Thank you, sir."

Jak savoured his own liquor, and sighed in satisfaction. "Triple malt. A good one."

Bennet couldn't tell the difference, but decided it was more than his life was worth to say so. He thought a *Yes, sir* would be safe, so indulged in it. Jak grinned and let him enjoy the drink for a minute. Bennet waited for the shoe to fall.

"It's difficult, sending you on this one when it's Warwick's command. But it's your operation, and you'll be needed." Jak put down his glass and rubbed at his eyes. "There is a lot happening at the moment, Bennet. A lot of people, powerful Ennead-type people, would have heart attacks if they knew about this mission. It has the potential for causing us a lot of grief at the very highest political and diplomatic level."

Another reason to despise politicians. Not that Bennet needed one.

Jak poured himself another and offered the bottle. "Too many of our colonies and settlement planets are in a state of unrest. The war isn't popular with the taxpayers, Bennet. We can expect a great deal more protest."

"Yes, sir. I know the Phoenix League has made political gains."

Starting out on Thorn after liberation from a Maess invasion almost thirty years before, the Phoenix movement, with all its emotion-packed symbolism of life and hope rising renewed from the ashes, was gaining ground in many of Albion's colonies with its agenda for peace and change. Its charismatic leader was becoming a person of note, a thorn—and Bennet had to hide a grin when his thoughts tended this way—in the side of the essentially conservative Albion government. Albion, of course, saw nothing to be gained in changing the situation where she was the premier planet, the mother-planet, the font of all power. Phoenix was a threat.

"Significant gains. Very significant. And Vines appears to know how to use the political capital and influence he's won. They're on the rise, demanding change. They want more autonomy, they want peace. They're tired of war."

Bennet shared Jak's sour grin. Everyone was tired of war. None more than the military.

"Perhaps it's not a bad thing," Jak said, "shaking up the political establishment and making the politicians think more deeply about what they're doing and why. But Vines has them nervous and jumpy, Bennet, because his party is a threat to the nice, safe status quo, and that doesn't make for good decisions. In the climate we have now, even the President hesitated about Makepeace, and the gods know he has no time for the Phoenix people and their demands. That's why it's taken so long to approve this job. You know, politicians are odd fish. They want us to win the war, of course, but then I get orders that the damage on this job is to be 'contained'. Destroy the base, bring us back a live one if you can manage it, but don't go beyond that. Limited damage, only. Those are your orders."

Bennet blinked. "Yes sir. I hadn't planned on destroying everything in my path on the way in or out. That's too noisy for me. I'm Shield. We sneak."

Jak grinned. "You do indeed. Just as well. It's like we're expected to lob marshmallows at the enemy, not bombs, and then they'll complain if the Maess get diabetes." Jak sounded too like Warwick for Bennet's comfort, but it was only for an instant. "Commander Warwick will enjoy commanding this mission, I think. He is, of course, an outstanding soldier."

Bennet put aside the resentful memory of Warwick's scornful voice, all those years ago when he'd been eighteen and at odds with his father about wanting to take his degree at the Thebaid rather than follow family tradition and enter the Military Academy.

A pity he hasn't got what it takes to go to the Academy, Caeden. Sioned can't wait to get there. She has more balls than he has. I'd be ashamed of any child of mine ducking out like that. It had hurt, but what had hurt more was his father's acquiescent silence and the knowledge Caeden was as ashamed, disgusted and disappointed as Warwick wanted him to be. It astonished Bennet, sometimes, that he and his father had retrieved any sort of relationship at all, although Warwick's spite had been a pinprick compared to the devastation that had been Joss.

Instead he focused on what he knew about Warwick's record. Warwick might have a strong regard for his own reputation and was never shy about promoting it, but Bennet couldn't deny Warwick had been the great hero of the previous generation. He was charismatic, full of braggadocio and had an unflinching belief in his own abilities, with a name for reckless courage few had matched. He had a kind of instinctive tactical brilliance. Even Caeden—and Bennet admitted his father was one of the best— even Caeden didn't have that spark. Warwick's achievements were admirable: the crushing defeat he inflicted on the Maess at Taxos, the battle at Brannus, the Coressian incident, to name but the three most famous. Warwick had earned his reputation the hard way. As a boy, Bennet had revered the great hero who was one of his father's closest friends, only seeing the faulty man behind the façade as he grew older.

Not to mention that in his book, tactical brilliance was a short-sighted virtue when set against the need for strategic understanding. Warwick wouldn't get strategy if it had him in a stranglehold.

Still, Bennet could say, with complete sincerity, "Yes, he is. Outstanding."

"He's very different to your father. Caeden's solid worth."

"I know, sir." It was true and it was a compliment Caeden would relish. Bennet cast about for something nice to say about his (thankfully) temporary commander. "Commander Warwick has a brilliant reputation."

"All the same, I'd like you on the *Caliban*, where you can keep an oversight of what's going on. No playing on the *Dhow* until you rendezvous for the drop itself."

What the hell? An oversight? "Yes, sir. No, sir."

"Three bags full, sir." Jak laughed, then said, more soberly, "Making the decision on the ground, Bennet... it's a nasty one. Very nasty. I'm sorry to lay the extra responsibility on you."

"It comes with the territory. I mean, if I wasn't prepared to carry through the plans and schemes Felix and I come up with, I wouldn't do the work for the Unit."

If Bennet had still been the wide-eyed little boy begging his Uncle Jak for sweets and stories, the Supreme Commander's next words would have been the equivalent of a lollipop offered as a reward for good behaviour. "You can wear your Shield uniform, if it makes you feel better."

Not a great idea given Warwick's outburst earlier, although Bennet appreciated the thoughtfulness behind it. "I'd better stick to Fleet dress while I'm on the *Caliban*, at least. It's less confrontational."

Jak's mouth twitched. "Dear me, we are growing up."

"I hope so, sir."

"Grown up enough to take your next posting without complaint?"

Bennet's stomach clenched. No. Please not. Please the gods not.

"Flight Captain Simonitz of the *Gyrfalcon* is retiring on medical grounds. You can fill the gap while we cast around for a permanent replacement, put what you've learned on the *Corvus* to good use."

Bennet's mouth opened a couple of times, and closed with the protests unsaid. His father and Jak had plotted this between them. Of course they had. He could only assume that the year before they hadn't had sufficient grounds to remove Simonitz, and Bennet's escape to the *Corvus* had been nothing more than a brief respite.

"Sometimes," Jak said, "I can run the military the way it pleases me. I may be an interfering old man, but it will do both of you a power of good to work together. Your father's the best I have, you know. Time he saw what you're capable of. Besides, I don't have anywhere else worth putting you for a year without wasting all the experience you got on the *Corvus*. I wouldn't want to give you anything less than a destroyer, and I don't have one of those in my back pocket right now. Look on this as a way of neatly killing several birds with one stone."

Bennet tried again. "But serving under my father... personalities aside, sir, that's going to make for more difficulties."

"It's hardly unknown for a son or daughter to follow their parents into the same ship. Isn't your sister there already? Fleet's a family orientated place, Bennet. You know that."

Bennet sighed. He did know that. He knew that the way Natalia had and Liam did: all things being equal, they'd end up in what most Fleet families considered the family firm, trapped a system where families would serve on one ship for generations. What was the point of arguing? He'd escaped it for eight years. Better than most managed.

Jak, not unsympathetic, grinned and offered him the bottle again. This time, Bennet took it.

"I don't think working with your father will be that bad," Felix said with a stunning lack of sympathy, the bastard. "You're getting on better with him now."

"It's not him." Bennet closed his eyes for a second, but he wasn't able to banish the face of the man he hadn't seen for two years now. Flynn's face. It stared back at him from behind his closed eyelids; mocking, nonchalant, smiling, eager, loving. A heart he'd thought cured started aching again. "It's not Dad."

"Ah," Felix said, and when Bennet looked at him, his expression finally showed a modicum of empathy. "Green-eyed Fleet lieutenants."

Bennet regretted confiding in Felix about his convoluted love life. The two of them had drunk too much the night they celebrated Felix's engagement. It had loosened Bennet's tongue too far. "Just the one."

"If you're lucky, it will only be for a few months. A year at most."

"If I'm really lucky," Bennet said, "I'll be killed on Makepeace."

CHAPTER FIFTEEN

28 Quartus 7490, Military HQ

"Warwick's waiting." Bennet closed the lid of the protective case holding an improved version of the Link he'd carried to T18 four years before, and pressed his thumb against the lock to seal it. The box fitted into the backpack Felix had ready for him. "We're due to take his cutter back to *Caliban* in a couple of hours."

"They'll hold the cutter for you." Felix took a handheld scanner from its box. "You're going to need this. I finished modifying it last night. I've been thinking about this ever since your little bombshell hit at Yule. An ordinary scanner will pick up the signatures of Maess-manufactured metals and compounds, but you'd have to be screening out everything else around you all the time and sometimes the signatures can be masked by other things or confused with stuff we use ourselves." Felix grinned and indicated Bennet's leg. "That could cause us to make some regrettable errors. You're not the only war hero gamely getting about on an artificial joint, you know, and it wouldn't do to mistake you for a Maess cyborg."

"Just a human one." Bennet ignored the hero jibe.

"We don't know, if you're right, how much—or, more to the point, how little—Maess material may have been incorporated into those people. You're going to need the most sensitive detector we can put together. We've taken apart enough drones over the years to get a good analysis of the metal alloys they use in construction. I've set the scanner to look for those specifics, and those specifics only. That means I've been able to increase sensitivity levels. Try it on your knee."

Bennet passed the scanner over his right knee. Nothing. The tiny screen was lit, but nothing whatever showed on it.

"This one should be easy." Felix reached into a large box beside his lab bench and pulled up a deactivated drone head. He plonked it, without ceremony, onto the bench top.

"Off the scale."

Drone body parts were gruesome in their obscene parody of the human form. The head was no exception, seeming to stare back up at him, mocking, despite the lack of eyes or any other facial feature. Bennet had to turn a threatened shudder into a deliberate easing of tense shoulders.

"And now this." Felix handed him a tiny, but heavy, ingot. "Lead. With some impurities taken from our deactivated friend here, present in quantities so small there's no point in trying to explain them to a mere historian who can't get his head around scientific measurement systems."

"Because I have more interesting things inside my head, thank you. It's reading metallic trilinium, free-base alloyed germacium, some hybridised fusion of solactinium and taeaciate."

"Some of the base materials for manufacturing Maess drones. We're still trying to reproduce them for ourselves. The chemical and metallurgical data you brought back from T18 wasn't as complete as it might be."

"I was pushed for time, and I had a lot of stuff to download. You should have given me a shopping list."

"I might have done, if I'd realised you can read." Felix grinned. "The metallic version of trilinium could come in handy, given its impressive tensile strength. We'll crack it one day."

"But until we do, anyone with a metallic trilinium knee is

more suspect than I am."

"I think we can safely say so, yes."

"If this can detect those metals in a lead ingot, then it'll have no trouble with seeing them…" Bennet paused, reluctant to finish.

"In flesh. No, none at all. So we know we have a way of spotting one, at least, of our possibilities—this will detect any human who has even microscopic amounts of Maess hardware implanted in their heads."

A headache pulsed into being behind Bennet's right eye. Gods, this bloody job was impossible. He rubbed his temple. "One option out of five is not good enough."

"Better than none and it's the best we can do. I've put half a dozen scanners into the backpack for you to hand around the ground force. You won't have time to check every prisoner yourself. Make sure you bring all the scanners back."

Bennet nodded. "No possibility we can scan for organic implants?"

Felix shook his head. He went to a refrigerated unit at the far side of the room and brought back a small jar. Inside, something greenish-grey floated in clear liquid, its scales overlapping like tiles on a roof. Thin, hair-like wires moving lazily in the preserving fluid. Air, vaporising against the cold jar, roiled like faint smoke.

"The node from our friend here." Felix swept the Maess head down onto the floor out of the way. It bounced away with a noisy rattle. Felix regarded the jar's contents with a look that was almost fond. "Reminds me of a pickled walnut."

"I'm allergic." Bennet would never eat nuts again now Felix had made the comparison. "It's in good condition. Mostly they start deliquescing soon after the drone's deactivated."

"If you can call a Maess drone alive in the first place, we took this from a live capture."

Bennet stiffened, made himself relax. He glanced down at the drone head on the floor. They weren't human. They didn't breathe. Felix was right: they weren't alive. They were machines with a few live cells wired into them. That was all. It couldn't compare to killing something that was alive.

"We're using a new preservative one of the Unit's chemists created. It's four, five times more effective than anything we've had in the past." Felix gave the jar a shake and the node bobbed around under the air-tight lid, a particularly loathsome piece of flotsam. "Looks good, doesn't it?"

Bennet frowned. "The scanner picked up the inorganic stuff all right. Why not Maess organic material?"

"The only organic material we've ever been able to examine comes from the nodes. We've made some advances in assessing their molecular and cellular physiologies, but the nodes aren't exactly giving us a lot in terms of their genetics, or morphology, or biochemistry or any other branch of biological science you can name." Felix put down the jar and threw up his hands. "We have so little to go on, it's laughable. I could maybe build you a scanner to focus on some of the Maess genome proteins we've found in the nodes, but you'd have to de-nucleate a few hundred cells to be able to do the tests." Felix rubbed a finger across the condensation on the jar's lid. "I don't think you'll have the time to do that while you're running around shooting at things, and you'd need a portable lab the size of a bus. I have tried to miniaturise the testing devices, but at the moment I can't build a handheld scanner that differentiates between human and Maess material." He hesitated, then shook his head. "Oh well. Here."

He delved back into the refrigerator and brought out another jar of preserved horror; another amorphous mass of cells, smaller than the Maess node but just as unattractive.

Bennet's heart thumped. He watched as Felix reached into the jar with forceps and lifted out the unappetising lump, letting it drain. "And this is?"

"You know what it is. Maess genetic material from a downed drone combined with human DNA using in-vitro microscopic techniques. We implanted each hybrid in an empty protein envelope taken from a de-nucleated human ovum."

"Felix, this is as bad as anything the Maess might be doing on Makepeace! You promised me you'd destroyed them all."

"I've destroyed most of the hybrids. This is the last."

"This frightens me more than what the Maess are doing. What in hell is the point of me blowing up Makepeace if you take up where the Maess leave off?"

"We had to see if it was possible to combine genetic material. How else could we have found supporting evidence for your theories?"

Bennet stared at him. "Fuck," he said, at last.

"This is the only remaining sample. I oversaw the destruction of the rest myself."

"Well, that makes me feel better."

"It should. You can trust me, Bennet. I'm as scared of this crap as you are, but we had to be certain."

Bennet raised his hands and let them fall again. "You managed to combine Maess and human genes. Bully for you, Felix. Don't expect me to cheer."

"I'm not cheering, either. We did it, but making it viable is another matter entirely."

"Thank the gods!"

Except that the Maess had more than thirty years of research on Felix and his band of mad scientists. That thought hadn't escaped Felix either. "If they've done it and found some way of making the hybrids viable, you may come across things on Makepeace that are mostly human—"

"But not quite."

"No." Felix dropped the thing back into its jar. "Not quite."

Bennet hefted the scanner in his hands. "And this won't help me."

"I wish I could say it did, Bennet, but I can't work out how to detect evidence of Maess DNA and be certain the scanner reads

Maess as opposed to human proteins and amino acids. I can't give you a way of checking out the prisoners before you risk bringing any of them back. Not if the Maess have gone down the route of creating and implanting a hybrid node."

"Just as we thought." Bennet scrubbed at his eyes with the heel of his free hand. "That's so great."

"Yeah. Sorry." Felix pushed at the jar with a forefinger, sighed, and resealed the lid.

"What would it look like, if they are going for a hybrid? Like that thing?"

"I don't know. That's what we managed to make with our technology. The gods alone know what their version might be like."

For a minute, Bennet despaired. "This is impossible, Felix. If I don't know what I'm looking for, how in hell can I bring any of them back?"

"I don't know that, either."

Bennet's knees shook. He sat down on a stool, supporting himself on the lab bench with his elbows. The little jar was only a foot or two away, to his right. He stared at it, swallowing down the nausea.

"We should have gone with your proposal to burn Makepeace from space," Felix said.

"Such a morally superior idea."

Felix shrugged. "We can't afford morals. Not this time."

Bennet said, his voice steadier than he expected, "This scares the fuck out of me. All of it. Makepeace, the nodes, what I might find. It scares the everlasting fuck out of me."

"Me, too." And Felix's voice shook more than Bennet's had. After a second, he cleared his throat. "I've downloaded details and holopics from our production process onto a datapad for you. If you see anything like that, it's evidence for which option the Maess have chosen."

"Oh sure, their lab is going to look just like this one! Come on, Felix. You've seen the data brought back from Maess bases, not to mention the stuff I got on T18. Most of the equipment isn't even half-way recognisable. Most of it looks like it was grown, not manufactured."

"Then just blow up everything." Felix handed him the datapad. "It's the best we can do, you know."

"I know." Bennet raised his head. "All the rest are destroyed?"

"Yes. I promise."

"And this one?"

"I'll destroy that, too. Trust me."

"Now would be a good time. Now would be a very good time."

"Gods, you have such a stick up your arse sometimes." Felix put the sealed jar with its revolting little mass of unnatural organic matter into a small incinerator. "Do the honours?"

Bennet pressed the buttons on the machine with shaking fingers. When he opened the incinerator again, the jar and its contents were little more than a puddle of slag. "Better."

Felix had taken back the scanner. He fitted it into a soft leather carrying case and handed it over. "It'll loop through your belt."

"Thanks."

Felix hauled a large carry-case onto the bench. "Bring back as many nodes as you can. This is refrigerated. Flick this switch here to activate the coolants."

"I'll try. But if we're a few days getting back, all you may have in the vials might be icy sludge."

"The vials are filled with the new preservative and the batteries will last a month. I'm not worried about that." Felix leaned up against his workbench. "What will you do with the prisoners you can't be sure about?"

"You've just told me I can't be sure about any of them."

"Yeah. Sorry," Felix said, again. "You'll be able to tell if any have Maess hardware inside of them, though."

"Not good enough." Bennet turned the scanner over and over. "Not if that's all I can detect."

"Sorry."

"And you know what I'll have to do with them."

"Will you be able to do it?" Felix looked at him, frowning. "Don't take this the wrong way, Bennet, but I've known you for what, nine years now? I think you can rationalise away killing drones because they're machines, basically. Killing one of them is like taking a computer off-line. Something organic is different. Killing humans...."

"I killed a Jack, once. In a fire fight."

"And you weren't exactly a happy little Shield warrior afterwards."

"I'll do what I have to do." Bennet concentrated for a minute on slotting the scanner into place beside his laser holster. His hands were quite steady as he re-buckled his belt.

Felix handed him another small case. "This may be useful."

Bennet's mouth tightened. "What is it?"

"Poison. It's fast acting and painless. Twenty shots in each hypo, ten hypos, all pre-loaded. I thought that if you had to leave any of them behind, this might make it easier."

Bennet swallowed. He kept his tone deadpan. "I see. You expect me to poison them before I blow them up."

"They won't feel anything."

"I fucking well will!" Bennet slammed down the box of slim, deadly little hypos, scattering them, and pushed himself away from the bench.

"It'll be kinder." Felix spoke to Bennet's back.

Just for a second, Bennet wanted to scream and yell and hit something, hard. He breathed deep to get it under control, letting the breath sigh out of him, turning back to Felix. "I want to bring as many back as I can."

"If you bring them back, they'll live the rest of their lives in a special penal colony. The Ennead could never authorise them to live free."

"Better that than being experimented upon."

Felix had collected the hypos. When Bennet turned, he was busy slotting them into the case. "You think?"

Bennet looked over to the incinerator and its pool of cooling slag. No. The only difference was likely to be who conducted the experiments. Slowly, he stretched out a hand and picked up the box of hypos. It fitted into the backpack, sitting neatly on the case holding the Link. The damned Link that had got them into this god-awful mess in the first place.

The only quiet place Bennet could find was the bathroom. He locked himself into a cubicle, dropping the carry-case and backpack onto the floor and losing lunch. And then he sat there for a few minutes, holding the modified scanner against the metal buried in his leg and wondering if the next human cyborg he came up against would be the one he had to kill.

"I wanted to wish you both luck." The Supreme Commander shook hands with Warwick, who was grave and quiet, and gave Bennet a folded piece of paper. "This came for you, from the *Gyrfalcon*."

Bennet hesitated.

"You can read it now. I copied it down myself as he dictated it. Nothing in there's going to shock me."

Only a few lines in Jak's distinctive script, but the tone was all Caeden: sorrow and compassion that this task had fallen Bennet's way, complete confidence he would do what was needed, pleased anticipation they'd be serving together when Makepeace was over. *Try to control your reaction to that in front of the Supreme Commander. The sound of gnashing teeth is music to his ears.* Ending with love.

Bennet folded the paper and slipped it into his belt pouch. He nodded at Jak.

Jak's eyes were bright and watchful. "Final orders, Captain. You will do what you have to, anything you have to, to keep our people safe. You and you alone know enough about this to be able to assess the risks. Can you deal with the consequences?"

The same doubts as Felix.

Bennet nodded, aware of Warwick's hard gaze. "Yes sir. Yes, I can."

What choice did he have, after all?

CHAPTER SIXTEEN

30 Quartus 7490: Dreadnought *Gyrfalcon*

"He goes at the end of next week, I heard."

Flynn looked up from the spread of cards in his hand to meet Jillia's gaze. "Sim?"

"Yeah."

"Shit." Flynn felt a stab of something that might be regret.

Simonitz had been a good captain once, before the booze won out. He'd had faith in Flynn, enough faith to fight the Lieutenant's corner when Flynn's first tour of duty on the *Gyrfalcon* had drawn to an end. If it hadn't been for Simonitz, Flynn would never have convinced the Commander and Colonel Quist he was fit to serve on the best dreadnought in the Fleet. Flynn thought the two still had the occasional moment of doubt, but on the whole he'd proved Simonitz right. He hadn't let the Captain down, and that wasn't something he could say about everyone in his life.

"I didn't think he'd last this long." Kyle peered at his cards as if intense scrutiny could make them better. By ESP or telekinesis or something.

"What grounds?" Flynn asked.

"Other than him being a drunk, of course," Lange muttered, only half under his breath.

"Other than that," Jillia said. "Medical retirement."

Flynn grimaced. "He'll hate that."

Lange's snort didn't signify compassion and sympathy. "He'll hate a court martial even more."

"In the circumstances, I'm surprised they haven't sent him straight off the ship," Jillia took the empty chair between Kyle and Lange. "He's on non-flying duties until he goes. This will be horrible. They should have shipped him straight out, as soon as they told him. What the hell are we going to say to him?"

Lange didn't glance up from his hand, focused on sorting the cards. "Cheers?"

Jillia choked. "What have you got against poor old Sim?"

"Having an abusive alco for a father saps your sympathy, believe me." Lange shrugged.

The others exchanged a look and Flynn grinned at Kyle. "You're senior. You get to be in charge, I guess."

"Oh joy." Kyle rolled his eyes, but the smirk betrayed how pleased he was. Always was a smug bastard. And ambitious.

Lange was evidently going out of his way to make friends that day. All it would need was for him to have a hand to beat Flynn's, and Lange could count Flynn in the ranks of people who'd cut him from their Yule-card lists. Flynn, though, was sure that Lange didn't have the cards to beat him, not if the scowl Lange gave his hand was any indication. So Lange did the next best thing. He annoyed Kyle instead, grinning at him and remarking, "Until we get a replacement."

"Well," Jillia said. "About that…"

It was impossible to hide from Cruz, not even on a ship as big as the *Gyrfalcon*.

She was too methodical, that was the trouble. She'd start with all the most likely places—the OC and the Hornet launch bay—and then work her way down the entire list of every possible haunt, every possible hiding place. It wasn't that she lacked imagination and intuition, but that she was reasoned and rational, too organised. She liked lists.

Methodical. That was Cruz.

He'd always known he couldn't hide from her. That he'd managed to evade her for what, three hours? Astonishing. It didn't surprise him in the least when she finally ran him to ground in the storeroom behind the starboard Hornet deck. He was at the back of it, lounging on a pile of spare deck-crew uniforms. She'd probably yell at him for littering up the place, making it look untidy.

"You've been missing for hours." It wasn't much of a greeting.

Flynn didn't bother with denial. "I put some effort into it this time."

"I'll say. I've been all over the place looking for you."

Flynn managed a tight grin. "Yeah?"

"Yeah." Cruz's answering smile was as thin and uncertain as Flynn's had felt, belied by the way her hands twisted in her belt. "I even checked out every men's bathroom on the ship. There are one helluva lot of prudes employed here. Anyone would think a woman had never seen their junk before."

"I wasn't in a bathroom."

"No. I guessed that. Even if you had the worst case of constipation this century, you were having it somewhere else." Cruz settled down beside him, getting her back against the wall, shoulder to shoulder. "I ended up having to admit defeat and ask people if they'd seen you. Jordan said you came in here hours ago looking for a new strap for your laser holster. I didn't expect you to be still here." She paused, leaned in against him. "I heard the news when I came in from patrol."

"Yeah. It's true, isn't it? Jilly had it right, what she said in the OC?"

"Yes. I saw Sim. He's still swearing up a storm. He thinks it's all a conspiracy, getting him off the ship. It may be, at that. You can see the Commander would want it."

Flynn nodded. "When?"

"Sim said he didn't know but it had damn well better be after he's gone or he'll keelhaul the bastard himself." Cruz obviously remembered who she was talking to and winced. "Sorry. Anyhow, not straight away, is what I heard. Kyle gets to boss us around for a bit. Don't know how long."

But Flynn laughed, very softly. It felt wrenched out him. "I don't think Sim will worry him. Bennet, I mean. He has other things to bother about. If he's worried at all, that is."

"The way you are."

Flynn stared at a ceiling he'd been contemplating for hours. "I'm not sure I'm worried, precisely. I don't know what I am. That's the trouble. It's been nearly two years, and no contact since the day I came back here and left him on Albion. I won't deny that I've missed him and it hurt like all hell. Shit, in the beginning I thought I'd die from it. But still, two years. Two years of never, ever expecting to see him again. You have to get on with things, when it's like that. I've had plenty since him."

"All girls."

"Yeah, well, I've never fancied men much since, to tell you the truth. I think he kinda spoiled me for anyone else."

"Well," Cruz said. She pushed her long dreadlocks back and tilted her head to one side. "Maybe when he gets here?"

Flynn laughed again. Wrenched out of him again, flat and without any amusement in the sound. "And how would you feel if you knew our Captain was sleeping with one of his pilots? You'd be really pleased, right? You wouldn't think about favouritism, or be looking at everything that happens for evidence he lets me off easy?" At Cruz's silence, he nodded. "And he'd be the first to agree with you, Cruz. It won't make any difference, him being here—not that way. The difference will be in wanting something you can't have and wanting it from parsecs away; and wanting something you can't have and wanting it from close up. I'm just trying to work out what I think about that."

"You can't be sure he won't want to."

"Oh, I think he might want to, but I know he won't do it." Flynn paused. "At least, I think he might want to. I don't know about that, either. He's been with someone else, you know."

"And how in hell was I supposed to know?"

"Figure of speech. The point is that I know."

"From Natalia," Cruz said, and nodded. "I remember you said that was one reason you went out with her, to get some intel."

Flynn sighed and leaned his head back to rest it against the wall. "Rosie. I met her when the Commander took me to Demeter to see him, when they got him back from Telnos. And later, when I was on leave, we had dinner with her and some Infantry guy. She was Bennet's Lieutenant in Shield."

"So, he hasn't wanted another man, either?"

Flynn turned to stare at her, then grinned. Bless her for finding the right thing to say. *Bless her.* "I never thought of that."

She grinned and gave his arm a light punch. "That's good, isn't it? He might still want to, and he might find a way."

"No. He's too damn conventional to break rules."

Cruz choked. "Conventional? If half that stuff in the news was accurate when he was missing, he left home when he was eighteen to live with his tutor. I dunno about you, but that's no convention where I was brought up. And he's Shield. They're not exactly conventional forces."

"Cruz, when you were seventeen or eighteen, and you discovered your cock was for more—" Flynn paused, grinned at her raised eyebrow and corrected himself hastily. "Well, if you'd been a boy and you just discovered your cock was for more than pissing through, would you go straight, and I mean straight, into a monogamous relationship that lasted for nine years? Or would you take a few practice runs at the target first? Or whatever the girl's equivalent is."

"Well..."

"Exactly. But he was brought up devout Theban. Where he comes from, you don't do things like that. You wait until you're married and then it's commitment. That's what's conventional in his little world. So, what does he do? He kicks over the traces, true, but he does it in a kinda conventional way."

"That doesn't make sense," Cruz said.

"It does. Think about it. You're eighteen, in a religious Theban family that's been dedicated for generations to public service of one kind or another, mostly military. You've had that all your life, Cruz. Everything you've ever done has been held up against it. It's in your damned genes. So, if you rebel against it all, if you were a repressed Theban boy leaping out of the closet, what would you do?"

"Me? I'd have a wild time to make up for all that church going."

"You would, yes. You'd spread yourself around, getting as much action as you can. You would not end up near enough married, for the gods' sake, and you wouldn't end up in the services anyway. You'd sweep the streets first, if you were that determined to wipe your family's nose in how different you are. That's because you're Cruz and not Bennet. That's not what he did. He went to Joss and he stayed with Joss, like they were married. It's rebellion, but not like we know it. It's like he's half-hearted about it."

"Well, I suppose that makes sense in weird kind of way. What you mean is he can't break the conditioning."

"That's it. He laughed about it sometimes. He said the family had worshipped the Triple Goddess for generations—Duty, Service and Honour. When he said it, you could hear the capital letters. He can't escape it at all. He jumped ship with Joss, sure, but he jumped straight into the kind of long-term commitment his family would have approved of, if Joss had had tits and no cock. He stuck it out with Joss when anyone with less of an eye to what was expected of him, would have chucked it in years before. He didn't touch Rosie for years because of the fraternisation rules and he was her senior officer, though I think he wanted her. He won't touch me because when he gets here because he'll be my commander, and those bloody frat rules will be right up there between us, like a wall—" Flynn stopped short.

Cruz let the silence thicken for a few minutes. She put her hand over his, lacing their fingers together, but she didn't speak. She was good like that. Quiet and steadfast, and he couldn't do without her. She was his right hand, his heart, and the gods knew, she was his conscience.

"So," Flynn said, at last. "That's what I think about it, I guess. I'm trying to set myself up for it. I won't offer, and he won't offer, and we'll have to try and make some fucking sense out of it." He sighed. "At least I got some warning. It's one helluva lot better than not knowing, and just seeing him get off the cutter. I have time to think about it and decide how I can handle it."

"You do your thinking in here?"

Flynn looked around the gloomy, grimy compartment. "I haven't been in here for years. I said goodbye to him in here, after the T18 mission. Seemed like a good place to say goodbye to him again."

CHAPTER SEVENTEEN

30 Quartus 7490: The dreadnought *Caliban*

"She's about a century older than the *Gyrfalcon*," Warwick said, and Bennet, fascinated, had a demonstration of something he'd always considered a hackneyed literary conceit: a man visibly swelling with pride. "She's the second oldest of the dreadnoughts. Only the *Merlin*'s older, by twenty years."

"Same general design, but I guess there's some slight differences in layout to the other dreadnoughts? While the Bridge and Flag Offices had a similar layout on the two I've been on, the commanders' offices were in different places."

Warwick nodded. "The differences aren't significant. They found the perfect dreadnought design when they built the *Merlin*, and they never saw the need to change. I don't think it will take you long to find your way about."

The journey out from Albion, cooped up on a cutter, hadn't been quite the trial Bennet had dreaded. Warwick had been quiet and introspective, leaving Bennet and Illych to their own devices without disturbing them, rarely joining in the desultory conversations and seeming to prefer visiting the pilots on the flight deck. Bennet and Illych played a lot of chess. Illych wasn't the greatest player in the world, but it passed the time.

Bennet had tried to catch up on his sleep. Without success.

When the cutter was dimmed down, he had divided each sleep period between dozing in short bursts and going over it all, again and again, when he couldn't even doze. For a lot of the time he had lain on one of the padded seats, rolled in blankets, watching Warwick staring out into hyperspace. The Commander had been as sleepless as Bennet himself.

Once they'd dropped off Illych at the *Hertford*, a few hundred miles to the rear of *Caliban*, Warwick's mood changed. He insisted on Bennet joining him in the cockpit of the cutter so they could watch the final approach, eager as a boy to show off his latest toys. The change in him as he arrived home was marked. He was full of suppressed excitement; expansive, jovial, constantly in motion.

Warwick was more bearable out here where the man was in his own territory, where he was king-pin and no one to compete with. He was no less overbearing, but jocular and avuncular, as if there was no malice in it. It still irked, being patronised, but Bennet had the advantage over the average junior officer: he wasn't patronised to anything like the extent that the cutter pilot was, nor was he expected to react with the same level of unthinking adoration. The pilot, the gods help him, blushed whenever Warwick spoke to him.

For once, Bennet was happy to sink his principles and make the most of being Caeden's son, welcoming the benefits. A lower level of patronage from Warwick and not being required to lick the hand that petted him, suited him just fine.

But he pleased the Commander by admiring the *Caliban* as they came into an approach vector. It was no hardship. The dreadnought class was a triumph of functional design. There were more graceful ships. There were more beautiful ships. But there weren't more brutally powerful ships anywhere in the Fleet. What you saw with a dreadnought was what you got: sheer strength and overwhelming might, and more clout to the cubic yard than seemed technologically feasible. *Caliban*, her hull scoured silver by six centuries of service in the cosmic dust swirling endlessly in so-called empty space and bristling with laser gun emplacements, was as glorious as a dreadnought came. Warwick was delighted when Bennet said so, and the two had a friendly five minutes discussing the finer points of Fleet ship architecture. Bennet enjoyed it.

Several people waited for them on the deck when the cutter landed, including Warwick's daughter. Good lords, Sioned had improved. She was prettier than Bennet remembered. She looked a great deal like her mother, but with the edges hardened and glassy.

Her surprise on seeing him, when Warwick released her from a welcoming hug, wasn't that flattering. He must have changed as much as she had. He hoped he was similarly improved. It was... what? Eight years, at least, since he'd seen her last. It must have been his graduation from SSI. Bennet had been focused on the rivalry between his father and Joss and had no more than a faint memory of her gazing adoringly up at Warwick, as usual. He'd probably been rude and certainly offhand; a habit from their childhood when Sioned, five years his junior, had tried to catch his attention. But either she'd forgiven it or forgotten. She hugged him and kissed his cheek, evidently so excited by her father's return that Bennet was included in the general spread of affection.

"Bennet! I haven't seen you for years!"

He kissed her back, the way he kissed Natalia when his sister allowed it. "It's good to see you, Sioned."

She smiled and preened for him, putting the goods on discreet but definite show. Her smile was brilliant. "Aren't you in Shield anymore?"

"I'm on rotation out." The Quartermasters on Demeter should hand out signs to wave along with the fresh uniforms. Having to say it each time was a painful reminder of his exile.

"But why are you here? Have you been posted here?"

Bennet hoped he didn't blench. "Just a temporary thing."

"Not now, Sioned," Warwick said, with such indulgence that Bennet could only stare. "Captain, this is my exec, Colonel Mateusz. Matt, this is Shield Captain Bennet."

"Welcome aboard." Mateusz, both remarkably tall and remarkably youthful in appearance, shook hands.

"Thanks. I'm glad to be here." Bennet noted the lines of strain about Mateusz's eyes, despite the youthful face. He didn't envy the man his rapid advancement. He wouldn't want to be Warwick's executive officer, even to get some colonel's crowns on his collar. He wanted the crowns badly, but not that badly.

"Kit." The *Caliban*'s Flight Captain offered her hand.

"Short for Kitten," Mateusz said, with a grin.

"Only if you want to lose that hand," Warwick warned him and turned to business. In a couple of minutes, he sent Sioned on her way, had a lurking crewman take Bennet's kit bag to whatever quarters they could assign him ("Make sure it's in the command sector, Sergeant.") and swept Mateusz, Bennet and Kit onto the travellator to get to the prow of the ship and the elevators up to the Bridge.

The suppressed excitement Bennet had noted on the last stages of their journey out from Albion was un-suppressing itself. Warwick zinged with it, like an enthusiastic boy forty years his junior. He reminded Bennet of Liam. He bounced on his toes all the way up into the ship, eyes bright, the fingers of one hand drumming against his thigh. Kit caught Bennet's amused gaze and smiled.

Bennet had spent time on two dreadnoughts. His father's Bridge always hummed with quiet efficiency, everyone knowing what they had to do and constrained by Caeden's presence to strive for the best. The *Corvus* had been looser, Dalton more humanly approachable than Caeden. There had been more chatter and laughter on the *Corvus*'s Bridge. The *Caliban* was something else again.

The Bridge crew exploded when they saw Warwick, leaping up to their feet, cheers and applause drowning out the Duty Officer's attempt to shout the traditional "Commander on deck!" The welcome was way beyond enthusiastic. Warwick, smiling and relaxed, acknowledged the cheers with a regal air. The man was popular, without doubt, and knew how to use it to bind people to him. They adored him. And Warwick encouraged it; the cutter pilot effect forty times over. He beamed at them, waving his arms like a conductor in front of an orchestra.

Bennet looked away, glancing at Kit again. Now her smile seemed mocking, the amusement at his expense. He stared back. Her smile widened, she opened her mouth and cheered. Right in his face.

Shield training held. He managed not to react, staring her out. He was the only one on the Bridge not cheering and jumping around. Hell. This was more than distasteful; this was personality cult. It was sick. The senior officers' complicity in it was sick. He preferred his father's quiet reticence. What was it Jak had said? Solid worth, that was it. Was this what had Jak on edge, had made him send Bennet here for 'oversight'? This adulation?

He kept his face straight, waiting it out, enduring the looks the crew gave him. Hell, he had to be sticking out like the proverbial sore thumb; the ghost at the feast. Odd man out.

It took a few minutes to reach the Bridge Office. Warwick paused en route to give the helm and navigational desk orders to lay in a course to Epsis-Acteon and get underway.

"Final messages home, sir?" Bennet said, when Warwick turned to lead the way into the office.

Warwick stopped and gave him an odd look. Bennet thought it was like Kit's: amused at his expense. But Warwick nodded, and gave the order. Kit said something to Mateusz that Bennet couldn't catch. She wore the knowing, mocking smile again. If he'd been a cat, his back would be arched and he'd be spitting by now. The momentary comfort he'd achieved with Warwick on the cutter had gone.

He straightened his shoulders against the instinctive urge to hunch them in defence, and followed Warwick into the office. Like its counterpart on the *Corvus*, the office was at one side of the Bridge. It was a relief to close the door on the scenes of delight outside.

Warwick waved everyone into chairs around the conference table. He sat back in his big chair at the head of the table, his colour high, a smile so wide it beamed. "We owe Shield Captain

Bennet a vote of thanks. We have the best opportunity I've seen in years to get out there and strike a blow before they strike us. Such a chance to do those bastards some real damage!" He added, with rather less incandescence, "The Shield Captain is established as second in command for this mission. To be noted and be announced to the crew when we brief them on our mission. Captain Bennet, I would appreciate you giving my officers a preliminary briefing, please."

Finding out he was Warwick's second appeared to dim their enthusiasm. Bennet could cope with the grimace Kit made at Mateusz because it had put her nose out of joint and he was petty enough to admit he enjoyed it. He settled into a chair at the conference table and took the coffee Kit offered with a stiff nod of thanks. It wasn't his day. On top of his personal discomfort over being on this ship at all, it didn't look like tea was in the offing. He decided it would be impolitic to ask for it.

"The first thing is that tomorrow we and the *Hertford* will be rendezvousing in the Epsis-Acteon frontier system with two Transport ships, currently on their way out from Albion. Except for several of our own unmanned listening stations, Epsis-Acteon is an empty system,. It's our starting line." Bennet sipped at his coffee and hid his grimace. Too strong and bitter. "As soon as the transporters reach us, we head into Maess space."

"See!" Warwick threw his arms wide and his smile brightened again. "We're taking the war to them at last. This is a raid, not another defensive ploy!"

Bennet turned his attention to Kit and Colonel Mateusz. Their expressions were open, smiling, showing the same delight as Warwick. He'd have preferred healthy caution until they knew what they were facing.

Mateusz matched Warwick, beam for beam. "I agree, sir. Now's our chance. And we're ready."

"We've waited a long time." Kit gave Bennet a dazzling smile. Bennet bristled. He didn't like her. He didn't like her, or Mateusz, or Warwick. Or anything on this bloody ship.

Warwick nodded. "I can't tell you everything. But Bennet here's in on it, and he'll tell you what he can. Over to you, Captain!"

Bennet quelled a sigh, smiled at them in as insincere a fashion as they smiled at him, and began.

Warwick escorted him to his quarters after the initial briefing.

The Commander's predilection for his company was odd. It wasn't expected, a senior taking such an interest in a junior officer not under his direct command. Unsettling. Bennet was allowed an hour to himself in his temporary quarters to clean up after their two-day journey out from Albion, but Warwick was at the door to escort him down to the Officers' Club almost before Bennet had the chance to turn around. Bennet's faint protest that he could have found his way to the OC unaided was waved airily away with the assurance that Warwick wanted to take Bennet there himself to introduce him to the *Caliban*'s officers, so everyone understood Bennet was the Commander's special and most favoured guest. Bennet, mentally holding his father to blame for this embarrassing level of attention, could only smile and acquiesce.

"Quarters comfortable, I hope?" Warwick looked around with a critical eye.

They'd given him a decent set of command quarters, as good as those he'd had on the *Corvus* and much bigger than his cabin on the *Hype*; a big room with the sleeping quarters closed off by frosted, shatterproof plasteen doors, a tiny spare room and the bathroom off to one side. Standard for the command sector.

"Fine, sir. Thank you."

"Good." Warwick turned the conversation—well, monologue; it was hardly a two-way chat—onto a more familiar topic. The Commander spent the short journey to the OC expounding on what was clearly a major obsession with him; the Good Ship *Caliban* and all who sailed in her. Bennet wasn't required to contribute more than the occasional admiring murmur. Plenty of scope to worry about what would be waiting for him in the OC.

They had arrived on the *Caliban* just after the first shift change. Like all Fleet ships, *Caliban* operated on a standard system of three nine-hour shifts, each overlapping by an hour; switching to thirteen-thirteen when on alert, to increase the number of pilots out on patrol watching for the enemy; and finally, running 25/10 when in battle, throwing everything into the air at once and keeping it flying for as long as possible while thanking the gods for the evil-minded man who'd invented stims.

Caliban was on normal running. Warwick would shift her onto alert status when they'd made the rendezvous and were on their way into Maess space, but until then, this was as normal a day as anyone could hope for. Now, in the hour before dinner, the OC would have about two-thirds of its officers there for Bennet to meet—the graveyard shift being responsible and restrained, sticking with soft drinks, mindful they'd be on duty at midnight and enviously watching the day shift, now off duty and free to indulge themselves with something more alcoholic. The poor sods on swing shift were out on patrol.

Warwick's reception in the OC was as rapturous as his welcome on the Bridge. Bennet stood to one side, trying to feel neither superfluous nor too overtly cynical. So much veneration! It was heavy and overpowering. People were all but genuflecting. He scanned the crowd, but couldn't see one face reflecting what he felt. If any officer there didn't adore Warwick, the feeling was well hidden.

He shifted position, catching a glimpse of a familiar face. For a second he battled with a recalcitrant memory, pushing away the things he didn't want to remember and allowing through the things he did.

Powell.

Hell's teeth, it was Lieutenant Powell, last seen on the *Gyrfalcon* expressing quiet outrage at what he considered Bennet's perfidy over the T18 mission. Powell saw him at the same instant, did an exaggerated double-take that would get him booed off-stage by any discriminating audience and, after a moment's hesitation, pushed through the crowd towards him.

"Bennet?"

"Hey, Powell." Bennet smiled, and offered his hand.

Powell grasped it. "What in hell are you doing here?"

"And it's nice to see you again, too."

Powell laughed. "Oh fuck! It's going to be one of those jobs, isn't it?"

Bennet grinned back, then straightened, stiffening as Warwick stepped up to them. The Commander dropped a hand onto Bennet's shoulder and raised the other to call for silence. Bennet tensed in dismayed apprehension.

"Everyone, a moment's quiet, please. This is Shield Captain Bennet, who's joined us for a specific job we'll tell you more about in a day or two. Until then, you're not to bother the Shield Captain with questions about it, please. We're very honoured to have him on board and I'm sure you'll make him welcome."

His face uncomfortably hot under the curious scrutiny of dozens of eyes, Bennet tried for an easy smile and knew he'd failed miserably, as usual. He responded as best he could to the greetings but gods! the relief when Warwick signalled normality could return by turning back to Bennet and herding him towards the bar was almost overwhelming.

"What's with the uniform?" Powell asked, while Warwick waylaid a steward and sent him to sort out some drinks. To give Powell credit, at least he hadn't buggered off and left Bennet to his doom.

"I'm in disguise." Bennet was grateful for the chance to recover what little sang-froid the gods had blessed him with. "Actually, I think I need to wear a bloody great badge, just about here"—his hand described a circle somewhere around where his medal ribbons ought to sit if he'd ever bothered wearing them— "saying something like *Don't ask. I'm on my rotation out and hating every damned second of it.*"

Powell laughed. "I remember you said you weren't looking

forward to it. Maybe it should say something more like: *Don't ask or I'm liable to cry in your arms.*"

Warwick's attention was back on them. "You two know each other?"

"We met on the *Gyrfalcon*, sir." Bennet took the liquor Warwick handed him with a smile of thanks.

"Yes?"

"Yes, sir." Bennet ignored the implied demand for more information. Powell though, squirmed, clearly uncomfortable. Bennet let Powell squirm and Warwick stare for a second or two, then compassion for Powell made him add, "Powell was my driver on the original job that got us the data we've discussed, sir."

Warwick's mouth tightened. "You mean the *Gyrfalcon* was involved? I thought it was a Shield job."

"It was, sir, but we were pressed for ships. It was when the Maess attacked Cetes, and all of our ships were involved in tracking their forces. General Martens arranged for the *Gyrfalcon* to take me in on the run."

"You mean, Caeden was involved with that raid and—" Warwick bit off the words, eyes darkening. His chagrin at having been beaten to a Shield job by another dreadnought was obvious.

Soothing was obviously called for, so Bennet soothed to the best of his ability. "You know what it's like with the security regulations, sir. They covered that job, just like they cover this one. He wasn't allowed to talk about it."

"And you were involved?" Warwick turned the basilisk-like glare onto Powell.

Bennet tried to take the flak. "As I said, sir, Lieutenant Powell was my driver. He took me in to the target."

"But I didn't bring you back." Powell glanced at Warwick, and although amusement shaded his tone, it had a companion. Resentment? Bitterness? A warning? "Shields sneak, sir. If this one's conned us into one of his little jobs behind the lines, I wouldn't trust him an inch. I was his decoy, not his driver."

"I had six of *Gyrfalcon*'s pilots down there with me, Powell. You were all decoys."

"Not all of us. Some of us were less decoy-ish than others."

Bennet's face grew hot again. No, not all of them. One in particular had been anything but a decoy, had been the one Bennet was targeting, the one Bennet had got. For a little while. Once again his dread of a posting to the *Gyrfalcon* rose up like bile in his throat.

Warwick, though, after one dark look at the pair of them, decided to be amused. He laughed and accused Bennet of being a dark horse, slapping him so hard on the back that he choked, and after a few minutes of less loaded conversation went away to spend some quality time with his officers.

Bennet, recovering, grinned. "Gods, Powell, if you could bottle what that man has, we'd have won the war years ago."

"He's great, isn't he?"

Bennet kept smiling. Powell meant it, the poor sap. "One of our best warriors."

"*The* best! I'm lucky they didn't kick up over me being late joining Third, after T18."

"Oh yeah, I remember. You weren't too pleased with me for holding up your transfer. I'm glad it's worked out well for you."

"I had to make my name, but I've done all right. Red Squadron leader."

"Great," Bennet said, and meant it.

"It's just…" Powell hesitated. Then he nodded towards the bar. "Another drink?"

"Okay. A beer will be fine."

"Wait here, then. I'll be back."

Bennet watched him, wondering at the tension. A minute or two later he let Powell corral him into a quiet corner, ignoring the curious looks from the rest of the assembled officers. "Well?"

"I haven't ever said why I wanted a transfer off the *Gyrfalcon*. I'd rather people here didn't know."

"Didn't know what?"

Powell made a tsking sound, showing too many teeth in something closer to a snarl than a grin. "Why I left. Don't tell them."

"Powell, I don't know why you asked for a transfer. How could I? I was there for, what, three weeks?"

"C'mon, you must have seen it! I was fucking stupid enough to let that bastard walk all over me."

"Oh." *Oh hell, yes.* The cause of Powell's distress on the *Gyrfalcon* was, in fact, the cause of Bennet's own. He'd been so focused on his own interest back then, he'd forgotten Powell's completely. Odd that his own discomfort now mirrored Powell's.

"Yeah. Oh." Powell's scowl was majestic. "I spent a lot of time trying to catch Flynn's attention. You didn't even have to try. That hacked me off more than you shitting on me over that raid."

"Right," Bennet said, too discomposed to protest at Powell's version of history.

Powell then treated Bennet to more broken, insecure sentences than he'd heard in a long time. "Thing is, this is a pretty straight ship... I mean, people on the *Gyrfalcon* wouldn't have... but I don't think everyone here would.... you know, understand... you know, it'd be awkward... there's someone I'm interested in and she... well, I couldn't tell her, could I, and still expect... you know..."

"Powell, it's none of my business what you do, who you do or why you do it." Bennet considered adding that he didn't care, either, which would at least have the merit of truth. But he remembered Powell had been sensitive, back on the *Gyrfalcon*. Maybe that had been rawness from his break up with Fly— with the person he'd been involved with, but Bennet decided against taking the risk. "It never crossed my mind to mention it."

"Thanks. I appreciate it. It was just a stupid infatuation"

"Your experimental phase." Bennet felt half-demented. He couldn't believe this conversation.

"Yes!" Powell said, clearly relieved. "Everyone has one."

Bennet finished his beer and pushed away thoughts of Joss, and Rosie, and other people. "My whole life's one experimental phase. And you really do not want to see the results."

CHAPTER EIGHTEEN

31 - 37 Quartus 7490: The dreadnought *Caliban*

At least Sioned and Powell were friendly.

Bennet wasn't blind to the fact that the only two prepared to cut him any real slack were the people who had known him before he came aboard. The *Caliban*'s officers were a difficult bunch.

If he sat in a quiet corner of the OC and watched them, they were, to the last one, thrumming with excitement and energy. They formed little groups, sitting with their heads close together, gossiping and laughing, the members of the groups shifting and coalescing again. All of them open, laughing, talking over each other and laughing again, with big sweeping arm gestures and animated, wide, easy grins. Classic stuff. The attitudes of those without a care in the world and eagerly anticipating what was ahead. These weren't people who were reflecting on being behind enemy lines with all the risks and dangers that entailed. These were people relishing the task before them. The ship was on silent running now, on alert, and the pilots sat out their duty hours in the launch tubes and ready rooms, and still they grinned and laughed. Even when told this was a rescue mission, they grinned and laughed. They were enjoying themselves. Thrilled, about being behind enemy lines, taking to heart the Warwick dictum of pushing the Maess hard.

Unless Bennet joined them.

Then the grins faded; still there, but not as open, not as wide and unguarded. They closed down the expansive body language, closed in on themselves. They had taken Warwick's injunction not to ask questions as a reason for not speaking at all, mostly, past the common courtesies or polite conversations about Tierce, say, and the chances of favourite teams in the various leagues. On his second evening, he was such a blight on their spirits he spent half an hour listening to a cacophony of throat clearing and watched the pained grimaces as the group he was with tried to find something to say. Their relief when he left was palpable. The instant he made his excuses and walked away, the babble of conversation behind him started. Pointed. Exclusionary.

Was every smile as derisive as Kit's?

Consequently, he jumped at Sioned's invitation to have lunch, three days after his arrival. At least she would talk to him.

"I'm sorry I haven't seen much of you." She said, hooking her arm through his as they walked to the commissary. She was warm against his side, in close. His arm brushed against her breast. "I was on swing shift until we switched to alert. I'm on the second shift now. There's nothing worse than swing for socialising. You're working while everyone else is having fun, and by the time you come off duty at midnight, most people are winding down for bed. Hate it."

"Being on alert is an improvement?"

"But it is, Bennet! It's more exciting. It means we're on our way and things can only liven up." She pointed out a quiet corner table. Once there, she signalled a steward for service, and sat opposite him, regarding him for a moment. The quiet smile on her face reminded him of her mother's. She had never looked more like Aunt Beth. "It's so good to see you. It's been so long."

"Years."

"Too many." Her knee pressed up against his. Bennet shifted slightly to break contact, his right hand stretching and clenching, stretching and clenching. She reached across the table, catching his hand in hers, laughing. "What are you doing?"

He glanced down at his hand. Frowned. "Oh. That. I injured it, a couple of years ago. I got into the habit when I had to do exercises to get some dexterity back. I don't realise I'm doing it half the time."

Her smile widened. She squeezed his hand. "I don't think I've seen you since you graduated from SSI, have I? I saw Aunt Meriel just after Yule…" She faltered, the smile fading.

Bennet turned his hand under hers and gripped it. "I know. I haven't had the chance to say anything, but you know how sorry I am. I'll miss Aunt Beth. More than I'd miss any of my real aunts."

She pressed her lips together, hard. Nodded. When she spoke again, her voice wavered for a moment. "I was so glad your mother was there, Bennet. I couldn't have… I'm glad she came. She was so kind and she listened. We talked a lot. You were on the *Corvus,* she said. How did you like it, being on a dreadnought?"

"It's not Shield." Bennet shrugged, allowing her the change of subject. Grateful for it. "But a good ship."

Sioned smiled again, more easily. "She said you were unhappy not to be allowed back in Shield yet. Poor Bennet! What have you been up to since you got here?"

"I hate being the stranger on the ship. No one ever knows what to do with you."

"You always were on the quiet side, always with your nose stuck in a book when we were kids. Just open up and join in. No one's going to bite."

"I'm still quiet." Bennet settled back and relaxed. *When we were kids?* He was five years older than her. She had always been a kid. "I'm dampening spirits all over the ship. They all join me in being quiet when they see I'm there. Your pilots are keen, aren't they? They're jazzed up and excited about this job."

"Of course they are! It's behind the lines and it's different for us, and it takes the war to those bastards, screwing with them in their own backyard." Sioned's words tumbled out, her eyes gleaming with the same excitement he'd seen in the pilots in the OC, in her father. "The most exciting thing we've done... oh ever!" She threw her hands up in the air. "It's real, Bennet. Real! We're not on the defensive anymore, not sitting around waiting for them to come for us, but going for them first. None of us can wait!"

She was her father's daughter all right.

Bennet was careful to try and dampen enthusiasm to something less frenetic. "This job involves rescuing a group of human prisoners. We'll be sneaking in there, breaking 'em out, and sneaking back. I don't have any plans to be noticed. If we don't see a single Maess fighter, I will be a happy man."

Sioned stared, and laughed. "Oh Bennet. Really! Are you always this prosaic?"

"Yes. Yes, I am." Maybe he was too prosaic, because the sparkle went from her eyes and her shoulders slumped. "I'm sorry, Sioned. Being behind the lines is just the day job."

When he was in Shield, anyway. Another year to go, and he could go home. Until then, he'd get through this crap and the *Gyrfalcon* and indulge people like Sioned, because they had no idea—no fucking idea at *all*—what they were talking about. She was so far off beam about this job that he pitied her. Careful not to show it of course, but he did.

"Mmmn." Sioned grimaced. She waited until the steward had served them, before saying, "Bennet, being in Shield must mean you see things like this mission differently, I get that. I do see you've done this sort of thing before, so it isn't as new and all right, not as exciting for you. Dad... I mean, the Commander, said we were lucky to have you with us. He said you'd have an awful lot to teach us about this sort of mission, how to survive behind the lines, how to scout targets. That sort of thing."

The Commander had said that, had he? Well, well.

"Shield operates differently to the other two services and we have different skills. Some of it's translatable across, sure it is. All the services should share, I think, rather than cling to their own traditions. But it's not likely that you'll have a chance to put it into practice unless you're thinking of transferring to Shield someday."

"I might think about that." She toyed with her food for a moment or two. "It's a shame you're going to the *Gyrfalcon* after this. You should stay with us and see some adventure."

"You don't think the *Gyrfalcon* will offer enough?" Bennet had to glance away for a second, grimace down at his plate. It would offer rather more excitement than he wanted, in one direction at least.

She laughed. "I love Uncle Caeden, honest I do, but he doesn't come over as adventurous!"

No. Solid worth was seldom flashy. Bennet smiled. "Your father has enough of that for half a dozen commanders." And wasn't that diplomatic? His mother would be proud of him. Even his father would give a wry grin.

"He does, doesn't he?" She took it at face value and meant it, too. Her chin came up and she gave him a knowing smile, tilting her head to one side. An only child, she always had adored her father. It looked like she'd never grown out it. "He has such courage and energy and vision! I love being here. It's going to be such fun."

Fun? No. She had no idea at all.

Her knee pressed against his again and the smile was brilliant. "I'll bet the pilots go quiet when you're there because you're too darn serious. You know, when we were kids, I always wanted to twitch that book out of your hands and make you come and play." She tapped the datapad that was never more than inches from his hand. "What would happen if I took this away? Would you come out and play now?"

She dropped her fork onto her plate and made a grabbing gesture with both hands, laughing. Good gods. What a waste of time. He had no more interest in her than she had in him, but she always did like to play games. Always. She'd been such a bloody nuisance on visits, abandoning Natalia to follow him around until he lost his temper and yelled. Pity he couldn't yell here. Instead, he forced a smile and put a protective hand over the pad. "Some books are serious, Sioned."

She sat back, shook her head. "They're Rets, Bennet. Rets. Yes, they've given us a good reason to make hell for the Maess and we're all jumping at the chance, but they're still just Rets."

Absolutely no idea.

He shrugged.

"At least, we're going to blow that base to hell, aren't we?" She sounded a touch petulant now, her mouth turning down and the smile dying away.

He could give her that much. "No matter what else happens, the base will go."

"That'll hurt them. That'll hurt the bastards. And we're taking the war to them, not sitting on our hands waiting for them to attack us. That's what has people here so stirred up. We've waited for this, for such a long time." She picked up her fork. "You know, you're awfully like your father. He's serious too."

Bennet grinned, and resumed eating. "I was just thinking you're very like yours."

"I'll take that as a compliment."

"Yeah." Bennet looked down at his plate and forked up some unidentifiable vegetable. "So will I."

"I do hope you aren't flirting with our Commander's only daughter." Powell's tone was light, but Bennet read into it exactly what he thought Powell intended him to read. A slight threat or a warning or both.

"I'm not very good at flirting. She's better at it." He accepted the mug of beer Powell offered him, trying not to let his repugnance show. His appetite had waned as the job approached, and the beer tasted too strong, too malty.

"Women generally are. It's the whole emotional intelligence

thing they're so proud of." Powell tipped his own mug to chink it against Bennet's. "Cheers."

"Well, I'm not sure I have enough of that sort of intelligence to understand what Sioned was after." Being open and friendly should deflect Powell's faint hostility. It appeared Bennet still wasn't forgiven for Flynn, despite Powell's claims that his affair with Flynn had been wildly experimental. And he most definitely wasn't forgiven for T18. Once assured Bennet would never mention Flynn to any of Powell's *Caliban* colleagues, the Lieutenant had felt free to refer to T18 about twenty times a day and never with affectionate remembrance. Bennet sometimes wondered why he was grateful Powell hadn't joined the rest of the officers and cut him dead.

"That may be because your sensors are off beam, of course," Powell said.

Bennet chose not to respond directly to the sting in Powell's tone. Far better to get one in of his own. "Yeah. Which is why I have to be mistaken in thinking she was trying to get me to elope with her." Bennet grinned at the way Powell's back stiffened. So, Sioned was Powell's new love interest. You couldn't fault the man's ambition. Bennet gestured to the other members of the OC. "Like most of them, she's excited about this job. I disappointed her there. She expected me to share it. She thought I'd jump at any opportunity to take off into enemy space."

"Wouldn't you?"

"Powell, even when I'm on my own ship—"

"Shield, you mean."

"Shield, I mean. Even then, I take off into enemy space it's because I need to, not because it's a fun thing to do to pass a quiet afternoon. I'm hardly likely to kidnap the *Gyrfalcon* or the *Caliban* or something to go play behind the lines."

"Oh I don't know. That's what you've done, isn't it, at T18 and here? Kidnapped us, I mean."

He had a point. Bennet raised a hand in the fencer's gesture, to concede it. "Only because there isn't a Shield ship big enough."

"That right? You must miss Shield."

Like a man would miss a hand, or a leg. "I'm okay at Fleet stuff, but it's not what I do best. One more year, and I go home."

Powell sipped at his beer, watching Bennet over the rim of the glass. He seemed oddly serious. "And you wouldn't take an opportunity to go home early?"

"What opportunity?"

"Kidnapping the *Gyrfalcon* or the *Caliban* or something, for instance."

Bennet laughed, his brief nostalgia for Shield dissipating in the first genuine amusement he'd felt for days now. Gods, what a stupid question. What use would that be to any self-respecting Shield warrior? He mirrored the grin Powell gave him.

"Don't be daft," he said.

The journey to the point where he'd rendezvous with the *Dhow* seemed endless. They moved through enemy space as fast as they could do it, the two Transport vessels close in behind and the *Hertford* as rear-guard, hard on the transporters' heels. Scant miles separated the ships, the little flotilla held in a tight formation eloquent of their tension and haste.

Bennet spent the days trying not to go over everything again and again. It was hard, because here on this ship he had no place, no duty, nothing of the grind of routine to keep him occupied, the way the routine on the *Corvus* had kept him busy. Here he had no patrols to fly, no picket duty to take. Others were doing the job of scouting out their immediate route or watching and listening for the enemy and for any hint they'd been spotted. All he could do was wait.

The tension racked up, but the *Caliban* people coped with it well. Whatever else he was, Warwick was an outstanding commander and trainer. His crew's performance didn't drop one iota, so far as Bennet could see. They were focused and efficient.

And yes, excited.

He didn't like them. A lot of it was down to Warwick, whose bluff heartiness jarred and twanged on his nerves. He disliked the man with enthusiasm. The vague indifference he'd felt for Sioned as a child didn't crystallise into anything stronger, either way. She was too much her father's daughter. He certainly didn't like Mateusz or Kit. The Colonel was snide, beneath a veneer of geniality, and Kit's barely hidden scorn stung. Powell, though, was a nonentity. A damn good pilot, yes, but a wishy-washy nobody who didn't have the courage of his sexual convictions. Sioned was welcome to him.

Bennet endured each day and night as best he could. Not having a job to do until he left for the *Dhow* meant he spent long hours wandering the ship. Warwick made him welcome on the Bridge and though he couldn't take a duty spell himself, it was interesting to see how Warwick ran his ship. Warwick was as different to Dalton as Dalton was to Caeden. That took up some of his day. For the rest, he took to spending long hours in the gym where he wore himself out on the treadmill or enlisted the drill Sergeant's willing help in rough hand-to-hand practice, until he was tired enough to sleep for a few hours at least.

He kept his reservations about the *Caliban* and Warwick's distasteful personality cult to himself. He focused on the job to come and trued not to think at all, as far as he could manage that almost impossible feat, of the *Gyrfalcon* and what would come after.

Boiling it down to essentials, he spent most of the time wishing he were somewhere else.

38 Quartus 7490: The *Caliban*'s Chapel

Final briefing had come and gone.

Illych, Mione and Willem had all come aboard the *Caliban* for it. Van Trion wasn't available. She was too busy scouting the old colony, getting as good an estimate as possible on Maess numbers and checking the planet hadn't sprouted more defences overnight. Bennet wasn't worried about Van's absence. He trusted her to be where he wanted her, when he wanted her there.

After the other captains had dispersed back to their ships and Warwick went to the Bridge to confer with Kit and Mateusz, Bennet spent his last hour on the *Caliban* in the little chapel on Deck Four. He'd left off praying long ago when he'd abandoned the outward practice of his childhood faith, but the constant internal plea, that he be as wrong as he possibly could be, was as close as he'd ever get to prayer. He sat very quiet, staring at the altar, going over it again and again.

In a few hours' time, he could be a murderer.

He didn't know if he would ever be able to come into a chapel again to face up to the gods he had trouble believing in. He wasn't sure he could face up to himself, for that matter.

But for all that, the dusty little chapel was a comforting place to be. The décor was simple, simpler than the plain church at home where he'd spent many a bored Tenth-day, but the imagery was the same. If he concentrated and shut off the little voice inside him pleading for it all to be a bad dream, then he could hear old Father Diogenes singing the prayers in his cracked, wavering tenor.

It was a memory he took with him to the flight deck to pick up his transport to the *Dhow*. Warwick had loaned him a Hornet. He'd got used to flying Hornets; he liked flying Hornets. He still preferred the smaller Shield Mosquitoes, but half of that preference came from emotional attachment and a loyalty to anything that smacked of home. There was nothing wrong with a Hornet.

No one came to see him off. Powell had wished him luck at breakfast, with the same polite indifference he'd feel if their positions were reversed and Sioned had added her good wishes as a careless afterthought. She'd been a little off with him for the last few days, since their discussion over lunch. It didn't bother him, Certainly, it didn't bother him enough to ask her why. It had taken him some time to notice.

He was so glad that Jak hadn't assigned him to the *Caliban*, he seriously considered kissing the old man's trouser turn-ups next time they met. Waiting for the *Caliban* Bridge to give him launch authority was a form of purgatory. And as the Hornet shot down the tube at last, the only emotion he felt, aside from the constant anxiety about what he'd find on Makepeace, was a profound and genuine relief.

SECTION THREE:

MAKEPEACE

38 - 39 Quartus 7490

CHAPTER NINETEEN

38 Quartus 7490: The Shield ship, *Dhow*

Van Trion met him on the *Dhow*'s flight deck, although she had to hop nimbly out of the way as the Hornet came to a stop in a space that could be described as snug about the shoulders. After more than two years away, one of them spent on the immensity that was a dreadnought, Bennet had almost forgotten how small Shield ships were. *Dhow* was smaller even than his own *Hyperion*.

He fished out his belongings from the space behind the seat: the backpack Felix had given him, the refrigerated unit and the kit bag he'd had the foresight to bring with him. He shook hands, taking the deep breath of someone who's finally stopped running, his whole system dizzy with it for a second.

"Good to be back?" Van Trion asked. "I took my rotation out in Infantry. The day I got back and they gave me the *Dhow*, I kissed the deck." Van frowned. "Right where your Hornet is dripping hyperdrive fluid."

Bennet forced a smile. "Sorry."

The look she gave him was sharp, assessing. "I know it's not quite home."

"It's close enough, Van. I've missed this."

"Well, welcome home. We'll reach Makepeace in seventeen

hours. We're smaller than the *Hype*, and we don't have much in the way of guest accommodation but if you want to get some sleep, you can use my bunk."

That explained the assessing look. He must look worse than he'd realised. "Do I look that bad?"

"The little I saw of Commander Warwick suggested very small doses would go a very long way. I thought you may need some R&R."

"He's bracing." Bennet followed her towards the back of the bay. He sought for something to say that at least bowed its head to the truth. "He wasn't too bad, I suppose. I had to spend an hour or two in the Officers' Club each night listening to the tale of how he won the battle at Taxos."

"Interesting story?"

"No. Though someone I know once suggested it might make for good operatic burlesque, complete with fireworks and patriotic tableaux."

Van laughed. "Sounds delightful."

"His officers never seemed to tire of hearing it. It's a funny sort of ship." Once more Bennet shook off the unease that had afflicted him on the *Caliban*. He was home in Shield: he could afford to stop worrying about the influence of personality cults and how they might stack up against solid worth. "I could recite it to you, if you like."

"Pass." She glanced about, opened up the decontamination chamber and nodded towards the benches inside. "Can we talk?"

"In there?"

"Well, no one's likely to disturb us in there. Like I said, *Dhow*'s a small ship and there aren't a lot of places to be private." She took the bench opposite him. "What can you tell me about this job, Bennet? I know you were hamstrung at that briefing meeting and couldn't say more than you did, but it doesn't smell right. At all."

It was a fair question and one he'd be asking in her place. Van waited patiently. He focused on the little room while he considered what was safe to reveal. A thin line of grease ran the length of the door down its edge, fluffy with dust, another grey among the myriad shades in what at first glance was a featureless little chamber, every slight dent and scuff mark varying the uniformity.

Displacement. He was remarkably good at it.

"I find it hard to believe they'd expend so much resource and energy on Rets," Van said, letting him have a minute's breathing space before returning to the attack. "A dreadnought and a destroyer? That's one helluva lot of firepower."

"Rets aren't worth the effort, you mean?" Bennet frowned. He'd have to tell her something. She and the rest of the *Dhow*'s warriors would be down there with him. They'd see it.

"No, I didn't say that, although a lot of people would. No one trusts a Ret. At the same time, we can't leave people to rot with the Maess, because those bastards will kill them eventually. I just can't imagine that we usually wheel out a dreadnought to go and get them, that's all." She watched him. "The base is an oddity, Bennet. You know as well as I do that most bases are purely military outposts, governing and protecting a slice of Maess space. They don't keep humans alive without good cause and it's always temporary. There's nothing on Makepeace to explain them being there."

"I know." Bennet hesitated only a second or two. "All right. For you only. No one else is to know until I do the briefing before we do the drop."

"Agreed."

"And I can't tell you everything."

She grimaced. "And why am I not surprised?"

"Only Warwick knows all of it. It's not that I don't trust you, Van."

"But I'm not Strategy Unit. And I don't have a high security clearance."

"No. Sorry." Bennet drew a deep, steadying breath. "You're

right about how odd the base is, and you're right that the few Rets we've ever got back in the past were lucky to be alive because the Maess rarely let humans live. The Rets on Makepeace have been there for years, at least a generation. We think Makepeace is scientific and the military presence provides a defensive force for the base alone, rather guarding an entire sector the way they usually do. You know yourself there's a standard base only three systems over. That one's the guard dog for this bit of space."

"Scientific." Van held his gaze, made the deduction he expected of her. "The humans are lab rats."

"Of some kind. We're going in to find out if it's true."

"And if it is? Do we know what the Maess are doing with them? I mean, it's not like the bastards don't already know a lot about our physical strengths and weaknesses. They've killed enough humans for that. Something psychological?"

"Maybe. We won't know until we get there."

"But you have a good idea. Come on, Bennet. I'm not stupid. This is serious, or you wouldn't have brought the *Caliban* into it."

"Of course it's serious. But until I can look around the base, I don't know how serious."

"Really."

Bennet sighed. She was as persistent as he'd be if their positions were reversed. "Really." He sighed again at the look she gave him. "I mean it, Van. I have some suspicions about what I'll find, but believe me, you do not want to know about it unless you want to have the same sleepless nights I do. But until we're in that base and can see for ourselves, I don't know. Not for sure."

Her mouth tightened, but she nodded. "That bad?"

"If it's what I think it may be, then it's worse." He leaned back on the bench, stretching the kinks out of his back.

"Then I don't know if this will make you feel better or not." Van held out a folded slip of paper. "I printed it for you, since it's so official it has General Martens' signature on it. It came for you an hour ago."

Bennet unfolded the paper. It was the General's authorisation giving him temporary promotion to major, for the duration of the raid. Well, that certainly explained Van's attitude and the faint air of offence.

"She said it would make sure there'd be no confusion when we were on the ground. The *Dhow* is under your command."

"She didn't need to do that."

"No, she didn't. You're already established as Warwick's second in the chain of command. I'd already assumed I'd be under your orders on the ground. You didn't ask for it?"

"No."

Van stared at him. It was a few seconds before she nodded acceptance. "It made me think about what we were going to find, if she thought I'd need that to co-operate, that I'd need to be forced."

It was to protect her, although a meagre protection at best. If they had to leave Makepeace without bringing any of the prisoners out with them, because he'd ordered they be left behind to die when the base was destroyed, then it was a fig-leaf of a legal defence that Van could claim she was only obeying orders. His orders. He wondered if, at the point when she realised that, she'd be able to square it with her conscience.

He knew he'd have trouble squaring it with his own.

She was older than he was, more experienced and had to have two or three years seniority over him. Half her disquiet had to be resentment at having a junior captain set over her, given authority over her and her ship and her people. Especially her people, if she was anything at all like he was himself, agonising over every injury and death, however unavoidable. And to have to hand over that responsibility to someone else, to have to rely on someone else's judgement on a job when it was her crew's lives and well-being on the line… well, he'd be seething. He was lucky she was politer and more restrained, more graceful, than he would be in like circumstances.

Mentally cursing the General's interference, he chose his words with care. "I'm sorry about this, Van. The decisions down on Makepeace have to be mine, because I'm the only one who knows enough about all this to make them. They may not be easy decisions to live with. I have to have command there, and I'm sorry that cuts across your command here. I do understand. They're your people. You know them and I don't. I'm looking for a ride to the base and backup while I do what I have to do. That's all."

She'd given him a sharp look when he'd hinted again at the significance of this raid. "I've got my orders. It's your raid. It always was, and we'll do what you want us to do to make sure you pull it off. But I don't like that no one will tell me what it's all about. And," she added, with a touch of venom, "hints that it's all too awful aren't helping."

"Sorry." He leaned his head against the wall of the chamber. "All I can tell you, and all I'll tell the crew before we hit dirt, is that depending on what I do find down there, we may not be bringing all the prisoners back up with us. We may not be bringing any of them back."

She frowned. "But the whole point is a rescue."

He shrugged.

"Bennet, we'll be blowing that base to hell!"

Bennet let his head roll back and closed his eyes for a minute. "Precisely."

Van Trion's cabin was tiny, the same size as his own back on the *Hyperion*. But it had a shower—sonic, but he'd take what he could get—and it had a bed. He dressed in tee and shorts after his shower, leaving the cherished black battledress to swing on its hanger on the closet door.

Another check before he slept. The refrigerated case first, fitted with its thirty jars of preservative, each already labelled in Felix's firm script. Felix had never been in battle, but even he realised it could be a little difficult to label up specimen jars in your best handwriting while dodging laser fire. He complained enough about Bennet's scrawl under normal conditions.

Besides the neatly-labelled jars, there was space in the middle of the case for more specimens, although, without the preservative, Bennet wasn't hopeful about getting more nodes back in one piece. The refrigeration unit showed as fully charged. He flicked the test button twice, to be sure.

Then the backpack. The Link sat snugly in its protective case, a row of shining data crystals beside it. Each of the five modified scanners were fully charged and ready; the sixth, the one he'd come to think of as his own, was charging in the power point at the head of Van's bed. Two small cases of tools, for collecting Maess neural nodes from the drones. Two large cameras and one small, along with several extra data crystals and power packs; he'd fix the small camera to the shoulder harness he'd wear over his jacket, flip it to vid mode and film everything he found. The little case of hypos... he closed that up again, quickly.

All ready.

Sixteen hours. He wasn't sure he could sleep, but here he could try. Here, home at last.

Van Trion woke him three hours out from Makepeace.

"I'm glad you were able to sleep." She turned her back to give him privacy as he got into his Shield blacks. "You look better."

He managed a tight grin back at her when she turned around again. "I needed it. Thank you. Did you manage to get some rest?"

"I've had most of the crew on down-time. I shared with Khaled, my Lieutenant."

"I could have bunked in with him. You didn't need to turn out of your own quarters."

Van laughed and shrugged. "Khal snores. I'm used to it, but you wouldn't have got a second's sleep. I'm leaving him up here to mind the shop."

Bennet gave her a thoughtful look.

"I want to keep him out of whatever crap you have lined up for us, Bennet. He's young yet."

"Yes." Bennet lifted the backpack and the refrigerated case onto the bed and left them there, ready. "Your office, to go over everything again?"

"How long have you been on a dreadnought?" she asked wryly, leading the way. "You do remember that my office is a computer station squeezed into the back of the Bridge?"

"It'll have a desk and we can print out the schematics and take a look at them. Most dreadnoughts have offices bigger than the *Hype*'s entire Bridge. I'd really forgotten how small Shield ships are."

"I'd have thought my massive cabin would have reminded you." Van stood back to let a couple of crewmen pass, nodding at their sketchy salutes. They both stared at Bennet as they passed. "I'm lending you my Sergeant. Haydn's a twenty-year veteran and as tough as they come. He'll watch your back while you do whatever it is you're going to do."

"Thanks," Bennet said, and meant it.

He followed her onto the Bridge. It was as tiny as the *Hyperion*'s and, for a second or two, he allowed himself to fantasise that this was *Hype*, this was his Bridge, and the Lieutenant turning to greet them wasn't a short, wiry native of Gallia who snored, but his own Rosie, who didn't. It only lasted a second. Rosie and the *Hype* were far away, Tarrant was *Hyperion*'s Captain now, and he didn't think Rosie was his own anymore. Even when he got back home to Shield for real, Bennet wasn't expecting to get the *Hype* back. He dreamed about it, but he wasn't expecting it. He didn't think he'd get Rosie back either.

Lieutenant Khaled greeted them, too discreet to stare as openly as the crewmen had. He cleared away various bits of flotsam from the small desk and returned to the command chair, giving his attention to the *Dhow*'s sneaking run in to the target.

"Where's the rest?" Bennet asked, while waiting for the

187

schematics to print.

Van turned the monitor and brought up the sensor array. "*Caliban* is where she should be, coming up from beta sector. We'll hook up with her in another hour. That group of signals is the *Hertford* and the two transporters; the *Bryson* there, and the *Smithfield* behind her. They should reach the shelter of the second planet in another couple of hours. Everyone's on target and on schedule."

"And no sign the Maess have picked up on us, yet." Someone handed Bennet a mug of coffee, and he thanked them, concentrating on studying the data from *Dhow*'s sensor arrays while the caffeine cleared the last remnants of sleep from his brain. Bennet noted the tiny spot that was this sector's main defensive military base, a good three systems away. No energy signatures to indicate they'd been spotted or that the defensive base was launching anything to intercept them. "It all looks quiet."

Van nodded. "As the grave."

"We should get a good run at Makepeace, then. Seven or eight hours, at least, if the defensive base doesn't get an early warning."

"I hope we don't need that long."

"Me too." Shield was used to fast runs in and fast runs out, and any prolonged time sitting on the ground tended to make the average Shield warrior nervous. Bennet was already nervous enough. "You have seven units here, right?"

She nodded. "Yes. Five warriors each unit, plus Haydn and me and Khal. I'll be leaving Khal and one unit up here."

Thirty warriors for the raid, then. It would have to be enough.

"It'll be dusk by the time we get there. Let's take another look at the place."

She took the schematics from the printer. "Here you go. This scan was taken at dawn three days ago."

Bennet could have drawn the base in his sleep, from several different elevations and with full artistic perspective, but he pored over the schematic anyway, checking and rechecking to make sure he hadn't missed anything.

"We never got close enough to do an accurate count on the prisoners, since we were ordered not to go in on the ground. Your orders, I suppose." Van Trion gave him a quirky little smile. "Number estimates fluctuate, depending on what we see on the day. Never less than one-twenty."

Bennet nodded. "One more thing, Van. Just for you and me, right now."

She raised an enquiring eyebrow. "You're letting me into your secrets, Bennet? My, I'm flattered."

He hoped his laugh was convincing. He'd pondered how to play this next part, but he had absolute trust in Van Trion and her abilities. The only certainty of Makepeace was that he had to explore the mysterious central building in the base. There was no certainty they'd find a real Maess there. He could leave that search to her. He doubted she'd find anything. They'd never found anything, not in a century of war.

"You may change your mind," he said. "We have more to think about than getting the prisoners and examining the centre building. There's a possibility we might find an organic Maess in command. If there is one, and it's not on the orbiting platform but down on the base, then every possible effort has to made to take it alive."

Her lower jaw dropped a fraction. "You're kidding. Wow."

"Yeah, I know. Thing is, I can't be in two places at once. I need to get into the central building and secure it. While I'm doing that, you and whoever you pick to go with you, will do a quick check of the other buildings. All the scans confirm there are no underground structures at the base. It's just those buildings and the holding pens. It should be a relatively easy job."

Van stared. "Easy! Well, I hope we can do it, Bennet, but what do they look like? How do we recognise one if we saw it? I don't suppose the drones are anything to go by, because they made them to look like us. What will I be looking for?"

Bennet's mouth was dry. He ran his tongue over his lips to

moisten them and swallowed a couple of times to get some moisture back. On T18 it had been a grey shape, iridescent, undulating, no fixed edges. Until it had seen him, and he'd watched cheekbones push out beneath blank black holes for eyes, a mouth open up to scream its hate at him. A parody of his own face.

"It won't look like much." He shrugged. "Or it'll look like you."

"This is Sergeant Haydn. He'll be sticking to you throughout the entire operation. This is Major Bennet, Sarge."

Bennet hid the twitch at his temporary rank and held out his hand. Haydn shook it respectfully, but his eyes were as watchful and as measuring as Van's. He wore the same expression Bennet's own Sergeant Tim would have worn, the respect masking a wariness that wouldn't be assuaged until Bennet had proved himself where it mattered, on the ground. That Bennet was Shield counted in his favour on whatever mental scorecard the Sergeant used to measure him against; but on the demerit side, he wasn't *Dhow*.

"I'm pleased to be working with you, Sarge. This is going to be messy and I'm glad to have you nursemaiding me."

"Whatever's needed, sir." Again, the stolidity was Tim incarnate, unwilling to unbend until this unknown officer had proved himself.

"You know this is a prisoner rescue mission. At the same time, we have to bring back some samples. They're as important as anything else we get. Who's your top team leader?"

"Corporal Danzer. She's next after me, Major."

Bennet nodded. The best corporal out of the lot, then, and the one marked for promotion. Danzer would be good. "I need her to collect some specific and important samples. You know each drone has a node of organic material—do you know how to remove it?"

Haydn shook his head. "No, sir."

"We usually try to collect stuff when we down a drone to send to you Strategy Unit types," Van Trion said. "But normally we only have time to collect heads to stick in the freezer down on the flight deck. It lacks finesse, but it gets the job done."

"Once we've taken the base, I want Danzer collecting nodes from as many drones as possible. Particularly EDA drones."

Haydn frowned. "I don't think she'll know how to extract the nodes either, sir."

"I'll show her how. It isn't difficult, just fiddly. Put her team on head collection duty." Bennet's hand drifted down to touch the scanner on his belt "I need another recommendation now. Once we've secured the base, we need to check on the prisoners. This operation isn't as simple as just herding them into the Transport ships. I need to know what we'll be carrying. I have six modified scanners to be used to check the freed prisoners and it has to be done thoroughly, no exceptions. Discounting Danzer's team, who are the six most methodical people in the other units, the ones who can be trusted to do this?"

The Sergeant flickered a glance sideways at Van Trion, the only outward sign of any perturbation he may have felt. "I'll pick you out the people you need. What will they be looking for, sir?"

"The scanners are pre-set." Bennet took the scanner from his belt. "Like this one. Remind me to hand it over when you kit out your six people. They're to sing out if anything dings on the scanner and put those particular prisoners behind a security wall."

Haydn's eyes narrowed. "Very well, sir."

"Thank you. It's important, Sarge."

Van glanced up as the rest of her small crew filed into the main compartment. As on the *Hype*, it served as recreation room, dining room and briefing room. Haydn went off to organise them, and Van turned to Bennet. "Is it a hobby of yours, cutting open drone heads?"

Bennet made a deprecating shrug with one shoulder. She turned away, shaking her head.

On the face of it, the plan for the Makepeace invasion was not complicated.

Hertford and the two transporters would take position behind the second planet in the system and wait, while the *Caliban* moved in closer and Bennet and the *Dhow*'s warriors went in and did whatever it was they had to do to give Bennet the chance to work out exactly how right he was. The *Hertford*'s job to protect the transporters at all costs. *Hertford*'s thirty Hornets would ride picket on the transporters, protecting them from stray fighters. A slow waiting game for Captain Illych, but they couldn't afford to leave the lightly-armed transporters vulnerable and unprotected. The Transport ships were crucial. There was no point in releasing the prisoners if they had no way of getting them off Makepeace, once freed.

Dhow and *Caliban* would go in together, *Caliban* to take out all the Maess outer defence markers and destroy the base fighter squadrons and the orbital platform. Three squadrons, Van's people had estimated; around sixty fighters. Par for the course for a Maess base, and plenty of playmates even for Warwick-the-Glorious.

As soon as *Caliban* engaged the fighters, the Shield warriors would hit dirt, take the base and free the prisoners. Not a lot of Shield warriors to do the job, and they'd wear ordinary battledress instead of Shield suits—no sneaking now—but they would have to be enough. *Caliban*, having defeated the fighters, would move into geo-stationary orbit above the base, a defensive position to protect the warriors on the ground and ready to pulverise the base from orbit when it was all over.

With Van Trion looking for real, organic Maess, Bennet would explore the factory and collect as much data as he could carry, while half of *Dhow*'s warriors checked the prisoners and readied them for transport, and the other half stood security. Warn them about the possibility of a live Maess and to be careful what they shot at. That would rattle even a hardened Shield warrior.

When the prisoners were checked, Bennet would call in the transporters' cutters: *Caliban*'s Hornets would meet them half-way, and take over escort duties from the *Hertford*'s fighters, and bring the cutters into the base to take off the prisoners and then escort them out again, handing them over to the *Hertford* half-way back.

Dhow's units would leave after seeding the rest of the base with solactinite explosive. Bennet, back in his borrowed Hornet, would co-ordinate the destruction of the base: blowing it up from below simultaneously with the *Caliban* striking from orbit and vaporising the surface with laser missiles.

Run for home. *Caliban*, the two transporters and *Hertford* in tight formation with their Hornets constantly in the air, the *Dhow* ranging ahead to scout their way back, watching for enemy reactions—because by then every Maess bases in the sector would be on alert and they'd have to fight their way home, probably.

And that was it. The Plan.

Bennet waited for Van to introduce him to her crew, put the projected schematic up for everyone to see, opened his mouth and started. He reckoned that if he rattled it off fast enough, blurring over the bits the Shield warriors didn't need to know, it might even sound convincing.

CHAPTER TWENTY

39 Quartus 7490: Makepeace

They came into the system at a point in opposition to Makepeace, using the sun to hide their approach. The flaring electromagnetic fields of the outer corona camouflaged the ships, deceiving and confusing the Maess listening stations until they were so close in, the Maess had little time to prepare a defence. The ionic 'chatter' screwed with their own comms and sensors too, of course, until they got out of the coronal edges and into the Makepeace system, but they'd planned the approach minutely.

Caliban led the way, Warwick completely focused on the job of tripping the base's defence grid and taking out the fighter squadrons. Sixty fighters were more than enough to keep Warwick happy; not to mention, Bennet said (if only to himself, and sotto voce at that), keeping the man gainfully and usefully employed. Warwick relished the job. At the edge of the system he launched all *Caliban*'s Hornets, seeking out and destroying the automated watching stations that formed the outer perimeter of the base defences. With her Hornets gathered around her, *Caliban* made a lunge forward to reach the base and engage the hastily-launched Maess defenders while jamming any and all transmissions from the orbiting platform and the base below.

Bennet, listening in to the communications traffic as *Dhow* followed in *Caliban*'s wake, left Warwick to it. The Commander certainly didn't need unsolicited advice from a mere captain on how to do his end of the job. He had attacked the defence lines with his usual gusto. And while Warwick played, the *Hertford* and the two transporters moved to take up their holding position behind the second planet in the system, an arid and unenticing ball of dust whose only useful purpose was to give the transporters something to hide behind.

Bennet and the Shield warriors were already on the ground by then. As soon as the dreadnought had engaged the Maess squadrons, Van had abandoned all attempts at subterfuge and had *Dhow* racing for the planet at full speed.

This was no usual sneaky, sneaking Shield raid. This was an invasion.

Small as the *Dhow* was, she was fitted with fifteen Mosquito fighters and two small, sleek cutters. They used them all, as well as the borrowed Hornet. Although the Mozzies escorted the cutters, guarding against the unlikely event that Warwick would let any Maess fighter stray away from him and the joyful game he was playing, their main task was to blast their way into the base and destroy the laser gun emplacements, creating confusion and getting as many holes punched into the ground defences as they could manage.

By the time the *Caliban* had sliced through the fighter squadrons and had locked into a course to bring her into close orbit to take on the orbital platform, Bennet and the Shield warriors had hit the ground running and were already inside the main perimeter, leaving their cutters and the Hornet parked a few hundred yards from the perimeter fence. The Mozzies flew guard over their heads, taking out as many drones as they could see.

Quite a juggling act, not to damage the buildings too badly and not to damage the holding pens at all, trying to spare the prisoners as much as possible.

Within five minutes of hitting the ground, they were inside the perimeter, scrambling over the tangled remains of the fence, all that was left after the Mozzies' laser shells had torn through it. The warriors all carried laser rifles: short, squat, compact and effective. Laser shells fried a drone's 'brain' on a head shot or essential circuitry in the chest. Bennet tended towards chest shots himself. More to aim for, less chance he'd miss. He didn't trust himself to go for the fancier head shots in the heat and speed of battle when all that mattered was that the fuckers went down and stayed down without damaging any of his warriors. He'd take no chances with the Shield warriors' lives if he could help it.

No more chances than he had to, anyway.

Bennet ran with Danzer's team, the one assigned to protect him, Haydn at his right hand and Van close by. The Sergeant was never more than a yard or two away. Danzer ran beyond Haydn, the refrigerated case slung over a shoulder broader than Bennet's own. Haydn was efficient and competent, every move composed and economical. Bennet didn't know whether or not to envy him that. While this was where he belonged, where his heart was, he couldn't be as unemotional about a job. His heart rate increased, his pulse raced and his mouth dried up. Elation, excitement, fear—he felt any or all of these, he didn't know which. He only knew he couldn't get through a job without the emotions that keyed him up, that heightened every sense and had his mind racing, computing the chances, the odds, the options, making constant adjustments to counter any threat or change. Beside him Haydn was stolid, seemingly unmoved, watching his back. A good sergeant.

What seemed now to be half a lifetime ago, Bennet had described Makepeace to Felix as an unpleasant kind of place. With hindsight, his judgement had been clouded by emotion. Even without knowing then what the Maess might be doing to their human prisoners, he had hated the idea they were being held on Makepeace at all. Telnos had taught him how terrible it could be, living under Maess occupation. However frightened and lonely and hopeless he'd been on Telnos, it would be worse for those on Makepeace.

But, unlike Telnos, Makepeace was not an unpleasant place, per se. True, the river was a dull greenish-grey under an overcast, darkening sky, but the valley was green with late spring, coarse grasses threaded through with small colourful flowers; and though the plants and animals were unfamiliar, the general feel of the place was, surprisingly, as hopeful as spring on Albion.

And in this strange, green, pretty spring-like place Bennet ran and fought and fired at the slower, clumsier cyborgs coming against them; breathless, excited, yelling orders, trying to see where every other one of the Shield warriors were, trying to ensure they got into the base with the fewest possible casualties, trying to count the enemy, trying to kill the enemy, trying to win, trying to be everywhere at once.

Trying to survive.

It didn't take as long as he'd feared. Maess drones were not the fastest moving, or the fastest thinking, creatures in the universe. Bennet had concluded a long time ago that whilst he couldn't hope to match one of the cyborgs for sheer strength and endurance, he more than outmatched them in wit and speed. His reaction time, any human's reaction time, made the drones look clumsy and sluggish in comparison. Adrenalin gave him the edge.

Adrenalin had brought him, unharmed, to the centre of the base, to the long low building he suspected held what he had come to see. He leaned up against the building wall, chest heaving to pull air into lungs still labouring with the strain of supporting a body so focused on the animalistic urge to run and fight that his heart had pounded until his chest ached. The blood thrummed in his temples, slowing now, giving him the mild headache he always expected after combat. He ignored it. It would clear on its own in a minute or two. He looked around, checking on everyone, kneading the tightening muscles above his artificial knee with one hand. It had held out well. He was slower, as his Tierce playing had shown him, but he'd regained well-nigh full mobility.

The noise was always the most difficult thing to assimilate when it came to a fire fight. He was only peripherally aware of it while the fight lasted, registering the shouts and screams and explosions and using the data they brought him as he assessed and reassessed what was going on around him. But he wasn't able, while he was in the thick of it, to analyse them and put them into their proper place. It was usually the point at which everything grew quiet again that his brain processed and replayed all he'd heard, as if the memories had been parked somewhere safe until he had the time to deal with them.

So it was only now, while he got his breath back and kneaded the kinks out of his knee, his mind added the audio track to the memories stored there: the whooshing whoop of short bursts of intense energy flung from the muzzle of his laser rifle, the flat boom of something exploding, the yells of fright and anger from the troopers. Someone had been screaming.

He looked around for the source, trying to do a quick head count. Thirty yards away someone bent over a huddled mass. The downed man's legs kicked, heels drumming on the ground. The screaming had died away into a pained gurgling.

Van landed beside him, slumping against the building wall with an audible whoof, sighing out a relieved breath. Bennet arched an eyebrow at her. "Status?"

"Two down, status unknown. The paramedic's checking." She glanced at the downed man and grimaced. "Maess hunting now?"

"Yes. Can you start the people Haydn picked out on scanning the prisoners? If you find a Maess—"

"I'll yell. Loudly."

"I'll hear you. If you don't find anything, come and join me in there." He indicated the building with a jerk of his head. She nodded and jogged away, calling on one of the corporals as she went. Bennet keyed open the comms link to the *Caliban*. The ship's Comms officer must have been on the watch for him and responded before Bennet finished identifying himself. Bennet waited only a few seconds for Warwick to come on the line. "Down and safe, sir. I'm going exploring now. Give me fifteen, twenty minutes to get back to you."

A klaxon sounded somewhere on the *Caliban*'s Bridge. Warwick acknowledged over the top of the noise and was gone again. The *Caliban* was in the middle of a battle, after all. The orbital platform may have lost its fighters, but it bristled with laser cannon. Warwick's distraction was understandable.

Bennet looked around for a drone. An EDA drone lay on its back a few yards away, chest-hit and immobile. Circuitry spilled from the hole in its chest, thin tendrils of smoke coiling up from the exposed wiring. Memory replayed to remind him he'd got this one himself. One of his kills. He walked over to it, calling to Danzer.

Both Sergeant and Corporal were beside him in a flash, Haydn helping Danzer ease the refrigerated storage box from her shoulders.

Bennet used his hand laser to take off the head and handed it to Danzer. She turned the featureless ovoid head around in her hands. "How do I get into it, sir?"

Bennet took the head back. "It can be hard to tell which is the front, once you've taken the head off, but you can see the back's more rounded at this point here. See this thin line running along it? That's the seal. Harder to see than in the older models, but it's your way in. Slit it with a knife"—Bennet replaced his laser with the knife that normally lived tucked into the top of his boot, and while Danzer held the head, he slid the blade down the length of the seal—"apply pressure here, and the head falls open."

Which it did, on cue, like a sliced melon. The node lay in a tangled nest of wiring and circuitry. Felix had provided a basic toolkit; a couple of cutters and small silicon-ended tongs. It was all he needed. Bennet cut through the wiring and used the tongs to lift the node, dropping it into the jar Haydn held out. He wiped his fingers on his pants, even though he hadn't had to touch the loathsome grey lump.

"That's all it takes. Okay?"

"Think so, sir." Danzer located another downed drone and came back with the head. Another EDA. They were definitely replacing all the older drones. "Nice knife, sir. Can I borrow it?"

Surprised she didn't have one of her own, Bennet handed it over.

"Thanks. Didn't want to ruin the edge on mine."

Bennet grinned, acknowledging the hit. "It had better be sharp when I get it back."

She chuckled, slitting the seal and levering the head apart. "Easier than I'd expected," she said, dropping the node into a jar.

Bennet straightened up, glanced at the door of the building. "As many EDA nodes as you can manage, Danzer. Leave me one intact EDA drone to take back with me, okay? Shove it in a body bag. If you have vials left over, pick up ordinary drone nodes and mark the vial in some way."

"Okay, sir. I got it. I can handle this."

Bennet and Haydn left her to it. Her team scattered to start head-hunting. The rest of the warriors fanned out across the base, checking for hostiles and working their way to the holding pens. Bennet could see the prisoners, a few braver ones moving up the fences now the short, brutal fire fight was over.

Haydn paused at the door and glanced at Bennet, waiting for instructions.

Bennet darted across to the other side of the door. He paused long enough to start the cam-recorder attached to the harness on his left shoulder. "Remember if there's anything in there, take a second before you shoot it, if you can. Unless it's a drone."

Haydn nodded. "All set."

Bennet wished he could say the same for himself. An instant to ready himself, and, "Now."

Haydn took out the door mechanism with his hand laser. When it slid open, they both flattened against the building wall, using it for cover, waiting. Nothing. No bolt of energy from a Maess photon rifle, no bulky drone bodies. Dead quiet and still.

Bennet went in first, moving fast, leaping to one side and

getting out of the bulls-eye the doorway made, flattening against
the inside of the wall this time, searching the gloomy interior for
any sign of trouble. Haydn leapt in behind him, laser ready, alert to
anything that moved.

"Seems clear," Bennet said. "Stay sharp."

The building was enormous. The lighting was dim and blue,
making little headway against the shadows. Dammit. Even on
night-settings, the camera-recorder on his shoulder harness wasn't
likely to pick up much in this light.

What little Bennet could see of the machinery in the gloom
didn't match the schematics Felix had provided. Most of the
equipment seemed to come up seamlessly out of the floor and
down from the ceiling, meeting at waist height to form long,
slender pods, each with a clear cover. Row on serried row of pods,
stretching off into the shadow. The dull blue light, occasionally
sparking with intense sapphire, came from something—fibre-
optics?—integrated into the machinery. The whole place hummed
with power, the low vibration just on the edge of hearing. It
resonated uncomfortably inside his bones.

He should get going. He had to see whether or not his fears
were justified, to see whether or not those poor sods in the holding
pens had been dissected, had been harvested into grotesque raw
materials to create monsters.

He didn't move.

"Sir?"

He glanced at Haydn. His ears were buzzing and he could feel
the sweat prickling at the corners of his eyes and on his upper lip.
He blinked rapidly.

"Sir?"

His left hand was slippery with sweat. Bennet shifted his laser
into his right hand, rubbing the damp palm against his pants leg to
dry it. His mouth filled with saliva, making him swallow hard. And
again.

"Wait here." He took a step forward.

Over to the right, something rustled and moved. Bennet jumped and swung to face it, heart pounding.

It swooped at him from behind one of the machines. Tall, taller than any human. Taller than any drone he'd ever seen. Human shaped, head glowing blue. It chattered at him, not machine noise but something with the cadence of speech. It raised an arm, the built-in photon pistol spitting at him.

Bennet threw himself to one side, yelling, bringing up his laser. But Haydn was faster. The Sergeant fired twice and whatever it was in the dim recesses of this place blundered into one of the pods and folded down onto itself, slipping out of sight. The chattering noise ceased.

"What the hell was that?" Haydn's voice shook. It surprised Bennet into tearing his gaze from the spot where the blue-headed drone had fallen, to stare at him. The Sergeant had paled, his eyes wide. "I've never seen anything like it."

"A drone of some kind. Definitely a drone." Bennet straightened tense shoulders that wanted to hunch in on themselves. "We'd better check." Bennet abandoned his original intention of leaving Haydn at the door and forced himself into a run, trying not to look into the pods as he passed and at the dark shapes under the curved, clear canopies.

He couldn't give them his full attention yet.

"Fuck!" Haydn had looked, then, more closely than Bennet. "Fuck! Major!"

"I know," Bennet said.

The thing, whatever it was, had fallen between two pods. It didn't move. Unlike the soldier outside, it didn't kick its legs or drum its heels. It felt nothing. Bennet bent over it, laser at the ready, his shoulders lifting to hunch protectively over his neck. He blew out a soft breath. Thank fuck. Thank *fuck*.

Not an organic Maess, at least.

Definitely a drone. Possibly a modified EDA? It had the same well-articulated hands, the same smooth plasticised skin over the electronics and metal underneath. But the metallic body had a bluish tinge.

The head was different. His first thought was it was translucent, the interior scattered with pinpoint lights. But no. The ovoid was bigger than usual but solid and opaque. Some sort of mesh covered the metal casing, the tiny lights woven into it at varying depths, giving the illusion he could see inside. Blue lights, the intense sapphire blue of the lights fizzing down the columns into the pods. Whatever this was, it was no ordinary drone.

The lights in its head dimmed. Flickered out.

The thing was deactivated.

It had shaken Haydn out of his previous calm. "What the hell is that?"

T18. Bennet had seen something like this on T18. Just a glimpse. When he'd seen that Thing, the real Maess, surrounded by drones, there had been something else. Something thinner than the usual drones, less bulky. Blue lights were involved, too. The Strategy Unit analysts never had worked out what it was. In the end they'd concluded it had been a problem with his camera, reflecting the lighting inside the base on T18. He'd had no reason to argue.

Well, now he knew it hadn't been the lighting.

Bloody hell. T18. He should have analysed those images more thoroughly. He should have—

"A drone." Bennet straightened. "Right now we do a fast run through, check for anything else in here that's still moving. Do not look in the pods!" He caught Haydn's arm with his free hand and shook it, hard, to grab the man's attention. "Are you with me here, Sarge? We need to check the rest of the place, fast as we can do it. I don't think there's anything else in this place but we need to do a quick recce, and look for any sign of lower levels. Can you do it?"

Haydn swallowed visibly and pressed his lips together hard. He nodded.

"You take that side." Bennet waved his laser to his left. "Stay in synch with me. Okay?"

"Okay."

They split up, working their way down the row of pods until they each reached a side wall. In the dim light, he could barely see Haydn. The all-black fatigues faded back into the dark and only the faint impression of movement betrayed where he was, a shadow moving among shadows. Haydn would be able to see no more of him as he ran along the wall towards the back of the building, checking visually down each aisle as he crossed the end of each row of pods, counting them. Once or twice he saw a pale oval blotch; the Sergeant's face, turning to make the same visual checks he was.

No indication this was more than a single-story building, no access points to other levels. True, nothing had shown up on the preliminary scans, but Bennet was too cautious to take that on trust. There may be no real need for verification, but he wasn't going to have a platoon of drones come at him from somewhere below because he was stupid enough not to be careful. But so far, this seemed to be exactly what the scans had suggested: one single-story unit with a considerable amount of high-energy-using machinery. No other doors, no elevator to lower levels and nothing in the roof other than machinery, with data monitoring stations in each corner. One of those would take the Link.

Ten rows of ten pods. No. Not quite. The last two rows weren't the same as the others. No pods, but long low tables, waist high, and the figures lying on them were too thin and attenuated for humanity. Two rows of these new drones, with open, empty heads. Waiting for neural nodes.

Bennet slowed, walking down the last row to meet Haydn, looking at the things on the table. The machines surrounding them were quiet and idle, powered down. Probably on standby. Mechanical production was at a halt, at any event. Probably nothing he or the *Dhow* people had done, though. It was more likely the drone carcasses were ready for their implants and the Maess were waiting for the neural nodes growing in the pods to… what? To ripen before harvesting and installation? He glanced at the rows of pods. Four times as many pods as drone bodies—that implied one hell of an attrition rate, a significant failure in the implant process. Maybe they hadn't perfected this process yet.

"Back to the door, Sarge."

Haydn gave him a grateful look. He ran faster than Bennet, getting there first. He leant up against the door stanchion, wiping his mouth.

Bennet joined him. "I saw nothing else moving. You?"

"No. Nothing else here." Haydn shook his head. "Just what's in those pods and that thing I shot."

"Right. Stay here, Sarge. Hold the door and don't let anyone else in, only Captain Van Trion. Get someone to bring me some refrigerated body bags. Half a dozen."

Haydn stared over his shoulder at the pods behind them.

"Sarge!" Bennet sharpened his tone. "Body bags, Haydn, and hold the door."

Haydn grimaced, but the sharpness had been enough to bring him back. "What is this place, sir? What have the bastards done to these people?"

"That's what I'm here to find out, Sarge." Bennet put his free hand on Haydn's arm. "All right?"

Haydn nodded. "You want me to hold the door?"

"For the moment. No one is to come in. Got it?"

"Just the Captain."

"Thanks. I'll be over at the drone."

Bennet's footsteps echoed. The only other sound was the faint humming from the machinery. It resonated in him, thrummed in muscle and trembled deep in his bones. Like a sort of tinnitus. He kept his eyes on the floor at his feet, looking neither right nor left.

It took some manoeuvring to stretch out the drone. He used an entire memory crystal in his camera on it, photographing it from every possible angle, close in, from a distance, blinking through each vivid flash.

More footsteps, steps that slowed and dragged. Van Trion, her face colourless, mouth drawn down.

She looked down at the thing for a second or two, using her foot to prod at it. When she turned the horrified, troubled gaze to him, she'd evidently dismissed it from consideration.

"Did you know?" She pointed to the pod the thing had fallen behind, hands shaking as badly as her voice. "Did you fucking know?"

Now he had to look.

Now he couldn't put it off any longer.

She was young. Maybe about the same age as Natalia, certainly no older than Liam. Once she had been so pretty she'd undoubtedly have caught the attention of his wayward little brother. Once she might have laughed and flirted, confident in her ability to use her looks and her slender young body to drive the Liams of this world wild, watching their frantic attempts to show off and attract her attention with demurely cast down, wicked eyes; enjoying the first tentative exercise of power. It wasn't only teenage boys who had hormones.

Here, her face was too pale for beauty, every last hint of colour drained from it. Even her lips were colourless. The flesh had fallen away from the bones beneath, cheekbones sharp as razors with the cheek below sunk so deep Bennet could see the shape of teeth beneath. The naked body stretched out in the pod was slender, too slender, with the belly concave beneath prominent ribs. Her body was as colourless as her face, the nipples on the small breasts barely flushed with tawny-pink. If the ribcage moved, it was so slight as to be imperceptible. Without medical scanners, Bennet couldn't be sure she was breathing.

He hoped she wasn't.

He leaned down, splaying his hand against the pod's

transparent cover, letting it take his weight, staring down at her.

She stared back, eyes open and unblinking. They were a pale blue. Not the bright blue of Rosie, or Liam or Natalia, but icy and chill and staring up at him as if it were all his fault she was lying there, starved and dead or dying, and abused in a way no sane man could even begin to fathom.

The top of her head was missing.

No accident. It had been removed surgically an inch above her eyebrows to expose the brain, the edges of the skin clean and scalpel-cut, the brain tissue wired directly into the pod. The same little lights that had danced inside the thing at his feet, were sparkling inside her head.

Blue lights.

CHAPTER TWENTY-ONE

39 Quartus 7490: Makepeace

"You fucking bastard!"

Bennet flinched, tearing his gaze from the girl's wasted face.

Van Trion shook visibly, her hands balled into fists. "You bastard! You knew!"

"This is not the time," Bennet snapped back. "Get a grip! We have a job to do." She choked, but he didn't give her the chance to come back. "Did you find anything?"

She glared. Shook her head. "Nothing. No live Maess."

Damn. Or thank the gods. He didn't know which.

"So if there was one, it may have been on the orbital platform. Warwick will have fried it by now. Great." Bennet glanced at his chronometer. Eighteen minutes. He'd only been in this hellish place for eighteen minutes. He had to call Warwick. "You or Haydn?"

"What?"

"In here. You or Haydn?"

Van's hands curled and uncurled with agitation. "Me."

"Then send him out to oversee the checks being made on the

prisoners. I'm not calling those transporter shuttles down until I'm sure what we're taking back." He softened his tone; not so much she thought he was ceding control, but trying to find some way back from the hostility. "Someone I trust has to do that. Get him out there. And tell him to keep his mouth shut."

"You can trust him."

"I know." Bennet kept his tone business-like, not letting the tempo slide. "Send him on his way, and move Danzer up to the doorway. She can stand watch from outside while she collects the nodes for me. The only thing I want coming through that door are the explosives and body bags."

She wavered, eyes drawn again to the pods.

"Now, Van! Don't look. Ignore everything."

She shot him a nasty glance, but did as he ordered. While she talked to Haydn, Bennet shrugged out of his backpack and left it propped up against the deactivated Maess drone. He took a moment to study the pod.

Like all the Maess technology he'd seen, it was curiously organic, as if it had grown. It thrummed with power, alight with diodes and incomprehensible dials and monitor screens. The bottom half flowed up from the floor—implying more machinery beneath his feet—growing into a long bench or table on which the girl lay. A dark metal stalactite came down from the ceiling, touching the clear cover dead centre, and then split into four long, sinuous arms that streamed down over the cover to merge seamlessly into each corner of the pod itself, holding the cover in place. Fibre-optic lines pulsed in the stalactite, glowing faintly blue and, occasionally, flashing with sapphire. He glanced up, but the roof was a dim mass of mechanical shapes and equipment, difficult to make out. A myriad machines or units making up one single machine?

He couldn't tell. He didn't have enough technical knowledge to know. He was the wrong man for this job. Felix should have been here, instead. Felix had a better chance of working it out. He reached up to switch on his com unit. The microphone dropped down into place. *"Caliban?"*

The answer was immediate, brusque and the man himself. "Warwick."

"Code Chimera, sir."

Confirmation they'd found what they were looking for, what he'd dreaded they'd find: irrefutable proof of Maess-human hybridisation.

A minor burst of static gave Warwick a respite before he had to reply. When he did, he was calm enough. "Yes, I see. You're certain?"

"Absolutely."

"The prisoners?"

"The facility does not, repeat not, appear to be creating cuckoos, sir." Bennet glanced around at the pods. "I'm looking at eighty incubators. Not retrievable. We also have over a hundred prisoners. We're checking them now. Their status is unknown."

The silence stretched out for a long moment. "Very well, Captain, your message is understood. Motherlode?"

"No, sir. If there was a live Maess, it wasn't down here on the ground base. The platform?"

"Gone. If it was on the platform, it's ash. Your recommendation, Captain?"

"We're scanning the live prisoners now, sir." His gaze found the girl's face again and he turned away. "I had better get on with collecting samples and documenting this facility. I'll call the shuttles in when I'm sure the prisoners are clear, sir—as sure as we can be, anyway. That may be some time yet."

Warwick grunted.

"How is it up there, sir?"

"Invigorating. We're clearing up the stragglers. We jammed all transmissions, of course, but we detected an energy surge from the nearest base. It may be something got through, or they monitor this place and picked up the jamming immediately. They're on their way." The undercurrent of suppressed excitement was back. Of course it was. The man would relish another invigorating encounter.

Bennet could roll his eyes in safety, unseen. He was careful to keep his tone neutral. "We still have a few hours, sir."

"Yes, Yes, you're right of course. Plenty of time for you to assess the situation there and evacuate."

"I think so, sir. Could you let me know when you're in geo-stationary orbit?"

"Of course." The suppressed excitement in Warwick's tone had been joined by the suggestion of sly amusement that had so annoyed Bennet on the *Caliban*. "Oh, and Captain? It's not a happy situation, I know, but well done. I have every confidence in your ability to handle everything. You appear to have things well in hand."

"Thank you, sir. I'd better get on with it."

Warwick wished him luck and cut the connection.

Van was back. She had taken his advice, if something so brusquely barked at her could be deemed advice, and avoided looking into the pods. She looked a lot steadier, anger getting the better of horror. "What's going on here?"

Bennet looked round at the two rows of drones, eight rows of mutilated humans. He glanced down at the downed drone with its human-grown brain.

"Bennet?"

He poked the thing with his foot, but it remained limp, its head unlit. Dead. No. It was off-line, deactivated. It was easier not to think of them as living beings, despite what they likely had inside their heads. "They're using the prisoners to grow the brain node for drones like this one. They're brooders. Incubators."

Van looked from him to the girl in the pod, eyes widening.

He nodded, certain he was right. This place was an

abomination. That his primary emotion was relief that this was about drones, and not the creation of cuckoos to infect the human nests—well, that was almost more horrible.

The blue fireflies in the girl's head danced on, indifferent.

"Oh Gods," Van said, and turned away to be sick.

She flung off the hand Bennet put on her arm, and bent double as she retched and retched, gasping in misery between each jarring heave. He watched for a second, helpless, before turning away to give her some privacy.

He'd stopped feeling sick after those first few seconds of hesitation at the door, before he and Haydn had been distracted by the drone. He didn't feel anything at all. He could look at the dreadful thing inside the pod and think about the pretty girl it must have once been and the terrible use she had been put to, but the horror and disgust affecting Van and that had even shaken the Sergeant, didn't affect him. Such feelings were so far away, so remote, they belonged to someone else. Perhaps to the girl in the pod.

He picked up the backpack and walked down the aisle back towards the door, looking at each pod he passed. He couldn't discern a pattern to the people in the pods. Male and female, young and old, every race and colour; the Maess appeared to be indiscriminate in the way they'd chosen the people for processing. The only thing the people had in common were the fireflies flickering inside their pollarded heads.

He stopped beside one pod. His breath caught, and in an instant his heart was racing, pounding, and every muscle tensed.

Luke!

It was a second or two before he could pull in air, the ragged breath juddering through his chest. Oh Gods. Not Luke. The boy in the pod was young, with a child's round face and wide, trusting brown eyes. So like Luke…. Two years now since he'd had those few weeks of surrogate fatherhood with Luke; one trust he had managed not to betray, at least. If he hadn't got Lukey home, if he hadn't got those farmers out… But he had. Luke was safe. It wasn't Luke in the pod.

Bennet turned away, flinching, and rode out the jitters by watching the lights in the head of the man in the next pod, looking for a pattern to them. He couldn't see it, if it were there. The flashes seemed random. If sequences hid within the apparent chaos, they weren't apparent and he didn't have time to spend in speculation. He rested the pack on the pod so it covered the man's face and he didn't have to look at it. He took out the second camera.

He kept his back to the dead child behind him.

Van joined him, wiping her mouth. She looked past him to what he couldn't look at himself, and her already wet eyes widened and filled with tears. She dashed them away, brushing at her eyes with shaking hands. "Fuck, Bennet, what did you know about this?"

"A little." The secrecy Supreme Commander Jak had insisted on was so irrelevant now he could have laughed.

"Oh, you bastard," she said, but there was no energy in it.

"I knew a little." It wasn't worth defending himself, but he did say, mostly to himself: "I prayed I was wrong."

It was enough to stop her. She paused, her hands slowly clenching and unclenching again. "When you arrived on the *Dhow*, you said it was horrible."

"Yes." No denying that.

"How long have you known?"

Bennet took out the Link and checked on it, getting it ready. It sat in its case, in protective padding, a dozen data crystals lined up beside it, lighting up the instant he touched the power button.

"Since Decimus, last year. I spent a lot of time going over the stuff I brought back from T18. I kept finding references to this place. They weren't easy to decipher and it took a while for me to guess at what it all might mean." He put the Link to one side. His right hand ached with tension, and he had to pause, copying her own gesture of clenching and unclenching his hand, stretching out his fingers until the nerves eased. He was careful, when he checked the cameras. He couldn't afford to drop one. He replaced the memory crystal in the one he'd been using and unseated the small one from his shoulder harness. A glance at the recorded film showed that the techs back home were going to have a field day trying to decipher the images—the lighting was too poor for clarity. Still, better than nothing. He changed the memory crystal for a new one and slotted it back into place on his harness. "We weren't certain, Van. I only suspected the Maess were using the humans for something to do with drone production. What that meant, how they were doing it... I had no idea. Not until we came to look."

"Are you sure that's what's going on here?"

Bennet indicated the rows of pods. "The drones on the tables at the back are all like that new one. It's a production process here."

"I've seen more EDAs recently, but that thing's new." She grimaced towards the deactivated drone.

"I might have seen one on T18. I'm not sure. And I had other things to look at." He glanced back towards the end of the room, where the metallic bodies lay. "Until we got the T18 material, we could only guess at how they make drones. I mean, apart from knowing there's that little node of organic matter inside each of them, we had no data on how it got there. I'm still not sure how they grow the stuff."

Van looked pointedly at the pods.

"No. Whatever is going on here is outside their normal production methods."

"You're sure of that?"

He nodded. "All the data points to this being an experimental station. I don't think they normally use humans as incubators for the organic material, but I'm certain that's what they're doing here. The whole set-up, what they're doing to the prisoners, the way all those empty drone cases are ready and waiting... it can't just be coincidence that the one Haydn downed had the same lights in its head as these people do."

Hybrid organic material, the thing he'd feared the most. At least, it appeared it was implanted in drones, not humans. Then he thought about the pens full of people outside and wondered.

Bennet rubbed at his temples as he tried to puzzle it all out. "We know, with the EDAs becoming more common, that the Maess evolve their drones. These have to be some variant bred for a purpose, experimental... I don't know, I haven't had a chance to think about it... they must be put together like this, with human tissue, deliberately, for a reason. I don't know what, yet." He stopped and shrugged, pushing his fingertips hard against his temple, trying to rub away the incipient headache. He thought back to the discussion with IntCom in the President's office, a lifetime ago. *They want something of us they don't have themselves*, he'd theorised, and now he wondered just what this new drone, this Chimera drone, would give them. He was sorry, now, that Haydn had had to down the only live one.

"What about the prisoners? Are they safe to take back?" Van Trion wasn't stupid. She was making the connections.

Bennet shrugged again. "The scanners I gave Haydn will pick up anyone carrying Maess hardware. That's the best we can do."

She twitched visibly.

"What's their condition? Did you talk to any of them?"

"I tried." Her tone was grim. "They aren't normal. I don't suppose I would be, either, in the circumstances but they're barely reacting at all. They're passive, indifferent. Even those who came out of their huts to see what the noise was all about are hard to talk to. They're struggling to talk. A word or two, that's all, and mostly disconnected, as if they can't find the words they want. Probably too traumatised. The rest appear mute."

"Drugged?"

"They grow most of their own food. I could see the gardens as we came in. I suppose it could be adulterated with something to keep the lab rats tamed."

"The paramedics on the Transport ships should have a better idea than us about what's causing it. We'll know if it's drugs if they start coming out of it on the way home."

Van pushed back her helmet and rubbed at the red line the edge left on her forehead, before settling it back into place. "They'll be docile enough, anyway. What about these people, the ones in here?"

Bennet let his shoulders sag. "They're dead already."

"But you wanted body bags—"

"For one or two of them, if I can work out how to take them out of the pods. One for that drone. If I can freeze it in time, we can get it back before its node decomposes. And one of the empty drones at the back."

Her eyes were round as pennies. "You're just going to leave the rest of them?"

Heat flashed through him, setting his heart pounding again. He caught her by the shoulders and forced her round to face the child that might have been Luke, if things had turned out differently on Telnos. She gasped and protested but he was stronger than her and he wouldn't let her go.

"Look at him, Van! He's dead. He's not breathing. And if by some miracle, he is alive, if I open the pod and try to take him out, how long would he live with the top of his head cut off like that and his brain full of Maess cells and technology? He's dead, the gods help him and us. He's dead. They're all dead. There's nothing we can do for them."

He released her so suddenly she stumbled, fetching up against the pod and making it shake. She recoiled as if it burned her, springing back.

He let his hands drop to his sides. "We have to get back with whatever we can carry and destroy the rest. When we blow this place to hell they won't feel anything." He stared, unwillingly, into the child's eyes. "But they'll be clean and free again."

She made a sound that may have been a sob.

"I'm sorry, Van," he said. "I know it's horrible. I've had longer than you to get used to the idea and it's still horrible. I'm sorry."

"Sorry!" She took a step away from him. "My sister's boy's about his age. Is that all you'd be able to say to her, that you're sorry?"

"Remember Telnos?"

Startled, she looked at him rather than at the horror in the pod. "What the fuck has that got to do with anything?"

"I got left behind there a couple of years back. Me and some infantry. We collected together the surviving settlers. One of them was a seven-year old orphan who stuck to me like a leech for weeks. When we got back, his aunt took him, adopted him. She wouldn't let me see him." Bennet's voice trembled with the slight stammer that always afflicted him when he was angry or afraid. "Well, who c-could blame her? He n-needed to settle with her. I was only in the way and I was still with Joss. I've not seen Lukey since. He's the n-nearest I'll ever g-get to a kid of my own." He grimaced, controlled the stammer ruthlessly, angry with himself for letting her provoke him. "He'd be this kid's age by now. You have no idea how sorry I am."

After a short silence, Van touched his arm, a fleeting contact, and said, quietly, "What will they do with the ones you do take back?"

"These people here, or the ones out there?"

"Both."

"The live prisoners will be taken to a holding centre, well away from Albion. It'll be a long time before we're sure they aren't carrying Maess components."

"You said the scanners would detect them."

"Hard components, yes. We can't detect biological tissue."

"Then what you mean is they'll be taking their prison with them. Poor bastards."

"Yes. Poor bastards. But at least they won't end up like this."

He glanced around at the pods. "As for these, if I can get a couple back, they'll go straight to the Unit's laboratory along with the new drones. We need to know what the Maess are doing here, Van. Then we've got a better chance of dealing with it before it deals with us."

"And the rest? The ones you have to leave in the pods?"

"I'll be putting one helluva lot of explosive in here."

She turned away, maybe to hide how her mouth was whitening with the pressure of compressing her lips. For a moment or two she stared down at the child. "Rather you than me."

"It will be me. I won't ask anyone else to do this." Bennet left her to think about it for a minute, turning back to the cameras. He put a couple of extra memory crystals into his pocket, keeping a couple aside for her.

After another thoughtful silence, Van sighed. "What do you want me to do now?"

"Take as many holopics as you can. I'm sorry, but it means taking pictures of these people here. Get as many as you can of the pods, the machinery, everything." He glanced at her, assessing the strain she was under. "Start with the drones at the back."

She shot him a look he couldn't quite decipher, took a camera and walked away. He waited for a second, looking down at the camera in his hands before slinging the strap over one shoulder and picking up the Link, fitting five of the little data crystals into the ports on the Link's side. He chose the data control terminal in a corner near the door and it took only seconds to locate the right slot and slide the Link into place. While it negotiated access with the Maess machine—a faster process than T18, in only four years they'd learned so much—Bennet hefted the camera in his hands and started work.

CHAPTER TWENTY-TWO

39 Quartus 7490: Makepeace

Danzer called him from the doorway, fifteen minutes later.

"This thing is full, sir." She showed him the case of drone nodes. "The Sarge is here and wants a word, and I've unloaded half a dozen body bags for you from one of the cutters. Want me to bring them inside?"

"No, I'll pick them up in a second. You guard that case with your life. Van!"

He let Van Trion out first and closed the door behind them. Danzer shrugged, moved back out of the way. Bennet was surprised at how dark it was. The sun had been setting when they'd arrived, and dusk was giving way now to true night.

"We've finished all the monitoring tests, sir. I had them run everybody through twice to be sure." Haydn, too, had put pieces of the puzzle together. An intelligent man, this. He was back to being stoic and calm. "Nothing. The scanners all came up clean."

Bennet wasn't as delighted about that as he'd first thought he would be. Not after seeing what was in the pods back in the building behind him. But at least he could cross one possibility off his list.

"I don't suppose we can do any more with them, down here,"

Van said.

"No." Bennet sighed, rubbing at his forehead, glanced at Haydn. "The Maess drones?"

"We're still doing a count. We got them all, sir."

"Just the usual basic soldiers and EDAs?"

Haydn nodded.

Shame there wasn't another one of the new ones.

Haydn had collected Felix's special scanners from the warriors who'd wielded them. Bennet fixed one on his belt and gave the rest to Danzer to look after. He glanced at Van Trion. "Well, let's go take a look at them. Lead the way, would you, Sergeant? Danzer, no one's to go in or out of that building."

Danzer grimaced. "Yes sir."

Van went with him, Haydn a yard or so behind them. "I wish I could have had the medics I wanted, to check them over," he said to her.

"What stopped you?"

"You met what stopped me in the Supreme Commander's office, dressed in a lot of gold braid. He wasn't keen on expanding the circle of people who knew about this place."

"What's his reasoning? They'll have to have medics on the holding base you mentioned. All the base personnel will have to know."

"Eventually, when the base is fully operational. But they won't be talking about it. The Official Secrets Act will see to that." Bennet looked over the patch of ground where the prisoners sat under the watchful eyes of a dozen Shield warriors. Silent, unmoving, hunched over themselves. Not even the children moved. He'd have given anything for them to be normal kids, running around and screaming and generally being childishly loud and obnoxious. "They're quiet."

"They're like sheep, sir," Haydn said. "Not a mite of trouble."

Bennet walked closer. He didn't think that most of them realised he was there. They sat on the ground, heads down; huddled lumps of inert humanity—at least, he hoped they were still human. One man frowned, his mouth working, and raised a hand a few inches. But whatever impulse he felt to try and react died away. The man's hand fell back into his lap and his face smoothed out into vacancy again. Probably they were kept docile through some chemical means. Bennet could see the attraction from the Maess point of view if it meant the prisoners wouldn't fight back when they became raw parts in the production process.

He glanced at Haydn. "How many of them?"

"Hundred and thirty-two, sir. A good few of them are kids."

With the eighty back in the factory, that tallied pretty well with his translation of the T18 data. "Have you talked with any of them?"

"They don't talk, sir. Some of them appear to understand us and did what they're told when we herded them out here. None of them talked to us. Or to each other. They're…" Haydn paused, appeared to be struggling to find the right word. "Slow," he said at last. "Sluggish. Doped out of their heads, I think."

Bennet moved closer to the prisoners. He wasn't sure what he was looking for. Shaved heads and surgical scars? He couldn't see anything like that, just tangled, dirty hair that in some cases may never have been cleaned. The gods knew what might be under the hair, mind. He wasn't reassured by the lack of visual evidence.

There were signs in plenty of deprivation, mistreatment and neglect. The prisoners—ex-prisoners—were scantily dressed and dirty. They gave off a stink of unwashed bodies and sweat, urine and shit, so powerful the evening breeze couldn't dispel it. Dulled eyes looked back at him as he walked amongst the crowd, pupils dilated, making the eyes dark holes in blank faces.

Haydn was right. They were doped out of their heads.

They had only muted reactions to him. They shrank away if he got too close, but their faces remained expressionless. When Bennet bent over the man who'd shown some awareness and tilted his head up, the eyes focused on him briefly before clouding over and sliding away again. He couldn't tell if the man had registered he was there. Possibly the man had seen something, tried to connect, but it had been too fleeting to be sure.

Bennet stepped back. He noticed they clustered together in little knots, often an adult with children huddled up against them. As he came closer, a woman, indescribably dirty and ragged, avoided his gaze but tightened her protective grip on the child in her lap. *Ah.* Not a complete tabula rasa, then, empty of all feeling. There may well be something salvageable in these poor people, because even here, some tiny scrap of humanity and human feeling remained. The Maess hadn't been able to destroy it altogether. That was hopeful.

He walked back to where Haydn and Van Trion waited, his head bowed under the weight of it all. He made his decision, the only one he could make. He glanced at Haydn. "Put the markers out for the transport landing field, Sarge."

"Yes, sir." Haydn waved an arm above his head, signalling a group of Shield warriors waiting at the remains of the perimeter fence. They darted away into the darkness. "It'll be about ten minutes."

"Thanks. It's getting cold, now the sun's gone down. See if you can find some blankets or something, especially for the kids. It'll be an hour at least before the Transports get here." He nodded at Haydn's acknowledgement and beckoned to Van to follow him, heading back to the manufactory.

"I'm not sure it's the right thing to do, taking them back," he said, rubbing at his eyes. They stung. Gods, he was tired. "It's one helluva risk."

"It's the only thing to do," Van said.

"I know. I need to get things moving there." He brought the com-link back on line. "Commander Warwick?"

A shrill burst of static made him wince. No answer.

"Commander?" A pause. Still nothing. "Commander?"

"Shouldn't he be in orbit by now?" Van asked.

"He should be." Bennet took off the headset and examined it. "Looks okay." He switched frequencies again and put it back on. "Captain Illych?"

"Illych." The *Hertford*'s Captain must have been crouched over the Comms desk, waiting.

"We're ready to move. Shuttles for a hundred and thirty-two. The markers will be out when they arrive and our passengers are ready."

"On their way. ETA: one hour, twenty."

"Thank you, Captain. I'm having trouble raising the *Caliban*. Can you try?" Bennet waited until Illych reported failure, a few minutes later. "Can you see her?"

"I've got this dust bowl of a planet between me and him," Illych said. "If you want me to take a look, it'll take me about twenty minutes to get out of orbit and into position to make a sensor sweep of Makepeace."

"Take a look, please."

"I'll get back to you."

"Thanks. I'll keep the *Caliban* frequency open in case it's just a fault and he gets back to me. Please switch to frequency 38.05."

"Done. *Hertford* out."

Fucking Warwick. Where the hell was he?

Van touched his arm, raised an eyebrow.

"I dunno. He should have been on station ten or fifteen minutes ago." Fucking Warwick-the-fucking-Glorious. Bennet switched to the *Dhow*'s assigned frequency. "See if you can raise the *Dhow*, Van."

"No problem," she said after a minute. "Khal, where are you?"

"Over the southern hemisphere, ma'am. Problem?"

It was where *Dhow* was supposed to be, out of *Caliban*'s way and watching the other side of the system for hostiles, until they

223

were ready to call the Lieutenant back to retrieve the Shield warriors.

"Move him closer," Bennet said. "Bring him close up and ask him to keep his eyes peeled and tell us if he sees anything out of the ordinary."

"But not tell him *Caliban* isn't answering?"

"Not yet. Tell him I'm getting nervous and want him ready to move in at speed."

She obeyed, trying to allay Khal's natural apprehension at the unexpected change by getting in a sly dig at their 'Major's' inability to keep to his own plan.

"I am listening in," Bennet pointed out to the pair of them, but it had the effect Van wanted. Khal sounded unfazed at the change.

"I don't like this," she said, after agreeing with Khal where he'd position the *Dhow* and sit it in geo-stationary orbit close by, and closing down the link.

Bennet shrugged. If they were lucky, it was nothing more than a brief comms blackout.

Van added, "Although I guess it's not likely something's happened to them."

"No. Not now they've got the platform. When I spoke to him, he said he was clearing up the last of the fighters."

Warwick had been so damned keyed up about this job. The entire crew had been keyed up about it. Excited. Odd they weren't where they were supposed to be, to finish it.

"Well, it'd take more than a few fighters to take out a dreadnought."

"I suppose. Maybe he saw something he needed to check out." In which case, why hadn't Warwick used the com-link to tell him? Bennet glanced, uselessly, at the sky. Nothing to see, nothing to be done. "Come on. We might as well crack on with what we have to do in there, and just wait for Warwick to get into position in his own good time."

Danzer sat in a pool of light from a portable searchlight a few feet from the manufactory door, an EDA drone's head on her lap. She pushed the two halves of it back together, shut the refrigerated case with a snap and grinned up at them.

"Can I keep this one for a souvenir?" She stroked the EDA's head.

"If you want." Bennet bent to flick the switch to activate the refrigerated case, waited until the monitors showed green before straightening up. He'd leave the case in Danzer's capable care.

Danzer looked at the head fondly. "It'll make a nice lamp base."

She had half-a-dozen body bags waiting. Although the military still used the term indiscriminately, what Danzer had with her were the rigid capsules specifically designed for taking bodies home, not the zip-up bags used to bury the dead planet-side. Fitted with anti-gravity suspensors and freezing units, the capsules were long, black, featureless ovoids that reminded Bennet of the pods inside the factory.

"I've put a whole EDA inside this case, sir." Danzer tapped the one nearest her. "I left its node in place. That okay?"

Bennet nodded. The case temperature was set at optimal level. Haydn was right. She was good at this.

Danzer had the explosive, too. Bennet assessed the amount. "Not enough. Double that, Corporal, and start setting it for me. I want at least fifty 150-gram bundles and detonators."

Danzer blinked. "Fifty. Yes, sir." She glanced at the building. "There won't be anything left but molecules."

"That's the idea." Bennet nodded his thanks and with Van's help he took the body bags into the factory.

They packed the new drone first, taking the opportunity to examine it more closely. It resembled one of the EDA drones, but for the head and the blueish tinge to the casing. It was heavier than it looked. Getting the long body into the capsule, bending the legs to fit took one helluva lot of sweating and cursing. Bennet closed the capsule down and set the controls. Condensation formed on the matt-black outer surface as the temperature inside plunged down to zero. When he touched the surface a second or two later, he could feel the frost. He pulled his fingers away before they could stick, hoping he'd judged the temperature right. He had to have the thing chilled to prevent decomposition setting in, the temperature at a fraction above freezing point. Anything more and Felix, not to mention the Supreme Commander, would kill him if the organic tissue was too damaged by ice crystals to be useful. It looked right.

Van pulled off her helmet and rubbed a hand across her temple, loosening the hair sticking to her forehead. She pushed her hair back and jammed the helmet back on. It appeared to be her coping mechanism of choice, fiddling with her helmet. "If I had any sense at all, I'd be out there doing the easy stuff herding those sheep, and Haydn would be in here using his brawn."

"I could do with some brawn myself." Bennet wasn't scrawny by any means but he didn't have Haydn's bulk, and brute strength had been needed to get the drone into the capsule, nothing more. They repeated the process with one of the unfinished drones from the end of the process. With no node in its head, keeping it cold wasn't an issue, but the body bag kept it hidden.

Bennet straightened up and looked about him. "I guess we try to work out how to open one of these things."

He left Van to float the two capsules over to the door while he looked again at the nearest pod, the one with the young girl in it. No visible catch that would open the cover, nor anything that looked like it might cause the top mechanism to retract and allow the cover to be moved. He couldn't feel anything, either as he moved slowly around the pod, using fingers and palms to map out the seal between table and cover.

"I'm beginning to think Felix is right," he said when Van rejoined him. "Historians are not best qualified for this kind of thing. I have no idea how to open it."

Van moved to the head of the pod, where the main control panel was situated—if that, indeed, was what it was—and touched one of the incomprehensible displays. "You think he'd know any more than you what all this stuff means?"

"He's the tech, not me. He'd make a better guess at it. I don't know where to start. There's no catch or switch along the cover seam that I can feel, and the gods alone know what would happen if you pressed any of those controls." He ran his left hand along one of the mechanical arms holding the cover in place. The fibre-optic cables vibrated under his fingers. The thing purred like a cat. The lines of blue light pulsed down from the machines in the ceiling and when a sapphire sparkle came, the vibration increased momentarily before falling back.

"I don't see how you can open the cover with all that equipment in the way." Van Trion ran a hand over the lid, grimacing.

"Something must make this whole thing retract up into the ceiling and take the cover with it."

"We could press something and see what happens."

Bennet managed a faint grin. "Choose a button. Any button."

She put her hands behind her back. "Oh no! You choose. This is your baby, not mine."

Bennet came to join her at the control panel. "I don't know," he said, after a few minutes of study. He had no idea at all. "These controls could be doing anything."

"And how do we get them out, anyway?" Van asked. "You can see quite clearly from this angle that there's all sorts of wiring going into their heads."

"I know." He'd photographed enough of them. "I'll have to cut the wires. No matter what I do, the scientists will tell me I've got it all wrong. Ideally we should take a whole pod back."

"Not a chance. We'd never get all the stuff above and below them, they weigh a ton, and…" Van hesitated. Winced.

"The bodies would decompose before we could get them home. I know. Okay, let's try this one."

Bennet pressed a button at random. Nothing seemed to

happen, other than the pulsing dull blue lights in the machine became a pulsing dull yellow. He and Van waited, then she looked at him and shrugged. Bennet tried another control. Again nothing.

"Shit, we could be here all night at this rate." He took out his laser. "There's only one way to do this."

He set it to concentrated beam, rather than pulse. If the laser could cut through the canopy, and if he was careful enough, he could slice through the cover down the edges where the mechanical arms flowed down to each corner, taking out a big triangular piece to allow him to slide the girl out and into a body bag. It would be awkward, but he could do it.

The laser sparked as it cut through, making him blink.

Van took a couple of steps away. "Doesn't look like there's anything critical in the cover, at any rate."

"No." Bennet put away his laser and pried away the covering.

Air hissed. The girl's body jerked and her mouth dropped open. "Ch-aaaaaaah."

"Shit!" Van sprang away to one side, out of the way. "Shit! I thought they were dead!"

Bennet, his hands trembling more than he liked, put his fingers against the girl's neck. Her skin was clammy, cold under his hand. Slightly greasy. "It may be gas escaping, or something."

"Fuck! I'm not touching that, Bennet!"

Bennet withdrew his hand. "I'll do it. Go back to taking more holopics, as many as you can get." He glanced at her. "As far away as you like."

"I can manage!" She turned her back on him, stalked away.

He waited until she was a few yards away, a shadowy figure in the poor light. Crouching by the head of the pod, he put his hand against the girl's neck again, inching his fingers past the obscenity that was her head, dreading having to touch that.

He couldn't be sure. That was the problem. The only scanner he had on him was a Felix special that would take too long to recalibrate, even if he had the tools and know-how to do it. He pressed his fingers into the cold skin and waited. If it was a pulse, it was impossibly slow.

He couldn't be sure.

He sat back on his heels. She had to be dead. She had to be. And what he had to do was insurance, a confirmation of an existing fact. That was all. Just confirmation.

The backpack was only a few feet away. It took only seconds to collect it and bring it back to where she lay. Felix's hypos were ready, slender little darts in their case. Felix had known as well as he had that he couldn't leave the prisoners to die in the explosions and fire, to die in agony.

Of course, the girl wasn't in that category. She was already dead. All of the people in the pods were already dead.

His hands shook as he readied a hypo. The fingers of his right hand tingled, a sudden onset of pins and needles that distracted him for a minute. Stress. The nerves he'd damaged back on Telnos two years earlier would always react this way when his body was pumping with adrenalin.

He pressed one of the hypos against the cold neck before his courage failed him. Again he felt for a pulse. Nothing. Definitely nothing.

The little lights in her head winked out, one by one.

He dropped the hypo back into the pack and rested his forehead against the edge of the pod, closing his eyes. He would take her home, this poor nameless girl who might once have caught Liam's eye, but he wouldn't let Liam see her. She wouldn't want Liam to see her now.

He got up. Off to his left, flashes of light showed where Van resumed taking pictures of a pod from every possible angle. Time to get on with it. His hands had stopped shaking by the time he took out the second toolkit, the mirror of the one he'd given Danzer. There were a myriad fine wires and needle-thin fibre-optic cables going into the girl's exposed brain. He snipped carefully through them all.

The girl didn't react. No more escape of gas or air from lungs that were stilled, no pulse from a heart that was silenced. Nothing.

He had a body bag ready. She weighed very little, but it was dead weight. Inert. He had to slide his hands under her arms and pull her out, head first, hoping to God everything inside her skull stayed where it was, holding her against his chest to brace her. It was awkward, without someone to help, but he managed it, easing her out of the pod and into his arms in a disgusting parody of a loving embrace, before lowering her into the waiting body bag.

Everything stayed in place.

He closed the lid down with a sigh and set the refrigeration unit going. He rubbed his hands down his jacket to get the feel of her off them. Disrespectful, somehow, to feel repulsed, but he couldn't help it.

He could only hope she'd forgive him. Wherever she was.

CHAPTER TWENTY-THREE

39 Quartus 7490: Makepeace

He was changing the data crystal in the Link for a fresh one when his com unit bleeped at him. It was Illych. "Shield Captain Bennet?"

"Here."

Illych's tone was grim. "That's more than the *Caliban* is. No sign of her. She's not in orbit, her Hornets are not at the rendezvous point to escort in the Transport cutters, and she's nowhere on my scanners. She may be masked by Makepeace itself, but I can't see her."

Bennet wasn't surprised, and that's what stunned him into a momentary silence. He wasn't surprised. He wasn't angry, yet, either, because how could he be angry about something he'd half-known already, something even the Supreme Commander had suspected: Warwick was not to be trusted.

"Bennet?"

Van drew closer, echoing Illych. "Bennet? What's wrong?"

"Are you sure?" Bennet knew it was stupid to ask, but he had to be certain.

"I'm sure. She's not there. I take it Shield can't see her either?"

Van touched his arm, making him jump. "*Caliban?*"

He nodded. "Yes. Or rather, no. No *Caliban.* She's not there."

Her mouth dropped open. Closed again. She swallowed. "He's gone? Just gone?"

Bennet shook his head, looking around him at what Warwick had left him to deal with. He'd told Warwick. Code Chimera, he'd said, and Warwick hadn't misunderstood and still the man had gone. For a moment he was dizzy with it, his head spinning, then his training kicked in. No time to agonise over it, no time to worry. "Warwick said the local base showed some activity and may be sending out ships."

"I think he's gone to intercept them," Illych said.

"Without a word to any of us?"

"All I have is a faint ion trail, some indications of plasma generation. He has to have taken her into hyperspace, heading for..." Illych bit off the words. He sounded stunned, his voice slow, as if he were operating on auto-pilot. He didn't finish. They could all imagine where Warwick had gone. "What in hell does the Commander think he's doing?"

"What do we do?" Van raised both hands and let them fall in a gesture betraying her shock.

Bennet only just stopped himself from copying the gesture. He couldn't afford to take the time to be shocked. "All right. Update the two Transport ships, Illych, and patch them into the comms line. Record all communications now."

"The Hornets? The ship and all its fighters gone?" Van closed her eyes. "Hell Bennet, getting home—"

"I know. We'll have to run for it."

Sitting ducks. They were sitting ducks. Bloody Warwick might as well have painted targets on their backs.

"Fuck." Van was grey-faced with shock. Her voice shook. "Something must have happened. Surely, something happened."

Sure it had. Warwick had happened. When they'd got to the

Caliban, with Warwick buzzing with excitement and delight, what was it the man had said to his Executive Officer and the Flight Captain who'd been so amused by Bennet? *We've got the best opportunity I've seen in years to get out there and strike a blow before they strike us. This is going to be such a chance to do those bastards some real damage.* He had been revelling in the prospect. But not the prospect of following the plan Bennet and Felix had put together. Oh no. Warwick had had his own plan. And he had said more, he'd said something even more significant: *We're taking the war to them.*

Not the war Bennet was fighting, or Illych or Van Trion; not the war Supreme Commander Jak was directing. This had to be personal. Warwick had his own war to fight, and be damned to Albion or anything else.

Gone rogue. Dammit, the man had gone rogue. It all fell into place now: the excitement, the sly amusement. The whole damn crew had been buzzing with it. They all knew, they were all in on it. And Sioned... bloody hell, Sioned! That lovey-dovey little chat. She'd been sounding him out, trying to see if he'd go with them. Warwick had planned this. He'd always planned to take off. To... What had he said back at the briefing? *...taking the fight to where it matters, kicking the Maess right in the balls... go out there and attack until we grind those bastards into the dirt...* He'd fucking well gone rogue! And the bastard had taken their safety margin with him. He'd taken all the fucking Hornets that were supposed to guard them on the way home. How the fuck was Bennet supposed to get these people home now? Fuck!

He said it aloud, grasping Van's arm. "We'll have a helluva job getting these people home safe. Fuck it, Van. He's left us wide open." In the background, Bennet heard Illych add Mione and Willem to the coms-net, explaining what had happened. He cut through their astonished questions and exclamations. There was no time for this. "Can every one hear me?"

When they acknowledged, Bennet squared back his shoulders. "Then let the record show that in the unexpected and so far unexplained absence of the *Caliban* from its assigned position, the sensor data appearing to show the *Caliban* has left the system, and the assumed absence or incapacity of Commander Warwick, I, Shield Captain Bennet, am invoking the provisions of Military Regulation 2.8 Section 1. I am taking formal command of this mission, until such time as we return to Albion and I can relinquish command to the appropriate authorities. Please acknowledge."

Van, eyes wide, nodded, and said "Yes, sir." Illych spluttered and hemmed for a minute, but in the end acknowledged the necessity, with another "Yes, sir. Acknowledged." The Transport captains mumbled agreement.

"Thank you, everyone. Listen up. We're going to have to make changes if we're going to get out of here without the *Caliban*'s escort. Captain Illych, you'll need to move in to take the *Caliban*'s place. *Hertford* just about has the firepower to hit this place with laser pulsars from orbit, and I want the base molten slag by the time we leave. Your Hornets will have to escort the cutters all the way in to collect the prisoners. Captains Mione and Willem, bring your ships into orbit with the *Hertford* and stay in formation with her. Without *Caliban* and her Hornets to act as escort, we can't leave your ships unprotected behind the second planet. We'll have to do everything differently. We need to move this up a gear, now. We get these people off as fast as we can do it, and then we fucking run for home."

"Acknowledged," Willem said, echoed an instant later by Mione. "I'm moving the *Bryson* into position now."

Van swept one arm around in a wide, expansive gesture, taking in the pods and the machines, and the poor sodding incubators with the tops of their heads sawn off. "Did he know?"

"Yes. He knew. I told him." Bennet scrubbed at his eyes to ease the stinging. Hell, he was tired. "Right now, though, we have a job to do and I can't worry about the *Caliban*. Except... Illych, keep on with the sensor sweeps and make sure you record and store them. I'll look at them later. We'll need them."

For the official inquiry. If they got out of there alive without the *Caliban* to help, if they got back in one piece, they'd all face an official inquiry.

Fucking Warwick. With luck, the Maess would smear the bastard all over the star systems. *Fucking Warwick-the-fucking-Glorious.*

May he die in flames.

In the end, it went smoothly. As smoothly as anything could go when he'd gone out there to rescue some tortured human prisoners and lost Albion a dreadnought in the process.

Bennet sent Van Trion out to ready the prisoners for transport while he took a middle-aged black man out of a pod, first ensuring, as with the girl, the man really was dead. An old woman came last. He emptied the backpack's deadly cargo of poison into the space where the old woman's destroyed head had lain for the gods alone knew how long. It seemed fitting, somehow. He didn't want to see the case of hypos ever again. He packed the cameras and the Link and the precious data crystals away. They were all he wanted to carry and they were appalling enough.

He sealed each of the closed body bags before putting them into Danzer's care, slipping plastic ties through the catches and crimping them closed. He made more changes to the plan as he went along. He no longer had any trust in Fleet or in the Transport ships: he would only put his faith in Shield. Danzer and her unit were going back with those bodies to the *Hertford*, he told her, and they would be guarding the body bags around the clock. The only orders she would take would be from him, no one else.

"Good," Van said, when he told her he was taking Danzer. She had returned to help him bring out the bags and had found the plastic tags to seal the black capsules in her Tech Corporal's equipment pack. "I don't want these things on my ship."

And she didn't want him on her ship, either, although she didn't say so in so many words. He knew, though. She was perfectly co-operative still, but what she'd seen in the factory behind them stood between them. It stood between Bennet and normality like a wall; and Van Trion and everything human was on the other side of it. He didn't have time to worry about it now, but he was, briefly, regretful. *Dhow* had been a powerful memory of Shield and home, but even that was denied him.

"I'll set the explosive here," he said. "What's our progress on mining the rest of the base?"

"Haydn has it all in hand. Fifty minutes and we'll be done."

"Thanks," Bennet said, and meant it. He watched Danzer arrange her unit around the six body bags and the refrigerated case full of Maess nodes and sent them all to the waiting cutter from the *Hertford*. "You'll be met by Captain Illych. He's set aside a compartment for you. Shoot anyone who comes within five yards of it. Anyone who isn't me, that is."

"Sir." Danzer had evidently decided she did not want to know what was going on and the best course of action was to play it, and him, by-the-book. She, too, was on the other side of the wall. She gave him back his knife and handed over the prepared explosive. "Enough, sir?"

It was more than enough. After changing the full data crystals on the Link for the next set, he spent the next hour setting explosive in the factory, interrupted only by Van Trion when the Transport cutters arrived and again when they left with their docile human cargo. He sent her and her Shield warriors back to the *Dhow*. She left without a backwards glance.

He spread the prepared charges evenly around the building, tucking the charges against walls and underneath pods. When it went up, there would be nothing left but a hole in the ground.

Nor was there.

He sat in his Hornet, holding it on a weaving figure-of-eight pattern, while the solactinite did its work. He couldn't hear the explosion, not from where he was, but it was absolutely magnificent against the night sky, lighting up the terrain for dozens of square miles, slicing into the darkness and making the night briefly as bright as a sun exploding. He fancied he could see the river boiling with the heat, sending spumes of steam up into the atmosphere. He felt the blast, the air currents around his ship making it judder and shake until he was fighting to keep the Hornet on an even keel; and when it was over and the explosions had stopped, he made one low pass over the base. Over the smoking crater in the ground where the base had once been.

Back to the figure-of-eight, but further off, and acting as gunnery spotter for the *Hertford*, as the laser torpedoes blasted down out of the sky to reduce the area to molten lava. The river did boil this time, no question, and when he sent his Hornet up to join the *Hertford*, he was as content as he could ever be that the abomination the Maess had created on Makepeace was no more.

Illych was waiting for him on the other side of *Hertford*'s decontamination chamber. He wouldn't meet Bennet's gaze at first, but tugged at his collar and reddened as he spoke. Disjointed little speeches along the lines of "I can't believe it." and "What happened to make him—?" and "Did he see something we couldn't, some immediate threat, some—?"

When Bennet glanced sideways, he saw a nerve twitching in Illych's cheek. Illych's mouth set hard after each truncated phrase. It wasn't Illych's fault. Ironic, though, that Illych evidently felt a responsibility that Warwick himself had cast off.

Bennet cut through a second iteration of Illych's mournful incomprehension. "I don't know what took *Caliban* off-station. Definitely no debris?"

Illych winced. "No. Nothing. I'll show you what I did find when we get to the Bridge."

"Can I see the Shield warriors first? Then after I've seen your scanner records, we need to talk about how we're going to make it home without the *Caliban* in support. It's going to be a nervous journey."

This time the wince morphed to fully fledged flinch.

Bennet had had time to make the arrangements with Illych while the Transport shuttles collected the prisoners. When Danzer and her unit had arrived in a cutter, carrying the body bags, they had been escorted straight to a nearby compartment. He and Illych diverted to check on them. Bennet examined each of the sealed ties and spent a moment to monitor each body bag's settings and temperature gauges, before setting an armed watch. Danzer accepted it all with an air of philosophical resignation. Bennet ignored Illych's open, if unspoken, curiosity.

The Bridge was smaller than a dreadnought's, but large enough to give Illych space for a decent-sized office carved out of the back of it. The monitor was already running when they got there.

"Here." Illych brought up an image on the monitor screen. "This is what we saw."

Bennet traced it with his finger, the faintest of ion trails, already degrading, leading out of the Makepeace system and heading towards the main Maess base in that sector and ending in the weak remnants of the plasma flare from engines moving into to faster-than-light mode as the ship jumped into hyperspace. *Caliban*'s electromagnetic signature, writ across the stars. Fading fast.

"Surely he must have seen something coming at us out of the base," Illych said. "Shouldn't we wait for him?"

Bennet traced the ion trail again. "No." He touched the storage pocket on his belt, where he'd secured the Link's data crystals and every image from the cameras. "No. We don't wait. What we've got is too important to risk."

"But… but it's Warwick!"

"Exactly. It's Warwick." Bennet stood up and stretched, rotating his shoulders to ease the tension in his aching neck, wishing he could relax enough to sleep.

"You can't leave him!"

Bennet shook his head. "We aren't leaving him."

Illych spluttered something, and waved a hand from the record on the screen to his crew at their stations on the Bridge. They were racing full-tilt for home, the two transporters tucked up in *Hertford*'s wake, barely a couple of miles behind her, and all of *Hertford*'s thirty Hornets roaming a tightly-defined perimeter around the three ships. *Dhow* was closer in than originally planned, just a few hundred miles ahead of the little flotilla. If it came to trouble, they'd need Van Trion's guns and the Mozzies.

Bennet managed a faint smile, wondering how, after this desertion, Warwick could still inspire such loyalty in those who'd followed him. Illych was shocked and grieving; Bennet wasn't even surprised. When it came to balancing tactical brilliance against solid worth, he knew which he wanted. He'd give half the universe to have his father there to depend upon. But Caeden was far away and it was up to Bennet to adjust some of the *Hertford* Captain's thinking.

"We aren't leaving Warwick," he said again. "He left us."

SECTION FOUR:

AFTERMATH

19 – 38 Quintus 7490

CHAPTER TWENTY-FOUR

19 Quintus 7490: Mendes, Sais City

It was late by the time the official car dropped Caeden in the suburb of Mendes, out on the coast, and the lower part of the house was dark and quiet. Only a few dimly lit windows showed in the upper storey.

The Supreme Commander had sent a car to meet him at the spaceport but he hadn't gone straight home, as he'd hoped. He'd been taken to Jak's office to be briefed, instead. *Briefed?* More like being hit by a runaway Transport shuttle. That Warwick would… that he *could* betray his oath of service!

"I've sent three Shield ships out looking for the bastard," Jak had said. "Not a sign. He's well away from Makepeace now, somewhere deep in Maess territory and not even Shield can see where he's gone. If I get hold of him—" And Jak's fist had thumped on his desk, his mouth tucked in and hard, lips pale with anger.

Caeden, stunned, could only nod. He couldn't comprehend it.

After listening to Jak and reviewing the terrible evidence Bennet had retrieved from Makepeace, he'd headed for home as soon as Jak released him, with one fruitless and worrying diversion on the way. It had to be close on two a.m. when he got home. Meriel woke with a start when he appeared, unexpected and unannounced, at the bedroom door. She stared at him for a second, unfocused.

"Oh thank the gods, thank the gods!" She scrambled out of bed with more speed than elegance and threw herself into Caeden's open arms. "You're home!"

"And glad of it." Caeden gave her a quick kiss. "Where's Bennet?"

Meriel clutched at him. "I don't know. In his room, I hope."

"He is here, then? Good. I checked his apartment on the way here, but couldn't get an answer. I'm relieved he's here."

Meriel pulled back and stared at him. "I wasn't expecting you."

"Jak called me back."

"For Bennet? Is he in trouble? Is that why he's so stressed?"

"It's complicated. How stressed?"

"I don't know, but I'm worried about him. There's something wrong and he won't tell me anything."

"The last job he went on went sour. Jak said Bennet was taking it hard."

"Taking what hard? He won't tell me. He got home two days ago but he won't talk to me. He won't eat and he isn't sleeping and he nearly scared the life out of me last night and the night before, wandering around the house all night like a ghost. I found him sitting on the stairs at four-o-clock this morning—yesterday morning now, I suppose. He was shivering to pieces, but he just kept saying everything was all right and he was sorry for waking me. He went back into his room like a lamb. I checked on him now and again. He didn't sleep. He walked around his room until dawn. And then he walked around the garden and the bay for most of the day."

Caeden felt something in his chest tighten. "That doesn't sound good."

"No. I had Thea call him and Liam come out here, but Bennet

wouldn't... Liam insisted on him going out and they walked around the bay for an hour or two, but even Liam gave up. He left Bennet to it in the end, saying Bennet just couldn't be bothered to talk to him. Bennet was the same with Thea on the com-link. You know how close he is to both of them, but he couldn't be bothered. The way he can't be bothered to eat and he can't be bothered to sleep."

Caeden sighed.

Meriel echoed it. "He's not cross or difficult, not like he usually is when he's hurt or ill. He's the opposite, terribly sweet and apologetic about it."

"That's worrying in itself."

"I just wish he'd tell me what's wrong." The hands still clutching at his tightened their grip. "Liam and I thought about getting a doctor for him, but Bennet didn't want to see anyone. Not even if it was Thea. He says he's not sick."

"I hope he isn't!"

Meriel shook her head, visibly calmer. "Well, no, I don't think he is, not really. He's upset about something, but he's not sick. What scares me is that if we let it go on, he might get sick, he might drift into a breakdown or something. I thought it might help if a doctor gave him something to make him sleep, to break the pattern he's getting into. But he wouldn't agree."

"It may not be a bad idea, though."

"I know. Thea's coming over tomorrow, regardless of what he says about it. I don't expect he'll be pleased." Meriel sighed. "He's just like you, you know."

Caeden raised an eyebrow.

She met the challenge with a terse, "He is every shade of stubborn and he got that from you."

Caeden smiled, and freed his hands to drop them onto his wife's shoulders. He turned her to face the mirror on her dressing table. "Take a good look, love, because genetics is a queer science and rarely one-sided. You're hardly spineless yourself, you know."

The smile she reflected back at him in the glass was fleeting, swamped by what he knew was real anxiety. "You can't force him when he's like this, and I can't get through to him, no matter how much I try. He won't talk to me about it." Her eyes narrowed. "He's more likely to talk to you."

"I hope he will." Caeden stooped to kiss her cheek and turned away, shrugging out of his flight jacket. "I expect it's reaction, that's all."

"Reaction to what? What happened? And why are you home?"

"I can't tell you a lot," he said, but she brushed that aside with an impatient gesture, used to his reticence about military matters. "Bennet went with the *Caliban* and some other ships behind the lines. I can't say much more."

She snorted. "Bennet would not like working with Warwick. He doesn't have a lot of time for him, you know."

Caeden nodded. He knew. He didn't have time for his old friend himself. Not now. "Bennet actually got back to Albion eleven days ago, but he's been held in a long debriefing session back at headquarters and he wasn't allowed to leave until it was over."

"A debriefing session? What sort of debriefing session takes what... nine days?"

"Keep this to yourself. Absolutely." He waited for her nod. Her eyes were wide with anxiety and fright. "The *Caliban* is missing, Merry, and there's to be a formal Inquiry. Jak wants me to be there."

He had been surprised, at first, at how fear for Bennet had pushed grief for one of his oldest friends into the background. And as he'd read the debriefing reports, particularly the dreadful record Bennet had written, anger had surged up to replace the grief and shock: anger at Warwick, at the astonishing irresponsibility he showed, the appalling impact this would have, both politically and militarily. It was a disaster. A calamity he could barely get his head around. And that selfish, self-glorifying bastard could still take Caeden's son down with him. If Warwick ever turned up again,

Caeden would take great delight in holding him down while Jak got his revenge. Even now, hours later, his pulse quickened and the heat surged through him again. He had to turn away for a second or two, to hide it from Meriel. Gods, he'd love to get his hands on Warwick's neck and squeeze. Hard.

The delicate colour drained from Meriel's face. "They're blaming Bennet?"

"Not exactly. But some Ennead members would take great delight in using Bennet to get at Maitland. And Jak. And me, I suppose. At least, with Jak's help, I can make sure he isn't unfairly blamed."

"Caeden, I'm not stupid and I won't be fobbed off. Is he in a lot of trouble?"

"Not if Jak or General Martens or I have anything to say about it. I don't think he'll be worried about the Inquiry." She chewed on her lower lip in unfeigned anxiety. He couldn't tell her that Bennet was far more likely to be worried about what he'd seen at Makepeace, so he added, as impressively as he knew how, "I promise it will be all right. You said he was in his room? I'll go and talk to him."

It took him a few minutes to reassure her and persuade her to let him go and see Bennet alone. Bennet's old room, the room that had been his when he was a child, was down the hall and across the landing, in the other wing of the house.

He knocked before going in, but if Bennet gave him permission to enter, he didn't hear it. He went in anyway. The room was dark and quiet, a dim light leaking in from the hallway behind him, but this was a big room and the hall light was muted, leaving the room full of shadows. For a second or two he thought Bennet wasn't there, but as his eyes adjusted to the dim light and dimmer shadow, he made out the silhouette. His son sat on the wide seat in the big bay window, knees drawn up, staring out at the sea. Caeden closed the door and made his way in the darkness to the window. There was enough space for him sit down, if he didn't mind being squeezed up against the edge of the window. Bennet didn't speak and he didn't look up, but he drew his feet in, to make room. It was enough to reassure Caeden that Bennet realised he was there and that he wasn't unwelcome.

They sat in companionable silence for long time, while Caeden leaned up against the side windowpane and thought about what he needed to say. He didn't push, waiting for Bennet break the silence first. He stared out past his son's dark head at the stars. It was a clear night, not a cloud in the sky. The window behind Bennet was open, letting in the soft, incessant susurration of water on the shingle in the bay below the cliffs, the sound of the sea gnawing at the land. Insatiable. Threatening. One day this house and everything in it would be gone, eaten up by a sea whose hunger could never be appeased.

He heard a clock strike half-past two: the dining room clock, he thought, from the mellow chime. Meriel must have left the window open, for the sound to have drifted up through the night air to Bennet's room. He shifted to manoeuvre a cushion into place to support his back and relaxed again, waiting.

The clock had struck three before Bennet spoke. "Were we expecting you?"

"I thought it was time I came home. Jak told me about Warwick."

"Mmn."

"Jak's taken me through the debriefing report." He waited, but Bennet wasn't willing to talk much; at least, not without prompting. "Can we have some light, Bennet?"

"If you like."

Caeden kept his tone casual, although he worried at the indifferent tone. "Thank you. My eyesight is bad enough at my age without straining it further." He got up and groped his way to the desk, passing his hand over a lamp on the desk top. It sprang into life under his palm. Too bright. He muted it, but it was more than enough, once his eyes had adjusted, for Caeden to see the way Bennet's face had thinned down to nothing but eyes and cheekbones, viciously dark circles under the eyes. The boy was exhausted, obviously; hollowed out. Caeden made his way back to the window seat and sat, letting out a soft sigh. "What do you think happened?"

"To Warwick?" Bennet shrugged. "Warwick happened to Warwick. He had a war to fight."

"Don't we all?" Caeden reflected that Meriel would be furious that she'd been right and that Bennet would rather talk to him than her. But then, warriors shared experiences she couldn't begin to imagine. Bennet had to know he'd understand a great deal more readily than she could, even if she were more likely to empathise.

"Not Warwick's war."

"There's a difference?"

"He wanted one of his own, one where he set all the rules."

That showed a surprising amount of perception. Bennet was smart. But unlike Liam, he was usually a lot smarter about things than he was about people. For Bennet, things were safer than people any day of the week.

"Did he say as much?"

"Say?" Bennet repeated. "Say? A lot of what Warwick says is crap. You have to add everything together to hear what he was really saying and then only after the event. He's cleverer than he looks."

Infuriating as he'd sometimes found the original, Caeden wasn't certain he was comfortable with this new, perceptive Bennet.

"He tried to get me to go along with them, I think. Sioned did, anyway, and Powell. They tried to find out if I would go. I didn't work it out at first. I thought they were just talking, just curious about Shield, the way everyone's curious about Shield."

And that was rather more like it. The oblivious Bennet, that was the familiar one. Caeden could cope better with the Bennet he knew. "Jak said he didn't take up position over the base, and *Hertford* picked up an ion trail leading out of the system."

"He saw what he wanted and he went for it. We weren't what

he wanted."

Sweat prickled at the corner of Caeden's eyes at the heavy going. "The evidence the *Hertford* gathered should be enough to show... well, even if we don't really know exactly what happened, we know the *Caliban* wasn't destroyed above Makepeace and Warwick abandoned the agreed plan. It's quite clear he took the *Caliban* towards the Maess military base in the sector. I'm sure the Inquiry will find Warwick deliberately abandoned the Makepeace mission. For whatever reason."

"Inquiry? Oh. Oh yes."

"On the twenty-second. I'll be there."

Bennet shrugged again.

"Are you worried about it?" Caeden asked.

"No."

"Then it's the base bothering you." Caeden had read Bennet's debriefing report with growing horror and disgust. If it had been him, he'd be as leery as Bennet was about it all, unwilling to sleep in case he dreamed.

Bennet looked at him for the first time. "You knew it was going to be horrible, didn't you? You sent me a message before we went."

"Yes. Jak promised he'd give it to you."

"Thank you," Bennet said. "It was nice."

Caeden repressed the urge to shake his son until Bennet snapped out of it, and kept his tone calm and uninflected. "I saw the holopics and film... and the other things you brought back."

Bennet unwound his long legs and pushed himself up onto his feet. Alarmed, Caeden jumped up to follow him, but Bennet only got as far as the bed before losing momentum. When Caeden reached him, he was trembling. "I'm tired, that's all," he said, when Caeden exclaimed about it. "I'm tired and I can't sleep."

"There were too many of them, Bennet. And they were beyond help."

248

Bennet sat down on the edge of the bed, loose-limbed, as if his knees had given way. When Caeden sat beside him, Bennet scooted around to sit with his back against the headboard. Caeden followed him and waited.

He didn't have to wait as long this time. It was only a few minutes before Bennet spoke. "The Maess were using them to grow nodes for a new kind of drone, did Jak tell you? Felix told me the preliminary tests were all positive. The new drone and the three... the three incubators I brought back, they had the same brains, Maess and human together. A hybrid."

"Yes. I know."

"A whole new class of drones. Chimeras. Did you hear about the people? The live ones?"

"Jak told me most are recovering some sense of self, now they're not exposed to whatever drugs they were being given. Most are more aware, some even able to be debriefed."

"Interrogated," Bennet said. "The word is interrogated. Felix is going out to the old prison colony next week."

"Not you, though. Your part's ended, Bennet."

"Is it?" Bennet dropped his head back to rest against the headboard. The curve of his exposed throat made him look more vulnerable than Caeden liked. "Did Uncle Jak tell you everything about the people I brought back?"

"He told me they had to isolate some of them, when the proper medicals were done."

Bennet glanced sideways at him and sat up again, running a hand through his overlong hair. "The ones who've had brain surgery."

"I know."

"That's the advantage of using an old penal colony. Plenty of places to keep the cuckoos in the nest secure."

"Jak said they're tractable. No trouble."

"Lobotomised, apparently. No evidence of anything put in,

just bits of brain taken away. They seem to be harmless, Felix said." Bennet's eyes gleamed in the dim light. "A new definition of harmless."

Caeden nodded.

"The ones I left behind were the lucky ones, after all. I'd thought nothing could be worse than having the top of your head sawn off for the Maess to play with, but I might be wrong there."

"It looked… well, I saw the holopics, of course."

"Eighty of them. There were so many of them. Men and women and—" Bennet broke off. "Eighty."

Jak had spread dozens of holopics over the desk earlier when he'd briefed Caeden. Hundreds of holopics. Images of the facility, of the new Chimera drone, of the machines, of every prisoner lying in his or her pod. Every single one, old and young. Caeden grimaced at the recollection. "I know. I was surprised you and Captain Van Trion photographed every one of them."

"They'll get no other memorial."

True. The dead were nameless and unknowable. Even when the dead are our beloved dead, loved and mourned and regretted, in the end they become nameless and unknowable.

"I left them," Bennet said. "I blew them up."

"I spent a lot of time this evening looking at what you brought back with you, Bennet, including the three bodies in the laboratory. They were beyond our reach. They were dead."

Bennet drew his knees up again, as if in protection and looped his hands around them. He stared down at his hands. All Caeden could see of his face was the gleam of eyes under the dark lashes. "Did you know I killed a man, years ago?"

"No. I hadn't heard that."

"We found some Jacks raiding a Dacian trading outpost, when I had the *Hype*. They'd killed the traders and I guess they thought they didn't have any choice about fighting it out with us. One of them tried to shoot me as we came through the airlocks. I blew his head off."

"And if you hadn't, he'd have killed you, right?"

"Yes."

"It was self-defence, Bennet."

"I know. But it wasn't self-defence on Makepeace, was it? How do I argue that one away?"

"They were dead," Caeden said, pleased with the calm certainty he'd achieved in his tone. He could only hope it would soothe his son. "All of them. They were beyond your, or anyone else's, power to save."

Bennet was silent for a moment or two, as if thinking. "Felix gave me a full set of hypos. I don't know exactly what was in them. I didn't want to know."

"In case you couldn't bring the people back."

Bennet nodded. "In case I had to leave them to be blown up. We didn't want them to suffer." He choked out something that wasn't quite a laugh. Something more cynical and humourless. "We didn't want them to suffer any more than they had already."

"No one would want that," Caeden said, after Bennet's voice had trailed off into a too-long silence.

"I only used the hypos on the three I brought back, not on the ones I left behind. I didn't have time to take eighty of them out of the pods and poison them to make sure. I left them to the solactinite instead."

Caeden chose his words with care. "Captain Van Trion was convinced they were all dead. She said so, in her debrief report; and so did Sergeant Haydn, based on the glimpses he got. It's clear from those holopics that they were dead. And from everything you and she and the Shield warriors said, you used two, three times the solactinite needed just to blow that place up. You made sure every single one of them went in the initial blast. I don't think they can have suffered, Bennet. I don't think they can have felt anything. They were already dead."

Bennet shivered. The bed shook in tempo with him. His voice was so low Caeden had to strain to hear him. "The lights in her head went out when I used the hypo on her. The girl. The first one."

Caeden grimaced, glad Bennet wasn't looking at him at that moment. Bennet wouldn't like to be pitied. It took him a second or two to gather his thoughts, and in the short delay Bennet seemed to shrink in on himself, waiting for the blow, the condemnation. "She was young, I think. About Natalia's age?"

Bennet's head jerked up. He stared, audibly catching his breath.

"I thought about Tallie when I saw her. I thought if it had been her, or Thea or your mother, they'd have thanked you for what you did, for releasing them from that torment." He paused, and added, sincerely, "And so would I, from my heart. I don't think that poor child would be anything but grateful to you, Bennet." Bennet murmured something and Caeden spoke over the top of it, not letting Bennet voice the futile guilt, putting everything he had into reassurance. He put his arm around Bennet's shoulders, feeling him shake, and pulled him close. "If, as you seem to fear, there was some terrible parody of life in her, then you gave her the peace the Maess denied her. I don't think there was—"

"I can't be sure!" Bennet was agonised. "I'm not sure!"

"She was dead. You did the right thing, and I'm not sure I could have done it myself. I'm proud of that... of you. I'm so very proud of you, Bennet."

Bennet was quiet after that. And when Meriel opened the door and woke Caeden from a doze, he wasn't at all certain how long he'd sat there with Bennet curled up beside him, the dark head resting on his lap the way Bennet-the-child might have slept twenty-five years ago. He had one hand on Bennet's hair, and as Meriel watched them, her expression rueful, he resumed the comforting stroking he hoped had helped soothe his son to sleep.

"He'll be all right. He just needed to tell someone. You go to bed. I'll stay with him."

Her expression softened into a smile. "He always was Daddy's boy."

She closed the door, softly.

Caeden leaned back and closed his eyes again, tired. Not always, he thought, remembering Joss. Not always.

CHAPTER TWENTY-FIVE

21 Quintus 7490: Strategy Unit Laboratory

Felix handed over a datapad with the first draft of their report. "I'm going out to the Boeotian system as soon as we've done the report back to the Intelligence Committee. I take it you got my message about them wanting to start on us tomorrow, as soon as the Inquiry's done?"

"Yes. Dad told me."

"Very protective, your father."

Bennet let his mouth curve in a brief grin. "Very."

"It didn't exactly help me yesterday. I couldn't get past him and I really needed to talk to you about the Committee. We need to prepare."

"The story's straight."

"But the presentation matters. I've started working on it. I need your help."

"I'm here for the rest of the day." Bennet concentrated on the datapad in his hand. "How many?"

"The tally has been confirmed at fourteen who show signs of invasive cranial surgery." Felix swung down from the lab stool to join Bennet at the table in the centre of the room. "They've been isolated from the others."

Bennet tightened his grip on the datapad to stop his hands from shaking. "They can't have been..." He stopped, because there wasn't a word to describe having the top of your head cut off. He remembered the agricultural simile that had come to him on Makepeace. "They can't have been pollarded like the ones in the pods. We'd hardly have missed that."

"No. You couldn't have seen it. It was some time ago. A considerable time, since they all had hair hiding the scars." Felix frowned. He touched the datapad in Bennet's hands. "You can see from this that they've been lobotomised. The entire frontal cortex has been severed from the rest of the brain, so they aren't capable of emotional or intellectual responses. They're sort of blunted, dull, with not much personality left. There's definite impairment."

"Was the frontal lobe severed or removed?"

"Soft tissue scans say removed. Sorry. Sloppy of me to suggest otherwise."

"Some variant experiment to hybridise the tissue? An early attempt to extract human brain material to use?"

"We can hope that's all it is, and not to create room to put something there in its place."

Bennet looked down at his datapad. He had to unclench his hands from it. They were aching. "It's just... it's just it all sounds so delicate compared to the crude way they were growing the hybridised tissue. Delicate operations that leave the skull intact and suture it all back up again to heal. It doesn't mesh."

"I know."

"It's anomalous and inconsistent. I don't like inconsistencies. You can hide too much inside them."

Felix snorted out a short laugh lacking any vestige of humour. "Yes. We'll know more when I get there. At the moment, the people are corralled into an isolation unit. I'll be doing all the tests and examinations myself."

"Lucky you." Bennet shook his head. "I don't like this. I don't like it at all."

"Me neither." Felix cleared the datapads to one side to rest his elbows on the table and prop his chin on his hands. "Has The Management said what you'll be doing after tomorrow?"

"Providing I still have a career? I'll be going to the *Gyrfalcon* when the Intelligence Committee's finished with these preliminary reports. I'm not a scientist, Felix. This next stage is up to you. But it's still our project. We'll work it long distance, as usual."

"I'll let you know what I find as soon as I can."

"Yeah."

For a minute they looked at each other.

Then Felix smiled, very slightly. "It's all going to hell, isn't it?"

Bennet nodded. "At light speed."

22 Quintus 7490: The Praesidium, Sais City

The formal Board of Inquiry met in the Praesidium, the huge, ornate building in the centre of Sais City housing the Ennead and all its administrators and officers. President Maitland would chair it himself, flanked by the Ennead members of the Intelligence Committee. *To intimidate us*, Supreme Commander Jak had surmised with some scorn during the last-minute briefing in his office, before going on ahead to take his seat and, Bennet hoped, terrorise and bully a few of his fellow judges in return. As Bennet commented (quietly) to his father, Jak was unintimidated with good reason since the Supreme Commander would be sitting in judgement on the safe side of the table.

Caeden left with the Supreme Commander after giving his son some last-minute exhortations about his manner and conduct for the day ahead, instructions that visibly amused Jak and which Bennet bore with remarkable filial patience. Given the shameful display of weakness that had had him clinging to his father for an entire night and the following day, Bennet didn't feel he had much of a leg to stand on when it came to declaring independence and saying he'd work out for himself the best tactics for getting through the Inquiry, thank you kindly. His father's unstinting support had had the twin effect of giving Bennet the space to start to come to terms with what he'd found and done on Makepeace and make him feel he'd been reduced to dependency status, sent back to adolescence or something. He was both grateful and resentful. He had just enough grace to keep the resentment to himself.

He travelled to the Ennead building with Felix. The other witnesses, as the summonses described them, would make their own way there. Felix settled back in the military car Jak had allowed them to have in order, the Supreme Commander had said, to impress upon everyone he'd back his people against the politicians any day of the week. Bennet was grateful, both for the transport and the support. It meant something, to have Jak on his side. He knew his godfather would do his best to ensure the Inquiry Board did not look at Bennet and see a scapegoat with a noose around its neck.

Felix seemed to be as relaxed about proceedings as the Supreme Commander. "You know, you're not the most socially skilled man I know but you're being unnaturally quiet, even for you. Don't let it bother you."

Bennet shrugged. "How can it not?"

"The whole Makepeace mission was approved by the President himself. We wouldn't have gone without his nod. The details of the job had the Supreme Commander's approval. You can't be held responsible for Warwick being insane. Okay, it's not going to be pleasant but I doubt they'll tear your balls off. There are plenty of other things to worry about."

Bennet said nothing, conveying everything in another shrug.

"You just worry that people wearing more braid than you won't think you're wonderful."

Bennet tried sneering, but Felix laughed.

"C'mon, Bennet. Reality check here. Little as you want to

accept it, you can't expect everyone in the universe to think you're the greatest thing since humanity left Earth."

"The fewer who don't think that, the better," Bennet said. "I do not want to be known throughout all three services as the man who lost a dreadnought."

"You aren't responsible for Warwick running off."

"It was my mission."

"But it was his decision, based on the gods alone know what reasoning. If any. He was in command, not you."

"Yeah. Well, I know that. I know there was nothing in hell I could do to stop Warwick leaving. I mean, it's not like I knew what he was planning, did I? They can't expect me to anticipate the man's treason. I do know that." Bennet shifted uncomfortably in the wide seat, fiddling with the seat belt to stop it slipping.

Felix watched him for a minute or two, until Bennet raised his head and stared back. "Can you do it? They'll want to pull all the details out of your head, and I know it shook you."

Bennet had to force his shoulders back from hunching up to protect his neck. Funny how old instincts had a man doing that, to protect the vulnerable areas from attack, whenever he was stressed or threatened. Going over the stuff with Felix the previous day had been hard. Today would be hard, cubed. "One of the good things about working with the Unit, you know, is that I like the problems we solve and, mostly, I like being right. I know I'm not stupid and I like getting the chance to show off." He looked away, staring out at the streets full of humans—unknowing, vulnerable, ignorant humans who had no idea. "I'd give anything at all to have been wrong about this."

"All you did was analyse the material," Felix said. "You didn't create Makepeace by finding out about it, by realising what the T18 data meant. You can't beat yourself up over that."

"No."

"Without that information, we would be vulnerable. You were right. It had to be done."

"Yes. I know."

Felix grinned. "Don't see what you're worrying about, anyway. It was my bloody plan."

"Our plan. We were in it together."

"So loyal! Determined to go down with me, huh?" Felix frowned. "Oh dear, that was inadvertently sexual."

"I'm trying not to think about it," Bennet assured him.

"Good. Because even if they throw the book at us and we end up as cellmates, I'm warning you now I'm not up for a change in my sexuality just to keep you sweet for the next twenty years. Though I admit you do look good in dress uniform."

Bennet choked, and laughed for the first time in days. From the smug expression on Felix's face, that was what his companion intended. Bennet chafed through a short delay as they were held back by the security detail around the Praesidium; a group demonstrating in the square blocked the road for a couple of minutes before security hustled them on. Their holo-banners, each decorated with a phoenix rising from flickering flame, flashed messages as the transport inched past.

End the war! End the bloodshed! Peace!

A banner was thrust at the side window as they passed. Bennet and Felix exchanged glances. The poor fools.

"Although you'd look better if you had your medals on straight," Felix said, as if there had been no interruption. The transport drew up at the foot of the Praesidium steps. "There's probably a regulation somewhere about putting them on squint. Disrespect for the honours granted you by an adoring public, or something."

"Most of mine come in the post." Bennet followed Felix out of the transport. "Shield isn't big on ceremony."

They started up the immense and imposing flight of steps leading to the columned portico.

"Just as well, given the rudimentary nature of your social

skills," Felix said. "At least they're letting us in by the front door. I'd have worried if we'd been sent around to the Tradesman's Entrance."

It was more of an effort to keep up the dark humour with every step Bennet climbed. "Although that's more our natural level, you mean?"

"Mine, anyway. My daddy's not a member of the Intelligence Committee."

"Be grateful mine is. At least he's on our side."

"On yours, anyway. I'm content to slipstream in behind." Felix sighed. "And no, that was not another double entendre."

"If you say so," Bennet said, and grinned.

The columned portico enclosed a wide marble pavement. Handy for making speeches, Felix said, and addressing the huddled masses. He waved a hand at the demonstration to show which huddled mass he meant, following Bennet across the portico to where the bronze doors, several times a man's height, were thrown back to allow them entrance—allow them entrance once they'd got past security, anyway, and security at the Praesidium was tight. Large, intimidating guards demonstrated to them how much of a privilege it was for hoi polloi to enter the building's august portals, even when they were the sons of rich military men and came summonsed by the President himself. The guards stared with blank-faced suspicion when they stated their business and subjected their summonses to intense visual and UV scrutiny. They had to prove through biometric analysis that they were the people named. They had to empty their pockets and account for every item in them. They were searched and made to parade through more than one scanner area to ensure they weren't secreting anything dangerous about their persons. And finally they were allowed in, with an escort who had been put together by the same construction company that built dreadnoughts. Felix voiced heartfelt gratitude that at least the security men had restricted the body searches to electronic scanning.

"We are a democracy, aren't we?" Felix ignored the guard

coming along behind them. "I mean, we do pay taxes for the upkeep of this place? The least they could do is bloody well let us in when we're invited."

"It's not always like this. They've heightened security." Bennet dredged up a snippet of information from the comforting monologues Caeden had graced him with over the last couple of days. His father knew when to be silent and when to talk to fill the gaps. "The demonstration. Dad said Phoenix was gaining in popularity, even here on Albion."

"I know all that. I see more of our democracy in action than you do. Wotisname, Vines, their leader, is all over the news these days. But you know, the most aggressive thing I've ever seen them do is wave a placard at me. They're no excuse for all this ridiculous security and if these goons snap on the rubber gloves for a body search then I am signing up to be a bloody anarchist. What's with you? You'd normally be the one complaining."

"I was thinking how useless it all is." Bennet glanced over his shoulder to the scanner area and the beefy Ennead Security officers who manned it. "If I'd been right about everything, if I still am right about everything, those scanners wouldn't show it."

Felix, too, stared back at the security control area, and scowled. "I'll have to work harder on some new scanners."

"You do that. Be sure to send me one."

"That reminds me! You were one short when you gave me back the scanners I was able to modify."

"Was I?" Bennet said. "I must have mislaid it."

Felix snorted. He and Bennet followed their escort into the designated waiting room, reprising the moment they'd walked into Jak's waiting room a month earlier. The other captains, all in full dress uniform this time, were already there. Illych shifted constantly in his chair. Mione glanced at Bennet, before going back to twisting one of her jacket buttons forwards and backwards, backwards and forwards. She'd be damned lucky if she didn't end up in front of the Inquiry improperly dressed. Willem's nervous habit appeared to be foot tapping.

Van Trion at least was still and quiet. She and Sergeant Haydn, who hadn't been summoned to the Inquiry, were slated to join the IntCom debrief that afternoon. Compared to the debrief, when everything they'd seen and done on Makepeace would be crawled over and analysed to the last jot, the formal Inquiry was a gnat's bite.

Bennet nodded greetings at them all and went to sit beside her. "All right?"

"I've been better. You?"

He nodded. "The same. I've not been sleeping much."

"Nor me." She gave him a tight smile. "I don't like dreaming."

"No."

"I asked you once, when you came aboard the *Dhow*, how you coped with both jobs. How do you do it?"

Bennet sighed and shrugged. "Just barely."

The two members of the Ennead who also sat on IntCom, Seigneur Jethric of Illuria and Madam Beatrice of Achaea, were on the Inquiry Board. Bennet didn't know either of them on a personal level, just as faces who occasionally sat on the other side of IntCom's table while he and Felix briefed them on something or other. Supreme Commander Jak was there, of course, and General Martens. The old man talking with Jak was Seigneur Etienne, the head of the Ennead Secretariat, and another of Caeden's allies.

They had been talking, in two or three little groups, when the captains trailed in. Caeden had said once to Bennet that it was in the margins where the shifting alliances were forged and broken; the shadows where political deals were done and undone, where backs were scratched or stabbed with all the delicacy of a stiletto between the shoulder blades. Bennet glanced at his General, who sat apart. Typical of her. One day, when he'd be the one sitting there with the Shield General's stars in his collar, he'd take a leaf from Martens' book and stay above the petty politicking. He could do a great deal worse

The President called them to order. It wasn't a big room and the witnesses sat in a tight-packed gaggle in the central section behind the lonely chair where each would be interrogated. The remaining members of the Intelligence Committee, Field Marshal Klára and Caeden, took seats off to one side. They weren't formal Inquiry members and wouldn't take any part in the proceedings. Their main part would come that afternoon, when IntCom met. At least they'd been allowed in to observe.

"This is a formal Board of Inquiry," the President said, when everyone was still, "constituted under the provisions of the Military Judicial Inquiries Act of 6837 as amended by Part II and accompanying legal Schedules of the Military Inquiry Deposition Regulations of 7003. In accordance with those Regulations, the proceedings and deliberations of this Inquiry will be recorded and encrypted, Griffin Beta Six and higher security access only. This Board is convened to inquire into the disappearance of the dreadnought *Caliban* and her entire crew on 39 Quintus of this year whilst in military action at the former Nicaean colony of Makepeace in the Firenze Quadrant. All proceedings and deliberations of the Inquiry are covered by the Official Secrets Act, and every one of you giving evidence here today will sign declarations that you understand and accept the Act's provisions as they apply to proceedings here, to you and to your future conduct. You are bound by those provisions in their entirety. Breach them, and you will endure the full penalty of the law."

He paused and looked around the silent room, and tapped his ceremonial gavel against the table.

"This Board of Inquiry is now in session."

CHAPTER TWENTY-SIX

22 Quintus 7490: The Praesidium, Sais City

The President of the Ennead was another old family friend. Well, a cultivated ally, at least, given Caeden's grasp on political realities and the need to have friends in all possible high places. It might mean nothing in the end if the Inquiry Board was determined to find a scapegoat for Warwick's insanity, but that it was chaired by one of his father's allies was enough to make Bennet feel slightly less hopeless.

Maitland was a big man. He had presence. All the authority of the Nine Provinces was vested in him and he was a consummate politician. He knew how to play that. Mostly, Bennet concluded, it was his voice. It was deep and rich; and it was with relish Maitland rolled out all that impressive rhetoric, the significant, legal phrases dropping like polished stones into the quiet room.

"Strategy Unit Personnel will remain for the entire Inquiry, please. As for the rest of you, when I am satisfied with your testimony, you will leave the Inquiry room and, after you have been taken to the security office and signed your declarations, you will return to the waiting room to await our verdict and our directions as to your future conduct."

Maitland called the first witness. All in a voice like rich honey. No wonder the man was a politician. It was either that or become some charlatan of an actor. Although there was not, in Bennet's view, a great deal of difference between the two professions.

With the exception of Felix, who would go first, the Board intended to question the witnesses in reverse order of their understanding and knowledge of what the Maess had been doing on Makepeace. Bennet would be last. He'd known all along, but he slumped back in his uncomfortable hard chair anyway, wishing for the first time in his life that he'd done as his father had wanted and gone to the Academy. He'd be safe in Fleet somewhere now if he had, a million parsecs away from the Strategy Unit and all the crummy jobs the Unit gave him. He'd like that. He'd really like that.

Felix was a precise and scientific witness, allowing the eminence of neither the Board of Inquiry as an institution nor the people who comprised it to concern him. He took the Inquiry through the plan he and Bennet had put together for getting the prisoners off the base. He had been allowed to bring some schematics and scanner holopics with him, the better to explain the topography of the Makepeace system and show where every ship should have been and at what stage. Felix always liked visual aids. He was principally examined on his assessments of the risks, and the countermeasures he and Bennet had put into place. When pressed by Jethric, he had to admit to a failure to anticipate that a dreadnought commander would abandon the plan and the rest of the rescue mission. "Next time, sir, I'll be sure to factor in the possibility."

Beatrice's mouth narrowed right down. "You seem remarkably certain you'll be allowed a next time, Captain."

"Experience, ma'am. The Strategy Unit's part in this war may be unsung, but we'd have lost long ago without the Unit's work."

"And yet with you, we may not have lost the battle but we have lost a dreadnought. Hardly an inexpensive, inconsequential piece of equipment to lose, Captain. Careless, don't you agree?"

"The debrief reports, ma'am, suggest Commander Warwick left of his own volition." Felix was polite but unmoved.

Beatrice's thin mouth curved into something that, in a poor light, may have been mistaken for a smile. "I think you'll find that's for this Inquiry to decide, Captain. No further questions."

Felix slid back into his seat beside Bennet. "She doesn't like us," he remarked, sotto voce, as the next witness was called up, her identity verified and her oath of truth-and-nothing-but was taken. "I can tell."

Transport Captain Mione next, a resentful and angry witness, followed by a calm and disinterested Transport Captain Willem. They gave identical accounts of the initial briefing meeting (interesting), their journey to Makepeace (uneventful), Bennet assuming command and the consequences of Warwick's disappearance (a surprise, but the plans had to be changed) and the run for home once they had the freed prisoners on board (nerve-wracking, without the *Caliban*'s guns but at least the prisoners were quiet). At which point they were dismissed to the care of the head of Ennead Security who would oversee their signatures to the declarations of secrecy. Both left with alacrity and without looking back. *Lucky sods.* Bennet amended his regret that he hadn't gone to the Academy. Now he wished he'd gone there and bombed out into the safe confines of the Transport Directorate. Tootling about the star systems ferrying safe and inanimate cargoes had a very strong attraction.

Captain Illych was bereaved, a witness in mourning. He didn't attempt to hide his sense of betrayal. Bennet wasn't sure whether Illych's pain was for the loss of Warwick and the *Caliban* or for being left behind, for being somehow unworthy of Warwick's trust. He suspected that the members of the Inquiry Board were left similarly uncertain.

Illych confirmed the sensor sweep records; yes, that was his seal and the Shield Captain's on the sensor tapes. They had both witnessed the seals being broken during the debrief session. He would vouch for it that no one had tampered with them in the interim. That was the sensor record as he remembered it. There's the *Caliban*'s ion trail, centre left, leading out of the Makepeace system towards the main Maess base in that quadrant and just before it reaches the orbit of the third planet, there's the plasma flare from the jump into hyperspace.

What did he think had taken the *Caliban* off-station?

Silence, then a slow uncertain response to the Supreme Commander's question: "I don't know, sir. I don't know. I can't believe—I mean, the Commander had to have seen something he had to act upon, something my isometrics and scanner arrays didn't pick up. We know there was activity at the nearest Maess base…" Illych paused, shook his head. "He had to have seen some threat, something that made him take off to deal with it and there was some comms problem that stopped him from telling the rest of us." Illych avoided the Supreme Commander's cynical gaze. "I can't think of anything else. There's no data to go on."

"And so," Beatrice said, tone smooth and oily, "you followed Shield Captain Bennet's orders to abandon the *Caliban*?"

Bennet's shoulders stiffened in sympathy with Illych's. Caeden had warned Bennet to expect attack but to be openly accused… Bennet ducked his head so no one could read his expression. *Damn.* Damn it.

Illych confirmed that Bennet had invoked Section 2.8 to take command in Commander Warwick's absence. All fully recorded and acknowledged, absolutely by-the-book. "He was in charge and we had a mission to finish, a job to do. Without knowing what had taken the Commander away, we couldn't wait for the *Caliban* to return, not when we knew there was activity at the nearby Maess base with every likelihood we had a battleship heading our way. Without the *Caliban*'s Hornet squadrons and her firepower, we were vulnerable. The *Bryson* and the *Smithfield*, the two Transport ships, were only lightly armed. Shield Captain Bennet was right. We couldn't wait."

"How very pragmatic of you," Beatrice said, and sat back.

No further questions. Illych, stiff and offended, got out of the inquisition chair. He paused by Bennet to nod and indicate his support to all and sundry—sundry being the politicians. He was a decent man. He deserved better than Warwick for a commander.

Van Trion was a quiet witness, calm and judicious. The stuff on the initial briefing was tedious, the fourth time they heard it, but Bennet listened to her carefully when her narrative reached Makepeace. She outlined what they'd found in the factory. She wasn't permitted to go into detail, but she made clear her belief it was a manufacturing plant, creating the new Chimera drones.

"And what, Shield Captain Van Trion, do you think of Shield Captain Bennet's decision not to bring back all of those poor people in the factory?" Beatrice's voice was pure silk.

Jak stirred, turning his head to give the Ennead councillor a considering glance. Bennet, straightening up in his chair, could see, out of the corner of his eye, Caeden straightening in his. His father's face was expressionless.

"This line of questioning may be more appropriate for this afternoon's meeting, Beatrice," the President said, mildly enough.

"Indulge me. I'm attempting to establish the new mission commander's state of mind and if it's germane to the decision to abandon the *Caliban*." Beatrice was still silken smooth. When the President made a gesture to continue, she turned back to Van. "Well?"

"They were dead," Van said. "We couldn't bring them back."

"Yet you brought three, I believe, along with the new type of drone, the so-called Chimera drone. You have no comment on the Shield Captain's decision to bring back the drone, rather than a human?"

"No, ma'am."

"Even though the Shield Captain's decision meant one more human was left behind to die?"

"They were already dead. There were eighty of them. We couldn't bring back eighty corpses. We couldn't help them, and we couldn't do anything else."

"And so you blew them up," Beatrice murmured. She glanced at Caeden, then at Bennet himself. "Or rather, Shield Captain Bennet did. He has quite a record of abandoning people, I see."

Bennet grimaced. The bitch. The ball-breaking bitch. Beatrice was definitely out to get him.

Van Trion glanced at Bennet when it was all over, a look of pity and comprehension. She, too, nodded to him as she passed on her way out, indicating her support as far as she could in the circumstances. Bennet nodded back, took a deep breath, and straightened up, looking the Board members in the eye. The President beckoned him forward. The chair seemed to be parsecs away. His knees were shaking by the time he reached it and he sat down rather hard.

"And now we come to you," the President said. "You are, after all, the reason we're here. We'll take my lecture on secrecy as read, shall we? Your security rating is as high as anyone's here." He glanced up to smile at Bennet, a display of teeth that made Bennet want to sit lower in the chair and hunch his shoulders. "Although we'll administer the usual oaths—"

At the President's nod, Bennet put his right hand over his heart and taking as his witness the gods in whom he had only a residue of his childhood faith, he affirmed that he would tell only the truth and nothing but the truth.

The President started off. "Have you anything to add to the accounts we've already had of the initial briefing session?"

Bennet swallowed, trying to get some moisture into his throat, remembering his father's instructions. After a second's consideration, he said, "It all accords with my memory, sir, except for one thing. Captain Illych mentioned the short conversation he and I had with Commander Warwick over lunch. He reported the Commander's reactions—"

"He said that the Commander was excited at the prospect of taking the action to the enemy."

"Yes sir. There's more to it, though. The Commander was agitated about what he seemed to see as inaction... at what he perceived as an unwillingness to risk direct engagement with the enemy. He didn't say so in terms, but that's what he meant."

"What terms did he use, then?" Jethric asked.

"He was scathing about the political reluctance to prosecute the war to its fullest, envious about Shield's role in proactive missions, sir. He was very excited by the prospect of this job. It's something I picked up on later."

"As we will, too," the President said. "To keep in sequence—did you remark on Commander Warwick's unusual reactions?"

"It wasn't... The Commander's an old family friend, sir, and I'm familiar with him. What he said was nothing new for him, but I was struck by the intensity and energy with which he said it. Even for him, it was vehement. I put it down to his recent bereavement."

"The bereavement that left him with no ties back here on Albion," Jethric observed.

Bennet glanced at him. Jethric wasn't as hostile as Beatrice, anyway. "Yes, sir. I thought it accounted for the emotion, the intensity, and so I ignored it. There were other, more pressing and important things to worry about, and there didn't really seem to be anything in it. Except with the benefit of hindsight, of course."

"Hindsight that is distorting your interpretation of your recollection now?" Beatrice asked in the silky voice Bennet was beginning to hate.

"I don't believe so, ma'am." He kept his tone as flat as he could.

Beatrice stared down her nose and turned away when Bennet stared back.

"Did his mood continue?" the President asked.

"No, sir. The private briefing he had when the other captains were dismissed, was sobering."

Maitland nodded. "Well, we're all familiar now with the presentation made to IntCom earlier this year. No need to repeat that here. Just run through the journey out to the *Caliban* and what happened up until the point you left for the *Dhow*. Any other little nuggets that may demonstrate Commander Warwick's psychological... er... position will be useful, if you have evidence for it."

And then they picked over his memory like ravens feasting on a corpse. Every single thing he could remember was pulled out, shaken up, probed and dissected: Warwick's uncharacteristic, quiet distraction on the cutter out; the increasing excitement when they reached the *Caliban*; the uncomfortable (for Bennet) atmosphere on the dreadnought; the excitement and anticipation showed by all the officers; Bennet's increasing unease at the veneration in which Warwick was held by his crew.

"I take it that you're too familiar with commanders to hold them in the same respect," Beatrice said, in the tone that had annoyed Bennet previously with its scorn. The woman was snide. And it was with the same snide expression that she was now looking at Caeden.

Bennet looked, too, and permitted himself a smile. "I respect them, ma'am, but I grew up with way too many of them around for me to genuflect every time I see one."

Caeden rolled his eyes.

"Then you are a remarkably privileged young man."

"I know it, ma'am."

And then his recollection of the approaches made to him on the *Caliban* went through the same dissective process. Bennet was honest about his own obtuseness. "Everything they said could be interpreted solely as interest in Shield. The other services don't see a lot of us and, well, they tend to have a romanticised view of what we do. When I thought about it later, I realised those conversations could just as easily have been attempts to sound me out about my willingness to join them. I didn't see it at the time."

Beatrice threw up both hands in a dramatic gesture. It was a wonder she didn't take Jak's eye out. "This is astonishing! This is Commander Warwick we're talking about. Warwick! Are you seriously suggesting this was a deliberate act of desertion by one of our most respected warriors?"

"I don't know, ma'am."

"You don't know? You throw out accusations like this and you don't know?"

"I haven't made any accusations."

"Then what are you suggesting?"

"I don't know what reason Commander Warwick had to take the *Caliban* off-station, ma'am, and I don't presume to guess."

"Yes, you are! That's exactly what you're doing, impugning one of Albion's greatest warriors!"

"The actions of more than one of the Commander's officers may be construed as an approach to me. That's all I've said, ma'am."

"Pure speculation!"

"I don't think I implied otherwise, ma'am. I don't know if that's what they were trying to do or if it was nothing more than the usual curiosity about how Shield works. It's only significant in light of what happened at Makepeace."

"We don't know what happened at Makepeace, Shield Captain, other than you lost us a dreadnought."

Bennet stared, his face burning.

"Pre-judging the outcome, Beatrice?" Jak said.

Beatrice huffed. Impatient. Intolerant. "I'm aware of your partiality and blind spots, Supreme Commander."

Jak smiled. "Such mutual understanding is rewarding."

"Beatrice. Jak," President Maitland said, very quietly. As soon as the Inquiry Board had recovered its equanimity, he turned to Bennet. "You had no such hints from Commander Warwick himself?"

"No, sir."

"You're very certain."

"I am, sir. I've considered it a great deal since Makepeace, going over every conversation I had with the Commander. While I'm still uncertain about the approaches from his officers, I'm very sure he did not attempt to recruit me personally."

"That must be a blow to the ego." Beatrice's sneer curled up one side of her mouth. It was not a good look on her. "And it blows a hole the size of the *Caliban* in this farrago of nonsense."

Bennet let his mouth tighten and relax again, all the stress relief he could allow himself in the circumstances. "As you said, ma'am, we're speculating."

"I don't appreciate speculation about the probity and reputation about one of our greatest commanders, Shield Captain, no matter how old a family friend he may be."

Bennet let his mouth tighten up again. He didn't know what to say. He glanced out of the corner of his eye at Caeden, looking for a clue. His father was sombre, mouth drawn down and a faint line between the eyes. Caeden shook his head slightly. A warning.

Jethric cut in, smoothly, "The Shield Captain's views on Commander Warwick's behaviour seem pretty germane to me, Beatrice."

"His views are insulting!"

Bennet had to relax his mouth again. "I don't consider I have insulted Commander Warwick by recounting what happened."

"No? Not even to cover up the extent of your culpability on Makepeace?"

It was hard to get the words out, given how hard his mouth was set. He had to force himself to unclench his fingers from the fists they were curling into, to relax shoulder muscles so tense that his neck was beginning to ache. "I know what I'm responsible for on Makepeace," he said, and for an instant he lost sight of the Board, and saw fireflies and wide eyes with no life behind them, like sun-faded blue shutters over the broken windows in a derelict house.

Jethric struck in again, before Beatrice could be snide about it being the Board's job to decide the level of his responsibility and culpability, not for him. But that was one thing no one other than he could decide. No one.

Jethric looked up from his datapads. "Shield Captain, can you cut to the point at which you spoke to Warwick when you were in the base on Makepeace? What did you tell Commander Warwick, once you were on the surface?"

Bennet nodded, grateful for the respite from Beatrice's hostility. "I called him as soon as we'd secured the base and I'd had time assess the facility. I told him it was Code Chimera. That was the agreed code confirming the Maess were indeed using humans and human tissue in drone production."

Martens struck in with a "You spoke to him personally?"

"Yes, ma'am. He answered the call and he acknowledged. He knew what it meant. He said he'd tell me when they were in geo-stationary orbit, and that's the last I heard from him."

She nodded and let it go. With a promise (a threat?) that they'd come back to the factory and its contents and dissect Bennet's actions there later at IntCom—"Reprehensible though they may be," Beatrice said with an audible snort—Jak took over then. He focused on Bennet's formal assumption of command and the destruction of Makepeace before going over the same ground he'd taken with Illych, and finished up with the same question. What did the Shield Captain think had happened to make the Commander take the *Caliban* off-station?

"I don't know. We do know there was an energy flare from the Maess base, but any threat was several hours away. You can see from the tapes there was nothing more immediate the *Hertford*'s scanners could pick up. Of course, Illych's scanner and isometrics arrays aren't as powerful as a dreadnought's, but the *Hertford* should have been able to detect anything within the system, or the adjacent systems, that posed an immediate threat. If Warwick saw it, we should have seen it. But whatever took Warwick away wasn't visible. As for where he was right then, when we were searching for him..." Bennet brooded for a minute. In hyperspace, half-way to the next base over, taking his war to the enemy. But he shrugged without voicing it, mindful of Caeden's (very sound) advice. "I don't know, sir," he said, tired.

"And your reasons for not searching and waiting longer?"

"I had a job to do, sir. I had to get those people back. I definitely needed to get those samples back, the evidence Captain Van Trion and I collected, because we have to know what the Maess are up to. The longer we sat there, the more vulnerable we were. We were sitting ducks. One destroyer and one Shield ship wouldn't be enough to hold the Maess off. They'd roll right over us."

"But surely that was what Warwick had left to prevent?" Beatrice said in another of those sniping attacks.

Tired as he was, Bennet wasn't falling into that trap. "I have no idea why he took the *Caliban* off-station, ma'am."

"With such reduced defensive firepower, it must have been a nervous journey back," the President commented.

"Very nervous, sir," Bennet said, sincere.

And finally the ravens had finished feasting on the corpse. Ravens were big birds; heavy birds, and powerful. They had to flap heavily to get off the ground but they did it, wheeling away, tired of the monotony of the thin flesh on dried bones. Bennet said so to Felix when they were finally sent out of the room—no need for either of them to sign a declaration given their security ratings, President Maitland said with a geniality that made Bennet's skin crawl with apprehension—and the Board members were left to argue amongst themselves until they came to a decision on how much blame to pin onto him.

"You always need carrion eaters." Felix followed him into the room where the others were waiting, more or less patiently, according to their natures. "They're a necessary part of the eco-system."

"Not when it's my eyes they're pecking out." Bennet was conscious he hadn't been at his best. Far from it, allowing Councillor Beatrice to needle him. His eyes stung with weariness. He rubbed at them, but it didn't do any good. "Not then."

CHAPTER TWENTY-SEVEN

Only a couple of hours, that was all it had taken. Just over two. Caeden tilted his wrist to glance again at his chronometer, surprised. It had felt a lot longer. It never did when he was on what Bennet had called the safe side of the table. Time flew, then, while you asked your questions and sifted the evidence and made your judgement—but it had crawled slowly and painfully while he watched Beatrice try to crucify his son.

"He did all right on the whole. It's a pity he let Beatrice needle him, but I suppose it can be hard to deflect when you aren't used to it. The councillor's an old hand at the game and I'd expect her to score a few hits. Your son fights a different kind of war." The corner of Klára's mouth quirked up. "A cleaner one, despite what he found on Makepeace."

"Bennet knows it's mostly aimed at others—the President, Jak, us. I warned him about the point scoring." Except Caeden had expected Jethric to lead the attack, not Beatrice. But Jethric was quiet and subdued and Beatrice appeared to be unusually angry. Odd how they'd traded places. Caeden watched the Board's discussions. They kept their voices down and he couldn't make out more than a word or two. He turned to Klára, adding, "He despises politics."

"And he despises politicians. So did Warwick, of course." Klára chuckled. "I can just imagine what he said about… what was it Bennet called it? The political unwillingness to prosecute war to the fullest?"

"Something like that."

"Yes. Bennet was discreet, but I can imagine Warwick was not. And so can they." She tightened her grip on the swagger stick in her hand and tapped it against her knee. "Warwick had a point. They do hamstring us, our civilian masters. We aren't nearly as efficient at doing our jobs, answering to them."

Caeden managed a smile. "The price of democracy, Klára. We are their servants."

"I know it. I don't have to like it." She stretched out her left hand, tapped the swagger stick against her palm. "The other thing that strikes me is they're agitated beyond what I'd expect. Don't get me wrong! Losing a dreadnought is a catastrophe, cataclysmic in both military and political terms. Not to mention economically. But there's something else. Maitland taking a Presidential executive decision over this and excluding the politicians from the discussions? That's unprecedented. Even though your son's theories were beyond disturbing."

"It's bothered me ever since IntCom. I got the brush-off from Jak and Etienne when I tried to find out what was behind it."

Her mouth curved into a slight smile. "Me too. I don't think Martens knows anything either. Annoying."

"More than that. We can't advise on what we don't know about." Caeden watched the tap-tap-tap of the swagger stick. A sort of nervous tic.

Maitland turned at the same moment Caeden looked up. They stared at each other for a moment, then Maitland nodded. "We may as well make this a general discussion," he said, and invited Caeden and Klára over to the table. "I don't think there's any doubt at all that Warwick left of his own volition. There was no debris, nothing but the ion trail out of the system. *Caliban* wasn't destroyed, she was taken away. Caeden, just how accurate is your son's impression of that ship likely to be?"

Caeden had half-expected to be asked and had prepared his answer with care. "Bennet's usually less good at reading people than he is at understanding more abstract principles. No one would deny that. But he's no fool. I have no doubt the atmosphere was one he would not be comfortable with, and he's analysed it carefully in the light of Makepeace. We'll likely never know if those conversations he told us about were as ambiguous as he now thinks, but the fact the *Caliban* isn't here is suggestive."

Martens agreed. "The Shield Captain was the only person on the *Caliban* who truly understood what it's like to operate behind enemy lines. His experience would be invaluable if Warwick has taken the war to the enemy. It would have been foolish not to try and recruit him, even if indirectly through Warwick's daughter and a pilot he knew formerly. I trust Captain Bennet's instincts here."

"Oh, let's cut this short," Beatrice said, with a glance at Caeden. "We all know Warwick took off, for whatever reason. I'm sure he planned this and took advantage of the Makepeace raid to kick off his personal campaign from well inside enemy territory. And we all know neither the Shield Captain nor anyone else could have stopped it."

Jethric was head down in his datapads again, but he glanced up long enough to say, "I'd add that without Shield Captain Bennet taking decisive action to bring the prisoners back, we might well be down a destroyer and a couple of Transport ships too. He did well to make it back with what he'd found." Caeden was struck by how strained the councillor looked. "And what he found was appalling."

What was going on here? Jethric and Beatrice had reversed roles. Neither was running true to form. Caeden had been dealing with politicians for his entire career. He was used to their narrow-minded focus on their own advancement, their own advantage. That it was Beatrice showing these traits and Jethric who was being reasonable, concerned him. He preferred his politicians to be predictable.

"We now have a rogue dreadnought roaming behind enemy lines, out of our control, causing the gods alone know how much damage, and at a very delicate time, politically. We have no way of getting Warwick back, of stopping him. That could be catastrophic to our interests." Beatrice turned her frown onto Maitland. "If we are looking at accountability here, then perhaps the Ennead should not have been kept out of the decision-making process."

Maitland was not visibly disturbed by the implied accusation. "A point we have discussed since we heard the news—and, I'd remind you, Beatrice, we've discussed it repeatedly and in some depth. I am aware of your views and concerns, and that you would not have supported the mission if I'd opened it to all of IntCom."

"Of course I wouldn't! In the current circumstances, the risks are just too great. Look how it's turned out, for the gods' sakes."

Caeden frowned. There was that word again: *delicate*. Maitland had used it at IntCom, now Beatrice. What was going on behind the scenes? The usual politicking between bickering politicians, the usual back-stabbing and jockeying for position or advantage? Or something more? Phoenix, maybe?

Maitland's tone was even. He appeared unaffected by Beatrice's vehemence. "We are at war. War is about risk. I don't downplay *at all* the consequences of losing a dreadnought. The costs are huge—economically, politically, militarily. Huge. But that's countered by the intelligence Shield Captain Bennet brought back with him. We had to go in."

"I disagree. It could ruin everything we're doing to hold on to the settlement planets. The costs alone are disastrous."

"This isn't the place to discuss other matters." Maitland rubbed at his eyes. "Indeed, we've done very little else but discuss them and the impact Warwick's action will have, ever since we got word of the *Caliban*. We can add nothing here. What we do have to decide, now, is two things. One, what happens to those military personnel who were involved in the Makepeace mission, and two, public handling of the loss of the *Caliban*. First, let's wind up this Inquiry and make a decision about the captains and ships involved. Supreme Commander?"

"It's quite clear Warwick deliberately and with aforethought took the *Caliban* off-station and abandoned the mission. He went rogue. Not one of those ships, or any of their officers from Shield

Captain Bennet down could have done anything at all to prevent Warwick's actions and he was, moreover, the commanding officer." Jak gave Beatrice a thin smile. "Commanders are responsible for everything their command does or fails to do, Councillor. Everything. Shield Captain Bennet is absolutely responsible for the conduct of the mission and the personnel involved after he formally took command. Not before. That was Warwick's job, and Warwick walked away from it. I don't know what other finding we can make."

"I agree." Jethric laced his hands together and rested them on the pile of datapads in front of him. "I can't fathom Warwick at all."

"He had no ties here, once his wife died," Etienne said. "He has always been one of the more enthusiastic commanders, shall we say. His reputation for tactical brilliance was at least seventy percent a willingness to take excessive risk and bull his way through the consequences. Couple that with his frustration over political constraints, it seems obvious he seized an opportunity to prosecute the war on his own terms."

Caeden had to close his mouth tight. He wasn't a member of the Inquiry Board and he had no right to speak here. He couldn't risk the concession the Board had granted by allowing him and Klára to remain for the discussion. His own views on Warwick's actions would have to remain unvoiced.

"The Shield Captain's assumption of command was quite legal, I take it?" Jethric asked.

"He'd have breached Regulations if he hadn't," Jak said, blunt and uncompromising. "It was his duty, as laid out in the Regs, to take command. The 'death, disability, incapacity, or absence of the Commander' it says. Warwick's desertion—and let's not fool ourselves, because it is desertion, dereliction of his sworn duty and a dishonourable breach of orders—well, it's covered, anyway. He was certainly absent. Shield Captain Bennet was honour and duty bound to take command and finish the job. Which he did."

"Despite the odds against them." Jethric nodded. "Their success in getting back at all with those prisoners and the data is commendable. I agree with Jak. None of them can be held responsible for the loss of the *Caliban*."

Caeden blew out a long, silent breath. Thank the gods. It would have been iniquitous for the Board to assign blame, but when it came to politicians covering their backsides, it wouldn't have surprised him.

Maitland looked around at them all, gauging them. "To summarise, Warwick deserted. He had overall command and overall responsibility. None of the captains could have anticipated his plans or prevented him carrying them out. They are exonerated of responsibility for the loss of the *Caliban*. Agreed?"

The heads nodded. Caeden, relieved, sat back.

Beatrice snorted. "There was never any real doubt of the outcome, but I suppose your golden boy gets away without so much as a reprimand, Jak?"

"On what basis would I deliver a reprimand?"

"How about losing us a dreadnought?"

Jak's snort was as derisive as anything Beatrice could manage. "Warwick lost us the dreadnought."

"The mission was hardly covered in glowing success, no matter what."

"I'll put a notation to that effect on the Shield Captain's file, if you like," Jak said.

Beatrice sniffed and turned away.

"And on mine, and Martens' and the President's. Caeden's and Klára's. We all agreed to this."

"Yes, we did," President Maitland said. "I did. The decision to go was mine." He rubbed at his forehead again. "A dreadnought. We lost an entire dreadnought. Sometimes the magnitude of the blow is overwhelming. What a disaster!"

Beatrice closed up her datapad cover with a decided snap. "Let's hope the price is worth the intelligence Shield Captain Bennet brought back, whether it's a price we can afford to pay."

"I don't know," Jak said. "I do know we couldn't afford not to know what he found there. The implications of that are equally overwhelming."

Maitland held up a hand, in a fencer's graceful acknowledgement of a point made. "Formal finding, the responsibility is Warwick's and his actions could not have been anticipated by his junior officers on the mission. The Inquiry notes and commends Shield Captain Bennet's assumption of command in Commander Warwick's absence. Indeed, the actions of all the junior officers in stepping up to carry out the mission objectives successfully are in keeping with the highest traditions of military service and reflect great deal of credit upon them and their individual services. The Inquiry formally notes that Captains Van Trion, Willem, Mione and Illych are to be commended for their service, their coolness in adapting to adverse circumstances and the sheer achievement of getting those people out against the odds. Their actions, patriotism etc. etc. are lauded by their grateful government and people. Their gallantry and devotion to duty under circumstances that would have unnerved many have been noted by this Board. Whatever awards you think are right, Jak. We'll need formal citations for the record."

The Supreme Commander nodded.

Caeden frowned. What about Bennet?

Maitland didn't keep him waiting long. "As for Shield Captain Bennet... well, yes. We wouldn't have anything back at all but for him and the record must reflect that. But I have to temper the commendation. You're quite right, Jak. A notation on his file and Captain Felix's to the effect the mission they planned was not a success since it cost us a dreadnought. A grey mark, if not exactly a black one." He glanced at Caeden, but his focus returned to Beatrice and Jak. "And that's final. You'll neither of you get anything better." He waited, nodded at their silent acquiescence. "Etienne, please draw up a formal declaration of our findings in the appropriate language."

"Of course." Etienne inclined his head. "By this afternoon's IntCom meeting."

"Thank you. We'll clear it there. And then bury it. Highest possible security rating."

Etienne's smile was gentle. "But of course."

Maitland's smile, in comparison, looked forced. "Thank you. Now then. The news about the *Caliban* can't be concealed forever. Etienne, I suggest we bring in Nathan. He has the expertise to deal with this." To the others he said, as Etienne used a comlink to obey the President's request, "Our new Director of Communications. Most of you will know him, I believe, from his time as the foremost political journalist and reporter on AlbionNews. Etienne and I appointed him to the Secretariat a week ago to oversee Ennead communications. He will bring a more nuanced, news-based approach to our communications with the public. Most opportune, as we move into a sensitive phase of our relations with the colony planets."

What? *That* Nathan? The name jerked Caeden from his brooding over the essential unfairness of Bennet carrying the can for Warwick. He stiffened, drawing himself up. Oh yes. He knew Nathan.

"Nathan will be here in five minutes," Etienne said in his usual even tone. And when the President suggested a recess, and there was a general game of musical chairs as people got up to stretch legs and move around, he changed his seat to an empty one beside Caeden and said, quietly, under the various discussions breaking out around them, "Not as bad an outcome as it might have been, Caeden."

"No. I know. It just burns me that Bennet's getting any blame for it. Shooting the messenger with a vengeance."

"It could have been far worse. The evidence was clear, though and the boy didn't do badly in his deposition. But he has no game face. His emotions are too obvious."

Caeden swallowed a sigh. "Bennet is not comfortable with politics, with compromise and prevarication. He does tend to see things in black and white."

"So I see. It won't do, you know, not with the level of game he's involved in now." Etienne's smile broadened. "We need to do something about it. I like the boy. He has a refreshing honesty and I am impressed by his analytical work—which, little as we like the outcome, has been first class. Beyond first class. I should like an opportunity to know him better."

Well now. Well, well, well.

Etienne may not have the word 'politician' in his job description, but he was the wiliest exponent of the art Caeden knew. He had been director of the Secretariat for the last fifteen years, and there wasn't a political body buried anywhere in the known universe that Etienne hadn't been aware of before it breathed its last. He didn't need the outward trappings of power and office. If he had an interest in Bennet, then he would be a very formidable ally.

"I would be delighted if you did, Etienne. Although I don't know when you'll have the chance."

"Not immediately, perhaps, but I don't think this project is finished with us yet. There will be opportunities for me to meet him outside of IntCom or here. We'll arrange something."

Caeden smiled. "I would be delighted."

CHAPTER TWENTY-EIGHT

Caeden eyed his political masters at the other side of the room. The discussion between Beatrice and Maitland looked heated. Jethric sat with his head bowed over the datapads, ignoring everyone.

Caeden shifted in his seat, turned himself sideways on to the rest of the Board and dropped his voice. "What's going on, Etienne? I've never seen Jethric so subdued or Beatrice so virulent."

Etienne's mouth curved into a faint smile. "You missed some energetic discussions when the news came through. Both Beatrice and Jethric were furious at being cut out of IntCom's discussions. I know Jethric threatened impeachment proceedings, and you could hear the shouting all over the Praesidium. Then Bennet got home with those bodies and dozens of dozens of photographs. It took the wind out of his sails. He's rather overwhelmed by it, I think. Beatrice is still angry, but I don't think she is gunning for Bennet. He's a convenient target, a means for her to snipe at Maitland. And at Jak."

"I've never seen her so difficult. She's usually the more reasonable of the two, more amenable to argument. I expected some hostility, but I thought it would be Jethric." He smiled. "It's worrying when our political masters switch the game on us like that."

"As I said, Jethric's overwhelmed and horrified, and will, I think—probably for the first time in his life—put the greater good over his own political ambition. I don't know how long it will last, but at least, today, he's seeing the bigger picture. As for Beatrice..." Etienne frowned. "I don't know. She has always been a moderate voice, one pushing for a more nuanced and conciliatory approach to the Maess. But her position in her own province is under severe pressure from the peace movement. She has to make some gesture in that direction if she's to stave off defeat at the next election. The major settlement planets and the colonies are increasingly restless about their financial ties to us and are looking for Ennead allies. The war costs us billions every week. Taxes are high, public spending is constrained. They resent paying for it."

"Wars don't come cheap."

Etienne huffed out a soft laugh. "No indeed. Still, she appears to be establishing herself as the Friend to the Oppressed. She's open to discussion with Vines and his Phoenix League. That puts her in direct opposition to Maitland. As you know, he has little patience with complaints from the colonies."

Caeden nodded. He'd heard Maitland's views before. "I suspect he'd tell them to sit down and shut up. He appears to have a rather centralist view of where power and authority should lie. He's always been a traditionalist."

"Yes. A definite exponent of the 'Albion is mother, Albion is father' point of view. But despite everything Maitland might cling to about Albion not being accountable to her colonies, the fallout from this could be very far reaching. We haven't lost a dreadnought for almost two hundred years, not since the *Morro Coyo* went in a collision near Demeter. The impact on public confidence is going to be profound. They could be more open to the siren song the Phoenix League sings. I don't say it will bring down the Ennead, or bring about early elections, but we can expect a very rocky political ride. Vines, in the Phoenix League, will be blessing the gods for this and the opportunities it will give him."

Caeden grunted. Bloody politicians.

"The fact it's Maitland's final term has made him a touch...

brave. Perhaps that's the word. He took a huge personal risk making it an executive decision and it may yet blow up in his face. At least, he's taking communications seriously now and sees the necessity for a stronger hand there. If we're to control the reaction, influence the media to see things the way we want them to and ensure we can guide public opinion, then Nathan's role will be pivotal." Etienne's eyes, a darker grey than Bennet's, focused on Caeden. "It appears to me you have a problem with him. With Nathan."

"I don't have much of a game face either, you mean?" Caeden returned the amused smile Etienne gave him. He sobered. "Yes, I have a problem with him. Look up his coverage of the Telnos incident, two years ago, and you'll realise why."

Nathan had been the anchor of AlbionNews' flagship daily news programme for the last decade, and when it came to the big events, it was Nathan everyone expected to present it. Everyone expected to see his face on their screens and his voice doing the observing, analysing, commenting. There wasn't a major political or military event in the calendar he hadn't covered.

For all his relative youth—mid to late thirties, perhaps? No more than that. Thirty-five, say. A young man, still. Nathan had made his name during Maitland's first election campaign, a good twelve years ago now. Since then, politicians, generals and Fleet commanders had come and gone to the accompaniment of Nathan's probing questions and analytical assessment of their achievements (or lack thereof). He fronted the news station's analysis of every election, was at the Praesidium for every major announcement from the Ennead, at Military HQ for every victory or setback. He had even covered the wedding of the Maitland's youngest daughter—lukewarm about the dress, but prone to a good deal of incisive comment about the guest list showing who was, and who was not, in political favour. And if they weren't in that particular in-out position before Nathan mentioned it, they probably were afterwards.

Caeden could accept all that. The man knew his craft as surely as Caeden knew his. Nathan would bring an incisive, analytical, biting approach to formal communications from the Ennead that the gods knew it had sorely lacked in the past. But Caeden couldn't yet dismiss the memory of the amused sneer on the journalist's face when news of the Telnos rescue had broken, two years earlier.

Telnos. For weeks he and Meriel had thought their elder son dead. And when Bennet and all the survivors he'd protected had been rescued and brought home, the best AlbionNews' premier political reporter could do in the way of the story hadn't focused on the Shield warrior who had been left for dead after evacuating colonists from a planet in the teeth of a Maess advance. It hadn't covered Bennet's success in gathering together the survivors and keeping them safely hidden from the Maess for weeks. Or that he'd sent them all onto the rescue ship before he'd step onto a cutter himself. Or how badly wounded he'd been, getting those people to safety.

Oh no. It had been a snide, jeering commentary on how Bennet, at eighteen, had left home to live with his tutor at the Thebaid Institute. His *male* tutor, Nathan had said, with a smirk and raised eyebrows. What did his upright, religious father think about that, do you think?

Well, what Bennet's upright, religious father had thought about it was that Nathan could dance naked on the pinnacle of the Praesidium's dome for a year before Caeden would ever again grant the oily little snake an interview or provide an opinion or sound bite. And even then Nathan would have to beg.

"That was aimed at you, you know," Etienne said, proving that once again he had an uncanny grasp of political realities. Of course. He'd have reviewed Nathan's relationships with the Ennead and the senior members of military before appointing him. Perhaps it was a lesson to Caeden in political realism that Etienne had appointed Nathan anyway.

"I do know." Caeden glanced at the door and watched Nathan's entrance. "That doesn't make me like him, or his nuanced news-based approach, any better."

Maitland called them all to order, seated Nathan at Etienne's other side, and sketched in some of the background. It was masterly. Maitland managed not to mention Bennet, or Bennet's theories, or what he found on Makepeace. "There are facts about this mission I can't share with you, Nathan. Not at this time. But I will tell you this much, because I've no doubt your former colleagues will speculate on Warwick's state of mind following the death of his wife earlier this year, and the better briefed you are to deal with any questions and speculation in that area the better. The *Caliban* was deliberately taken off-station."

Nathan's jaw dropped at the realisation that Albion was not only down an entire dreadnought, but the dreadnought's Commander appeared to have deserted and taken his entire crew with him. He looked around the table, searching all the faces watching him. Caeden followed suit. Every face there was grave. Nathan swallowed visibly and nodded.

"You understand there can be no hint this was a deliberate act. I don't think the public will be able to stomach it. The unrest about the war and the tax burden it imposes, while still contained, sours the political landscape. We can't afford to stoke that fire, not with colonial administrations facing elections and fighting the growing popularity of Seigneur Vines' Phoenix League." Maitland waved a hand to the window and the square beyond. He didn't bother hiding a sneer. "The details of Makepeace must remain confidential, and we do not want a focus on the unfortunate prisoners, whose health has been destroyed by their captivity and who need time to recover. What do you suggest?"

The ex-journalist had been typing madly on his datapad throughout Maitland's briefing. "If I have this straight, what we need is a story that accounts for the disappearance of the *Caliban* somehow and yet leaves Commander Warwick's reputation intact?"

"Very intact." Maitland's expression showed nothing of what his opinion might be.

"You said there was a surge of energy from the nearby base." Nathan looked up from his datapad. "It showed up on the sensor records? Verified and on footage we can share with the press?"

"Yes and yes," Maitland said. "We can prepare footage, complete with verifiable identity codes for the *Caliban* and the recording ship."

"Good. That all helps. We have to pitch this as being helpful, but not so helpful we raise suspicions we're being too accommodating and must be hiding something. Nor can we offer them so little we leave room for them to go digging. Balance, that's what we're after here. Giving them the footage will draw some of their teeth, hits the right note. Who was in command after Warwick went? The Captain of the destroyer?"

And suddenly everyone was looking at Caeden.

"No," Etienne said. "It was, in fact, the ranking Shield officer, who was in command of the ground operation."

Martens gave the ex-journalist a wintry smile. "We prefer discretion. Do not name my Shield officers."

Nathan grimaced. "It's better to be upfront and honest, if we can."

The hypocrisy was breath-taking. Even the politicians appeared awed.

"The key is to hide misdirection in the truth." Nathan glanced at his pad. "The loss of the *Caliban*'s the big story. Most people have only minimal concern for Rets, and we might get questions about whether sending along such a large rescue operation was, in the light of what happened, a fair and reasonable use of resources. The Phoenix League will seize on that. Vines' public profile is gaining daily in credibility and strength and he carries the entire League with him, in the colonies as well as here on Albion. He will be the key person to brief—privately, before the news breaks. I'll need something on the actual costs in monetary terms and we'll do some comparisons on other budget spends to put it into proportion."

Good luck with that, thought Caeden. The cost of a new dreadnought would wipe out the planetary economy for a decade and put an intolerable burden on the settlement planets and colonies whose taxes flowed into Albion's coffers. In the midst of an expensive war, it just wasn't possible. They were forever a dreadnought down, now. Warwick had blown a bigger hole in

Albion's defences than the Maess had ever managed.

It appeared Nathan grasped that nuance. "The costs of the rescue, I mean, not the cost of replacing the *Caliban*."

"We couldn't do it," Beatrice said, tone snappish. "We can't afford it."

"No, ma'am, I agree. I have a line into the Finance ministry. Guaranteed discreet, and helpful. Some of our arguments have to be around the human cost of not getting people back from the Maess, adding a reminder that it's Fleet's duty to protect lives and that in any battle we could lose more than one dreadnought. Didn't the *Brandenberg* have a close call twenty years back and spend two years in repair and refit? We need to remind people about that sort of risk. Dreadnoughts are not invulnerable." Nathan paused for breath, and Caeden eyed him with a smidgeon of respect. The man knew his trade. "What happened to the Rets, sir?"

"They're in a holding facility, awaiting debriefing." Etienne's tone was cool. "Shed as little light as you can on them, please, Nathan, consonant with not stirring up suspicions and interest."

Nathan nodded. "I can cobble something together to play on the heartstrings, although that might provoke some of the more liberal news outlets to explore the human interest angle. We can divert that, I think, by a suggestion these Rets are some sort of health risk at the moment."

"Which they most certainly are. Although we are, of course, still assessing how and to what extent they might pose a general risk to public health, we are being cautious and careful in our analysis of their physical and mental condition. We have no idea, yet what they were exposed to during their long captivity and they themselves are fragile." Etienne was quite as nuanced as ever Nathan could hope to be. Caeden was impressed. "Work around it, please."

"But of course." Nathan's fingers worked the datapad with brisk efficiency. "And they will be quarantined for some time, I take it? That should work, although better if you can find me a photograph of someone in an isolation capsule as visual reinforcement."

"No problem." The corner of Jak's mouth twisted with something—disgust, knowing him—but he smoothed the expression out.

Caeden shared the feeling. News-based nuances took some stomaching. It was impressive, but not in a way he felt was entirely honourable.

Nathan glanced back at his datapad. "Then I think we have enough to take them out of the main focus, and with luck, we can play that element out until the interest dies down and it's yesterday's story. The spotlight will be on Warwick and the *Caliban*, anyway. I think that's all I need. There will have to be a formal announcement, President Maitland—you or the Supreme Commander?"

"Both of us," Maitland said.

"Good. A united front." Nathan glanced around the table. "I'll get the statements and the press releases ready. I have a bio of Warwick on file I can use as background and I assume there's something there on the *Caliban*. We'll have to be upfront about it being a rescue mission and Rets were brought back. The general thrust of the story is very simple. At the Battle of Makepeace, with his usual courage and tenacity, Commander Warwick ensured the success of the rescue. First, by taking out the orbital defences and destroying squadrons of Maess fighter craft. And second, by facing, alone, the threat posed by a nearby Maess base. Contact with the *Caliban* was lost during the struggle to secure Makepeace. The other ships, knowing they were in a much weaker position when it came to firepower and tactical capability, took advantage of the post-battle confusion to slip away and bring the prisoners home. Thanks to Warwick's brave action, covering their retreat, they were successful. We have not been able to re-establish contact with the *Caliban*, and Shield's careful reconnaissance of the area has thrown up no sign of *Caliban*'s whereabouts, nor of debris or wreckage. The fate of the ship and its crew is still unknown, although we have to assume the worst and she's lost to us in an act of exemplary courage and heroism, sacrificed to save the prisoners and ensure that Shield and the destroyer could get the Transport ships out safely. No less than we would expect of one of Albion's most courageous, heroic sons; a legend and a role model for all of us; an everlasting example of leadership, courage, strength, valour, fearlessness and service before self. Laudatory praise from you, Mr President and suitably patriotic noises as you honour his sacrifice. You'll have to announce posthumous awards, of course. I'd suggest a Lion of Thebes for Warwick."

"Would you?" Maitland's mouth twisted. His gaze met Caeden's and slid away again. Caeden shook his head. It appeared Nathan had found a way to devalue even their most venerated award for valour. That took real talent.

"I think we have to, sir, to add to the story. Something for everyone else, down to the lowliest crewmember. Something significant. At least Orders of the Star of Gold, I think. Are there one or two we can bump up to Orders of Honour? I'll need a crew list for the background note and choose one or two of them for a higher Order. The press will concentrate on Warwick and we can gloss over the prisoners, and trot out the quarantine story when needed." Nathan shook his head. "It's thin. It's damned thin, but I'll pad it out and smooth it down, of course, and cover all the angles my former colleagues are likely to home in on. I'll have something substantive to run past you in an hour or so, sir."

There was a murmur of agreement. It was a thin story. There was no doubt about it. But Maitland nodded, and dismissed Nathan to carry out the herculean task of creating something convincing out of so little. "Bring it to IntCom this afternoon, Nathan. Etienne will tell you where and when. We'll approve it there."

Once Nathan was gone, Maitland sat back, rolling his shoulders. "Good. Let's get this charade over with, have some lunch and then start on the real work with a preliminary meeting of the Intelligence Committee."

And that was that. The Inquiry Board was over with surprisingly little bloodshed. All things considered, a good outcome

"So Warwick's heroic reputation is to be left intact," Klára said.

"Our people need heroes." Jethric's manner remained quiet and subdued.

"And so we manufacture them?" Klára frowned. "Pity the society that needs to have its heroes manufactured for it."

"No." Caeden ran a hand around the inside of his collar and put up a silent prayer that Bennet would keep his mouth shut when he found out what the official story was to be. Because there was no doubt at all but this story would infuriate Bennet, not least because of the implication he sneaked away with the prisoners while the brave Warwick and the *Caliban* fought bravely to cover his escape. "Pity the society that needs them at all."

CHAPTER TWENTY-NINE

37 Quintus 7490: Demeter Transfer Station

The regular Transport shuttle out of the Sais City spaceport carried a consignment of around fifty warriors, bringing them out to that great military melting pot, Demeter Transfer Station, on their way to re-join their units or their ships. It was late, dammit.

Boring way to travel. Even worse, if it was your job to drive the shuttle. The last time Rosie had taken a Transport fleet shuttle, it had come into Demeter with all the innate excitement of a man parking a bus. The pilot had been asleep for most of it, she'd swear. If she'd had to spend her entire career literally shuttling backwards and forwards, she'd sleep too. It was terminally boring.

She gripped the key tight in her hand and pushed her fist into her pants pocket, out of sight. Surely he wouldn't be long? The crowd was pushing past her now, but the big Shield trooper to her right stood quiet, not bothering her, bulking large and keeping a pocket of Shieldness around them that had the other people in the arrival lounge veering off to give them space. The other services were always leery of Shield.

A couple of dozen people waited in the small room beyond the security gate, and more than one loud (if not rapturous) reunion blocked her view of the passengers disembarking from the shuttle.

There.

She dodged past a group of outstandingly raucous Infantry, avoiding both their calls and the arms outstretched to impede her. Bennet didn't see her at first. It was only when she caught at his arm and called his name that he appeared to realise she was there. He stared when she touched him, frowning.

He was beautiful. Gorgeous. His hair was untidy, as usual, pushed carelessly back from his brow and falling into his eyes in a way that would have most women—and quite a few men—itching to brush it back for him. She gave in to temptation, raising a hand to push his hair back so she could see his eyes, read the expression in them. She loved his eyes. Such an unusual silvery shade of grey. Now they looked tired, with little lines about them she didn't like. He'd lost weight, too. But as he realised it was her, his slow smile started, making his mouth curve up and his eyes lose their dullness and brighten into life. Now the little lines looked more like laughter. The frown vanished.

"Rosie."

That was all. Just her name, on a breath and something like a laugh. She couldn't manage to get his name out past the lump in her throat. She let him pull her in, let him wrap her up. She ignored the laughter and catcalls around them, the open curiosity and amusement and be damned to officers being expected to show military decorum to enlisted. Be damned to it. She hadn't kissed anyone like this since he'd left for the *Corvus* a year ago. She'd missed this.

The gods alone knew how much later it was before they let each other go, how long they just held on and caught at each other. The room had a lot fewer people in it when she finally took a step away to look at him properly. He was too thin, and too tired, but he was here. At last.

"Rosie," he said when he released her. He let go with one hand to cup her face with it. She pressed up against his palm, rubbing her check against it.

"Hello, love." She rested her forehead against his for a second, and smiled.

"I never expected—" He stopped, laughed, shook his head. He slid the hand down the side of her neck, his fingers tracing the fine gold chain to the pendant he'd given her.

"I never take it off." She reached up to close her fingers over his. Gave him a decisive little nod to push the point home.

He kissed her again. "I never expected to see you!"

"I know. Surprise!" She stood back, took both his hands in hers. "How long do you have?"

His smiled vanished. "Shit. The *Gyrfalcon's* cutter is waiting for me. I'm going straight out."

"Oh." She pulled out the room key, looked at it, and pushed it back into her hip pocket. "Oh. I got us a room. I hoped... Oh, well."

He put his hand over the pocket. She remembered what it felt like to have his hands hold both hips as she straddled him, hot and damp with want and need. The fluttery feeling in her chest quickened.

"No time, Rosie."

"There never was, was there? Sums it all up for us." Her breath came hard, her chest tightening. It would be good to droop, to allow the heaviness to pull her down. She shrugged, tightening her mouth, but still it trembled, dammit. She could feel it. "I've missed you." So much. She put her hand over his, pressing it against her hip. "All we can do is make the best of what we have. Which gate?"

"Eighteen."

"So if we take it slow, we could have half an hour? Oh, Bennet. Not quite the reunion I had in mind." She tried to make it light, but it came out sad. And bitter.

"No." Bennet looked rather helplessly at the kit bags beside them. He'd have his hands so full, he wouldn't even be able to hold hers. Well, she'd thought of that.

"I'll deal with that. I thought some brawn may be needed."

Rosie beckoned forward the trooper. He'd be a stranger to Bennet, she remembered. "Will here arrived on the *Hype* after your time," she explained as Will saluted. Bennet kept one backpack, shrugging into it while she loaded up her human mule with Bennet's kit and sent him on his way to deliver it to the waiting cutter.

"I've missed my efficient Lieutenant," he said, when she slipped her hand into his.

"And Rosie?"

"I've missed my Rosie more. It's been a long year."

"Letters don't do it," she agreed.

"Better than nothing."

"Only just." Rosie sighed and tightened her grip on his hand.

They followed Will out into the main corridor running the length of Demeter from prow to stern. More people out here for them to dodge, people on their way to their ships or Infantry quarters or dotting in and out of the small shops, restaurants and bars lining the corridor.

Rosie let Will go ahead; he knew where to take Bennet's kit. She tugged Bennet over to the left hand corridor wall, to one side of the main flow of traffic. She glanced at him sidelong. The brief delight—she was sure it had been that—at seeing her had faded. He looked tired and worn again, his eyelids drooping and his mouth a straight line. She would have liked to kiss it back into curves. Instead, she opted for a direct assault. "I heard the last job was a bad one, Bennet."

"What? How?"

"Your mother keeps in touch with me, didn't you know? She told me you'd been on a bad job for the Supreme Commander and you'd be arriving on Demeter today on your way to the *Gyrfalcon*. She wanted me to try and meet you. I didn't expect I could, but the Hype needed some minor repairs and we brought her in a couple of days ago." She looked at him sideways again. His mouth had hardened. Not a good sign. "Your mother didn't say what it was, but I figured it had to be something big, if she's that worried about you. I've seen the news reels. The *Caliban*?"

"I can't talk about it." His hand tightened on hers. "But yeah. The *Caliban*."

Something in her chest contracted at his tone, the lost look in his eyes. He dropped his gaze, wouldn't look at her. Really not good, then. She looked around. A couple of compartments down the corridor, a sign advertised a coffee shop. She pulled him into it, despite his protests, and pushed him into a corner table. "Your cutter can wait a while. Stay here."

The staff provided her with tea with little more than an eye roll. It didn't look like good tea, too strong and black, but it would have to do. It was a coffee shop, after all. She couldn't expect gourmet leaves here. She put the cup onto the table top in front of him and took her seat, sipping at her own cup. She hid the wince, looking over his head to the flat screen monitor showing programmes piped in from Albion. A soap opera, with the sound turned off.

She took another sip of tea and winced again. Yes. Too strong. "There's been nothing else on the news for the last week and a half. It's making the whole Ennead look shaky and people are het up about it. There was talk this morning of impeaching the President and calling early elections. Terrible loss, a dreadnought."

His mouth twisted. That was interesting.

"The accounts all mention that Shield was involved and the ranking Shield officer took command on Makepeace when the *Caliban* was lost. Was that you?"

He nodded. Sipped at his tea. Grimaced.

Shit. That would have meant an Inquiry when he got home. He was here and he was still a captain and on his way to a new posting, so he'd got through it, but it must have been... she couldn't find words hard enough and powerful enough to imagine what it must have been like. 'Stressful' didn't begin to cut it.

"I can't tell you anything much about it, Rosie. It was a Strategy Unit job." He dropped his voice and she had to strain to hear him. "I ended up thanking the gods about whose son I am, and whose godson, and how many political friends my father's made a virtue out of cultivating. Because I reckon if I'd been just any Shield officer, I might be facing a court martial right now. They'd have railroaded me, if they could. Some of them, anyway."

She shoved her cup into its saucer and grabbed at his hands. "Bennet!"

"And the worst thing? Not the Inquiry. That was bad enough. But sitting there that afternoon in IntCom, listening to the crap they were going to say about it, about the *Caliban*. That was worse." This time, when his mouth twisted, it was into a full-blown sneer. "I had to listen to their new Director of Communications"—his scorn for the title was scorching—"tell the world I sat back and let Warwick-the-fucking-Glorious sacrifice himself to save the mission, while I ran away home to Albion. And it is a load of—"

He stopped abruptly, pressing his lips together so hard they were white.

Rosie's mouth was dry. She had to work it a couple of times to get enough moisture to dampen her lips, to find her voice. "They didn't hold you responsible?"

Bennet's brief flare of energy was over. He sagged back. Shook his head. "No. They couldn't. The evidence was all there, what happened. One of the politicians was out to find someone to blame, that's all. All the weasels are running scared. They're scared that more colonies will start griping about taxes, they're scared they'll face Phoenix League candidates at the next elections, they're scared they'll be booted out." He caught her hand, but his smile was a painful, thin travesty. "I'm sorry, Rosie. You don't need to hear this. I'm all right."

"Of course you can tell me! What did your dad say? Does he know?"

"Oh yes. He was there. Not part of the Inquiry Board, of course, but he was there." Bennet's smile twisted. "He was good about things. Supportive. Although he did tell me to get over myself when I complained to him about what was being said. He kept telling me it wasn't about me, but it felt bloody pointed at the time."

"I'll bet! It's official though? They exonerated you?"

"Yes. Mostly. Although what difference does that make? I planned a mission, Rosie, and it cost us a dreadnought. The bosses aren't going to forget that in a hurry."

What could she say? Because the gods knew he was probably right there. So while he stared down at the tabletop to hide, she held his hands and smoothed across the backs of them with her fingers, making soothing noises and trying not to give way to the weight pressing on her. Her throat ached.

When Bennet looked up again, his eyes were bright but he was back in control. "I hadn't realised my mother wrote to you."

Well, the gods knew she wouldn't want to talk about it either if she'd been the one in an Inquiry. She let him change the subject, but kept her grip on his hands. "I get on very well with her, you know, and I've had lunch with her a couple of times over the last year. I think she's trying to keep me sweet for you. She's a born matchmaker."

Bennet straightened. His eyes narrowed. "She might have the right idea. We should get married. Why don't we?"

Her breath caught on a gasp. "What? Be serious!"

"I am serious, Rosie. Marry me."

Oh gods. Oh gods. The heaviness pressed down until she wanted to wilt under it. The flutters in her stomach wore lead boots. "We can't even manage a decent affair! I haven't seen you for over a year. Long distance marriage wouldn't work for me, Bennet."

"It doesn't have to be long distance."

"It'll always be long distance!" It came out too loud. She looked around to see if anyone had heard her. No, the rest of the patrons were too involved in their own dramas. She lowered her voice. "You're in Fleet and I'm not; and I'm due my rotation out later this year and we'd be split up again because I'm going to

Infantry. But when you do come back, it won't be to the *Hype*."

Wherever Martens posted him when he got home to Shield, she wouldn't disrupt the *Hyperion*'s command, not after three years under Tarrant. He had to know that.

His mouth twisted. "No. I won't get the *Hype* back."

She pulled one hand away, touched her throat and felt the fluttering in her pulse. Breathing was harder. "It won't work."

"We don't have to stay in the military."

Rosie stared. She opened her mouth, closed it, opened it again.

"You're overdoing the astonishment," he said. "I've been thinking about it for the last few weeks. The apartment's mine outright, so we'd have somewhere to live. I could work at the Thebaid. Be an academic. If there isn't a Fellowship available immediately, I have enough income from the family trusts to live on, more than enough. More than the military pays me. We could resign."

"What would I do? Stay at home and have babies?" She couldn't keep the sharpness from her tone, but maybe he didn't hear it. Maybe he didn't want to hear it.

"Sounds like a plan to me."

Her eyes stung. Breathing hurt and her heart pounded. She dropped one hand to splay it out and rub her chest, to ease the tightness there. A flush of heat stung her skin from the inside out. Bennet was brighter, energised, more alert. She had to press her lips tight shut to trap the words behind them, to stop it all from tumbling out.

She dropped both hands to the edge of the table, gripping it tight. She used it to give herself momentum, jerking her arms straight and standing up. The chair skidded away behind her. She wouldn't look at Bennet. She wouldn't.

"Rosie!"

Every step to the counter was so hard Rosie's boot heels rang on the steel floor. The guy behind the counter had wide eyes and one hand over his mouth. *What the hell was wrong with him?* He looked like he'd wet himself any second.

She relaxed the tightness around her mouth enough to speak. "Coffee. Please."

The guy jumped to obey. The coffee was strong and black, the way she liked it. She dumped in a packet of sweetener too, and only then could she turn and walk back to the table, steps quieter now because she didn't want to spill her coffee. She glanced at Bennet. He stared back at her, his mouth pressed shut as hard as her own was. His eyes narrowed when she jerked the chair back into place and sat down, but she looked over him at the screen. Soap opera gave way to the news bulleting. *Caliban* again, and Vines pontificating to camera. A blessing the sound was muted. She turned her attention to stirring in the sweetener with savage little jabs of the spoon.

"Rosie?"

When she could trust herself, she said, "I won't be second best."

His mouth had dropped open. Astonished she didn't fall into his arms?

"You aren't!"

The coffee tasted like heaven. If she were honest, she'd admit she didn't like tea.

"I mean it, Rosie." He was hurt, too. Surprised and hurt.

"I don't think so." She had to look away. "It's not me you really want, and I'm not going to settle for being your consolation prize. I love you, but I have more pride than that."

"I've just asked you to marry me!" His voice rose, hard with indignation.

"You didn't mean it." She took another sip of her coffee and savoured it, watching him over the rim of the cup. He already looked so beaten down, she gave him some leeway. "What time we had together was pretty damn good. But if he walked in here now, if Flynn walked in, you wouldn't even notice I was here."

He jerked back, shaking his head. "That's not true—"

"Yes, it is. I know you love him."

"I love you."

It might hurt more to be knifed in the chest, but she doubted it. Thing was, according to his lights, he wasn't lying. "I know you do, but it's not the same. It was good last year, when we weren't long distance. Although I do sometimes wonder if we ever got over the real distance of me being a girl."

His shoulders hunched up, defensive. His voice was shaky and soft. "Gender isn't the first thing I think about, you know."

"Really? Am I the only woman in your life?"

He shrugged, his face reddening. "You know it."

"Then that's as good as it'll ever get. It'll do. It'll have to do."

"I do mean it," he persisted.

"You think you do." Gods, he looked as if she'd hit him. The whole Makepeace thing had him seriously rattled. "It must have been a very bad job with the *Caliban*."

"Yeah."

It was difficult to speak. The ache in her throat was a lump, hard and painful. "I get that. And I also get that you don't want to go to your father's ship. But you don't get to use me like that. You ask a girl to marry you because you can't imagine life without her, not because you're scared of life without Flynn. It's not on. It's insulting."

He was scarlet and wouldn't meet her gaze.

Her anger drained away. Gods, she was tired. As tired as Bennet looked. "Whatever has you so beaten down, whatever happened at Makepeace and whatever will happen on the *Gyrfalcon*, marriage isn't the cure."

"I wasn't looking for a cure. I was looking for something else."

"Well, I'm not your something else. We both know that."

One of Rosie's previous captains had been a poet. Shield, he'd said once, was perspective and nobility and tradition, and blood and guts and a sheer bloody-mindedness that wouldn't recognise defeat. Shield never gave up, never surrendered. Shield was a hard place, a terrible place; a place that forced you to find courage and endurance. Shield was both hammer and anvil, beating keen-edged weapons from the base metal.

She was no poet. But being Shield was the only thing to keep her going now, that opened her mouth to speak the truth and not a stupid lovelorn assent to his proposal.

She forced a smile, put a hand on his. He turned his hand in hers, gripped it until her fingers hurt. "I do love you, Bennet. But I'm not big enough for you to hide behind. Time to call it a day."

Hammer crashed down on anvil, and only Shield was left.

CHAPTER THIRTY

37 Quintus 7490: dreadnought *Gyrfalcon*

Flight Sergeant Danae brought the little ship into *Gyrfalcon*'s cutter bay, dead centre in the ship between the port and starboard Hornet decks. She'd been agitated and antsy by the time he'd finally arrived at the right deck in Demeter, hours late. She hadn't quite flounced at his lateness, but she left him with the distinct impression she'd have liked to. Instead, she'd left him to himself for most of the journey out from Demeter, calling him up to the tiny flight deck only when the *Gyrfalcon* was within visual range. Bennet hadn't minded the neglect.

It was four years since he'd seen the *Gyrfalcon* last, only then she'd been growing bigger in the view from the Mozzie's cockpit until she'd loomed so large she'd blotted out entire galaxies. Then he'd worried about having to be on his father's ship and how that would impact on the job he had to do to get into T18, apprehensive about how they'd manage without his mother there to keep the peace between them.

A laughably inconsequential issue now.

So, four years since T18.

Two years since Telnos. Two years since leaving Joss and finally abandoning a compromise as dead and desiccated as one of his beloved mummies. Two years since those incandescent weeks

ut, not with the *Gyrfalcon*'s silvery-grey bulk filling the
heavens.

One year since he was sent to Fleet, escaping today's fate by a
hair's-breadth, because *Gyrfalcon*'s lush of a Flight Captain hadn't
yet hit the bottom of his own particular barrel. Great timing on
Simonitz's part, and a damned pity he hadn't stayed sober a few
months longer.

One month since Makepeace, and the discovery that there
truly was a fate worse than death.

And twelve hours since he'd lost Rosie.

He shook his head, trying to take hold of himself, to stop the
rot. It sounded like a countdown, each beat of the count another
disaster, another mistake.

"Not much used to dreadnoughts then, sir?"

Bennet let his mouth close. He'd been staring as if he'd never
seen a space ship before. He must have looked moronic. Moronic
enough to have amused Danae, anyway. "I always forget what big
buggers they are and it gets me, every time. She's huge."

Danae grinned. "You'll soon get used to her, sir."

Bennet hoped so.

She was a good pilot, he noticed, capable and sure, deftly
adjusting the controls to coax the cutter into a textbook landing on
the central deck. She'd do well in a Hornet, with that sort of
precision flying.

There was no one waiting for him. Last time he'd had a
welcoming committee that had worn colonel's crowns and a stern
expression, with a gaggle of pilots hanging around to see him
arrive. They'd been unknowns, nothing more to him then than the
people whose records he'd scour to find the right pilot for the job
of getting him into the Maess base on T18. There had been no hint,
as he'd glanced at them, that among them was the right pilot for
him. The only pilot for him.

Nothing this time. No one. Neither known or unknown, right

307

or otherwise. No one.

Nothing at all.

He was relieved. He was nervous enough with having people watching for him. Really, he was relieved there was no one there.

"I'll have everything taken to your quarters, sir," Danae said, following him down the ramp. "I know Corporal Bren's been assigned to you by the Quartermaster, and he's getting everything sorted out. A crate of your stuff came through on last week's freight run. I think the Deckmaster put it into storage, unless Bren's already located it. Want me to check?"

"I'd appreciate that, thanks. Books, mostly, but I don't want to lose them." Along with the paintings Rosie had given him and his favourites from the collection of antiquities in the apartment. Not to mention his Shield suit and his uniform, carefully pressed and neatly folded until it was time to take off this silly disguise and get back to who he really was.

He left the two kitbags with Danae, keeping only the satchel of datapads with him, keeping all the terrible knowledge safe, slinging the strap over one shoulder. Danae was protesting innocence to the Starboard Deckmaster as he walked into the main body of the ship. "Not my fault, Maire, honest!" and her voice cut off abruptly as the door slid shut, shutting him into silence.

No decontamination necessary, since he hadn't been dirtside. Shame. He would have welcomed the ten minutes it took to get through the cycle, welcomed the delay as a chance to think about what he felt and deal with it. He practiced the slow, even breathing the Shield psychs had said would help calm the flutters. He couldn't remember when that advice had come. Part of the debriefing from the job when he'd had to kill the Jack? Years ago. At least five long years ago, when it was only one death that defined him.

They usually worked, the breathing exercises, clearing his mind and leaving him calmer, more grounded. He couldn't say the psychs' nostrum was effective this time, though. There was a coldness in his gut, like a hand closing about them to yank them, and he had to concentrate to keep his breathing calm and level. The flutters were so un-calm they were wearing lead boots and turning somersaults. They somersaulted all the long way up to the Bridge.

When he stepped out of the turbolift and onto the Bridge, faces turned towards him in open curiosity. He knew a few of them. The tall Bridge Captain standing at Colonel Quist's shoulder... What was his name again? Omaha? Orion? Something like that.

And Natalia, looking trim in her engineering uniform, her expression guarded. She sat at the engineering desk. Her mouth curved into a brief smile, but she kept a wary eye on the Colonel. It looked like even the Commander's children didn't get away with too much familiarity on duty. He smiled back, pleased to see her.

Quist raised an eyebrow. Looked him up and down. "How nice of you to join us, Captain."

The day he'd first stepped aboard this ship, Quist's welcome had been cool. Second impressions were little better than the first, then. Bennet opted for discretion over valour, lowered the satchel to the deck and offered a snappy salute in lieu of a defence.

"I'm glad to be here, Colonel," he said, perjuring his immortal soul without a second thought.

Quist looked him up and down again, and snorted. "The Commander's waiting for you in his office. When he's finished with you, come and see me."

"Ma'am."

Natalia smirked at him. He wasn't at all sure if it was sympathetic or not, so he kept the return grimace light, grabbing his satchel again.

The office looked just the same. The same painful tidiness, the same group of holopics on the desk, the same commander sitting behind it regarding him with marked disfavour.

"You're late," his father said.

The flutters made an effort to be full-blown quivers, and he had to take a calming breath to beat them into stillness again. As a precaution, he stiffened into a salute. Not perhaps, as snappy as the public one he'd given Colonel Quist, but acceptable, he hoped. "I was held up on Demeter. Shield business, sir," he added, as the cool glare continued to intimidate.

Caeden scowled. "Martens is not getting you back any earlier!"

"No. She hasn't tried it. It was just something I had to do. I'm sorry."

"Not the best impression on your first day, arriving eight hours late."

Bennet went for both rueful and self-deprecating. "So Colonel Quist has already intimated, sir."

And finally, his father laughed, got up and came around the desk to embrace him. Bennet submitted to it as gracefully as he could, pleased he was so welcome and remembering, too, the support Caeden had given so unstintingly.

Caeden didn't let him go, just moved back enough to be able to look at him properly, one hand smoothing down the back of his hair. "All right?"

"Fine." Bennet endured the hair smoothing. He met the watchful, measuring gaze and smiled. "I'm okay."

"It got to you badly."

"I'm fine. You know. Dealing."

"Good." Caeden hugged him again. "I'm sorry you couldn't have travelled back with me after IntCom."

"Too much work to do, tidying up."

"I know. I'm glad you're here now."

Translation: where I can keep an eye on you. Bennet sighed. He wished he could feel the same, but he dreaded the year to come.

"I know you're more doubtful," Caeden said. "But we will make it work. I remember when I was first posted here all those years ago I wasn't that thrilled to be serving with your grandfather."

"I don't remember him."

"Unfortunately for you, I'm very like him." Caeden grinned, and finally released him. He noticed the satchel for the first time and frowned.

"Yes," Bennet said. "I'm still working on it."

Caeden shook his head. "Look, I'm serious about this. Don't let it get to you to that extent again, do you hear me? Come and talk to me if you need to."

"Yes. It'll be all right. But, yes, okay."

Another long searching glance before his father nodded. "All right. Now, then, I know you've had a year with Fleet and I'm sure being under Dalton's command has taught you a lot, and yes, I did see her report and very flattering it was too, although no more than I'd expect, but—"

And for the next ten minutes his father talked dreadnoughts at him until Bennet, making valiant efforts to keep up, thought the old man could write the manual. He made interested noises and welcomed the diversion, allowing the part of his mind that wasn't pretending to be attentive, to pass literary criticism on the Caeden book of instructions. He'd just decided on how he would run the publishing and marketing plan for *The Care and Feeding of Young Dreadnought Captains* when his father drew the lecture to a halt.

"We'll adjust, you know," he said again. "This will be a good posting for you, Bennet, and I promise you won't regret it. And now you'd better go and settle yourself in, and you're having dinner with me tonight, you and Natalia. We'll discuss then how we'll get through the next year without murdering each other."

Bennet nodded. "Fine. I have to see Colonel Quist first." He sighed. "No doubt to explain myself about being late."

"She'll want to give you her usual welcome speech. It's different to mine. You don't have to listen to it. After all, you weren't listening to me just now."

Bennet felt his face burn with juvenile guilt, as if he were ten years old again and having to confess he'd got less than perfect marks on his maths test.

"But please don't yawn in her face or I'll never hear the end of it. All you need to know is it's about duty and discipline and decorum, and respect for the regulations, of course."

"Is it that alliterative?" Bennet said, in as admiring a tone as he could manage.

"And respect for your elders and betters," his father said, raising a quelling eyebrow. "She'll tell you what she wants you to do for the rest of the day, what's left of it. Go and get that over with and I'll see you at dinner." He waited until Bennet was almost at the door. "I am glad you're here, son."

"There's a 'but' hanging at the end of that." Bennet turned, the flutters reminding him of their presence with an impromptu tap-dance against his ribs.

"There will be difficulties here, I realise that. Over and above the adjustments we have to have to make personally if this is going to work out."

"You're the one who connived with the Supreme Commander to get me here, so if it's difficult, you can hardly blame me."

Caeden hesitated. "The rules help. That's what they're there for."

Bennet let himself stiffen up. "I don't recall breaking any. Sir."

"No. And I'm sure you won't."

Just for a second, Bennet trembled on the edge of a retort that would likely see him sitting out his first day in the brig. He cut it back to a coldly official, "It's reassuring to have your confidence, sir."

"Bennet—"

"If I might be excused, Commander? I'd better go and get my lecture from Colonel Quist."

Caeden sighed. "I'll see you later for supper. We'll talk about it then."

"I don't think so, sir," Bennet said, and marched out before his father could say anything else.

He stashed the satchel beside Natalia and listened to Colonel Quist's welcome talk with only half an ear, still seething. He'd thought they'd made a lot of progress over the last few years, since T18, but there it was again, echoes of everything Caeden had said all those years ago in the library at the Thebaid. He'd be willing to bet Caeden wouldn't say anything even faintly as insulting to a straight-A heterosexual officer. Of course not.

He spent the next hour taking the tour of the Bridge and the Flag Office, trying to absorb the information being fired at him, keeping a watchful eye on his datapads, fuelling his anger at his father and trying to get the flutters—by now, evolving into fully-adult jitters—under control. He must have managed the multi-tasking, because Quist warmed as the hour progressed, looking approving once or twice. She smiled once. That was, frankly, scary.

The Commander returned to the Bridge about thirty minutes in. Although no one had to snap to attention when the duty Sergeant roared out the timeless "Commander on deck!", they did all straighten in their seats and turn to look at him, until he told them to stand easy and return to their duties. Quist nodded at Caeden, but didn't stop her lecture on the need for more rigour in the patrol schedule. Bennet listened dutifully and kept his attention on the Colonel until he was dismissed, pretending his father wasn't standing on the command dais watching him with the disconcerting gaze that was measuring and anxious and, somehow, full of trepidation.

As if, thought Bennet, the old man was finally facing up to the fact that he might, just might, have made a monumental mistake.

The quarters had been Simonitz's, but there was nothing there to hint at their previous owner. Not even an empty bottle was left. The place was bland and empty and still smelled faintly of new paint. It had to be better than smelling of old booze.

Colonel Quist had told him they'd sent Simonitz back early. We let him go, she'd said, as if talking about freeing a prisoner on licence, granting him probation for good behaviour. Bennet had wondered if Simonitz had viewed the *Gyrfalcon* as a prison, or if it was his own peculiar circumstances that made the strong metal walls close about him, trapping him where he dreaded to be.

Still he was glad not to have to deal with the man's probable and understandable resentment. Back on Albion for the Inquiry, all his father had said about it was that Simonitz had not taken it well.

No! Really? And his pilots wouldn't be feeling lost and bereft, either, then, with their Captain tossed aside to make room for the Commander's son? Bennet was astonished his father didn't realise the impact of that. Or did realise and thought it wasn't important?

Bennet had brooded about it all through Quist's long monologue. The way he'd brooded about his father's lack of faith. The way he'd brooded about other things. He'd been quite relieved when Quist had dismissed him and told him to go and get settled in. At least here, with the door closed, he could do his brooding in peace.

A member of the Quartermaster's staff had been summoned to the Bridge to take him to his quarters. Corporal Bren, young and rather shy, had reassured Bennet he'd already overseen the delivery of Bennet's kit and the box of books. He'd been assigned to be Bennet's batman, he'd said on the way to the command quarters deck and *Just page me whenever you need anything, sir, and I'll have the place cleaned up daily while you're on duty.* Bennet preferred looking after himself, but he'd known better than try and alter ship's procedures this early in the game. It could wait, and in the meantime he allowed Bren to set the place to rights and put his kitbags into the sleeping quarters for him to unpack at his leisure. The Corporal must have spent the day giving the rooms one final clean up—there was a faint scent of polish competing with the paint—and scurrying back and forth to the Quartermasters to collect all the supplies Bennet might need to start housekeeping; linen, and enough basic foodstuffs to stock out the tiny kitchen area. He had everything he needed.

When Bren had gone, Bennet looked the place over with more care. The quarters had the same layout as the *Corvus* and the *Caliban*: one large room with the sleeping quarters off it, divided off by sliding opaque doors; a fresher with real water in the turboshower (a blessing and a boon to be prized beyond rubies, and the biggest benefit of being assigned to Fleet); one tiny spare room with a couple of bunk beds in it, relics of the time when Fleet officers' families would join them for extended periods. He'd shared a very similar room with Thea, Natalia and Liam for a week, not long after his father had taken command of the *Gyrfalcon*. Liam had been what? About three? Appallingly noisy and energetic, anyway and a damp bedfellow. Bennet had envied the girls in the top bunk. A couple of years later he'd slept alone in the same room, visiting his father for a birthday treat and discovering his sexuality by falling in adolescent love with one of Caeden's dashing pilots.

Well, and hadn't that started a habit he didn't seem able to break. That he didn't want to break.

He sighed, thought regretfully of Rosie, settled onto the sofa with a cup of tea in his hands, and faced up to it. One hurdle past, a hurdle that a few years ago would have seemed insurmountable, but now... well, on the cutter he'd decided it was laughably inconsequential. That wasn't doing his father any disservice, but recognised the distance they'd come in four years. Or rather, the distance he'd thought they'd come, until, with a flash of his earlier resentment, he remembered that insulting reminder.

His father didn't really know him at all.

That aside, they would find a way to work together. He would let his father know exactly what he felt about the insult and they'd probably have a yelling match, and then they'd be stiff as two alpha dogs around each other for a few weeks until it all settled down. There was no way he was going to let Caeden get away with it. Compromising everything to keep the peace—shit, he'd done enough of that with Joss. He wasn't about to start with his father.

If it was still a hurdle, it was one that didn't intimidate him.

The other one, the real one, though... he sighed and sipped his tea, savouring its delicacy. That one he didn't even know how to begin to deal with. So many sleepless hours spent worrying over it, agonising over it, and he still didn't know what to do.

Except he knew he couldn't bear it if his first run at the hurdle was in public, in the briefing room or the OC or somewhere equally full of people to wonder at his reaction. He wasn't sure how he'd react, that was the trouble. He knew how he wanted to react, but wishes weren't horses and he wasn't sanguine about his own acting abilities. He didn't think he'd be able to hide what he felt.

The door chime sounded.

He froze, the cup half-way to his lips. He looked sideways at the door.

The door chime sounded.

He got up. The cup rattled on its saucer when he replaced it. He glanced around, but there was nowhere to go, nowhere to hide.

Breathe. Deep and slow and even.

Breathe.

The door chime sounded.

He wet suddenly dry lips, and metaphorically started his run, heart pounding in his chest, muscles bunching for the effort, for the reaching leap to take him over this last, immense hurdle.

"Enter," he said. His voice was surprisingly steady.

The door slid aside.

"Hey," Flynn said, and smiled.

~end~

Continued in *Taking Shield 04: The Chains of Their Sins*

ABOUT THE *TAKING SHIELD* SERIES

Earth's a dead planet, dark for thousands of years; lost for so long no one even knows where the solar system is. Her last known colony, Albion, has grown to be regional galactic power in its own right. But its drive to expand and found colonies of its own has threatened an alien race, the Maess, against whom Albion is now fighting a last-ditch battle for survival in a war that's dragged on for generations.

Taking Shield charts the missions and adventures of Shield Captain Bennet, scion of a prominent military family. Bennet, also an analyst with the Military Strategy Unit, will uncover crucial data about the Maess to help with the war effort. Against the demands of his family's 'triple goddess' of Duty, Honour and Service, is set Bennet's relationships with lovers and family. When the series opens, Bennet is at odds with his long term partner, Joss, who wants him out of the military and back in an academic, archaeological career. He's estranged from his father, Caeden, who is the commander of Fleet's First Flotilla. Events of the first book, in which he is sent to his father's ship to carry out an infiltration mission behind Maess lines, improve his relationship with Caeden, but bring with them the catalyst that will destroy the one with Joss: one Fleet Lieutenant Flynn, who, over the course of the series, develops into Bennet's main love interest.

Over the *Taking Shield* arc, Bennet will see the extremes to which humanity's enemies, and his own people, will go to win the war. Some days he isn't able to tell friend from foe. Some days he doubts everything, including himself, as he strives to ensure Albion's victory. And some days he isn't sure, any longer, what victory looks like.

The Taking Shield books in order:

Gyrfalcon

Heart Scarab

Makepeace

The Chains of Their Sins

Day of Wrath (to be published late 2017)

ABOUT THE AUTHOR

I love space opera, with spaceships and laser pistols and humanity fighting for its survival against unknowable, unfathomable aliens and, at the same time, against itself and humans' own worst traits. Yes, I'm hopelessly old fashioned!

I am currently working on two, quite different, series of books:

- The Taking Shield series is a classic space opera with handsome young men wielding lasers—a love story, but not a romance.

- The *Lancaster's Luck* series is a classic m/m romance, but with the added twist of a steampunk world where aeroships fill the skies of Victorian London and our hero uses pistols powered by luminferous aether and phlogiston.

To keep in touch with publication of new books in each series, you can follow my blog and sign up for my quarterly newsletter at my website www.annabutlerfiction.com. Or email me at annabutlerfiction@gmail.com

GLASS HAT
PRESS

67813341R00180

Made in the USA
Charleston, SC
22 February 2017